APR 1 5 1999

D1046694

WITHDRAWN
from Toronto Public Library

A Sense of
Belonging

Also by Erica James

A Breath of Fresh Air
Time for a Change
Airs & Graces

A Sense of Belonging

ERICA JAMES

ORION

Copyright © Erica James, 1998

All rights reserved

The moral right of Erica James to be identified as the author
of this work has been asserted by her in accordance with the
Copyright, Designs and Patents Act 1988.

First published in Great Britain in 1998 by
Orion
An imprint of Orion Books Ltd
Orion House, 5 Upper St Martin's Lane,
London WC2H 9EA

A CIP catalogue record for this book
is available from the British Library

ISBN 0 75280 747 1 (cased)
0 75281 244 0 (trade paperback)

Typeset by Deltatype Ltd, Birkenhead, Merseyside
Printed and bound in Great Britain by
Clays Ltd, St Ives plc.

To Edward and Samuel

ACKNOWLEDGEMENTS

This book couldn't have been written without the help and support of so many people and whether or not they want the credit (or the blame) they're going to get it.

Life-saving thanks must go to Big G for those quiet, calming moments.

Glass-raising thanks to Helena who listened to numerous silly ideas being tossed around her kitchen while I poured the wine and she cooked the lunch.

Side-splitting thanks to Maureen for saying, 'Come on, that's just not on!' As ever, she made me laugh at just the right time.

Courteous thanks to Morris Phillips for allowing me to pry into his business.

And the same to Susan Howard of Avocado Cards in Huddersfield.

Respectful thanks to Jane Wood at Orion, along with Selina Walker and Sarah Yorke.

Appreciative thanks to Helen Spencer for the over-the-phone consultations.

Humble thanks to all those people who shared their personal experiences of MS with me, especially Sue Argent who never minded me ringing her with yet another query. Her outlook on life, together with her extraordinary strength of character, is a truly inspiring example to us all. Thank you, Sue.

Devoted and adoring thanks to the two back-room boys, Edward and Samuel, who know exactly when to run for cover when things are going badly, and whose survival skills are improving with each book I write.

And, finally, forelock-tugging thanks to Jonathan Lloyd at Curtis Brown for being nothing like Piers Lambert!

*A novel is a mirror which passes
over a highway. Sometimes it reflects
to your eye the blue of the skies,
at others the churned-up mud
of the road.*

Henri Beyle (called Stendhal)
1783–1842

THE BEGINNING

Chapter One

THE END

Jessica Lloyd looked at what she'd just typed, considered it for a few seconds, then allowed herself a small wry smile.

This wasn't because she had at last finished her latest novel, or indeed that these two perfectly innocuous words would irritate the hell out of her exacting agent – 'I know when it ends, Jessica, there's no need to tell me, I'm not a fool' – but because, and heaven forbid that anyone would accuse her of spouting high-sounding humbug, she happened to believe that there was no such thing as an ending. In her experience life was all about beginnings.

And today of all days she had to believe that this was true.

She switched off the laptop, stood up, stretched her arms over her head and went and leant against the white-painted wall that separated her small terrace from the rocky drop below. She rested her elbows on the sun-warmed stone and gazed out at the sweep of bay with its crystal-clear water that was holiday-brochure blue. It was a breathlessly hot June morning and the sea was calm and tranquil, benign even, but Jessica knew well enough that by early afternoon there would be a strong wind blowing in across the water, bringing with it the kind of crashing waves that wind-surfers delighted in and for which this part of Corfu was renowned.

But for now, all was still.

She went back to the shade of her vine-covered pergola, to the wooden table she had been working at, and gathered up her things and took them inside. She plugged the laptop into the printer, which squatted incongruously next to the bread bin on top of the fridge in the tiny kitchen, and set it to print her final chapter of *A Carefree Life*. While she waited for the machine to do its work she poured herself a glass of ice-cold mineral water and gulped it down. It was eleven o'clock and she had been working on the terrace since a little after seven, having got up early to finish her novel. And now that it was done she could use the rest of the day to say her goodbyes.

She had lived on Corfu for six years and for the most part she had cherished every magical timeless day that had drifted by. She had come to the island not long after her thirtieth birthday and had fallen for the charming, carefree way of life the Corfiotes so enjoyed. It had suited her own temperament perfectly.

She had also fallen in love, or what she had thought was love at the time. Now she wasn't so sure.

First there had been Christos who, if nothing else, had tried to teach her to cook, or rather his mother had. But when it finally dawned on Christos that she had absolutely no interest in cooking, and that if he wanted anything worthwhile to eat he either had to do it himself or go home to his mother, he went in search of a nice local girl who would know exactly how to produce his favourite meal of arni brizoles. There had been no bitter recriminations between them when they'd parted, just a shared sense of better luck next time.

Luck had given her Gavin.

Gavin, so sure, so confident and so amusing. He was the original free spirit, as he'd never stopped letting her know.

He had come to the island some two years before, to work as a sailing instructor, and when they'd met, like Christos, he had set about teaching her what was important to him. In his case it was sailing. She hated sailing almost as much as cooking, but had been so captivated by Gavin that she hadn't let on and had tried her best to listen to his enthusiastic instructions. She'd then tried even harder to carry them out. But it had been hopeless. Tacking into the wind was a concept she never mastered. Each lesson she would capsize the small boat at least half a dozen times – it didn't help that Gavin would shout from the shore that a child of ten could sail the wretched thing. 'Then let it!' she shouted back at him one day, abandoning the boat and swimming away from it in a monumental sulk.

If the sailing was a nightmare, the sex was a dream.

And always afterwards, whether they were lying on her bed in the moonlight or in the sun on her secluded terrace, he would sing to her or tell her jokes.

But the sex, the singing and the jokes – and thank goodness, the sailing – were all about to become things of the past.

She hadn't told Gavin what she was doing because she knew what his reaction would be if she did try and explain to him why she was leaving. There would be that little-boy-lost look, accompanied by the words, 'But you can't really mean it' – in Gavin's world, nobody ever meant what they said. He would then open a bottle of wine and insist

4

they discuss it on the terrace beneath the stars and moon, where he knew she'd be unable to stay angry with him for more than two minutes. And because of his arrogance he would assume she was going because of him and he'd say, 'But it's just the way I am, it doesn't mean anything' and lead her to the bedroom. Then, once they'd made love, he would whisper in her ear, 'Stay, Jessica, don't go.'

And she'd give in. Just like that.

She sighed. It wasn't good to think about Gavin too much. Not at this stage. Not when she knew how weak he could make her feel. His greatest skill, she had long since decided, was that he knew exactly how to keep her dangling. She was ashamed to admit it, but basically it was all down to sex. And it wasn't even that Gavin understood her body and knew all the right things to do with it that made him so appealing, it was more a case of the sheer force of his energy in bed that had her gasping for more. Without a doubt, if sex were ever made an Olympic sport, Gavin would be the Mark Spitz of the event.

She smiled to herself and imagined Gavin putting his latest round of infidelity down to essential training.

She poured another glass of water, quickly drank it, then decided to have a swim before taking her motor boat into Kassiopi. She went in search of her swimming costume. Just as she had changed, the phone rang.

It was her mother.

Instantly Jessica was filled with alarm. Her mother rarely called. It was always Jessica who did the phoning. The last time Anna had phoned was six months ago and it was to announce that she was being admitted into hospital for a heart bypass operation. Very calmly she had said, 'Don't go doing anything silly, Jessica, like rushing over, but I'm going into hospital for a few days. There seems to be a problem with my heart. A lot of fuss over nothing, very probably.' Within hours of the call Jessica was sitting on a plane bound for Manchester, panic-stricken that she might never see her mother again. It was a thought that had stayed with her throughout the flight and had reduced her to a tearful, sniffling wreck, much to the consternation of the man in the seat next to her.

They had never been overtly close, not like other mothers and daughters Jessica knew, who needed constantly to be together, but their love for one another was just as strong. Unfortunately, so was the need for both of them to live independently of each other.

'What is it?' Jessica asked. 'What's happened?'

'Don't fuss. I'm fine. I just wanted to see if it wasn't too late to make you change your mind.'

'No chance,' Jessica said with a light laugh. 'Everything's arranged this end and you know jolly well that I've exchanged contracts on Cholmford Hall Mews, so you can expect me as I'd originally said.'

'Remind me.'

Jessica tutted. 'Does that mean you've lost the letter I sent you?'

'I might have.'

'Honestly, Mum, you're hopeless.'

'I'm nothing of the sort. After years of having a head for paperwork I've given it up. Now get on and tell me what time you'll be arriving tonight, this call's costing me a fortune.'

'With a bit of luck I'll see you some time after eleven.'

'As early as that?'

'You really know how to make a daughter feel loved.'

'I'm working on it, Jessica, but it's not easy.'

A few moments later, when Jessica put down the phone, she found herself almost wishing the hours away until her flight. She wanted to go home. Which was strange because England hadn't been home for years.

She picked up a large towel from the back of a chair and made her way down the steep hillside path at the end of her sun terrace. At a sharp turn she paused and stood still in the fierce heat, and gazed across the expanse of sparkling water. In the distance was the Albanian coastline, its mountainous bumps blurred and hazy in the baking sunshine. All around her was the sweet smell of cypress trees and the ever present noise of cicadas hidden in the olive trees. Surely she should feel something, she thought, as she stood taking in the view and the moment. Shouldn't there be at least some feeling of regret at leaving all this, this island that had once been such a blissful paradise?

But that was the point, she supposed. It no longer was a blissful paradise.

She carried on down the path, taking care where she placed her feet on the stones that in places were loose and wobbly.

When she reached the tiny sheltered area of pebble beach that she called her own, where she kept her small boat tied to an overhanging branch of a eucalyptus tree, she placed her towel on a rock and slipped into the clear turquoise water. It was wonderfully cool and refreshing, and leaning her slim brown body forward she began swimming away from the shore, moving her arms and legs slowly and rhythmically.

Perhaps this might be something she would miss when she returned to England.

But even the thought of a chilly chlorine dip at the local swimming baths back in Cheshire could not persuade her that what she was doing was wrong.

It was in January, when her mother had gone into hospital, that Jessica had begun to feel uneasy. It was the first time that she wondered whether she hadn't been a little selfish all her adult life.

The trouble was she had been brought up by a strong, clear-minded and very independent woman, and raised with the expectation that she would be the same. Which had meant that at the earliest opportunity she had been encouraged to fly the nest and spread her wings. At no stage had she thought about marriage or ever having children, the two things just didn't come into her thinking. As a child there had been no bedtime stories of young girls being rescued by handsome princes on the look-out for a compliant, pretty wife, instead there had been tales of heroic women battling against the odds; of Joan of Arc, Amy Johnson, Florence Nightingale and even Ginger Rogers who, according to her mother, did everything Fred Astaire did but backwards and in high heels. 'Whatever you want to do,' her mother would say when kissing her good-night, 'believe you can do it and you will. And more important than anything else, make sure you enjoy what you do.'

Which might well have provoked some children into becoming high-flying achievers, but not Jessica. What it did was convince her from an early age that whatever she did it would be because she wanted to do it. She grew to be extremely single-minded and able to turn her hand to anything she chose. Her scholastic education came to an end at the age of eighteen and because she already had a passion for skiing, but couldn't afford to fund it, she decided to work as a chalet maid in a ski resort in the French Alps, where she spent what little free time she had on the slopes perfecting her technique. She'd then gone to live in Colorado, where she worked as a skiing instructor. From there she'd returned to Europe and while island hopping round Greece, with only a bulging backpack to her name, had chanced upon a holiday company desperate for an extra rep to help them out for a couple of weeks on Corfu. By the time the job came to an end Jessica knew that she had chanced upon a place that she had no desire to leave. She began working in a taverna, which was where she had met Christos, and when she wasn't serving plates of moussaka and feta salad to the tourists, along with retsina and ouzo, she was to be found on the beach with a notebook and pen.

7

Quite unexpectedly she had discovered she had a new craving and was instantly keen to satisfy it. She had started writing a novel. It took her a year and when it was finished she posted the set of notebooks to her mother to read. Unbeknown to Jessica, Anna had then secretly typed it out and sent it off to an agent in London. Several months later, not long after Christos had given up on Jessica, she had received a letter from her mother with the news that a publisher was interested in her book. 'They're offering real money,' she wrote, 'not buttons, but hard cash. You'd better come over right away and see what you think.'

And she had. First she had met the agent to whom her mother had sent the manuscript, then the publisher. A contract was signed and when she flew back to Corfu a week later the first thing she did was to give up working at the taverna and buy herself a new set of notebooks and pens, and start writing another novel.

Now, as she climbed up the steep path to her small whitewashed house that nestled comfortably into the unspoilt hillside, she thought of the third book she had completed today, which she would take with her to England that evening on the plane, along with just a few carefully selected possessions that would remind her of Corfu. The house was rented, as was the furniture, and much as she'd come to love her locally carved olive-wood knick-knacks and brightly coloured rugs and wall hangings, it was only right that they should stay behind. They would look out of place in her new house; it would be like taking holiday souvenirs home and finding they looked silly away from their own environment, just as cheap holiday wine was best enjoyed *in situ*.

She threw her wet towel over the clothes line tied between two olive trees and experienced the uneasy feeling that her decision to leave Gavin and her idyllic life-style and return home to England was all about her finally growing up.

No more could she justify her carefree life. No more could she ignore what she felt she owed her mother. And whether her mother was prepared to admit it or not, Anna needed her daughter's help.

Just occasionally, though, Jessica had the strange and dangerous feeling that perhaps this wasn't so, that in actual fact, by some quirk of human nature, it was she who wanted her mother to need her.

Either way, it didn't matter. The truth was, at the age of thirty-six she had discovered that Corfu could not offer her what she now found she wanted more than anything else.

She went inside the house to shower and get ready to go out, more convinced than ever that what she had suspected for some time was true – she had outstayed her welcome on this lovely Ionian island. It was definitely time to move on, to go back to England where she had a new home waiting for her, not with her mother – that would be a disaster for them both – but somewhere close by, where she hoped to be able to keep a surreptitious eye on Anna.

And maybe she might even find what it was she was looking for, that setting up home at Cholmford Hall Mews would satisfy the very real sense of belonging that she was now seeking.

Chapter Two

Kate Morris stared with pleasure through the large arched window in the sun-filled sitting-room of 5 Cholmford Hall Mews and experienced the sensation of having died and gone to heaven. She wondered how she would ever get anything done in the house with this beautiful view of rolling fields and woodland to gaze at all day.

Well, one thing was for sure, today was not the day to stand and dream. There was such a lot to do and she wanted most of it done before Alec came home from work that evening. She wished to surprise him, wanted very much to make their new home together perfect.

They had only moved in yesterday, so she knew that it was just possible that she was setting her sights too high, but she badly desired everything to be right.

She moved away from the window and turned her attention to one of the large packing cases in the middle of the room. She opened it, took off the protective layers of scrunched-up paper and pulled out a parcel to unwrap. It was a framed photograph of Alec and his family – the McLaren clan as she called them – taken last Christmas. There was Alec's daughter Ruth, who wasn't much younger than Kate, and her husband Adam, and their son, little Oscar, four years old and utterly adorable; dark-eyed and winsome, and Kate's favourite member of the McLaren family, other than the man she loved. And looking very much the patriarchal figure, Alec was in the middle of the picture, his tall frame dominating the photograph as he stood proudly, surrounded by his family. She ran her finger over his face, taking in the flecks of grey at his temples, the smile that had put her so thoroughly at ease when they'd first met and the new pair of gold-rimmed glasses she had helped him choose the week before Christmas. She was in the picture too. She gazed critically at herself and saw a tall girl in her late twenties looking more like a gawky schoolgirl with shoulders slightly stooped as though this would make her less visible and less out of place among a family in which she felt she didn't belong. It was a sad truth, but it was exactly how she'd always looked in her own family photographs. The final figure in the group portrait was perhaps the most important member of the family . . . in terms of Kate's future happiness, she suspected. It was Melissa McLaren.

Melissa and Alec had been divorced now for over two years, but Kate was astute enough to know that a formal piece of paper could never fully untie the bond that existed between a couple who had not only been married for as long as Alec and Melissa had, but who also still saw one another on a daily basis running their jointly owned company together. Kate recognised all too well that some women in her position would be unhappy with the situation in which her partner still had so much contact with his ex, but Kate was determined never to let something as petty as jealousy ruin what she and Alec had between them. Though they had only known one another for less than a year their love was as precious to Kate as anything she'd ever known.

She placed the photograph on the mantelpiece, along with some other ornaments she'd already unwrapped after seeing Alec off to work earlier that morning. It was a shame he'd needed to go in to the office today of all days, it would have been lovely to have had him here with her setting up home together.

They had met last autumn through, of all things, a dating agency – a fact that nobody in the McLaren clan was ever to know about. 'I couldn't bear for Melissa to know I'd resorted to meeting somebody this way,' Alec had told Kate. It wasn't perhaps the most flattering thing for him to say to her, but she knew and understood what he meant, and had respected his need to protect his pride. Hadn't she felt exactly the same herself?

In theory they should never have met, because of their age difference, but that particular week the computer at the agency had had a glitch and had sent out hundreds of profiles to mismatched prospective partners and, with curiosity on both their parts to blame, she and Alec had arranged to meet for a drink in a wine bar in Knutsford.

'Excuse my lack of originality,' he'd said on the phone, 'but how will I recognise you? I've never done this kind of thing before.'

'I'm tall for my age,' she'd joked, 'and I have rather a lot of hair.'

She had liked the look of him from the very first second she'd seen him enter the wine bar, without even knowing that he was her date. He'd been dressed in a loose-fitting raincoat over a linen suit and pale-green shirt that later in the evening she had realised had reflected the colour of his eyes. She had liked him even more when he'd approached her without hesitating and said, 'You have to be Kate Morris, I love your hair, it makes you look like an ethereal Burne-Jones beauty.'

According to the advice offered by the dating agency, when two people meet for the first time they should plan to spend a maximum of thirty minutes in each other's company. She and Alec had spent all evening together. They'd had a couple of drinks in the wine bar and moved on to a nearby restaurant. She had found his manner easy and comfortable. He was softly spoken, with just the merest hint of a Scottish accent, and appeared confident and perfectly composed, even though he admitted to her the following day that he had been terrified that she would think him old and boring. But there was nothing old and boring about Alec, he was spontaneous and fun, and she had fallen in love with him by the time they'd finished their meal. Later, when he had walked her to her car and had said how much he'd enjoyed the evening, he'd added, 'I don't suppose there's any hope of you humouring a middle-aged man and having dinner with me next week, is there?'

'No,' she'd answered, 'no, I don't think so.'

He'd lowered his eyes, disappointed – ever since that moment she'd never seen him look so downcast. 'I just thought it was worth asking,' he'd mumbled awkwardly, staring into the shop window behind him, 'but I quite understand, I suppose that's how this dating thing works.'

She'd reached out and rested her hand on his coat sleeve. 'You don't understand at all,' she'd said, 'I said no because I can't wait until next week. How about tomorrow evening?'

His handsome face had instantly broken into a delighted smile. 'You mean it?'

'Yes.' She'd smiled back at him. 'Why wouldn't I?'

He'd thrown his arms in the air. 'A million and one reasons why not. Like I'm twenty years older than you.'

'Actually you're twenty-one years older.'

He groaned. 'That bad, eh?'

'Old enough to be my father.'

'Doesn't it bother you?'

'So where shall we eat?'

'Here? Wherever. Wherever you want. Oh Kate, give me something that belongs to you so that I don't wake up in the morning and find you were nothing but a dream.'

Kate smiled and hoped she would never forget the memory of their first meeting. She carried on with the unpacking. When she'd cleared another two boxes she was interrupted by the sound of the doorbell. She clambered over the chaos of yet more unopened boxes in the hall and opened the front door. She was met by the sight of a woman holding a large bouquet of flowers.

'Kate Morris?'

'Yes, that's me.'

'For you.'

Kate took the flowers and watched the woman turn her florist's van round in the gravelled courtyard in front of all the mews houses and drive out through the central archway. She closed the door and walked through to the kitchen. She laid the flowers on the table and read the small accompanying card. *To my darling Kate, sorry I can't be with you on this special day. Please don't work too hard. All my love, Alec.*

Kate swallowed back tears of happiness. Nobody had ever treated her so lovingly.

Chapter Three

From the kitchen window of 2 Cholmford Hall Mews Amanda Fergusson watched the florist's van drive away and felt a stab of jealousy at the sight of such a beautiful bouquet of flowers. Tony wasn't a flower person, chocolates yes, occasionally, but rarely flowers. But then that was all right, because she wasn't a sentimental person either.

She closed the dishwasher and moved on to tidying up the breakfast bar. But her thoughts were still with the pretty young girl over in number five, who she decided was probably sickeningly sentimental and was on the receiving end of similarly romantic gestures all the time from her ... Amanda hesitated. Her what, precisely?

Husband?

No. The man who had stood on the doorstep that morning kissing her goodbye as though he couldn't bear to be parted from her was no husband. Amanda had one of those and she knew the difference: in broad daylight husbands pecked, while lovers embraced.

On the other hand, they might be newly-weds. That was it, probably. Recently married and still going through the honeymoon period. It would soon be over, just as it was with her and Tony. It hadn't slipped her notice either that there was a considerable age gap between the happy couple.

She carried on with the clearing up. In the adjoining family room she could hear the sound of Tony's six-year-old daughter Hattie, singing along to a programme on Children's BBC. Amanda listened to the little girl. She sounded relaxed and cheerful. Which wasn't always the case.

When Amanda had met Tony eighteen months before, he was still trying to get over the loss of his wife, who had died in a car accident the previous year. He was also finding it difficult to cope with the demands of his job and his young daughter. A succession of unreliable nannies hadn't helped either and had served only to disrupt Hattie's life further.

But now, at least, thanks to her, both Tony and Hattie seemed to be on a more even keel, even if at times Amanda felt she was out of her depth. Marriage to Tony wasn't all that she'd imagined it would be, but she was working on it. Tony, however, wasn't her real problem, that was Hattie. She wished at times that Tony would trust her more with his daughter. He was too prone to step in and undermine her when she was trying her best to discipline the girl.

They had argued again last night. Hattie had been in and out of bed, one minute claiming she was thirsty, the next that she was too hot. 'I can't sleep,' she'd said. Tony had immediately suggested that Hattie come downstairs and sit with them for a while, but she had known the answer was to be firm and make Hattie realise that grown-ups needed their time together. Tony had had his way, and Hattie had sat between them on the sofa and had consequently refused to go back upstairs. Eventually she had fallen asleep, lying across Tony's chest, and he had carried her up to her room. By which time it was nearly midnight and they too had gone to bed, exhausted and bad-tempered.

'May I have a drink?'

Amanda turned round to see Hattie standing in the doorway. 'Please,' she said. '*Please* may I have a drink?'

'Please,' repeated Hattie in a bored tone.

Amanda poured out a plastic cup of apple juice. She placed it on the breakfast bar. 'Climb up on to your stool, then.'

'I want it in there,' Hattie said, pointing towards the family room and the television.

'In here or not at all. What's it to be?'

Hattie stared back at her.

Amanda sensed a battle of wills looming. 'You know the rules,' she said, 'where there are carpets, new carpets at that, you're not allowed to eat or drink.'

'Daddy lets –'

'Then Daddy's wrong.'

Hattie's eyes opened wide.

Amanda was cross with herself. Once again, not only had she cast herself as the wicked stepmother, but she had broken the cardinal rule: Daddy was never wrong. And the only way out of the problem now was either to give in – which she wouldn't – or provide a distraction. 'Why don't we go out,' she said. 'Let's go and meet the nice new lady who moved in yesterday.'

Kate had almost cleared the sitting-room of packing cases and was just considering a well-earned coffee break when she heard the doorbell for a second time that day and went to answer it.

It was the little girl she noticed first. She decided that she was a couple of years older than Oscar.

'We thought we'd come and introduce ourselves,' said the woman behind the small fair-haired child, 'we live in number two over in the corner. I'm Amanda and this is Hattie.' Hattie immediately tried to hide herself behind Amanda.

'Come on now, don't be shy,' Amanda said, giving her a little shove. 'I'm afraid she can be very silly at times.'

Kate bent down and smiled at Hattie. 'Hello,' she said, 'I'm Kate. Would you like to come in and help me unpack a few boxes? I've got so much to do, it would be lovely to have another pair of hands.'

Hattie considered Kate for a moment, then pushed past Amanda and followed her inside the house.

'I was just going to make myself a cup of coffee, would you like one?'

'Please,' Amanda answered, 'but only if we're not keeping you. I can see you've still got a lot to do.'

Kate led the way through to the kitchen and swept her long hair up from her face. She held it in that position for a few seconds and looked back at the mess in the hall, which she had yet to make an impression on. 'You're so right.' She sighed, letting go of her hair and sending it cascading down her back. 'But not to worry, I'm sure I'll get it all done by this evening, especially now that I've got Hattie to help me.' She smiled down at the little girl who was busy staring at her.

'You've got lovely hair,' Hattie said unexpectedly.

'Thank you and so have you.'

'No I haven't, mine's horrible. I'd like it long like yours, but Amanda says it's easier to keep it short like this.'

'And Amanda is quite right,' Kate said diplomatically, wondering what Amanda's relationship was to this sweet girl – aunt, stepmother or child-minder? Surely not her mother. 'But maybe when you're a big girl and can look after your own hair you'll be able to have it just as you want.'

'I will,' Hattie said flatly. She gave Amanda a sideways glance.

'Now what would you like to drink?' Kate asked, aware that the rapport between her two visitors was not all that it could be.

'May I have some apple juice, please?'

'What beautiful manners you have, but I'm afraid I've only got orange juice or grape juice. Or how about some milk?'

'Milk please.'

Amanda watched the scene between her new neighbour and Hattie. If she had been jealous at the sight of the flowers arriving in the courtyard earlier this morning, she now felt an even greater sense of envy witnessing the ease with which this willowy beauty could strike up such a friendly alliance with her stepdaughter. It had taken Amanda the best part of six months to get Hattie so much as to smile at her.

'There now,' Kate said, picking up the tray of drinks, 'I think that's everything we shall need. Oh, Hattie, could you carry that tin of biscuits for me? Yes, that's the one, the large red tin. Can you manage it? Splendid.'

'Where are we going to have our drinks?' asked Hattie.

'In the sitting-room, it's the only tidy room in the house.'

'Is there a carpet in there?'

'Yes,' Kate said, puzzled. 'Why?'

Hattie didn't answer but she threw another look at her stepmother.

Amanda followed behind, feeling cross and slightly left out. 'What lovely flowers,' she said, when they went into the sitting-room and she saw the enormous arrangement on a highly polished corner table. 'I saw them arrive earlier, lucky you.' She went over to take a closer look and to read the card propped up in front of the vase. When she looked back at Kate she was surprised to see that she was blushing.

'Alec is very romantic, he does things like that.'

'Is Alec your husband?' asked Hattie, taking off her shoes and making herself at home in a large comfortable wing-back armchair.

'Sort of,' Kate said, handing Amanda her cup of coffee. 'Milk?'

Amanda shook her head, hoping that Hattie would ask what 'sort of' meant.

'Sugar?'

'No, thank you.' She waited for Hattie to oblige, but the silly girl was too busy smiling at Kate, who was now passing her a glass of milk. She almost wished that Hattie would misbehave and spill the drink all over the expensive-looking fabric of the chair in which she was sitting, as she did at home sometimes, then they'd see how this beautiful serene creature would handle things.

'So when did you move in?' Kate asked, as she settled herself on a low footstool beside Hattie's chair and offered her a biscuit.

'Last week. We were the first. It's been strange being here all on our own. It's very quiet. I'm just so glad I've got a car or I'd feel completely isolated.'

17

Kate stared out through the large arched window that took up nearly the entire width of the far end of the room. 'But it's wonderful, isn't it? The countryside is so pretty. I don't think I shall ever want to leave. There's such a good feeling about the place. Do you feel it too?'

'Ah . . . yes,' lied Amanda. All she had felt since they'd moved in was a colossal sense of exhaustion. Running herself ragged over unpacking, then gathering swatches of fabrics and wallpaper samples was not her idea of fun, especially as she was now looking after Hattie full time because they'd taken her out of school before the end of term so that they could move house and area. For the first time since her marriage to Tony, when she'd given up her job in the building society in order to be a stay-at-home mum for Hattie, she longed for her old way of life – chasing unpaid mortgage payments was a doddle in comparison.

'Is there anybody else living here, or are we the only ones to have moved in?' Kate asked, offering Amanda a biscuit.

Amanda had a pretty good idea what was going on with the development as she'd made it her business to befriend Sue, the sales negotiator who worked in the show house three days a week. Though even Sue hadn't been entirely sure what the set-up between Kate and Alec was. 'Contracts have been exchanged on number one and completion has already taken place on number four,' she said.

'Any idea what the other people are like?'

'Apparently your immediate neighbour is a well-known author, a romantic novelist, but I've never heard of her, not that I read that kind of book. I prefer something with a bit more substance when I do have the time to read.'

'How interesting. Do you know her name?'

'Jessica . . . Jessica Somebody or other. I can't remember her surname, which just goes to show she can't be that well-known.'

'Her name's Jessica Lloyd,' Hattie said, her mouth full of biscuit crumbs.

'Hattie,' reprimanded Amanda, 'don't speak with your mouth full.' She then turned to Kate. 'I think Hattie might be right though.'

'I know I'm right,' Hattie continued, 'because when the lady in the show house said her name yesterday I thought of Vanessa Lloyd at my old school. Is she famous?'

Kate smiled. 'I don't know about that, but I used to work in a library and Jessica Lloyd's books were never on the shelves, they were always out on loan. She's very good.'

18

'Oh, well then,' Amanda laughed, 'we shall have to watch ourselves and be on our guard, or we'll all end up in her next novel.'

'And what about number one, do you know who's moving in there?'

'According to Sue in the show house, he's a lonesome bachelor. She thinks he's the sort to keep himself very much to himself.'

Chapter Four

'You're out of your mind!'

Josh ignored his brother and continued to drive along the narrow lane with its high hedges that in places were brushing both sides of his Shogun. He hoped they wouldn't meet an oncoming car, because if his memory served him correctly there wasn't another space to pull in for at least a quarter of a mile.

'I mean it,' Charlie persisted. 'You must be mad thinking of living out here, there'll be no night-life other than owls tu-whit, tu-whooing all hours and driving you round the bend. What's got into you?'

Still Josh didn't say anything. He had anticipated this reaction from Charlie, which was why he had deliberately only brought his brother to see the house when he'd exchanged contracts and had set a date for the removal men to move his stuff out of his flat in Bowdon. And he knew very well that his brother wasn't at all concerned about the lack of available social life that there would be out here in the country. The real line of Charlie's argument was yet to come. He didn't want to hear it, but he knew there could be no avoidance. It was inevitable. Just as so many other things in his life were inevitable.

'Is there any chance of you answering me?'

'And is there any chance of you keeping an open mind?' Josh said evenly, slowing the Shogun to negotiate a small bridge that crossed the canal. He stopped the car to admire the view, hoping it might impress his brother – that it might disarm Charlie of some of his resounding disapproval. To the right of the bridge and moored further along the tow-path was a brightly painted barge and on the bow of the boat was a Jack Russell terrier with a red spotted scarf tied round its neck; it was barking frantically at a swan passing serenely by. On the other side of the bridge and to the left was an attractive white-painted cottage with a garden that was in full flower, which led down to the tow-path where willow trees dipped their elegant branches into the water.

'Well?' said Josh.

'Okay,' Charlie muttered crossly, 'an open mind it is.'

Josh drove on. The narrow lane began to open out and the hedges shrank sufficiently to reveal fields of ripening corn swaying gently in the rippling breeze. They came to a turning to the right, which took them through an avenue of chestnut trees so large and majestic that the branches reached out across the road and formed a long leafy tunnel.

Charlie continued to sit in the front passenger seat unmoved by all the picture-postcard settings they were driving through. For the life of him he couldn't work out what Josh had been up to. Why in heaven's name had he done this crazy thing? And in secret. What had possessed him to buy a house out here in the middle of nowhere? 'Is that it?' he asked, seeing a large building ahead of them.

'Yes,' said Josh. He slowed the car and drove through the archway of Cholmford Hall Mews. He parked outside number one, which was the end property on the left-hand side of the horseshoe-shaped barn conversion. 'I'll get the keys,' he said.

He walked slowly and stiffly across the courtyard to the show house where he found the sales negotiator in the kitchen. She was perched on a bar stool reading a magazine. She closed it and slipped it under a property brochure as soon as she saw him.

'Okay if I have the key?' he asked. 'I want to show somebody round.'

'Of course, Mr Crawford. No problem.' She went to a filing cabinet tucked into a corner of the kitchen and pulled out an envelope of labelled keys. She handed him his set. 'You're moving in next week, aren't you?' she said, hoping to engage him in conversation. He really was quite good-looking, in that smooth, clean-cut kind of way you usually only saw on the telly. He had a neat dress sense too, but then she'd always liked a man in black. A shame she could never get him to talk, though. He was always polite, but not what she'd call forthcoming. He thanked her for the keys and left.

There was so sign of Charlie when Josh went back across the courtyard, but the small gate to the garden of number one was open. He found his brother standing in the middle of the recently turfed lawn. This garden mirrored exactly number five's and they were the largest plots on the development, both extending to almost half an acre, and the views across to Bosley Cloud and the Peak District were stunning.

'Admiring the view?' asked Josh.

'Not particularly, I'm getting agoraphobia. Give me the suburbs any day.'

'Philistine. Come and see inside the house.'

As they moved from one empty, echoing room to another Josh waited for his brother finally to get to the point. Charlie was rarely quiet and the uncomfortable silence growing between them was getting on his nerves. It had been the same at work recently. Without a word, Charlie was syphoning off jobs that would normally come Josh's way. Even when they had been planning their last trip to Hong Kong, Charlie had assumed that Josh would stay behind. He'd tried to make out that Josh was needed in Manchester to make sure everything was in order for their next trade fair.

'Okay,' Charlie said at last, when they'd done the full tour and were back in the sitting-room where they'd started. They stood in front of a large arched window and stared out at the garden and hills beyond. 'I'll concede that it's a great house. I'll even go so far as to say I like where it is. It has a certain countrified-meets-chic charm to it, though I couldn't see myself here, not ever. I'd feel too cut off.'

'But?'

A couple of moments passed before Charlie spoke. 'Oh, come off it, Josh, you know perfectly well what the "but" is.'

Josh shook his head. 'Please. Explain it to me.'

Charlie kept his eyes on the patchwork of uneven turf outside. He couldn't bring himself to say the words. How could he? How could he tell his brother – his best mate – that the odds were against him, that one morning in the not too distant future he could wake up unable to manage the stairs in his own home, never mind push a bloody great mower round that huge garden out there.

'You're not saying anything, Charlie. Don't tell me you're struggling to find the right words.'

Charlie turned away from the window. He faced his brother. 'Don't taunt me, it's not fair.'

Josh's face hardened. 'You're right,' he said, 'you're absolutely right. It isn't fair. It's not fair that I've got multiple sclerosis and that I should want to live in this house. I should behave myself and conform, and become the disabled person you want me to be. I should throw in the towel and move into a crappy, depressing little bungalow and have the whole place kitted out with ramps and God knows what else.'

'I didn't say that.'

'No. You didn't need to. It's been written all over your face ever since last night when I told you about this place.'

Charlie ran his hand through his hair. It was nine months now since Josh had been diagnosed as having MS and he knew he should be getting used to these sudden outbursts of anger from his younger brother, but he wasn't. If anything he was finding it more and more difficult to come up with the right response. If he were honest, he found his brother's anger frightening because he knew that it betrayed Josh's fear of his illness.

'Who said anything about a bungalow?' he said, trying to make light of Josh's accusation. 'And anyway, what was so wrong with your flat? Why the sudden need to up sticks and be so far away from everyone you know?'

Josh moved slowly across the room and went and leaned against the carved oak mantelpiece. He could feel the underside of his left foot beginning to tingle, which he knew in a matter of hours would turn into full-blown pins and needles and would spread up his leg, leaving him with barely any feeling in that part of his body. If he was lucky it would be gone by the morning. If not, it could last for days, maybe even weeks. 'If you must know, I'm tired of you all staring at me,' he said, 'you, Mum and Dad, and everyone at work, you're all giving me those same pitying looks. Poor Josh, you're thinking, only thirty-seven and destined soon to be little more than a vegetable in a wheelchair.'

Charlie flinched at his brother's words, but he couldn't stop his concern now turning to anger. He stuffed his fists into his trouser pockets. 'It's because we care about you, you ungrateful bastard!'

'And I'm sick of it,' Josh shouted back at him. 'If I haven't got much worthwhile life left then I'm bloody well going to enjoy what I have got, which means living out here in the country and being allowed to be *me*, and not some stereotyped image of a crippo that you've got in mind.'

'But it's so isolated here,' Charlie tried to reason.

But Josh was past reason. 'Good,' he shouted, 'because then you won't hear me screaming when I've had enough and done myself in!'

Chapter Five

Before heading for Kassiopi, Jessica steered her boat towards a secluded bay that contained nothing but a couple of extravagantly large holiday villas surrounded by bushes of purple-flowering oleander and soaring cypress trees. Both villas had direct access on to the small sandy beach where Jessica could see and smell a lunch-time barbecue in progress. Exuberant English voices drifted across the water as children chased and splashed each other in the rock pools and parents, stretched out on sun-loungers, instinctively called out to them to be careful.

Jessica smiled at the children as they waved at her and carefully manoeuvred the boat alongside the rickety wooden jetty that had been built to serve the two holiday properties, as well as her friends' more modest house higher up the hillside. She switched off the engine, hopped out and tied the boat to the post Helen and Jack used. She then began the climb up the steep wooded slope to where they lived.

She was hot and short of breath by the time she reached their little house with its buttermilk walls partially draped in bougainvillaea and topped with a delicate coral-coloured roof. She found them both lying languidly in deck-chairs in the shade of the terrace that Jack had spent the winter months constructing. For once, Jack was wearing shorts, but as usual, apart from a sun visor, Helen didn't have a stitch on.

'Hi there,' Helen said when she saw Jessica. 'You look like you could do with something to drink.'

Jessica flopped on to a nearby chair and fanned herself with her hand. 'Please,' she said, lifting off her sun-glasses and wiping the sweat from her face, 'a keg of water should just about do it, along with the same quantity of ice that sank the *Titanic*.'

Helen laughed, which had the effect of making her large tanned breasts wobble. Jessica had always been fascinated by Helen's body: splendidly Rubensesque and the colour of terracotta, its voluptuous form compared with her own, which was a rather straight-up-and-down affair with just a hint of a bump here and there, had made her feel slightly less of a woman than her friend. Before Helen and Jack had made their home here on the island Helen had dressed in what she herself described as mumsy chain-store separates. Looking at her now, it was difficult to imagine that such a sensual, generous body could ever be restrained by anything so criminally dull. Helen's body was made for being on show and these days she chose to do exactly that, and proudly. She'd told Jessica how when she and Jack had arrived and they'd first stripped off their inhibited Englishness, Jack had been in a permanent state of arousal, which Helen had further boasted had done wonders for their sex life, which she said had begun to run out of steam back in Huddersfield.

'You just never learn, do you?' Helen said. 'How many years have you lived here and you still go rushing about in the heat of the day when any sensible-minded person does little more than open a bottle of wine.'

'Not sure we've got any icebergs lurking in the freezer, Jessica,' Jack said, getting to his feet, 'but I'll see what I can rustle up for you.'

Jessica watched Jack go inside and not for the first time wondered what his ex-work colleagues from the bank in Huddersfield would make of his current life-style.

Forty-eight-year-old finance managers didn't normally go in for such bohemian mores, but when Jack and Helen had come to Corfu on holiday three years ago they had returned home to Huddersfield after two weeks of bliss and decided that their lives were no longer suited to the confines of a nine-to-five existence on a smart housing estate on the edge of town. Jack had told Jessica how one morning, with his resignation neatly typed up, he had gone in to work ready to end twenty years of company loyalty and to discuss the effect this decision would have on his pension. What he hadn't been prepared for was a generous redundancy package being solicitously offered across his boss's desk. He immediately feigned disappointment and desk-thumping outrage at such treatment, then rushed to the staff toilets to dispose of his resignation.

They quickly sold their executive five-bedroomed house and moved to Corfu, and with Jack's redundancy money they bought a couple of tiny villas; one to live in and the other to rent out to tourists. And to go the whole hog, Helen rekindled an old hobby from her pre-teaching days and started painting. She now sold tasteful water-colours of the surrounding area to the very same kind of holiday-maker she had once been. Jessica affectionately called them the Tom and Barbara Good of Corfu.

'Do you think you'll ever leave here?' Jessica suddenly asked Helen.

Helen looked at her. 'What an absurd question. Are you feeling okay?'

Jack joined them on the terrace, carrying a tray of drinks. He handed Jessica a large beer mug of water with several cubes of ice, as well as another glass which contained white wine. He passed a glass of wine to his wife, who said, 'Jessica's just asked me the strangest of questions. Go on, Jessica, ask Jack and see what kind of response you get from him.'

'Fire away,' Jack said, settling himself in his deck-chair.

Jessica smiled. 'I only asked if you could ever see yourselves leaving the island.'

'It's a possibility, but only to go somewhere equally perfect.' Jack stared at Jessica. 'So what's the deal? Why the question?'

Jessica drained her beer mug of water and let a few ice cubes slip into her mouth. She crunched on them noisily.

'Well,' Helen said, 'like Jack says, what's the deal?'

'Not much, it's just that I've come to say goodbye.'

'Goodbye?' Helen and Jack looked at each other, horrified. 'What do you mean?' they said together.

'I'm going back to England.'

Helen sat up aghast. She leant forwards, her legs akimbo, completely oblivious to her nakedness.

'A-hem,' Jack said, raising his eyebrows, 'you're showing your sexy bits, Helen.'

Jessica smiled, amused that Jack hadn't lost all of his nine-to-five conventions.

Helen tutted and to please Jack slapped her legs together. 'Why, Jessica?' she asked. 'I don't understand it. It's paradise here.'

'I know,' Jessica said, 'but I think that's part of the problem. It's all too easy living as we do. It's as if we're all caught up in this wonderful balloon of a life that encapsulates the very best of everything we could ever want and . . . and I've got the feeling my own particular balloon of perfection has burst.'

Helen looked confused. 'I'm not sure I understand. What's wrong with enjoying ourselves?'

'Nothing . . . so long as it feels right.'

'And it doesn't feel right for you any more?'

Jessica turned to Jack and shook her head. 'Not any more, no. It's not enough.'

'How much paradise do you want, for heaven's sake?' cried Helen.

'I don't think it's paradise I'm searching for. Perhaps it's the opposite. I feel like I haven't earned myself a proper slot in life yet.'

'Oh, my fathers, you're not on some kind of guilt trip, are you? Don't tell me you're about to embark on some personal crusade of masochistic pleasure. You've had it too good and now it's time for a bit of punishment, is that what you're after? A hair shirt and a steady job?'

'Helen,' warned Jack, 'stop trivialising what Jessica's got to say.'

'I'm not,' she said crossly.

Jessica suddenly laughed. 'Stop it, you two. And Helen, for goodness sake stop looking so thoroughly indignant, it doesn't suit that wonderful body of yours.'

'So come on, Jessica,' Jack said, 'why the Shirley Valentine in reverse? What's brought it on?'

'I'm not sure I can explain it to you. All I know is that I no longer feel a part of life here. I don't feel I belong.'

'What does Gavin have to say?' Helen asked.

'Er . . . he doesn't know I'm going.'

'What?'

'When are you leaving?' asked Jack.

'Tonight.'

'*What!*'

'Helen, will you stop saying *what* all the time.'

'Listen, Jack, I'll say what as many times as it takes to talk some sense into this girl. She can't go, she simply can't.'

Jessica said goodbye and left her friends to carry on their bickering. She took the steep path down to the beach, untied her boat, started up the engine and headed towards Kassiopi where she hoped her next round of farewells wouldn't be quite so interrogative.

When she reached the busy harbour with its myriad fishing boats jostling for position with the many caiques waiting to take tourists for a trip along the coast she made her way to Costas's restaurant and decided that, to be on the safe side, she would simply tell him and his family that she was returning to England to look after her mother. A Greek man like Costas would understand all about family duty and responsibility.

Costas hugged her warmly when he saw her. He kissed her many times over and slipped his arms around her waist. He took her to the back of the restaurant away from all his customers. He kissed her again and asked her in one breath how she was, how her writing was going and when was she going to get around to casting him as her next romantic hero? His English was perfect, if slightly American-ised, having been learnt while working in Chicago in a restaurant owned by one of his many cousins. He called through to the kitchen at the back of the restaurant. Instantly his mother appeared through the beaded curtain and shuffling behind her came an even older woman, Costas's grandmother. The two women beamed at Jessica. They were very fond of her, especially as she had immortalised them both in the opening chapter of her first novel which had been set in Corfu. They spoke hardly any English and even though Jessica could speak passable Greek, Costas always insisted that she spoke in English so that he could practise his interpreting skills. Jessica suspected it was because he liked to show off in front of his womenfolk.

'I can't stay long,' she said, refusing his offer of a drink and a plate or two of mezéthes, 'I've just come to say goodbye.'

'Goodbye?' he repeated, 'why?'

'I'm going back to England.'

Costas forgot all about translating for his mother and grand-mother. They waited patiently for him to speak to them. But he didn't. 'For good?' was all he said to Jessica.

She nodded. 'I think so.'

He smiled.

'You don't seem surprised.'

'I'm not. I've seen it many times before. For visitors to the island its magic only lasts for so long.'

Jessica kissed him.

'What's that for?' he asked.

'For being the first to understand. Thank you.'

After leaving Costas and his family Jessica walked along the crowded harbour and crossed the square to Dimitrios, the owner of her house who, with his wife Anastasia, ran a noisy bar that unashamedly pandered to the needs of a particular type of English tourist. They served up steak and kidney pudding with mushy peas, even in August when the heat could be in the high nineties, and in the evenings they didn't bother playing bouzouki music, but showed videos of *Fawlty Towers* and *Men Behaving Badly* to amuse their customers over their beers.

Jessica chatted for a while with Dimitrios – unfortunately Anastasia was out visiting her mother – then handed him her spare set of keys to her house. She signed the necessary forms and returned to her boat.

When she finally reached Coyevinas she found Gavin waiting for her on the sun terrace.

Having said goodbye to her closest friends and dealt with the formalities of relinquishing her home, Jessica was already mentally flying back to England, ready to start her future.

But here was Gavin. Here was the present.

And just one look at him was enough to make her undo all her well-made plans.

He was leaning lazily against the wall, looking down at her as she approached the last few steps. His shoulder-length, sun-bleached hair was blowing in the afternoon sea breeze that had just started to pick up and his white T-shirt was rippling across his chest. She couldn't make out the expression on his face because he was wearing his favourite Ray-Bans, but she had the feeling that he had been waiting for her for some time and that he must have seen her little boat appear round the rocky promontory from Kassiopi and that he must also have watched her climb the steep hill path. She wondered what had brought him here at this time of day when normally he would be out teaching tourists to sail before the sea became too rough.

'Why aren't you working?' she asked, going straight inside the house.

'Pete's covering for me,' he said, following behind her and pushing his glasses up over his head.

'Why?' She frowned. *Why* was a word she'd heard too often today.

'Helen phoned me.'

'Oh.'

'What were you going to do, Jessica, write me a letter?'

She thought of the envelope in her bag. 'I'm sorry,' she said guiltily.

'No you're not.' His face took on an expression of bewilderment and reduced him to the hurt boy she had predicted.

'And are *you*?' she asked. 'Are you sorry I'm going, or are you just put out, a little inconvenienced perhaps?'

He didn't answer her. 'Helen didn't seem very clear about your reasons for leaving.'

Jessica smiled. 'She wouldn't be, she's too busy being punch drunk on Ionian nectar.'

Her metaphor was lost on him. He frowned and came towards her. 'Are you okay?'

'I think so,' she said, suddenly aware of the warmth of his body next to hers. She held her breath, knowing that if she breathed in the smell of him she would be caught in his spell and be reminded of all the pleasures soon to be denied her.

'Is it me? Is that why you're going?'

His arrogance gave her the strength she needed. How typical that he should think the world revolved around him. She took a step back from him and went outside to the terrace. He followed her and to the sound of the cicadas chirruping noisily in the nearby olive trees they both stood gazing at the sea and the shimmering outline of Albania where so much needless fighting had recently taken place.

'Your sleeping with other women did hurt me at first,' she said, determined to be honest with Gavin, but equally so that her last memory of him wouldn't be an acrimonious one. 'But then I began to realise that it wasn't our relationship that was bothering me. It was something much more significant. I woke up to the fact that there's nothing here for me any more.'

'Not even me?'

Still that arrogance! 'No, Gavin, not even you. Besides, there are plenty of other women for you, you don't need me. And I'm afraid that's something I want, I want somebody to need me.'

'Like your mother?'

She smiled. 'How perceptive of you ... and how very out of character.'

He shrugged. 'All things to all men, that's me.'

'Don't you mean all things to all women?'

He had the grace to turn away.

'By the way,' she said, sensing that their conversation was coming to an end, 'I know you don't approve of boats with engines, but you can have mine anyway. Do with it what you want.'

'Thanks.' He placed his hands on her shoulders and kissed her. 'Good luck, Jessica, I hope you find what you're looking for. Do you want a lift to the airport?'

Chapter Six

Alec thought of ringing Kate to let her know that he was on his way, but he was in such a hurry to see her he didn't want to do anything that might slow him down, so he locked up the office, threw his briefcase into the rear of his Saab 900, pushed back the soft top and headed for home along the A34 going south.

It was strange not to be driving in a northerly direction on this familiar stretch of road – through Alderley Edge, then on to Wilmslow – as he'd done for as long as he could remember, but he guessed that his new route home would soon become second nature to him. He passed Capesthorne Hall on his right with its extraordinary turreted façade and toyed with the idea of getting tickets for him and Kate for the open-air summer concert that would be held there next month. Thinking of Kate again made him want to get home even faster and he pressed down on the accelerator.

He wondered if he'd ever lose this feeling of euphoria every time he thought of her. He still couldn't believe his good fortune, that a girl like Kate would even be interested in him, let alone love him.

But then so much had happened to him that he was convinced that no matter how predictable one thought one's life was, it was anything but. He for one had never imagined he would end up running such a successful greetings card company.

Neither had he ever considered ending up a divorcé.

While he would admit that his marriage with Melissa had never been perfect, he had thought that there had been enough common ground between them – namely their daughter and the jointly owned business – to keep them together no matter what. There had been the usual conflicts that life bestowed so generously on any married couple, especially a couple who lived and worked together, but he had accepted the arguments and irritations as all part and parcel of marriage. Looking back on it, perhaps he had been too passive, too inclined to remember his vows of *for better or for worse* and had simply gone along with things. But in the end Melissa had not. Melissa had seen fit to give up on what she referred to as a bad job.

She had likened their marriage to a rather tedious book that one is told to read because it's a classic and never mind the boring bits, one must stick with it and see it through. Rather graphically, she'd told him that she had grown tired of wading through the same book, she wanted something new to read. 'There isn't anybody else,' she'd told him, as if this would make him feel better, 'I just don't want to be married to you any more.' Her pragmatic approach, he realised later, had at least made them both behave in a civilised manner throughout the divorce.

Initially, though, shock had rendered him unable to comprehend a life without Melissa when, one wet, miserable November evening she had moved out of their house in Wilmslow. 'I shan't be one of those grasping women,' she'd told him in the office the following morning. 'I shall just expect what is currently mine: half of the house, half of the savings and half of the business. Here's the name of my solicitor.'

That was the thing about Melissa, she was very businesslike, very organised and very together. Nothing fazed her.

No. That wasn't quite true. He had seen Melissa floored once, completely so. It was last Christmas when she'd first set eyes on Kate.

He'd heard the intake of breath, as well as the comment that followed. 'Pretty enough wrapping,' she'd whispered to their daughter Ruth, 'but is there anything worthwhile beneath those liquid eyes and the bewitching smile?'

He smiled, turned off the main road and drove through the avenue of chestnut trees towards Cholmford Hall Mews. 'Oh yes, Melissa,' he said out loud, a triumphant note to his voice, 'there's something more worthwhile than you'll ever know.'

He parked the car in front of the house and through the kitchen window that faced the courtyard he caught sight of Kate. She must have just taken a shower for he could see that she was wearing her white towelling bathrobe and a towel wrapped around her head.

He let himself in and placing his briefcase at the foot of the stairs in the hall he called out jokingly in true Hollywood style, 'Hi, honey, I'm home.'

She came and wrapped her arms around him. 'So you are.'

He held her tightly, pressed her slight body against his own and kissed her slender neck. He breathed in the perfume of her fragrant skin. 'You smell wonderful.'

'So does supper, I hope. It's nearly ready.'

He kissed her and began loosening her bathrobe. 'Can it wait?'

'Can you?'

He pulled the towel away from her head and let her wet hair fall to her waist. 'No,' he said and took her upstairs.

Later, when they sat down to eat, Alec poured out some wine and handed Kate a glass. 'A toast,' he said, 'to our first proper meal in our very own home.'

They chinked their glasses and smiled happily at each other in the candle-light.

'You don't mind eating in the kitchen, do you?' Kate asked. She had hoped to have had the dining-room sorted out in time, but in the end she had been too exhausted to start unpacking all of Alec's cut glass and china. Even so, she had gone to great lengths to make everything just right for them in the kitchen, setting the table perfectly for a romantic supper; napkins, scented candles, even a few flowers taken from Alec's bouquet.

'Of course I don't mind.' He laughed. 'This is wonderful. I don't know how you managed to get so much done today and cook a meal. The house looks fantastic. You're a marvel, you are, really.' He leant over and kissed her.

'So what was your day like?' she asked, basking in his praise.

'Busy. We've got trouble in the warehouse down in Oxford. I shall probably have to go and take a look some time in the next few weeks.'

'Can't Melissa go?' Kate knew it was silly, but she didn't want Alec going down to Oxford, not if it meant he might spend the night away from her.

'She could, but I'd rather do it myself. Why don't you come with me?'

'Are you sure?'

'Of course I am. We could stop the night in a nice hotel. It would give you a break from all the hard work you're putting in here.'

'I wouldn't be in the way?'

'Not at all. I'd much prefer it if you came. And besides, expensive hotel rooms have an aphrodisiac charm all of their own.'

She smiled. 'My own charm wearing thin already?'

He covered her hand with his. 'Not in a million years.'

Amanda tipped the remains of Tony's uneaten supper into the bin. Another disastrous evening was behind them. If only Tony didn't always give in to Hattie. Surely he could see that the child had him tightly wrapped around her little finger? How many bedtime stories did it take, for heaven's sake?

She went back into the sitting-room, switched on the television and began sorting out the swatches of fabric and wallpaper samples that she had collected over the past week. She really had to decide what colour scheme to have in the sitting-room. She was fed up with not having any curtains.

Upstairs in Hattie's bedroom Tony was sitting on the floor alongside his daughter. They were leaning against her bed looking at a book all about dolphins, which they'd bought on their holiday in America last year when they'd visited Sea World in Orlando.

'Do you remember when we were all splashed by that huge whale?' Hattie asked her father.

He smiled, remembering the holiday with fondness, not because it was supposed to have been his honeymoon with Amanda, but because it had brought his daughter such pleasure. 'Yes, we were drenched good and proper, weren't we?' He drew her closer to him.

'And then the whale came round the pool a second time and splashed us some more. Can we go again?'

Tony closed the book and placed it on Hattie's bedside table next to a framed photograph of her mother. 'Come on,' he said, 'time your pretty little head was on the pillow.'

Hattie reluctantly climbed into bed. Tony covered her with the white frilled duvet.

'So can we go again?' Hattie asked, looking up at him, her arms outstretched, waiting for a final hug.

'We'll have to see,' he said. He leant down and kissed her soft cheek. She quickly reached out to him and held on to his neck and pulled him down so that he ended up lying beside her.

'We went to see the new lady who moved in yesterday,' she said, hoping to keep her father's attention for a little longer.

'And is she nice?' he asked.

'Very nice. She's got lovely hair. It goes all the way down her back.'

'I'll look out for her. Now you really should go to sleep.' He kissed her again and made his escape.

He turned out the light and went downstairs, his head aching with tiredness. He was exhausted. He'd been up since five that morning and on the road by half past in order to see a customer in Reading for nine o'clock. The meeting had gone on until two, then he'd driven to Birmingham for another appointment. He'd finally reached home just after eight, only to find Amanda cross and out of sorts because Hattie had played her up over tea.

'Fancy a drink?' he said, when he found Amanda in the sitting-room watching the television.

'I'll make us some coffee, shall I?' she said, rising from the sofa.

He shook his head. 'I need something stronger.'

'There's some wine in the fridge. I'll get that.'

He collapsed on to the sofa, pushed aside the mess on the coffee table in front of him and put his feet up. He closed his eyes to some poor devil of a politician having his bones picked clean by a predatory Jeremy Paxman and tried hard not to think of what lay ahead after the weekend when he had an all-day meeting with one of the company bigwigs who was flying over from the States to determine the effectiveness of their UK office. 'Nothing to worry about, Tony,' Bradley Hurst had said on the phone yesterday morning, 'I want you to know that Arc is deeply invested in the UK. All I want to do is simply have ourselves a head-to-head to clarify our position.' The last time their position had been clarified by Bradley-Dewhurst-the-Butcher's-Boy, as all the sales guys in the office referred to the recently appointed vice-president of Arc Computers, their numbers had been dramatically reduced. As director of sales in the UK, Tony was only too aware that no matter how well the figures looked they would always be vulnerable to another attack from Bradley Hurst. The man was ruthless and probably went to bed at night chanting his own personal mantra – one employee less equals a dollar saved; two employees less equals two dollars saved; three employees less . . . It was a short-sighted way to run a company and long term it couldn't work.

When Amanda came back into the room with a bottle of wine and two glasses she found her carefully ordered wallpaper and fabric samples scattered all over the floor and Tony fast asleep. 'Happy bloody families,' she muttered to herself.

The flight had been delayed by nearly an hour and Jessica hoped her mother wouldn't be worrying. She had tried ringing from the airport at Corfu to warn her that she'd be late, but she hadn't been able to raise an answer. She had tried again when she'd landed at Manchester, but still there was no reply from Willow Cottage. She had fought against the rapidly forming image in her mind of her mother lying prostrate on the floor, her hand inches away from the phone. Instead, she had forced herself to picture her mother doing some late-night weeding in her immaculate garden, happily ignorant of the time or of the ringing telephone inside the house.

Now, as she sat in the back of a taxi driving at a snail's pace through the dark Cheshire countryside and with only a few minutes to go before her journey would be completed, Jessica chided herself for her stupidity. Her mother had managed just fine all these years without having anyone fretting over her, especially the kind of fretting that was turning her daughter into a neurotic idiot.

Idiot had been the word that Helen had used so vociferously at the airport when she and Jack had seen her off. Gavin had offered to come as well when she'd told him that Jack was driving her to the airport, but she had said she'd rather he didn't. 'Tears and sentiment would do me no good at this stage,' she'd told him.

There had been no danger of tears or sentiment with Helen, though. She was still cross with Jessica for leaving. 'You're an idiot, Jessica. A complete idiot. But mark my words, when you've been back in England for a few months you'll wonder what you've done.'

'You're probably right,' Jessica had said, 'but I'm going anyway.'

'And another thing,' Helen had gone on, 'why didn't you tell us what you were up to?'

'Because you would have tried to stop me.'

And that was the truth. She knew she'd hurt Helen and Jack with her secrecy, but she couldn't have taken the risk of letting them know what was in her mind. If she'd told them that on her last visit to England, when her mother had gone into hospital, she'd seen a house that she was considering buying they would have gone out of their way to dissuade her.

'Been on holiday, then?' the taxi driver asked, opening his mouth to speak for the first time.

'Yes,' she said, not wanting to explain yet again why she was returning to England. The pair of chatty young lads sitting next to her on the plane, with their scalped heads, noserings and sunburnt faces and bulging carrier bags of duty free, had been at a loss to understand why she didn't want to live in Corfu for the rest of her life. 'Give me a life of sun, sex and ouzo any day,' one of them had said.

'Somewhere hot and nice?' the driver asked her.

'Very hot and very nice,' she said truthfully.

'Ah well, it'll be back to normal and the real world now, won't it? That's the thing about holidays, there's nothing lasting about them, just a few out-of-focus photographs.'

Too tired to add anything of any worth to the conversation, Jessica let the man ramble on with his personal philosophy and anxiously watched the road. Now that the driver had opened up the floodgates of dialogue he seemed to have lost interest in keeping his eyes on the dark, narrow lanes and kept turning round to emphasise a point to her.

'You'll have to slow down here,' she said, suddenly leaning forward in her seat, 'there's a small bridge and almost immediately there'll be a turning to the left. That's it.'

In the clear moonlit sky Willow Cottage looked enchanting with its white rendered walls almost hidden beneath a swathe of sweet-smelling blooms from several ancient climbing roses, as well as a clematis that had competed for space over the porch. It was exactly how Jessica always pictured the house in which she'd grown up. Her own life might have taken a few twists and turns, but Willow Cottage had not.

The taxi driver was impressed. 'If I lived here I wouldn't need to go on holiday.'

Jessica waited impatiently for the man to amble his way round to the boot for her things. Come on, come on, she muttered to herself. 'How much do I owe you?' she asked, when finally a collection of overstuffed holdalls was gathered around her feet.

'Call it twenty-four.'

I'd sooner call it highway robbery, Jessica thought as she watched the red tail-lights of the car disappear. She looked up at the house and wondered why her mother hadn't already come to the door.

No! she told herself. Keep that writer's brain firmly under control, your mother is not lying dead on the Axminster!

She tried the doorbell, but got no response. In the end she let herself in with the key that was kept hidden beneath a large stone that Anna had brought back with her in her hand luggage after one of her stays in Corfu.

She found her mother upstairs in the spare room; it was stripped of all its furniture and old flannelette sheets covered the floor. Anna was standing on the top rung of a pair of step-ladders, a paintbrush in one hand and a pot of undercoat in the other; beneath her, a ghetto blaster was blaring out *The Three Tenors* and Pavarotti was 'Nessun dorma'-ing.

Jessica went over to Pavarotti and turned him down. Her mother suddenly caught sight of her and visibly jumped out of her skin. She gave a loud scream. 'What are you trying to do, Jessica, creeping up on me like that? You frightened me to death.'

'I'm sorry,' Jessica said, immediately horrified at what she'd done – *good grief, she could have killed her mother with shock*! 'I should have thought. I'm sorry. Are you okay? Do you need to sit down?'

'I'm fine,' Anna said irritably. She came down the step-ladder and put the pot of paint on a piece of newspaper. She then looked up at her daughter and, seeing the distress in her face, thought, poor Jessica, how fragile she thinks I've become. 'It'll take more than a little bit of shock to finish me off,' she said more good-humouredly. 'Now let me put this brush in a jar of white spirit, then I'll make us a drink. How was your flight? Oh, and by the way, welcome home.'

Chapter Seven

It was a difficult weekend for both Jessica and Anna. Jessica spent most of it hovering anxiously over her mother, watching her every move. In turn, Anna took every possible opportunity of trying to escape her daughter's infernal gaze.

'Should you be doing that?' was Jessica's automatic response to almost anything Anna did. She said it when she found her in the spare room finishing off the undercoating to the picture rail that she had started while waiting for Jessica to arrive the night before. She said it again when she found her mother standing on a chair in the downstairs loo, changing a light bulb.

'Look, Jessica,' Anna said, 'this can't go on.'

'You're right. It can't. Now get down from that chair and let me do that.'

By Sunday afternoon the strain was really telling. Jessica found Anna struggling with a heavily loaded wheelbarrow in the garden. 'What on earth do you think you're doing?' she cried out, running across the lawn to her mother. 'You have Dermot twice a week to help you in the garden. Leave him to do the heavy work.'

'This is not heavy work. Now kindly leave me alone,' Anna said, gripping the handles of the wheelbarrow through her tattered gardening gloves and doing her best not to lose her temper. 'Go and do something useful. Go for a walk. Go and look at your new house. Anything. So long as you leave me to dig in this manure in peace.' She then pointedly turned up the volume on the Walkman that she had strapped around her waist and staggered further down the garden listening to a piece of Chopin, which Jessica could hear tinkling through the headphones.

Jessica stood and watched her mother angrily tossing fork-loads of manure on to the rose beds and, realising that her own anger needed to be assuaged, decided to go for a walk. She stamped off across the lawn towards the front of the house and to the willow trees either side of the brick steps that led down to the canal.

At first she marched furiously along the tow-path, snatching out at long blades of grass and swishing them against the undergrowth of dock leaves and buttercups, at the same time mentally shouting at her mother for her stubbornness and her stupidity, but gradually the calming effect of the canal worked its magic on her and she felt herself beginning to think more rationally.

It had been the same when she'd been a teenager. The canal had been the perfect place of refuge after she'd argued with Anna over something as trivial as the colour of her hair or the skimpiness of her clothes. They'd shout at one another, each convinced the other was wrong, then she'd race out of the house in a fit of adolescent angst and make for the tow-path. But always by the time she'd even reached the first sweeping curve in the waterway and her favourite tree, her temper would have fizzled out and she would lean against the sycamore and wonder what all the fuss had been about.

She reached the sycamore tree now and as she leant against its huge trunk, a pretty red-and-green-painted narrow boat came into view. Its occupants smiled and nodded at her. She smiled back and watched them slowly chug on with their journey.

Her anger and frustration now gone, she admitted to herself that it was obvious she would have to move into Cholmford Hall Mews sooner than she had originally planned. The idea had been for her to stay for over a week at Willow Cottage, then move into her new home, but even a weekend was turning out to be too nerve-racking an ordeal for them. She suspected that her mother was trying to prove a point with all her displays of independence and that it was merely a device for marking out the territory that belonged to Anna, which she clearly wished to retain.

With this in mind, the first thing Jessica did the next day, Monday morning, was to phone the sales negotiator in the show house at Cholmford Hall Mews. 'I know I said it would be the following week I'd move in and we'd agreed that you needed the show house for as long as possible, but is there any chance I could arrive sooner?'

'You're in luck. We've finished work on number three and we're going to use that as an impromptu show house. It's not a patch on this one, but at least it'll be somewhere for me to sit. I'm actually in the process of moving my stuff across at the moment. I should be finished by this afternoon. I don't see why you couldn't move in tomorrow if you can get your solicitor to arrange for completion to take place by then. Everything's ready for you, the carpets were cleaned on Saturday and the furniture not included in the sale has been shifted across to number three. Do you want to come and check anything?'

Jessica's first reaction was to say no, but then, thinking that it would do her and her mother good to have a break from each other, she said, 'Yes, I'll come down later, about two.'

She phoned her solicitor who said he'd arrange everything in time and after lunch she set off for Cholmford Hall Mews, which was little more than a mile away from Willow Cottage.

The day was warm and sunny, and as Jessica strolled along the lane and entered the cool tunnel of chestnut trees she found herself remembering all the times she'd played here as a child. With her mother's help she had even learnt to ride a bike properly on this flat stretch of road. Anna had never tired of telling the story of the day when Jessica had demanded that the stabilisers be removed from her bicycle. This act of 'big girlness' had meant that her poor mother had had to spend hours running alongside her, one hand on the saddle, the other nudging the handlebars whenever Jessica starting going too fast and out of control.

'Let go, let go,' she had screamed at Anna. 'I can do it, take your hand away.' And of course, the first time Anna had let go, Jessica had tumbled straight off the little bike and had ended up in a heap, with two grazed knees and a blow to her pride.

Jessica smiled to herself, thinking that her mother would probably view her as no better now than that skinny, demanding, four-and-a-half-year-old.

When she'd been that horrible child, Cholmford Hall Mews had been nothing but a sad, derelict stable block – the only surviving bricks and mortar from Cholmford Hall, which according to the local history books had originally been a grand shooting lodge. Just after the First World War the Hall was completely burnt down to its eighteenth-century foundations and for years after nobody saw fit to rebuild the house – the Cholmford family had long since run out of money. In the fifties the land was finally sold to a neighbouring farmer, who immediately cleared away the great pile of rubble and used the land for grazing. The stable block was then relegated to housing tractors and other assorted agricultural equipment and it wasn't until last year when a local building firm, on the look-out for a suitable conversion project, discovered the now thoroughly dilapidated barn and made an offer on it.

When Anna had first told Jessica about the development that was being built she had felt pangs of sorrow that her childhood haunt was to be spoiled and turned into a hideous eyesore. But then, when a few months later her mother had had her heart operation, Jessica had quickly made the decision to go and take a look at the building work. Far from spoiling the barn and the surrounding area, the builder had gone out of his way to create five good-sized homes of considerable quality that blended in perfectly with the incomparable setting. Jessica had come away impressed and within days had made up her mind to buy one of the houses. She didn't tell Anna straight away what she was doing – she needed the shock of her own actions to settle down before she could start explaining herself to her mother.

When Anna had been admitted to hospital, all Jessica had been able to think about was how much she loved her and what a happy childhood she had given her. Even her father's death when she was six years old had done nothing to dent the rosy picture she had of her formative years. She supposed it was because Anna had more than made up for the potential deficit in that area.

And now it was down to Jessica to make sure that her mother's love and kindness were returned.

Jessica moved in to Cholmford Hall Mews on Tuesday afternoon. Anna helped her. They were both the happier for it, knowing that the sooner Jessica was installed in her own home, away from Willow Cottage, the sooner they would start adapting to having each other around.

In terms of moving in there wasn't much to do. The only things that needed unpacking were the holdalls Jessica had arrived with from Corfu, along with several carrier bags of supermarket provisions and a bag of basic crockery borrowed from her mother for Jessica's empty kitchen. Between them they carried everything into the house from the boot of Anna's Fiesta parked outside in the gravelled courtyard.

'It's quite lavish, isn't it?' Anna remarked when everything was in and they'd closed the front door and she looked about the place.

'You said that the first time you saw it.'

'I know. I suppose I was hoping it might have calmed down a bit since then. It's all a bit chichi, don't you think?'

Jessica laughed. She knew exactly what her mother was getting at. The show-house-style furnishings and décor were not at all to her liking, but at the time she'd made her offer on the house it had made sense to Jessica to have everything all done – it was a bit like moving house the *Blue Peter* way; *and here's one I made earlier.*

'And those sofas will be a nightmare to keep clean,' Anna said, going over to inspect the two enormous cream sofas that were placed either side of the fireplace with a distressed-oak table between them.

'It's straight out of *Homes and Garden*. I'm not sure it's really you, Jessica.'

'What, you think I'd be better suited to something a bit more down-market? Some sawdust on the floor and a couple of barrels to sit on?'

'Don't be clever. I only meant it's hardly what you've been used to.'

'That's true enough. Come on, let's go upstairs, the bathrooms are quite something. You'll be green with envy.'

'Why do you need two bathrooms?' Anna said when she followed her daughter up the stairs.

'I don't,' Jessica said, opening a door at the top of the landing. 'It's what builders think people want nowadays. Now what do you think of that, it's the last word in des. res. luxury, isn't it?'

'Goodness, what a lot of edges and corners,' Anna said, peering in at the Wedgwood-blue bathroom with its white tiles and dado border decorated with Grecian urns. Opposite the bath and built around a low-level toilet and a pair of basins was a bank of cupboards and drawers. She went over and opened them all, one by one. 'What on earth will you keep in all these?' she asked.

'I've no idea. Old manuscripts, perhaps. Come and see my bathroom, it's even grander than this one. It looks over towards Mow Cop and the builders have set the cast-iron bath on a raised platform, so I'll be able to enjoy the view while having a soak.'

When they had finished inspecting the bathrooms and Anna had marvelled at the jacuzzi facility to Jessica's bath they went back downstairs. 'How about a cup of tea?' she suggested.

'Good idea, I'll put the kettle on. Oh, but I can't. I don't have one.'

'Oh, well, we'll go shopping later,' Anna said, forever practical, 'meanwhile I'll fill the teapot with water and boil it in the microwave.'

'What microwave?' Jessica asked, looking about the streamlined kitchen and seeing only a row of light-oak cupboards and a runway of spotless work surface.

Anna went over to the built-in cooker unit. 'This one,' she said. She pressed a button and a small door sprang open revealing the spotless interior of a microwave. 'You'll have to get yourself better acquainted with modern-day kitchen equipment, Jessica. I never did like that kitchen of yours in Corfu, it was so basic. The ancient Greeks were such a go-ahead lot, but I'm afraid their descendants are way behind in the white goods department these days. Ooh look, you're not the only one moving in today.'

They stood at the window and stared at a removal van as it rumbled its way into the courtyard and came to a stop outside number one. A few seconds later it was joined by a dark-blue Shogun. Anna and Jessica watched the driver get out. He was quite tall, with a slim build, and was dressed entirely in black – black T-shirt tucked into black jeans, a black denim jacket slung over his shoulder and black shoes with thick chunky soles. He started walking across the courtyard, his progress slightly hampered by a limp to his left leg.

'I do believe he's coming here,' Anna said as the figure in black drew nearer.

'I think you're right,' Jessica concurred, slipping out of view from the window. 'I wonder what he wants.'

They waited for him to ring the doorbell. But he didn't. To their amazement they heard him turn the door handle and suddenly he appeared in the kitchen.

'Keys,' was all he said. But then he looked about him and when he'd taken in the sight of Jessica's few possessions already making themselves at home on the breakfast bar his face coloured. 'Ah,' he said uncomfortably.

Jessica was a nanosecond ahead of him. 'This isn't the show house any more,' she said helpfully, 'it's number three you want.'

He looked at her as though he were going to speak and certainly Jessica could have sworn she saw his mouth open, but something must have made him change his mind, for he quickly turned and left.

'What a rude man,' Jessica said as they took up a discreet position in front of the kitchen window once more and watched him make his way over to the new show house. 'He didn't even have the manners to apologise for barging his way in here.'

'I thought he was rather dishy,' Anna said, 'in an awkward, boyish kind of way. He reminds me of that chap from *The X Files*, you know, the one with the lovely skin and the silly surname.'

'Oh, stop being so modern, Mum. Now come and show me how this blasted microwave works.'

Josh collected his keys from the woman in the show house, thankful that she'd been on the phone and had been unable to try and engage him in conversation. It was the last thing he needed right now. It hadn't been able to believe it when he'd woken this morning and found that today of all days, when he needed all his faculties to cope with the move, the power of speech was to be denied him. It was like that some mornings. He never knew what he would wake up to.

Sometimes it was his hands that refused to work properly. Other days it could be his legs and this morning it had been his speech. He could form a sentence perfectly in his head, but when he actually said the words they came out all joined together like a string of sausages. It was so frustrating.

And so bloody demeaning.

He dreaded to think what those two women must have thought of him. Bad enough that he had barged his way into their house as he had, but even worse that he couldn't apologise for what he'd done.

He joined the removal men who were now all out of the van and were having a quick smoke before unloading his things. He let himself into the house. From his jacket pocket he pulled out a pen and a pad of yellow Post-its and on each page began writing: sitting-room, dining-room, study, kitchen and so on, until he had identified each room. He then went round the house sticking the appropriate piece of paper on each door. That way he hoped the men wouldn't have to keep asking him where everything had to go as each packing box had been appropriately labelled. He'd spent most of the day trying to keep himself to himself so as not to invite conversation, but there had been times when they'd been packing up at the flat when it had been impossible not to answer their questions. He'd tried his best to give them clear instructions, but he knew that they either had him down as a drunk, because his speech was so slurred, or worse, had concluded that he was a half-wit.

It was nearly seven o'clock when the removal men left Josh alone. He found the emergency box of supplies that he had packed himself – coffee, milk, tea-bags, biscuits, Mars bars, pain-killers and some Southern Comfort. He pulled out the bottle and without bothering to look for a glass he slowly climbed the stairs, taking each step with infinite care, steadying himself with his free hand against the white-painted banister. When he reached his bedroom he had to fight his way through the packing boxes to where his bed had been placed. It was exactly where he didn't want it. But no matter. He sat on the edge of it and took several large gulps of Southern Comfort. It burnt his throat and left a warm glow of apparent strength there. He knew he shouldn't drink, that the alcohol would make his co-ordination even worse, as well as slur his speech more than it already was, but he didn't care. He was exhausted and had no intention of talking to another soul that day. He planned to sleep for at least the next twelve hours. He drank some more, then tried screwing the lid on the bottle, but this simple task took all his concentration and when he'd managed it he dropped the bottle on the floor and collapsed back on to the bed.

He was asleep within seconds.

The phone rang an hour later. It wasn't easy to find as somebody – one of the removal men – had placed it under the bed. He eventually located it and fumbled with the receiver.

'Josh, it's Charlie. How's it going?'

'Iwasleep.'

'What? You're not very clear. Do you need a hand? I could come over if you want.'

'Sodoff!'

Josh banged the receiver down and lay on the bed. He tried to go back to sleep, but in spite of his exhaustion he knew he wouldn't be able to. He knew also that Charlie would ring again.

He was right. The phone rang almost at once.

'Sawry,' he managed to say.

'It's okay,' Charlie said, 'don't worry, is it a bad speech day?'

'Yess.'

'Do you need any help?'

Josh could hear that Charlie was suddenly emphasising his own clear diction, as if this would in some way help Josh's words come out right. He knew that Charlie couldn't help it, it was a knee-jerk reaction, like clearing your throat for somebody else. The last time they'd been in this situation Josh had felt angry and humiliated by Charlie talking to him as though he were a simpleton, but tonight he was too tired to feel anything.

'Josh, are you still there?'

'Yesss,' he said wearily.

'Are you very knackered?'

'Yesss.'

'Would you like some company?'

'No.'

Chapter Eight

Amanda wondered what on earth she was going to do.

Her mother was supposed to be baby-sitting for Hattie that evening and she had just rung to say that she couldn't make it. Tony would go mad. The relationship between the pair of them was bad enough without Rita further worsening the situation – one that had developed from the day she had taken Tony to meet her parents for the first time: the dreaded Sunday-lunch scenario – roast boy-friend and apple pie. Her mother didn't have a very high opinion of men and was never slow in publicly declaring them a species incapable of making a commitment. 'Commitment my foot,' she would often say, 'men don't know the meaning of the word. A piece of soggy loo roll has more staying power than a man.'

When she had uttered these familiar words in front of Tony he had laughed politely and asked where that left Amanda's father. 'You've been married for over thirty years, Amanda tells me, that's quite a commitment, wouldn't you say?' Since then Rita had viewed Tony with suspicion. She didn't like to be questioned.

Even on their wedding day, Rita had approached Amanda while she was slipping into her dress and suggested that it wasn't too late to change her mind.

'But I don't want to change my mind,' she had told her mother.

'Then maybe you should consider it. I'm not entirely sure you've thought this through. Is he really the right man for you? It's all been so quick.'

'A two-year engagement would be too quick for you, Mother. Now help me with my zip. And please don't worry, I know exactly what I'm doing.' Which was true, she was not the sort of woman to leave things to chance. Her mother might not realise it, but Tony was perfect for her.

She had thought that moving to Cholmford, where they would be only a few miles away from Rita, would perhaps ease the situation between the three of them. She had had visions of Rita becoming more involved with her and Tony, and especially with Hattie. She had seen her mother in the role of doting grandmother wanting to spend time with her newly acquired granddaughter. 'That's all right, Amanda,' she had imagined her mother saying, 'I'll take charge while you and Tony have some time to yourselves. A long weekend alone is just what you both need.'

She must have been crazy thinking that life could be that simple.

And what was she going to do about tonight? In an hour's time she was supposed to be having dinner with Tony and Bradley Hurst and his wife. It wasn't often that Tony discussed his work with her, but she knew that his all-day meeting with Hurst was an important one. She was aware, also, of the importance of tonight's little get-together and the part that she was expected to play. Which, if she was honest, she enjoyed. The role of corporate wife appealed to her. If she herself couldn't work, then making a career on the back of her husband's was quite possibly the next best thing. And it was another reason why she didn't want to lose this evening's opportunity of presenting herself and Tony as the perfect couple to Bradley Hurst. She quite fancied the trappings that came with Arc Computers, more important, she had her eye on the perks that came further up the organisation. Currently Tony was the UK sales director for Arc and while he seemed happy with his lot, she had other ideas. Who knows, if only Tony could show a bit more ambition, one day they might end up in America where the standard of living was so incredible.

But all this was pie in the sky. So much for being the force behind the successful husband, she couldn't even organise a baby-sitter for that evening. There just wasn't anybody to whom she could turn. Having moved here to the back of beyond where they didn't know a living soul, apart from Rita, there wasn't anyone to whom she could shout for help. Everyone they knew lived at least twenty-five miles away. It was hopeless. Well, there was nothing else for it but to ring Tony and explain. She would have to lie through her teeth and make out that her mother was, at the very least, at death's door. Which would probably bring a smile to Tony's face.

'When will Grandma Rita be here?' asked Hattie, coming into the bedroom where Amanda was staring out of the window. Hattie was all ready for bed, dressed in her Beauty and the Beast nightie and chewing on her toothbrush.

'She's not,' Amanda said flatly. 'She can't make it.'

Hattie sucked on her toothbrush. 'Does that mean you can't go out?'

Amanda moved away from the window. She went and sat in front of the dressing-table mirror and began taking out the heated rollers from her hair. 'Got it in one.'

Hattie came and stood next to her. 'Are you disappointed?'

Amanda stared back at Hattie in the mirror. 'Yes,' she said truthfully, 'yes I am, and I think your father's going to be more disappointed. In fact, I'd better ring him now while he's still at the office, before he leaves for the restaurant.'

'Isn't there anybody else who could baby-sit?' Hattie didn't like the idea of her father being upset.

Amanda took the last of the rollers out and shook her hair. She started brushing it. 'We don't know anybody else here, that's the problem.'

'We know Kate.'

Amanda stopped what she was doing. She thought of last Friday when the sickeningly *lovely* Kate had had Hattie eating out of her hand. She had certainly shown that she had a knack for dealing with small children, which was more than Amanda had, and she had come away after their visit consumed with jealousy that anyone could be that good with her stepdaughter. When they'd finished their cups of coffee Kate had let Hattie plunder several packing cases of books out in the hall and had even allowed her to play with her jewellery box – little more than a cheap trinket box as far as Amanda could see – which she had brought down from her bedroom. 'I'd be so grateful if you sort it out for me,' she'd said to a smiling Hattie, 'the move has made it all topsy-turvy. Do you think you could manage that?'

Amanda turned and faced Hattie. 'You're right,' she said, a glimmer of hope twinkling in the far distance, 'we do know Kate, but do you think she'd do it?'

'She might, she was very nice to me.'

The words 'to me' were not lost on Amanda. 'She's probably got plans for tonight already,' she said, brushing her hair once more. 'And anyway, what would your father say about somebody he doesn't know looking after you?'

Hattie kept quiet and carried on chewing her toothbrush.

Stupid question, thought Amanda, if there was one person who could convince Tony a bad idea was a good one it was Hattie. 'Okay,' she said, getting up from the padded stool and stepping into her black patent shoes. 'I'll go across and see Kate. It's worth a try.'

The taxi dropped Amanda off just outside the restaurant. She couldn't believe her luck that Kate had agreed only too readily to help out.

'Alec won't be home till late, so I'd be happy to look after Hattie,' she'd said. 'Let me write a note for him and I'll be over.'

Not being a child person herself, Amanda couldn't understand anyone being so keen to spend an evening cooped up with somebody else's offspring. But she was more than glad that there were people like Kate who were fool enough to do so.

She saw Tony attracting her attention from the far side of the busy restaurant and she weaved her way through the maze of tables to reach him. He kissed her cheek and introduced her to the Hursts. She had never met Bradley Hurst before and she was taken completely unawares by the sight of him. He was one of the best-looking men she had ever had the good fortune to meet. He was tall, very tall, with piercing, icy blue eyes behind a pair of rimless glasses and he had a head of thick blond hair that made him more Robert Redford – in his younger days – than the man himself; he also looked and smelt the very epitome of power and success. His wife complemented him exactly – she could have been straight out of *Murder One*; a smart-arse lawyer type, all suit, lipstick and shiny hair. They made a glamorous couple and in comparison Amanda felt like little wifey who'd forgotten to take off her pinny and slippers.

'So great to meet you,' Bradley said, up on his feet and clasping her hand in his, 'Tony's told us all about you. We even know your shoe size.' He laughed warmly and Amanda didn't doubt his words for a minute. She knew how Arc operated from the way Tony had to spend hours genning up on the people who worked for the company.

'Hi, I'm Errol,' the suit and lipstick said, now taking her turn to shake hands.

As in Flynn? Amanda wanted to ask, but she knew better than to question an American about his or her name.

They sat down and Amanda waited to see which way the conversation would go, now that she had arrived. Would there be the routine polite questions about her busy day as a stay-at-home mother? She hoped not. It was too tedious for words.

'Tony's been telling us about the new home you've just moved into,' Bradley opened up with. 'Sounds kinda interesting. A converted barn. Errol and I would just love something like that, out in New England perhaps. Connecticut would be great. Ever been to New England, Amanda?'

'No.'

'Sure thing? Tony, you'll have to fix that. Amanda would love New England, I just know it. It's the neatest place for a vacation.'

Tony made the appropriate response and retreated behind the

head-nodding diplomacy he'd employed for most of that day. He'd like to fix Bradley-Dewhurst-the-Butcher's-Boy good and proper. How dare the man sit here in this bloody expensive restaurant telling him to take his wife on a lavish holiday to the States when he'd just informed him today that three of his best men would have to go. 'We're reshaping things as we head towards the millennium, Tony,' he'd started with first thing that morning, before Tony had even removed his jacket and sat down at his desk. 'We need to create a new vision, a new direction. It's all about concentrating the focus. You should see what we're doing back home, it's an exciting time for Arc. Tough, but exciting.'

Exciting for whom? Tony wanted to know. For the fortunate few who still had a job? And how the hell was he going to keep up morale in the office with everyone terrified about what would happen next? He'd be treated as a leper. He would become the enemy. Nobody would want to speak to him for fear that raising a head above the parapet would be reason enough to have it blown off.

Tony drove home listening to Amanda talking about how much she'd enjoyed the evening. 'You never told me what an interesting man that Bradley is.'

'I never told you that because he isn't.'

Amanda laughed. 'Nonsense.'

'I'm serious. The man's ruthless.'

'That's his business persona. If you're running a company like Arc you've got to be tough and stand up to people.' Secretly Amanda wished that Tony would show a bit more backbone. He'd been a right wet rag round the table during the meal, hardly opening his mouth, and when he did speak it was to come up with something as tactless as questioning Bradley's views on the state of the world's economy. Of course Bradley knew what he was talking about. As vice-president of Arc he was certainly better placed to understand these things than Tony.

'Now tell me about this woman who's looking after Hattie,' Tony said, breaking into her thoughts. 'You did leave a phone number with her, didn't you, just in case –'

'Don't worry. Of course I did. And believe me, there wouldn't have been a problem. I've never seen Hattie behave so well as she does with Kate. We should thank our lucky stars that we've got her living so close, she'll prove to be an absolute godsend, especially as your daughter seems to have fallen for her in such a big way.'

There were no lights on in the house upstairs when they reached home and when they let themselves in, all was quiet. Either Hattie was fast asleep or . . . or there was something wrong. Tony hurried through to the sitting-room, which was lit by a single lamp. When he saw Kate rise from the floor where she'd been sitting cross-legged reading a book in the soft light cast from the lamp behind her he could understand perfectly why Hattie had fallen for her. She was beautiful. Stunning.

And though the situation was completely different, he was reminded of the very first moment when he had met Hattie's mother Eve.

It had been love at first sight.

Chapter Nine

About an hour after leaving Tony and Amanda, Kate got into bed. She snuggled up close to Alec and laid her head in the crook of his arm. 'You didn't mind me not being here when you got home, did you?'

'Of course not,' he answered. 'What a silly question to ask.'

But Alec had minded, more than he cared to admit. He knew it was irrational, but when he'd let himself into the house and called out Kate's name and there'd been no response – only the message propped up by the microwave where his supper was waiting for him – he'd felt deflated and let down. Ever since their relationship had begun, and more particularly since Kate's job as a librarian had come to an end, he'd become used to her always being there for him when he came home from work.

Within weeks of meeting one another he had asked Kate to move in with him, to the cheerless house that he'd been renting after he and Melissa had sold what their solicitors had coldly referred to as *the matrimonial home* – he could have bought out Melissa's share in the property and stayed where he was, but he hadn't seen any point in remaining in the large family house, not when every room, every square inch of it, would remind him of the past. In what seemed no time at all after Kate had moved in with him the small, ugly house had undergone a magical transformation, it was suddenly alive and felt like a home; a proper home that was comfortable and inviting. It was as if Kate had bottled her unique, understated charm and liberally sprayed it around all the rooms. He realised very soon that the house had responded to Kate in exactly the same way that he had when she had saved him from a life that was leaden and interminably dull.

And it was that old life that he had been reminded of this evening when he had waited for Kate to come home. The empty house had dredged up memories of his being on his own after Melissa had left him. He had hated the long solitary evenings when all he'd had for company was the television and a meal for one on his lap. He had

53

been wretched and depressed. Inevitably, it hadn't taken him long to slip into the bad habit of staying late at work, then going home for a liquid supper followed by an early night.

Melissa had been only too quick to point out that he was letting himself go. 'You're a mess, Alec,' she said one morning at work, when he'd turned up late and heavy-headed. 'And your clothes stink of whisky. Go home and change, and take a good look at yourself.'

Melissa had never believed in pulling her punches. But she had been right, as she so often was, and with more strength than he'd known he possessed he'd hauled himself out of the trough of despair and begun to think about his future. And while clearing up several months' worth of self-pitying squalor from around the house, including a bin liner of old newspapers, his eye had fallen upon the 'Encounters' page of the *Sunday Times*. Was this the answer? he'd asked himself as he'd run his finger over the numerous dating agency advertisements. In a moment of decisiveness he'd picked up the phone and rung one of the numbers. Afterwards he'd regretted what he'd done and had needed a large whisky to calm himself down. His sense of shame and embarrassment was enormous, that he, Alec McLaren, had sunk to such a pathetic point that he was prepared to meet a total stranger in the belief that somehow his life would be miraculously improved by such a meeting.

But it had been. And how!

Kate was his life. He never wanted to be apart from her, which was why he had been so miserable all on his own that evening.

Of course, he could have simply strolled across the courtyard and joined Kate at number two, but in a way he had wanted to test himself. Just how dependent on her was he?

'So tell me about your day,' Kate said, slipping over on to her side and looking into his face.

He kissed her forehead and held her close. 'Nothing special,' he said, 'though I managed to convince our friends at W. H. Smith to give us more shelf space later in the year. You wouldn't believe how tight the whole thing's becoming. Oh, and by the way, Ruth phoned.'

'What did she want?' – other than more money, Kate wanted to add, but she had promised herself that she would never criticise Alec's family, no matter how tempted she was. In her opinion, Alec's daughter was a spoilt brat; a spoilt ungrateful brat at that, who shamelessly used her father whenever she needed to.

A few months before, Ruth had told Alec that Adam's one-man-band architectural firm was going through a lean time. 'People are so miserly these days,' she had moaned to Alec over Sunday lunch, 'they just don't seem to understand that to invest in one of Adam's exclusive designs is the best investment they could ever make.'

Alec had dutifully helped out in the only way Ruth understood and had parted with a large amount of cash. 'It's only money,' he'd told Kate, when a few weeks later Ruth announced that she and Adam were leaving little Oscar in the care of a child-minder and taking a holiday in St Lucia for a couple of weeks.

'She's after a favour,' Alec said, shifting his hand from Kate's neck and following the contour of her shoulder and then planting soft kisses on her throat.

'What kind of favour?' Kate asked nervously, raising Alec's head to her own. What on earth could Ruth want from *her*?

'I'll tell you in the morning.' He smiled and went back to kissing her.

When Tony awoke the next morning he found that Amanda's side of the bed was empty. He turned over and looked at the alarm clock. It was half past six. He closed his eyes, wishing the clock were wrong. Then he wondered where Amanda was. She was never up before him. 'You'll find I'm not a morning person,' she had told him the first night they'd slept together.

It was just one of the many little incompatibilities between them.

He pulled the duvet up over his head and wondered at the mess he had made of his life. He should never have married Amanda. Anyone could see they were wrong for each other. But then, how many other men in his position wouldn't have done the same?

Nothing could have prepared him for coping with the shock of Eve's death. One moment she had been on the telephone saying that she was just on her way to pick up Hattie from nursery and the next she was dead.

A freak accident.

A lorry with a man asleep at the wheel. It could have been anyone crushed to death on that wet, windy afternoon.

But it hadn't been anyone. It had been *his* wife. *His* Eve.

For months afterwards he'd gone around as if he too were dead. Nothing had made any sense any more. Even little Hattie had meant nothing but another problem for him to cope with. His work colleagues had helped as best they could by covering for him and continually making allowances. Friends, too, had played their part, but even the closest of them had gradually tired of the same sad story being replayed over and over.

In the end, and quite understandably, he had been left to stand on his own feet. Then he'd met Amanda at a party that his friends had insisted he went to. 'You've got to get out, Tony,' they'd repeatedly told him.

He'd given in, on the basis that after an hour he could leave if he wanted, and five minutes before his allotted time was up Amanda had walked into the kitchen where he'd been occupying himself arranging the magnetic letters on his hostess's fridge to form the words *I've had enough.*

'Enough of what?' she had asked.

If he'd been drunk he would have told her the truth, that he'd had enough of life, but because he was stone-cold sober, he'd said, 'Enough to eat.'

'Me too,' she'd said. 'Does Julie always force-feed her guests this way?'

'I wouldn't know. I've never been here before.'

'We've a lot in common then, me neither.'

Tony pushed back the duvet and thought that Amanda couldn't have been more wrong. They had nothing in common. He could see that so clearly now. He had married her because he had been a fool, a calculating fool to boot. He had seen her as a mother for Hattie, someone to organise his private life while he kept his professional one intact.

Poor Hattie, he thought as he got out of bed and went through to the bathroom for a shower. Poor, poor Hattie. He had thought he was doing the right thing in providing her with a mother, but the truth was he'd made things worse. He knew Hattie would never view Amanda as a proper mother and in a way he felt sorry for Amanda too. She was no Mary Poppins, but then neither was she Cruella De Vil. She was just Amanda, a woman who had made the mistake of getting herself involved with a man who still hadn't got over the death of his wife.

His first wife, he corrected himself. For better or for worse, Amanda was his wife now.

Downstairs in the kitchen Amanda was busy making breakfast. For a non-morning person she was feeling surprisingly cheerful. Her good mood was directly attributable to the previous evening. Late last night in bed, while Tony was asleep, she had made a few resolutions. From now on things were going to be different.

She had known all along that Tony had married her because he thought she would make his life easier. She had never deluded herself over the role she had been expected to play in his life and, more to the point, the role expected of her in Hattie's life. And that was fine, she liked nothing better than to know where she stood. But Tony had to be prepared to accept that as much as he was using her, she would use him. It was a fair bargain, in her opinion. If it was her job to take Hattie off Tony's hands, then in return it was only reasonable that his was to provide her with the life-style she wanted.

But after last night she had come to the conclusion that to get the best out of Tony – and ultimately the life-style she craved – she was going to have to work at their marriage a little harder than she'd originally imagined. She would have to appear to be giving him her unfailing support in everything that mattered to him – his daughter and his career.

It was listening to Bradley and Errol describing their 'honey pie' marriage that had made her reconsider her own. The gist of what they were saying was that if she were to shoulder the greater part of Tony's life, the more there would be for them to gain as a couple. 'I always treat Bradley's job as much mine as his,' Errol had said.

Amanda's initial response to such a comment was to scoff – only an American could have such a crass and idealistic view – but then she'd begun to wonder at what they were saying.

'Success is down to sharing the commitment of a career,' Bradley had said, 'I rely on Errol one hundred per cent. She's at home so that I can function at my best and be the success I am. Old-fashioned values keep it together, am I right, hon?'

'Absolutely,' Errol had said, 'I've had to make a few sacrifices here and there, but the rewards have certainly made up for anything I thought I'd lost.'

'And she's not just talking about the rewards of a perfectly cooked muffin.' Bradley had laughed.

Looking at the woman across the table in her smart-arsy suit, Amanda had found the image of Errol at home with a tray of blueberry muffins at the ready rather an unlikely picture.

'Brad's right,' Errol had said, 'I used to work as an attorney, but we soon found that we were pulling against each other and we just weren't getting anywhere. I suppose you could say we're centred on Brad now, we've invested my skills into his.'

'But hey, hon, you're talking to the converted. That's exactly what Tony and Amanda have done. Am I right, Amanda?'

The notion of centring herself on Tony had never before entered Amanda's head – what woman in the nineties *would ever* think of doing that?

In bed, she had asked herself the same question over and over –

was it really possible that by turning herself into an Errol she could make Tony a power-hungry executive like Bradley? In the end she had decided that it was worth a try . . . even if she did only pretend to be doing all that centring rubbish.

She scooped out Tony's egg from the pan of boiling water and took it to the table where she carefully placed it in the china egg-cup. Hearing footsteps on the stairs, she hurriedly poured out a cup of freshly made coffee.

Tony stood in the doorway amazed.

'Good-morning,' she said brightly, 'did you sleep well?'

He came over and continued to look amazed. He had never known Amanda to be up this early and he had certainly never heard her talk to him as though she were an air stewardess. 'It's not some kind of anniversary, is it?' he asked warily, looking at the table where he saw mats, napkins, glasses of orange juice, a pot of proper coffee and even a boiled egg. What was she up to?

She laughed and guided him to his chair. 'It's a celebration of sorts,' she said, 'it's the start of me getting my act together. Now tell me what you'd like for supper tonight.'

Supper! Good grief, it was as much as he could do to contemplate the egg in front of him. He knew he was being ungrateful, but more than anything he wished that Amanda were upstairs in bed as she usually was at this time of day, leaving him in peace with his normal hurried bowl of cereal while hovering over the sink looking out at the surrounding countryside with nothing but his own troubled thoughts for company.

Sinking into his chair and taking a fortifying sip of his coffee, he let his thoughts turn to last night. To that incredible moment when he'd first set eyes on Kate. She looked absolutely nothing like his first wife, but his whole body had responded in the same way as when he'd met Eve. His heart had jolted and his pulse had quickened, and as he'd crossed the room and held out his hand to her he had felt as though they'd met already. 'This was so good of you. I hope Hattie wasn't any trouble,' he'd said, holding on to her hand and not showing any sign of letting go of it.

'Not at all,' she'd answered, 'we chatted and then I read to her.'

'Let me guess. *The Secret Garden?*'

Kate had laughed. 'Yes, a few chapters, then we had *The Tale of Mrs Tiggy-Winkle.*'

Tony had been shocked. Not since Eve's death had Hattie let anyone read that book to her. She had loved the way her mother had read the story. Amanda had once tried it and Hattie had snatched the book out of her hands.

'We ought to thank Kate properly for last night,' he heard Amanda say.

He snapped out of his reverie. 'Yes,' he said, 'yes, you're right. How about some flowers?'

'Flowers,' Amanda repeated, her hand poised over the cafetiere to top up his coffee – flowers for a complete stranger, but rarely for her, she thought. 'We could do that, but I'm not sure it's the right thing to do,' she said slowly, thinking that Errol's marital professionalism would never allow her to stoop to anything as base or unworthy as jealousy. 'I know for a fact that her partner Alec has just bought her some.'

'Oh,' Tony said flatly. Partner. Alec. *Her partner*. He didn't want to hear words like that.

'I've got a much better idea,' Amanda carried on. 'Why don't we invite them for supper one evening, that way we can start being more neighbourly. Living out here and being so isolated it makes sense to build up a rapport with people whom we might need to rely on occasionally. What do you think?'

'Fine,' he said, pushing away his half-eaten egg. 'See what you can fix up. I'd better get going. Bradley wanted to see me in the office early this morning before he heads off to the airport.'

'Oh, well, give him my best and tell him to stay longer next time so that we can see more of him and his lovely wife.'

Tony grimaced. The less he saw of Bradley-Dewhurst-the-Butcher's-Boy the better.

Chapter Ten

When Alec had left for work and Kate had finished the toast and marmalade that he had kindly brought upstairs on a tray for her, she thought about what they had discussed while Alec was getting dressed.

'You don't have to do it, if you don't want to,' he had said, 'you mustn't feel duty bound to accept because it's Ruth who's asked you.'

But Kate had known that she would accept Ruth's proposal. That it was irresistible. Looking after Oscar would be a delight. In fact, it was just what she needed until she had decided what she was going to do about getting another job.

She got dressed and went downstairs, and found that the postman had been. A scattering of assorted-sized envelopes lay on the carpet in the hall. She picked them up and carried the pile through to the kitchen where she switched on the radio and was met with a snappy John Humphrys berating some poor soul for being incompetent. She turned the dial until she found Terry Wogan being accused of the same crime by one of his loyal listeners and to the sound of the Irishman's mock outrage she began opening the mail. The envelopes were all addressed to *Mr Alec McLaren and Miss Kate Morris* and were cards wishing them well in their new home, except for one which was addressed to her only. It was from Caroline with whom she had shared a tiny terraced cottage in Knutsford before she'd moved in with Alec, and with whom she'd also worked for two years at the library.

'I've lost your new phone number, so have resorted to this – let's get together for an evening out.' Caroline had used a green felt-tip pen to scrawl her message on the inside page of the card and her writing was large and loopy – not unlike Caroline, Kate thought with a smile. The card itself was also typical Caroline and the picture showed an oil-smeared, bronzed, muscly man in the skimpiest of leopardskin swimming trunks and to one side of his bottom her friend had written, 'Now he's what I call a man!'

To say that Caroline was interested in men was a huge understatement. She was pretty much obsessed with the male species. 'I'm always hungry for a good man,' she would joke, 'the only trouble is most of them are like a Big Mac, you have one and then a few hours later you're ready for another.'

No man ever stayed long in Caroline's life.

'I don't know what's wrong with men these days,' she would complain after the door of her love life had been slammed in her face yet again.

'You frighten them to death, that's what's wrong with them,' Kate had told her. 'Try not to be so pushy. Let them come up for air occasionally.'

'I'm only being me,' she would retort, 'I'll be damned if I'm going to pretend to be something I'm not.'

And if there was one quality about Caroline that Kate was in awe of it was her friend's incredible self-confidence and her implicit assumption that she was right and others were wrong. Whereas Kate had grown up believing it was she who was usually to blame for anything that went wrong and that it was her place to yield to those around her in order to make a situation work, Caroline was convinced of the opposite. The word sorry never appeared in her vocabulary, nor did the concept of being helpful, biddable or compliant ever occur to her, as her behaviour at the library showed only too plainly.

Caroline hated *the public*. She saw them as an unpleasant nuisance that got in the way of her carrying out her job as she roared about the shelves with a sense of urgency that frightened some of the more timid browsers who liked to while away their time quietly flicking through the papers and magazines. They certainly weren't up to being physically moved on when Caroline felt the need to tidy up the tables of paper-strewn reading matter. She didn't care that some of the braver users of the library called her the Gestapo behind her back.

Untidy customers Caroline could just about tolerate, but people who interrupted her and expected an answer to a daft question were the kind she had no time for. One afternoon an elderly pensioner had taken his life into his hands and had approached the desk where Caroline was hiding behind the computer reading the latest Penny Vincenzi and had asked, 'I wonder, have you got that book, you know the one all about life in a Cheshire village during the war?'

'How the hell should I know,' Caroline had snapped back. And seeing the poor man almost reduced to tears Kate had stepped in and taken him reassuringly by the arm to the selection of local history books.

Another time Caroline had caught a woman furtively eating a prawn and mayonnaise sandwich while reading a book in what she had thought was a quiet corner in among Travel and Careers. Unfortunately she had chosen a book that had made her laugh out loud and Caroline had pounced on her, not just for disturbing fellow library users, but for defacing council property by smearing page fifty-eight of *Caught in the Act* with a blob of mayonnaise.

Kate was just recalling the look of shock and bewilderment on the face of the woman when she remembered that *Caught in the Act* was one of Jessica Lloyd's novels.

Kate had noticed signs of their new neighbour moving in yesterday and she had badly wanted to pluck up the courage to go and knock on the door and introduce herself. Perhaps today she might.

But first she had to ring Ruth. She looked up at the clock – her Ikea station clock that her colleagues at the library had given her on her last day – and saw that it was nearly a quarter to nine. She went through to Alec's study and flipped through the address book to find Ruth's number. She pressed the buttons on the phone and prepared herself for a conversation with Ruth by taking several deep breaths. When the phone was picked up at the other end she was greeted with an explosion of noise. It sounded like an angry scene from a soap opera on the television, but Kate quickly realised that it was Ruth and Adam arguing. So who had answered the telephone?

'Hello,' she said cautiously.

'Hello,' said a small voice.

'Oscar, is that you?'

'Yes.'

'It's Kate.'

'Hello, I've just had my breakfast. I had a big bowl of Honey Pops.'

'Mm . . . delicious, do you think I could speak to Mummy?'

'She hasn't had her breakfast and she's very cross with Daddy. He used all the milk.'

'I'm sorry to hear that, but can you tell her I'm on the phone?'

Kate listened to Oscar banging down the receiver on something hard, then strained her ear to catch him interrupting the shouting match that was still in full flow. She couldn't hear his gentle voice, but she caught Ruth's loud and clear.

'Who's on the phone? Well, why didn't you tell me, Oscar? Really, you can be so naughty at times. Kate, is that you?'

'Hello Ruth, I hope I haven't called at an awkward time.'

'It's always an awkward time in this house,' Ruth said bad-temperedly, 'it's called being married to a fool. Now has Dad put my proposal to you? He did explain that I want this done on a proper footing? I'll be paying you.'

'Yes, Alec did mention that.'

'And?'

'I'd love to help out.'

'But?'

'There is no but,' Kate said. Poor Ruth, she was so cynical and unhelpful herself she couldn't imagine anybody wanting to help her.

'You mean you'll do it?'

'Of course I will.' And feeling in control with a member of Alec's family for the first time, Kate added, 'Why don't you and Oscar come over for lunch today and we can sort out the details?'

They agreed a time and said goodbye, and after Kate had tidied up the kitchen and found that she was still feeling flushed with success at having managed a conversation without Ruth making her feel slightly less worthy than a toe-nail clipping, she decided to introduce herself to Jessica Lloyd.

Jessica took one look at the stunning girl in front of her and wanted to reach for her notebook and pen. As classic images of romantic heroines went, this one was the princess of them all. Peas under the mattress, mirrors on the wall, mislaid glass slippers, she could show them a thing or two!

'I'm Kate and . . . and I don't want you to think I'm an interfering neighbour,' she said hesitantly, 'but I live next door and thought I'd just pop round to say hello. If you're busy I could come back another time.'

'I'm not busy at all. Come on in. I'm Jessica, by the way.' *Yes, come on in and let me get a better look at you!*

Jessica took Kate through to the sitting-room. 'Now before you say anything about the furniture and décor,' she laughed, 'I didn't choose any of it, so in no way does it reflect my character.'

Kate laughed too. 'It must be strange knowing that so many people have walked through your home just for the Sunday afternoon experience of poking about in a show house.'

Jessica pulled a face. 'Do you know, I hadn't thought of it quite like that. But you're right. What a horrid thought. Would you like a drink?'

'Tea would be lovely, but only if you're sure I'm not stopping you from doing anything.'

'You're not interrupting, honestly.'

Out in the kitchen Jessica filled the kettle – newly bought yesterday afternoon with her mother – plugged it in and reached for the nearest piece of paper to hand, which turned out to be an envelope from British Gas. She wrote quickly and spontaneously on the back of the envelope, trying her best to capture the stunning girl in the sitting-room. *Hair to die for*, she scribbled, *masses of copper waves right down to her waist – colour of a good sweet sherry. Tall and very slim – does she eat? Long, long legs hidden beneath faded jeans. Looks about twenty-one and makes me feel about a hundred and twenty-one! Pale complexion, probably never had a spot in her life! Greeny eyes, sort of misty in a sad kind of way. Irish background? Reminds me of those girls from* Riverdance. *Dread to think what Gavin's reaction to her would be!*

She crossed out this last comment and wrote, *Gavin Who?*

When she was satisfied with the thumbnail sketch, she made a pot of tea, grabbed a couple of her mother's cast-off mugs and slopped some milk into a cracked jug, also from Willow Cottage. Sooner, rather than later, she simply had to do some serious crockery shopping.

'Sorry I was so long,' she said when she joined Kate in the sitting-room. 'And I apologise for the state of this china. It's all borrowed from my mother until I get myself sorted. These poor old mugs look dreadful in here among all this chic furniture, rather out of place. A bit eccentric even. One could almost feel sorry for them.'

Kate wanted to say that everything looked fine and that anyway writers were allowed to be as eccentric as they wanted, that it was expected of them, but instead she said, 'Where have you moved from?'

'Corfu.'

Kate's eyes widened. 'Corfu? How wonderful. This is going to feel very different then, isn't it?' She suddenly lowered her gaze, conscious that Jessica was staring at her.

'I'm sorry,' Jessica said, realising that she'd been caught out. She quickly turned her attention to pouring the tea. 'I have a terrible habit of staring at people. An occupational hazard you could call it. I watch people all the time. They fascinate me.' She passed Kate her mug of tea.

'Thank you. Perhaps that's what makes you such a good writer.'

Disarming as well, thought Jessica. 'I don't know,' she said, 'am I?'

'A lot of people seem to think so, including me.'

Jessica looked awkwardly at her mother's chipped teapot. She found praise difficult to handle. Probably because she never trusted it. 'So how did you know I was a writer?' she asked.

'The woman over in number two told me ... and the sales negotiator told her. But I'd already heard of you. I'm a librarian, or rather I used to be.'

'Used to be?'

'I was made redundant. I was the last to be taken on and so naturally when all the cutbacks came into force a few months ago I was first to be asked to leave.'

'Any idea what you'll do next?'

Kate shrugged. 'I don't hold out much hope of getting another librarian job locally, but for the time being and perhaps until I really know what I want to do next I'm going to be looking after my partner's grandson.'

'Ah,' said Jessica – and thereby hangs a tale I'd like to know more about, she thought. But instead of immediately pursuing that particular line of conversation, she decided to keep it for when she and Kate knew one another a little better. She tucked her legs up underneath her on the sofa, reached for her mug of tea and settled herself in for a good gossiping session about her new bedfellows. 'When did you actually move in?' she began.

'On Thursday last week.'

'And were you the first?'

'No. There's a family over in number two –'

'With the woman who'd spoken to the sales negotiator, who'd told her all about me?'

Kate smiled. 'Yes, they were first to move in.'

'So what are they like?'

'They've a little girl called Hattie. She's really sweet.'

'And the parents, are they as sweet?'

Kate wasn't a gossiper by nature and she was reluctant to pass on what Hattie had told her last night while she had been looking after her, but having recently spent so much time alone she now found it almost impossible not to chat away with her new neighbour. And it wouldn't be gossip, really, would it, because Amanda had told her herself on Friday last week that she was Hattie's stepmother? It wasn't as if it were a secret. If it were, Amanda wouldn't have told her. 'They're very nice,' she said, 'she's his second wife ... the first was killed in a car crash. From the little I've seen of her I think

Amanda finds the role of stepmother difficult. It can't be easy if you don't have a natural rapport with children.'

'And she doesn't?'

Kate shook her head, then regretted it. 'That was probably very unkind of me.'

'No worries,' Jessica said, 'I shall strike it from the record.' She was amused at Kate's discretion. Beauty as well as a conscience. A beguiling combination.

They fell silent for a moment or two, until Kate said, 'We could lend you some china and anything else you're short of, if you like. Alec and I have got plenty of stuff we probably won't ever use.'

Jessica was touched. And intrigued. She wanted to know more about this Alec. She knew she was being unashamedly nosy, but meeting somebody for the first time often gave her an insatiable appetite for a dose of interrogation, especially when she was on the verge of writing a new novel and therefore on the look-out for a likely source of inspiration. 'That's really kind of you,' she said, 'but tell you what, would you like to come shopping with me this week and help me choose some things?'

Ruth finally arrived for lunch with Kate. She was over an hour late, uptight and overdressed in a Jackie Onassis-style cream suit with matching handbag, high heels and sun-glasses. She was cross, having just wasted an entire morning on an unsuccessful shopping trip to buy herself a suitable wardrobe for her new career, and while she took out her temper on her father's new home, tutting at the unimaginative design – Adam could have made so much better a job of it – Kate took Oscar outside to set the wooden table for lunch in the garden. Normally she would have had everything all neatly arranged, but she knew how Oscar liked to help her.

'Shall I put this knife here?' he asked.

'Yes please,' Kate said, 'and can you put the napkin next to it?'

They worked happily together until Ruth, tired of tutting inside alone, came out to the garden and tutted some more, saying that it was foolish to consider having lunch outside. 'The wasps will be swarming round as soon as we sit down.'

Kate held her ground and, as it turned out, the only person the wasps annoyed was Ruth. A pair hovered menacingly around her, dive-bombing her glass of orange juice or threatening an assault on her salad with its honey-and-mustard dressing. In the end they grew bored of the sport and flew away.

Kate ventured to enquire about the arrangements for Oscar. 'How many days a week will it be for?' she asked, watching Oscar who had finished his lunch and was now exploring the large empty garden.

'To begin with just two, that's until things pick up. But eventually I see myself working more or less full time. Adam needs somebody to get to grips with the administrative side of the business. The woman he's got now is hopeless. I know she's got problems at home, but these days one has to rise above that kind of thing and be the complete professional, otherwise there's simply no point.'

After hearing the sparring professionalism of Ruth and Adam arguing that morning, Kate couldn't help but wonder what the effect of their relationship might have on the business. It appalled her enough imagining the effect it must already be having on their son.

'So what time will you be wanting to drop Oscar off in the mornings?'

'Quite early, so you'll have to get your skates on. There'll be no more being spoilt by Dad bringing you breakfast in bed.'

Kate coloured and wished the wasps would come back. How did Ruth know these things? Surely Alec didn't tell her?

'Then in September, when he starts school, you'll have to take him. He's to be there at nine and he'll finish at three thirty. When you've collected him he'll need his tea. And by the way, I don't want him eating any old rubbish when he's here with you. He's to have fresh vegetables and fruit, plenty of fibre. I've got a list in my bag of meals he's to have. He's not to have any red meat, or fish fingers, or orange squash, fresh juice only. And definitely no sweets or biscuits.'

Poor Oscar, thought Kate. 'What time will you be picking him up?' She was wondering how much love she could cram into the precious hours Oscar would be with her.

'Heaven knows, to begin with. We'll both need to be flexible if this is to work.'

'Just a rough idea?' Kate persisted.

'Now don't try and pin me down, Kate. It's all very well you having worked in a cushy library where the hours are set, but outside the world of subsidy, in the real world, people have to graft all hours to get things done. I'm sure we'll soon slip into a pattern.'

'I'm sure we will,' Kate said, glancing over to Oscar who was fully absorbed in gathering buttercups and daisies by reaching one of his tiny hands through the picket fence to the weed-infested area of the neighbouring field.

'Oscar! Stop that at once,' called out Ruth, 'you'll get horrid stains all over your new Osh Kosh trousers. Now come back here where I can keep an eye on you.'

Oscar slowly withdrew his hand and wandered over to where they were sitting. He smiled up at Kate and handed her his bunch of squashed flowers.

'Thank you,' she said and gave his sun-warmed cheek a kiss. She was looking forward to having Oscar all to herself. It would be like having a child of her own.

Chapter Eleven

More than a week after he'd moved house Josh drove through the central archway of Cholmford Hall Mews and set off to work.

It wasn't yet eight o'clock, but already the day was warm. He activated the sun roof and as it slid back he switched off the radio. He wanted to enjoy his drive in to work that morning and had no desire for his good mood to be jeopardised by the tedium of listening to bad news. He didn't want to hear another word from some unknown MEP whinging on about why Britain should or should not touch a single currency. Neither was he interested in the latest round of Northern Ireland peace talks breaking down again.

On the other hand, nor did he want any good news to eclipse his own.

It was nothing short of a miracle that he was feeling better than he had for days. This morning he'd woken up with nothing more annoying than a stiff leg to bother him. Now that was what he called bloody fantastic news! Sod the government's latest employment figures – the lowest on record for years – and to hell with the pre-summer bonanza of high street spending, he, Joshua Crawford was up and running!

Okay then. He wasn't exactly running, but he was up and ready to get back to work.

He drove through the suffused green light of the avenue of chestnut trees and thought how it was that in such a relatively short space of time his expectations had been so dramatically reduced. It wasn't that long ago that if he'd have woken up with a stiff leg he would have been filled with fear, panic and anger.

When he reached the small bridge that spanned the canal he slowed the car and looked over to the pretty white cottage that he admired whenever he was passing. He envied whoever lived there. It was an idyllic spot. But then for that matter so was Cholmford Hall Mews. He drove on.

He would never admit it to his brother, or his parents, but the effort of setting up a new home on his own had been more debilitating than he'd expected. They'd all offered to help him, but he'd turned them down, wanting to prove to himself that he could manage. For the first few days after moving in he'd cursed his weakened body constantly, then he'd cursed himself for having collected so much junk. He made several trips to the council tip and jettisoned piles of stuff that should have been thrown away before the move, if not years before that. He also paid a visit to the nearest charity shop and donated countless bags of clothes that no longer fitted him because of the weight he'd lost in the past months. As well as this he handed over a bag of unused Christmas presents, including a Whistling Key Finder; some Resonating Energy Chimes, designed to relax and uplift; a Mini Carpet Bowls set and a rubber-sealed radio designed to be listened to while in the shower. They were absurd gifts and were all from his father, who took a perverse pleasure in browsing through the hundreds of mail-order catalogues that came his way. His taste for the impractical meant that for some time now both Josh and Charlie, as well as their mother, had ended up with a series of ludicrous presents.

It was while he was at the charity shop that his ego had taken an unexpected battering. He'd asked an elderly white-haired assistant whether the things in his car would be of any use. 'Always glad to have whatever's going,' she'd said and had promptly raced outside to his Shogun parked on the double-yellow lines, eager to help him unload the bags of clothes. It was a while before she realised that he wasn't able to keep pace and that he was still inside the shop, limping his way through the racks of second-hand goods. 'You should have said something, you poor old duck,' she'd said, looking pointedly at his legs, 'we'd have arranged to collect this lot from you, it would have saved you all the bother.'

His sense of frustration was enormous as he was then forced to watch a woman, who had to be at least thirty years older than him, manhandling the heavy bags from the back of his car. He'd hated himself and his situation.

Worse was to come later in the day when he started unpacking yet more boxes and came across his squash and tennis rackets, along with his skis and boots. The objects lay on the floor in the hall, reminding him, just in case he'd forgotten, that they would be of no use to him now. He banished them to the garage where they could no longer sneer at him. He hid the offending items behind an old blanket. He'd then spent the rest of the day struggling to put together a simple rack of shelves, but with each turn of the screwdriver his hands and wrists had burned until, two hours later, when all sense of feeling had gone from them he'd finally put in the last screw.

Triumphant, but knackered, he'd slept on the sofa that night, too exhausted to contemplate the stairs.

'Multiple sclerosis,' he'd been told last year by the neurologist, who had confirmed the illness to Josh, 'will take over your life and destroy it if you let it. There are certain things that you are going to have to face up to, like the chaos it will bring. Each day will be different. There's not a lot you can do to stop the unpredictable nature of MS, so the best advice I can give you is to take each day as it comes.'

The doctor had gone on to explain how the central nervous system worked and how his own was unable to send out and receive messages, which was why his body didn't work as it should. And as Josh had listened to what he was being told a feeling of relief had swept over him – he wasn't going mad after all. He hadn't imagined the weakness in his arms and legs; the occasional loss of balance and co-ordination; the heavy tiredness that without warning would suddenly come over him just as if he'd been drugged; the pins and needles; the numbness. For nearly two years he had experienced all these problems off and on, but because they came and went so quickly, as if by the flick of a switch, he had kept them to himself, but had always wondered after each occurrence whether he wasn't turning into some kind of hypochondriac. He had tried all this time to ignore what was going on, but when one morning he'd woken up and found that he couldn't see properly – everything through his right eye was blurred – he'd been terrified that he was going blind. He rushed to the nearby busy health practice, where he was quickly referred to an eye specialist, who in turn sent Josh to a neurologist. A whole series of tests followed. By this stage he had convinced himself that he was dying.

'You'll be with us for a few years yet,' the neurologist had said, when Josh had voiced his fears after he'd been given the diagnosis. 'But first things first. We need to set you up on a course of steroids to sort out the inflammation of your optic nerve.'

'Is that what's causing the blurred vision?'

'Yes. It's quite common in MS. Often it's the first conclusive evidence we have as to what we're dealing with.'

'And will it go back to normal? Will I be able to see?'

'Yes, the eye will be fine. Don't worry.'

But that was exactly what Josh started to do. Once the initial feeling of relief, that he now knew what was wrong with him, had gone, he realised that though the neurologist had given him varying degrees of help and advice, he had omitted to explain to him that there was no cure for what he had. When pressed, he admitted that there wasn't even a drug he could take to stop the illness from getting any worse.

Worry kicked in.

And anger.

How could this have happened to him? He'd always been so fit. He'd rarely been ill, not with anything significant. So why should he have multiple sclerosis? And what was there to come? He began to read up on the illness, and what he discovered only fuelled his anger and his ever-growing terror of what lay ahead.

But now, as he drove into the centre of Manchester and headed towards Deansgate, he was determined not to think about the future. It was too depressing. He joined the slow-moving queue of cars at the traffic lights and suddenly wished he weren't there, that he were back in Cholmford, in his new home.

Charlie might have joked that the place gave him agoraphobia, but Josh knew that he'd done the right thing in buying the house. He loved it already. He loved being in the sitting-room overlooking the fields of corn, bright and golden, and sharply contrasted against the adjoining fields of lush green grass, edged now and then with rows of hawthorns, oaks and beech trees, and all set against a magnificent backdrop of soft-focus hills.

What had appealed to Josh, when he'd first driven out to Cholmford after reading about the barn conversion in *Cheshire Life*, was the sense of freedom the house offered. Its isolation had immediately struck a chord with him. He had a desire to be alone, or at least to *feel* alone – given his circumstances, the coward in him reasoned that having a few people living close by wouldn't be a bad idea.

For some time he had been wanting to move as far away from Manchester as he sensibly could – the daily drive in to work had to be a realistic journey – and not just because he wanted a bit of space around him. He needed to distance himself from those closest to him.

Since his illness had been diagnosed he had felt confined – trapped even. He knew that Charlie meant well, his parents too, but their constantly looking out for him was beginning to have a suffocating effect. Trying to accommodate their response to his MS, as well as his own, was too much for him; it was like having to cope with yet another symptom of the illness. He believed, and hoped, that by moving away from their good intentions he would be able to sort himself out. God knows, he needed to.

All this he could see so clearly on a day like this when his body didn't feel as heavy as lead. When he felt comparatively well and normal it was easy to think logically and marshal his thoughts and fears. But it wasn't always so. He knew that. Too often he was irrational and as moody as hell.

He parked his car alongside his brother's TVR in the car-park behind their offices. Crawford and Sons was situated on the second floor of what had once been a Victorian warehouse, but had been converted into office space in the seventies. The first floor was occupied by a firm of solicitors and the top by a company of financial advisers. Josh had always joked that he and his brother were the only honest souls among a den of thieves.

Josh and Charlie had never considered working in anything other than the garment industry and when, thirteen years ago, their father had decided he wanted to retire early, he'd handed the business over to them. 'It's yours now,' he'd said, 'and I promise I shan't poke my nose in, it's up to you how you run it.' He'd been true to his word. Not once had he interfered with any decision they'd made.

They had worked for their father since leaving college and before that, spending all their vacations learning their craft from him, as well as developing a crucial sixth sense for a potential quickest selling line – an asset which had proved invaluable during the heady days of the Thatcherite era when there were fast bucks to be made in the garment trade and even faster bucks to be lost.

Crawford's had gone from strength to strength during the eighties and at one stage they'd had as many as forty employees. But that was then. Now things were different. With margins as tight as they were, the traditional layer of middle management had been removed from the company and they had pared themselves right down to the bone, numbering just fourteen employees to date. It was at least satisfying to know that, given the medicine they'd forced down their throats, they were still turning over the same profits as they had in the years of plenty, whereas many of their competitors who had resisted any honing down of their businesses had gone under.

Josh was convinced that their current success was due as much to their father as it was to the way in which he and Charlie had guided Crawford's through the recession and had then had the courage gradually to broaden the base of high street stores whom they supplied. The reputation and longevity of the company were just as important. Crawford's was well-known in Hong Kong where the bulk of what they sold in the UK was produced and as a consequence of their good name they were seen as a low risk. Maybe they were even liked. A few of their suppliers, the older ones in particular, still asked after their father. One always asked the same question: 'How's William?' he'd say, 'still pruning his roses?' He thought that was what all Englishmen did when they retired.

The other contributing factor to their survival was that Josh and Charlie knew their strengths. They were not innovators in the world of fashion, but followers. It was a clear distinction and so long as they remembered it Josh was sure they would continue to be a success.

He took the lift up to the second floor. When Mo, their receptionist, saw him she quickly stuffed a book under her desk. Josh was amused. For ages he and Charlie had known that Mo did most of her night-school homework during office hours, but so long as she kept doing her job as well as she did, neither of them had any complaints. He could also see that she must have raided the rail of finished samples in his office while he'd been away, for he recognised at once that she was wearing a knitted top that was part of next spring's line, as well as a pair of black PVC trousers – currently their fastest selling item. She grinned at him. 'Couldn't keep away, eh?'

'Got it in one.' He tried to sound as upbeat as he could, then attempted to stride past Mo, but the stiffness in his leg wouldn't let him. 'Charlie in his office?' he asked.

'Yes, but I've just put a call through. Shall I get you some coffee?'

'Thanks, that would be great.'

Charlie was still on the phone when Josh pushed against his door. When Charlie realised he was there he hurriedly brought his conversation to an end.

'Josh, what are you doing here? I thought you were off for another week?'

'I was getting bored,' he lied. He hadn't been bored at all. What had made him come in to work was something quite different. It was fear. He was frightened that if he stayed away too long there might not be a proper job for him to come back to. He wasn't worried that his brother would take advantage of his illness and try and squeeze him out of the business – Charlie would never do that – it was more that he was concerned that people would get used to him not being there. He was conscious, too, that for the past few months his brother had been working ridiculously long hours in order to cover for him. It couldn't go on.

He sat in the chair opposite Charlie and Mo brought in their coffee. She placed the mugs on the desk between them, which was almost buried beneath a tidal wave of faxes, contracts and specifications.

'So, how about you bring me up to date?' Josh said when Mo had left them. 'What's happened over that faulty batch of black jeans? Have they managed to get the dye fixed?'

Charlie leant back in his chair. 'Yes, after much verbal abuse they agreed there was a problem. I gave them an ultimatum by the way; one more cock-up like that and we ditch them. Is that okay with you?'

'Sure it is.' Josh felt the net of good intentions creeping over him. A year ago and Charlie wouldn't have put that question. 'And how about the problem at the warehouse?'

'I'm still dealing with that one.'

'Well, seeing as I'm back, let me sort it out.'

'Actually,' Charlie said slowly, 'I thought I'd go up there later today.'

'Meaning what?'

Charlie began sliding bits of paper across his desk. He didn't look up. 'Meaning exactly that. I'll go there later.'

Josh felt his body go taut with angry frustration. He got to his feet, placed both hands on the desk and leant forward. 'Meaning poor old Josh isn't up to it, I suppose. For pity's sake, Charlie, I'm quite capable of driving to Failsworth.' Then, summoning every ounce of energy, he marched out, slamming the door behind him. He ignored the stares of curiosity from everyone in the design area as his footsteps banged out angrily on the wooden floor. When he reached the safety of his own office he sank into his chair, sick with bitter exhaustion. He clasped his head in his hands.

A few moments later he looked up to see Charlie standing in the doorway. He came in. 'I'm sorry,' he said.

'Yeah, so am I.'

They fell silent. Then Josh spoke. 'Listen, Charlie, we need to talk. We can't go on like this . . . apart from anything else I don't have the energy. And what strength I do have I don't want to waste proving to you that I'm still capable of pulling my weight around here.'

Charlie nodded. 'Point made. Do you want to go out for lunch later and put me straight?'

'No, I've a better idea. Come back to my place tonight for supper. Meanwhile, I'll drive up to Failsworth and sort out the warehouse. Okay?'

Charlie nodded. 'Okay.'

Chapter Twelve

Jessica had a surprise call from her agent.

It was a surprise for two reasons: one, it was so early in the morning – early enough for Jessica to be dozing in bed still – and two, to her knowledge Piers rarely called anyone until late in the afternoon – not because he was still dozing in bed, but because he'd always given her the impression that he was far too busy a man to pick up the phone before lunch-time.

He was a curious agent, with none of the smooth-tongued charm Jessica had come across in her limited dealings with the world of publishing, and his opening gambit to their conversation now was a typical example of his complete disregard for the social conventions usually employed in such circumstances.

'Jessica, is that you?' he demanded – he never announced himself; if Piers was benevolent enough to ring somebody they were supposed to have sufficient wits about them to know who he was. At the other end of the line she could make out a strange vibrating noise. Then she recognised what it was. It was Piers shaving. The cheek of the man! He was too stingy to give her his undivided attention. He was probably sitting at his desk, his phone on monitor, one of his hands guiding a Braun multi-shaver across his coal-face craggy chin and the other scrolling through an author's royalty statement on his computer screen.

'Hello, Piers, how are you?' she said defiantly. She might be in bed and still not fully *compos mentis*, but she was prepared to give the social conventions an airing, even if he wasn't.

'Flat out and with no time for small talk. I finished *A Carefree Life*.'

'And?'

'Not bad.'

Praise indeed, thought Jessica. For Piers to offer up such a charitable comment was quite something. 'Thank you,' she said.

'Much better than the previous one you churned out,' he said, the sound of the Braun still whirring away in the background.

'Kind of you to say.' *It had only reached the bestseller lists!* Why the hell did she stay with him? There were plenty of other literary agents in London she could switch to. Why did she put up with him?

Easy. She put up with him because he was dead straight with her. There was never any beating about the bush. No fawning. No bullshit. No literary snobbery. No ego massaging. And if there had ever been the merest hint of any skin-crawling sycophancy she would have dropped Piers like the proverbial hot brick. Or was it a hot potato? Well, whatever. Something mighty hot.

There was also the small matter of his undeniable talent for negotiating a cracking good contract. The advances Jessica had received since writing her first novel had been more than enough to satisfy her modest needs and had enabled her to buy her house in Cholmford Hall Mews. She had no delusions that Piers was partly responsible for her good fortune. It was just a shame he couldn't employ a touch more sweetness in his manner. A few words of encouragement wouldn't go amiss.

'I want you to come down and see me,' he said.

She sat bolt upright, terrifyingly *compos mentis* now. A summons? What had she done wrong? Did he no longer want to act for her, was that it? Or worse, had her publishers decided not to offer her another contract? Had they found themselves a new Jessica Lloyd? After all, no writer was indispensable.

'When were you thinking?' she said calmly, already worrying about her next mortgage payment.

'Day after tomorrow.'

'Day after tomorrow?' repeated Jessica, more convinced than ever that the summons was in order to impart bad news. 'But I've just moved house,' she said, grasping at any excuse to put Piers off, 'I've got so much to do. I need to –'

'I know all that, Jessica.' His tone of voice implied, don't bother me with domestic details, I'm a busy man. 'But this is important.'

'Okay, what time?'

'Be here for twelve thirty. I'll book us a table for lunch.'

She heard him switch off the razor, which was all the goodbye she received.

She went downstairs and made herself a cup of coffee, and determined not to fret over her conversation with Piers she took a kitchen chair and went outside to sit on the unimaginative rectangle of patio. She stared at her empty plot of garden and tried to visualise how it would look by the time her mother had taken it by the scruff of the neck. Anna was full of enthusiasm for creating all manner of curvy-shaped beds and filling them with seedlings and cuttings from Willow Cottage. 'I'll plant some rudbeckia against the fence for you,' she'd said only the other day, 'and then I'll throw in some campanula and verbascum. Maybe some columbine as well, though not too much, it can be very short-lived. And a hibiscus would love the sunny aspect as well as the rich soil.' Jessica was no gardener and she was more than happy to let her mother's green fingers take charge, just so long as she didn't overdo things.

She yawned and stretched out her legs in the warm early-morning sun. She glanced down at the T-shirt she was wearing and the words written across her chest – *Wind Surfers Do It Wet And Standing Up*. It was Gavin's and had been part of a small selection of his clothes that he had kept at her house. It was months since he had worn it, yet Jessica could smell him in every fibre. She had intended to leave it behind in Corfu, but at the last minute, and in a moment of weakness and indulgence, she had relented and tucked it into one of the bags. Then last night, while lying in bed unable to sleep, she had pathetically sought it out. Slipping the garment over her head, the soft, well-worn fabric had felt familiar and comfortable against her skin, and had brought back happy memories of Gavin. Within seconds she had fallen asleep.

But this morning – and before Piers's phone call – she had woken up to the smell of Gavin and had longed for him, every bit of her missing him. Well, perhaps only the physical bits – she didn't miss the mental pain he'd inflicted on her by refusing to commit himself to their relationship. But really the missing and longing had started ages ago when she had become conscious of the loss of what had attracted her to him in the beginning. When they'd first met, Gavin's sense of fun and happy-go-lucky nature had matched her own carefree persona. They had been in perfect accord with the shared view that life was best enjoyed with no more thought given for tomorrow than for yesterday.

But then things had changed.

She had started wanting to plan her tomorrows.

And it had proved fatal.

She drank the rest of her coffee, then ran a lingering hand over the front of Gavin's T-shirt. She hadn't expected to feel his absence so keenly. She had imagined that she would simply start a new way of life and that it would be without Gavin. After all, she had done it before. Each time she had moved about the world she had managed quite easily to piece together a new existence on her own. But she suspected that this time it was going to be a little more difficult because the memory of Gavin was going to be more persistent than she had anticipated.

She had thought that she would miss Corfu itself, but strangely she didn't. Every now and then she would think fondly of the quiet bay that had been home for so long and of the friends she had made. Sometimes she would recall Helen and Jack and imagine them on their terrace happily bickering like a couple of noisy cicadas. But for how long would they remain so happy? was the question that came into her mind. Might even their contentment turn on them one day and poison their bickering into something altogether more damaging? She hoped not. She wanted them to be happy.

She wanted Gavin to be happy, too.

She smiled. Who was she kidding? Gavin would always be happy. He was too straightforward to be anything else. Nothing ever troubled him because he was incapable of taking anything seriously. That was why he was able to be unfaithful and not wonder at his actions. If it didn't matter to him, then why would it matter to anybody else? was his unspoken philosophy.

She hadn't thought of it before, but Gavin and Piers were quite similar. In many ways they couldn't be more different, but in other ways they were worryingly alike. It probably never crossed Piers's mind that a chance remark on his part – *Much better than the previous one you churned out* – would be deeply hurtful.

She thought now of her impending day to be spent in London and the thought appalled her. It would be stinking hot and horrendously crowded, full of worn-out tourists pointing at screwed-up maps and asking her for directions. Which would be futile because she knew London about as well as they did. On any previous trips to see Piers, or her editor, she had afterwards flown back to Corfu desperate for her little house and the peaceful tranquillity it gave her. She wasn't a city person and a day in London was just about as much as she could take.

She began to worry again what it was that Piers had to tell her. What was so important that he couldn't discuss it on the phone? Was it something to do with her recently delivered manuscript? She wondered about ringing her editor, but remembered that Cara would still be away on holiday and that *A Carefree Life* would be lying unread on her desk, awaiting her return.

Well, whatever it was that Piers had to tell her would have to wait until Friday, today she was going shopping with Kate. It was a funny thing, but the more times she saw Kate, the older and more worldly she felt. In the past all her friends had been older than her and she

79

had been happy to play her part accordingly. But Kate was almost ten years her junior and being in her company forced Jessica to behave quite differently. So what did that say about her? The trick cyclists might mutter something about her suffering from that well-known Peter Pan syndrome and that Corfu had been her Never-Never Land. Well, the trick cyclists could say all they wanted. They could pedal themselves up their inner tubes for all she cared. She wasn't afraid of adulthood. Wasn't that the very reason she had left Corfu? Responsibility for her mother had fairly smacked her in the face and made her see where her duty lay.

And on that grown-up thought she went indoors to get dressed.

Kate was just turning the key in the lock before going to call on Jessica when she heard footsteps coming across the courtyard. It was Amanda.

'I'm so pleased to have caught you,' Amanda said, hurrying the last few paces. 'I've been meaning to have a word with you for days. Tony and I wanted to thank you for helping us out the other night and we wondered whether you and Alec would come for dinner on Saturday.'

'There's no need to go to all that trouble,' Kate said, 'it was a pleasure looking after Hattie.'

'Well, come for dinner anyway. We'd love to see you both. About eight o'clock?'

'Thank you,' Kate said. She hoped that her voice conveyed at least a hint of sincerity. 'Would you like me to bring anything?'

Amanda laughed. 'Yes, some of your magic to work on Hattie, at least then we'll get an evening without her bothering us. She can be such a nuisance at bedtime.'

'I'll see what I can do,' Kate said stiffly. She suddenly decided that what she'd suspected from her first meeting with Amanda was true. She didn't like her one little bit. She started to move away from her front door.

'Off out, then?'

The enquiry was perfectly reasonable, but Kate was reluctant to satisfy Amanda's curiosity. Just because they were neighbours it didn't mean that they had to know one another's business. And besides, she didn't want Amanda suggesting that she come along for the ride as well. She had been looking forward to her day out with Jessica and had no desire for Amanda to spoil it.

'I'm just going shopping,' she said, in an effort to be economical with the truth.

'Anywhere nice?' asked Amanda.

Before Kate could reply Jessica's front door opened and she appeared on the step. Now we're for it, thought Kate.

Amanda looked over to Jessica and gave her a little wave. She hadn't yet had an opportunity to introduce herself to this supposedly well-known author – of whose supposed fame she was yet to be convinced – and she immediately seized her chance. She moved towards Jessica. 'Hello,' she said, 'I'm Amanda and I live in number two, over in the corner.'

'Hi, Kate tells me you were first to move in. How are you getting on?'

'Slowly getting things straight, you know how it is.'

Looking at Amanda in her commodore outfit – navy blazer and perfectly pressed knee-length white shorts with creases standing to attention and two-tone blue-and-white shoes – Jessica had a sneaky feeling that Amanda's idea of getting things straight would be entirely different from her own.

'I just came over to invite Kate and Alec for dinner on Saturday,' Amanda went on, 'I don't suppose you'd like to join us, would you?'

Kate hoped that Jessica would say yes. She didn't relish an evening of Alec talking to Tony and her being stuck with Amanda. Her wish was granted. 'Thank you,' she heard Jessica say, 'I'd love to come. What time?'

'Eight-ish and don't feel you have to dress up, it's casual.'

'One man's casual is another man's Sunday best,' Jessica said with a light laugh.

Amanda stared blankly at her, then returned her attention to Kate, 'I hope you enjoy your shopping.'

As they drove through the archway in Kate's little Mini, she said, 'Thank you for saying yes to Amanda's invitation. I'm not sure I could have coped with a whole evening of her without some kind of moral support.'

'Well, don't you dare back out at the last minute and leave me on my own. But tell me, and bearing in mind that I've known Amanda for all of two minutes, does she have the same effect on you? Does she make you want to say or do something outrageously rude, just to see how she would react?'

Kate smiled. 'Not exactly. To be honest she makes me feel awkward and nervous. But then lots of people make me feel like that.'

'What an extraordinary thing to say.'

'But it's true.'

'I hope I don't make you feel awkward.'

When Kate didn't reply Jessica said, 'Shall I take your silence as confirmation that I thoroughly put the wind up you?'

'No. No, I was quiet because I was just thinking that you don't make me feel nervous and I was trying to work out why.' She slowed down to negotiate the bridge over the canal and noticed that Jessica was craning her neck to look at the cottage on the right. She remembered then that Jessica had told her that this was where her mother lived. 'It's a beautiful house,' she said as they drove on.

Jessica wrenched her gaze away from Willow Cottage. She knew perfectly well that Anna wasn't at home, that she was staying with friends for a few days, but she couldn't rid herself of the need to be continually checking on her mother. It was quite alarming that in such a short space of time she had become a fanatic worrier about her mother's well-being. She realised now, with a sense of very real shame, that previously she had worried less over Anna because it had been a clear case of out of sight, out of mind.

'And did you grow up there?' asked Kate.

'Born and raised, as the expression goes.'

'It's lovely,' said Kate, 'I wish I'd grown up somewhere like this.'

Jessica caught the wistfulness in Kate's words. 'Don't be fooled by a few pretty roses round the door,' she said lightly. 'Now come on, tell me where we're going.'

'I thought perhaps we could go to Macclesfield. It's fairly easy to park there and I'm sure you'll be able to get most of what you want.'

'Brilliant, the sooner I get this over and done with the better. And thanks, by the way, for driving. Mum was all set to lend me her car, but then she was invited to spend a few days with friends over in Abersoch. And that's another thing I've got to arrange.'

'What's that?'

'A car. I'll go mad if I don't get one organised soon.'

'Did you have one in Corfu?'

'No. I either walked or used my boat.'

'It sounds very romantic. Don't you miss it all? This must seem quite ordinary in comparison.'

'It's all relative. Even shopping by boat becomes ordinary in the end.'

'I suppose so.' After a while Kate added, 'I hope that's not true of love.'

'That's quite a leap of thought,' Jessica said, intrigued and hoping for some further comment.

But Kate didn't say anything else. She kept her eyes on the road and her thoughts to herself. There were times when if she thought about how much she loved Alec she became convinced that something so precious could never last. She wasn't a pessimistic person by nature, but it was as if she were waiting for their relationship to go wrong.

Chapter Thirteen

Kate and Jessica finally returned home just after six o'clock. Kate's tiny car was brimming over with carrier bags, and boxes of china and glassware and bed linen, and the larger items that they hadn't been able to squeeze into the Mini were being delivered a few days later.

Kate helped Jessica carry everything inside and after she'd said goodbye she went next door to find a message on the answerphone from Ruth telling her – not asking her – to call back immediately.

Kate took the unprecedented step of ignoring a member of Alec's family and started preparing supper. She crushed a clove of garlic, put it into a frying pan along with a large spoonful of olive oil, then chopped up an onion and while that was softening in the hot oil with the garlic she peeled and chopped some tomatoes and added them to the pan. She was just reaching for the pot of fresh basil on the window-sill when the phone rang. She had forgotten to turn off the answerphone and Ruth's voice bellowed at her from the hall.

'You can't surely *still* be out,' Ruth said bad-temperedly.

Kate was tempted to ignore Ruth again, but remembering that, to all intents and purposes, she was now an employee of Alec's daughter she decided she'd better answer the phone. She took the frying pan off the hob and went and put Ruth out of her misery.

'Sorry about that, I've just got in,' she said, stretching the truth by about twenty minutes. 'If it's Alec you want to speak to I'm afraid he's not back yet.'

'No, it's not Dad I want, it's you. I need you to look after Oscar tomorrow. I'll drop him off at about half past eight.'

'But I thought you didn't want me to have him until the week after next.'

'I know that's what we agreed, but something's come up.'

Yes, thought Kate, lunch with a friend probably. 'I'm sorry, Ruth,' she said, 'but I can't help you, not tomorrow.'

'What? What do you mean you can't do it?'

'Alec's got to go down to Oxford to the warehouse tomorrow and I'm going with him.'

'Well, surely you can go another time; Dad's always going down there.'

Kate gripped the receiver. She really mustn't let Ruth push her around in this way. 'Alec was quite keen for me to go. We were going to stop the night in a hotel and then come back the following day.'

A loud snort from the other end of the line told Kate exactly what Ruth thought about her father spending a night in a hotel with a woman twenty-one years his junior.

'Well, all I'll say on the matter is that poor Oscar is going to be devastated,' Ruth went on. 'I promised him he'd be spending the day with you and now he'll probably cry himself to sleep with disappointment. If there's one thing children need, Kate, it's stability and consistency. I didn't think I'd have to remind *you* of that.'

Kate flinched. She'd known that she would regret ever letting Ruth wheedle out of her the details of her unhappy childhood. It had been a chance remark on Boxing Day when she had met Alec's family for the first time that had led to the mortifying disclosure. She had spent all morning in the kitchen preparing lunch and trying to take her mind off the impending show-down, and while she had been willing the day not to happen Alec had been insistent that all would be well. His calmness had surprised her. She hadn't expected him to be as nervous as she was, but his jovial manner – to the point of seemingly enjoying the prospect of his ex-wife meeting her – had only added to her own anxiety. The words *trophy girl-friend* had entered her head as he'd helped her choose what to wear. By the time they arrived she was rigid with fear and she let Alec greet his family while she hid in the kitchen and listened to him taking coats and offering drinks.

'They'll love you,' he whispered into her ear when inevitably he came to find her, 'who could fail to?'

'Melissa for one,' she whispered back.

He kissed her and took her by the hand to the sitting-room.

'This is Kate,' Alec announced, his arm around her shoulder. Predictably all eyes – especially Melissa's – were on her and, wishing herself anywhere but in that room, she made a few polite noises and sought refuge in Alec's grandson Oscar, who was sitting on the floor looking at a book.

'Hello,' she said, going over to the little boy and slipping down to the floor beside him. 'Is that a Christmas present?'

He raised his head warily, stared at her with his large, thoughtful brown eyes, then said, 'Yes. Will you read it to me?'

She didn't need asking twice and leaving Alec to entertain the rest of his family she took the book from Oscar and began reading aloud to him, but in a lowered voice so as not to draw attention to herself. After a few minutes, Ruth came over and joined them. She sat in the wing-back chair in front of Kate and Oscar, and with a glass of wine in her hand she watched the pair of them closely. She also listened. Kate struggled to keep her nerves at bay and continued reading as best she could. When the story was over Oscar, who was now sitting on her lap, turned the pages back to the beginning and said, 'Read it again, *please*.' She smiled and gave him a hug, glad that she had at least made one friend in Alec's family.

'Do all children lap you up in this way?' Ruth asked.

'I . . . don't know,' she answered.

'I've always thought that it's the childlike who relate best to children. Wouldn't you agree?'

The insult was glaringly obvious and Kate said the first thing that came into her head. It proved to be entirely the wrong thing to say. 'I just like children to be happy. I know what it's like to be unhappy.'

The expression on Ruth's face changed. She snapped forward in her chair and began the process of interrogation that she must have been dying to do ever since she had learnt of her father's scandalously young girl-friend. Kate tried hard to parry the questions that were being fired at her, but her nervousness and natural distaste for deception rendered her incapable of defending herself against such a determined inquisitor. By the time Ruth had finished with her, the full details had been drawn out of her and an unspoken conclusion reached – not only had Kate's unstable upbringing set her on a course of seeking out a lover to make up for the father she had never known, but her love of children was to compensate for the love she'd never received from her own mother, who had flitted from one disastrous relationship to another. But what was wrong if that was the case? Did it really matter? Wasn't it true that everybody's actions were attributable in one way or another to their upbringing? But any amount of self-justification wouldn't quell the tide of unhappiness Ruth's questioning was causing her.

Several times during Ruth's cross-examination Kate had looked across the room for help, to where Alec was talking to Melissa, but he had been unaware of her distress.

In the end it was Oscar who came to her rescue. 'I'm hungry,' he announced. 'What's for lunch?'

'I'd better go and see,' she said, quickly lifting him off her lap and getting to her feet. He had followed her out to the kitchen and they had remained the best of friends ever since.

But now as Kate thought of her little friend her heart ached at the distress she would cause him if she didn't do what his mother wanted. She couldn't bear the thought of him crying himself to sleep that night. She tried to think of a way round the problem; a solution that would suit them all. She didn't want to let Alec down, but neither did she want to hurt Oscar. An idea came into her head. She wasn't sure how Alec would take it, but Oscar was his grandson after all, so he couldn't object too much, could he?

But Alec did object.

'What?' he demanded, later that evening when Kate told him what she had agreed with Ruth.

'Ruth wanted me to look after Oscar and I said if it was all right with her he could come with us to Oxford . . . I thought he'd enjoy it,' she faltered. 'I thought you would, too.'

'You mean, you thought *you*'d enjoy it.'

Kate was dumbfounded. She had never heard Alec's voice so cold, or so sharp. 'I . . . I don't understand, you know I enjoying having Oscar around, I love him dearly.'

Alec turned on his heel and marched out of the kitchen. He went upstairs to the bedroom, yanked off his tie and threw it on the bed, followed by his jacket. He went and stood in front of the window and gazed out at the distant hills. After a few minutes, when his anger had subsided, a far worse emotion took hold of him. Shame. He was shattered at his sudden outburst of anger.

He didn't need to try and reason out his actions. It was all about his own insecurity. He was so terrified that he would lose Kate he was becoming irrationally possessive. He couldn't handle her wanting to spend time with anyone but himself.

Hell! He was even jealous of her spending time with Oscar.

He'd heard people talk about the demon of jealousy and what a powerful destructive force it could be, but he'd had no idea until now just how destructive.

All he wanted was to have Kate entirely to himself while they were in Oxford. He'd planned to get his visit at the warehouse over and done with as quickly as possible, then spend the rest of the time with Kate. He'd even ordered champagne to be waiting for them when they arrived at the hotel. He'd had in mind a night of seduction.

Not a night of baby-sitting!

He banged his fist down on the window-sill and Kate's small china trinket box close to his hand rattled its lid.

From downstairs he heard the sound of a door shutting and as he continued to stare out of the window he caught sight of Kate walking away from the house. He knew he ought to rush out to her, but he stayed where he was. Motionless. Bewildered. He had never known such pain. He watched her cross the courtyard and walk past the block of garages. Then she began to run, her beautiful hair fanning out behind her as she ran across the field where the nearby farmer sometimes grazed his sheep. She went into the darkness of the small copse and vanished out of sight.

'What are you staring at?'

Charlie turned away from the window and faced his brother who had just come into the room.

'You never told me you had such terrific-looking neighbours.'

'I didn't know I had.'

'Well this one was a beauty and she was running into the sunset like a frightened gazelle.'

Josh thought of the only female neighbour he'd met at Cholmford Hall Mews, bearing in mind that he'd felt like death when he'd encountered her. All he could recall of the woman from number four was that she was slim, with a terrific tan. He had the feeling, though, that she wasn't what his brother would describe as a beauty. He knew Charlie's taste in women and they were usually of the very tall, curvy variety. And as far as he knew there wasn't anybody of that description on his doorstep. But then he hadn't exactly gone out of his way to meet his neighbours, having kept himself to himself since moving in.

'So what did she look like?' he asked, going over to the leather sofa and settling himself down, glad to take the strain off his left leg, which had been hanging off him like a dead weight for most of the day. He picked up his can of beer from the glass-topped table in front of him.

Charlie came and joined him. 'I think I've just fallen in love with an angel straight from heaven.'

Josh nearly choked on his beer. 'You what?'

Charlie smiled. 'Okay then. Maybe not. But she was all willowy and gorgeous, like something out of a picture, you know, one of those Pre-Raphaelite paintings.'

'What, the ones where the women look like they've got disjointed necks?'

'Yeah, those are the ones.'

'So let me get this right. There's a woman out there in the fields with a broken neck and you fancy her?'

Charlie sighed. 'You put it so well.'

Josh got to his feet. 'I think you need another beer.'

Charlie followed him out to the kitchen and while Josh opened the fridge he lifted the lid on the pan of curry gently simmering on the hob. 'When's supper ready? I'm starving.'

Josh tossed him a can of beer. 'When we've had our conversation.' He went and sat on a stool at the island unit in the middle of the kitchen.

'Oh, it's the serious stuff now, is it?'

'Got it in one.'

Charlie sat opposite his brother. 'Look,' he said, 'I'm sorry about this morning.'

'Yeah, and so am I, I over-reacted. But if we're going to avoid any repeat performances of that little fiasco we've got to come to some kind of understanding. My body might be doing its best to convince me – and everybody else – that I'm about as useful as a chocolate teapot, but there's nothing wrong with my brain. Okay?'

Charlie nodded. 'I know that, Josh. It's just that –'

'I know what the just is, it's you thinking that you've got to cover for me. But how long do you think you can keep that up? You're shattered with all the extra work you're taking on and I don't know whether you've looked in the mirror recently, but your looks are definitely going.'

'Cheeky sod!'

'Yeah, well, do something about it. Stop treating me like a charity case and let me do my job as best I can, and get yourself home and in bed at a more realistic time each night. Otherwise we'll end up with no company to run because we'll both have blown it.'

Charlie took a long swig of beer. He looked thoughtfully at his brother. 'I hear what you're saying and in principle I agree. But . . .' he raised his hand as Josh opened his mouth to speak, 'don't leap down my throat, but how long do you think *you* can keep this up?'

'Honest answer?'

'Yes.'

'I don't know. Some days I feel fine, as if I could plod on for ever. Other days, I feel like death. But you know that already.'

'You don't think, then, that by easing off work you might . . . you know, you might prolong . . .' But he couldn't finish the question.

Josh did it for him. 'You mean, if I give up work and take it easy will I live to be sixty instead of perhaps snuffing it when I'm in my forties?'

Charlie swallowed. 'I wish you weren't so bloody blunt.'

'But that's the gist of your question, isn't it? Well?' Josh prompted when Charlie didn't answer him.

'Yes,' Charlie muttered morosely. He kept his gaze firmly on the can in his hands. He couldn't begin to imagine life without Josh. It was inconceivable. They weren't like other brothers. There was an extraordinary affinity between them that had enabled the pair of them never to tire of one another's company. They had grown up together; played together; studied together; worked together and even holidayed together. Some might say it was an unnatural relationship, that siblings could never be that close without there being something strange or sinister going on. But the truth was quite straightforward, he loved his brother and would do anything to protect him. He looked up, suddenly realising that Josh was answering his question.

'I have no idea if by taking it easy now my life will be extended, but I can only do what feels right. And what's important to me at the moment is to be able to carry on as though this whole nightmare had never started.'

'So how can I best help?'

'By supporting me, I guess.'

'That's what I've been doing.'

Josh shook his head. 'No. You've been feeling sorry for me. Pity's the last thing I need.'

Charlie crushed the empty beer can in his hand. 'Okay then. I'll try my best.' And wanting to lighten the mood – there was only so much of this he could handle – he said, 'But in return you've got to introduce me to your neighbours. I want to meet that fantastic girl who's just taken flight across the fields.'

Josh stared at the crushed can in front of him and felt a bit demolished himself. 'She's probably not real,' he said, slowly getting to his feet. 'It's just some mythical vision your body has created to taunt you with.'

It was almost dark when Alec heard footsteps on the stairs. Soft, wary footsteps.

He hadn't moved since Kate had fled. He was still standing in the bedroom, his head slumped against the cool glass of the window. He turned and faced her when she came in. She stared at him, the hurt on her face only too visible. She looked pale and fragile, her eyes wide with the pain he'd inflicted on her. He could see that she had been crying and his heart twisted with shame and guilt.

'I'm sorry,' she murmured. 'I should have asked you first about Oscar. I should have thought.'

That she could think herself in the wrong appalled Alec and in an instant he was across the room with his arms around her. He held her so tightly he heard her gasp.

'It's me who should be sorry,' he whispered, burrowing his face into her lovely hair and keeping it there. He couldn't look at her expression. Not because he couldn't risk seeing the anguish he had caused, but because he didn't want her to see the tears in his own eyes.

Chapter Fourteen

Thanks be to Richard Branson, thought Jessica as her train pulled into Euston Station precisely on time; the journey from hell was over.

The fat man in the seat directly opposite her – the cause of two hours and fifteen minutes of purgatory – closed his laptop and began tidying away his portable office, which, as the train had hurtled its way through the sun-dried countryside of Middle England, had steadily encroached further and further towards the small space that Jessica had tried in vain to claim as her own.

As far as Jessica was concerned journeys had a peculiar tendency to bring out the territorial, if not the killer instinct in the most passive of people. Motorways were bad enough with every driver seeing himself as king of the road, but there was nothing like a train journey really to threaten somebody's personal space. Especially if the very latest in high-tech weaponry was being employed – the mobile phone.

And the fat man opposite her must have been a top gun in the use of his.

Of course, she should have known better than to occupy a seat in the same compartment as Porky, never mind sit barely three feet away, but it had been a choice between him or a screaming baby further down the train.

Once she'd made up her mind where to sit she had offered up a smile in the hope of at least setting off on the right foot. But he had ignored her. Fine by me, she had thought, settling herself into her seat and sorting out where to put her large leather bag, which was loaded up with reading matter for the journey.

But it was clear from the word go that nobody but Porky was going to get a moment's peace all the way to London. If he wasn't shuffling through sheaves of paper or rattling the keys on his laptop, he was on the phone. And there was nothing discreet about Porky's manner of conducting business.

'Yah!' he would holler into the small phone pressed into the pudgy flesh of his face, 'Yah. Yah. Yah. Yah, just do it. Yah, thanks. Let me know how you get on. Speak to you soon.'

By the time the train reached Watford Gap, Jessica and her fellow passengers had had enough. But nobody, it seemed, was brave enough to do anything. One or two people shook their newspapers, hoping that this might be enough to shame Porky into quietening down. Someone even tutted. But it was Jessica who decided it was time for action when the horrible man heaved himself out of his seat and headed towards the buffet car. When he was completely out of sight, she leaned forward, reached for one of his yellow Post-its and wrote in large letters – *One more noise from you, Porkster, and you're DEAD!* She stuck it on the screen of his laptop. Her immediate neighbours read what she'd written and smiled their thanks and support.

'Couldn't have put it better myself,' said a tiny grey-haired lady who had been sucking Polo mints all the way from Stoke.

Porky returned with several paper carrier bags of food and drink. He squeezed his bulky frame back into his seat. But just as he'd levelled off he saw the note. He snatched it off the laptop and held it up. 'Who's responsible for this?' he demanded, glaring round at the compartment like a teacher with a class of fifth-form pranksters.

Nobody spoke. Nobody even looked at him. It was as if he didn't exist.

The remaining half-hour of the journey was wonderfully quiet.

As soon as she could, Jessica squeezed past Porky and bolted off the train. She made her way along the busy platform towards the escalator for the underground. She was in luck, a train had just pulled in and she found herself a space jammed up against a George Michael look-alike, extraordinary whiskers and all. He smelt delicious and was rather good-looking, but then after two joyful hours of Porky, Robin Cook would have scored a ten-out-of-ten rating on the hunkometer.

She got out at Charing Cross and began the short walk to Piers's office, which was situated just off Haymarket. It was now, as she made her way through the tourists sunning themselves on the steps of the National Gallery, that she began to worry – at least the awful train journey had kept her mind off her impending doom.

Jessica was convinced that her writing career was over. Last night in bed, she had tossed and turned – even Gavin's T-shirt had been of no use – as her mind had worked through the same scenario again and again: her publishers were no longer interested in her and Piers was unable to find anybody else to take her on, which was probably why he had been so uncharacteristically generous about *A Carefree Life*. Though convinced that this was the case, there was the small voice of reason suggesting that if so, Piers would be the last person to have any qualms about breaking the news to her over the phone. If an author was past her sell-by date Piers would have no problem in sending her packing. 'Jessica,' he would say, 'it's time to clear your desk. Pick up your P45 on your way out.'

By the time she reached the glass-fronted building where Piers hung out on the second floor she was sweating and her stomach was somersaulting a treat. She could barely breathe and there was a dull ache clawing at the back of her head. Nervous tension was a real killer!

She pressed the button and when the doors opened she stepped into the mirror-lined lift and hunted through her bag for a strip of pain-killers. But all she found were a couple of loose Paracetamols, chipped and coated in fluff. She gave them a rub and put them in her mouth and swallowed. One went down, but the other stuck to her tongue and at the foul taste her face twisted into the kind of distorted shape a champion gurner would have been proud of. The lift came to a sudden halt, the doors opened and in front of her stood an immaculately dressed Piers – pin-stripe trousers, light-blue shirt and Old School-style tie. Through her discomfort she was conscious that he blended in nicely with the navy-blue carpet at his feet.

'Les Dawson, I presume,' he said, when he saw her grimacing face.

It was the nearest she'd ever heard Piers get to making a joke. 'I need a glass of water,' she croaked. The tablet was firmly lodged at the back of her throat now and her taste-buds were sending out emergency distress signals. Mayday! Mayday! Poison alert! Prepare to abandon ship. Which was a smart way for her body to say that if something wasn't done soon, Piers would have a revolting mess on his office carpet.

Stella, Piers's assistant, was sent for and was given the task of sorting Jessica out, and when she finally emerged from the toilet she composed herself and allowed Stella to escort her to Piers's office. He was waiting for her.

'Sorry about that,' she said, 'it must be the air down here in London, it doesn't agree with me.'

He gave her a look as if to say, are you quite finished? Then lifted his jacket from the back of his chair and pulled it on. 'Let's go and eat.'

Jessica had rather hoped that Piers would put her out of her misery before they went to the restaurant. Perhaps he was such a sadist that he was enjoying the moment of keeping her in an agony of suspense. Oh well, if that was the case, she'd have the most expensive meal the restaurant had to offer. That would serve him right.

He took her to the Caprice.

'I was here with Nick Hornby last week,' he told her as they perused their menus.

'Who?' Jessica asked, knowing full well whom Piers meant; she'd read *Fever Pitch* as soon as the book had made it to the shelves in Kassiopi. It was the first time she'd known Piers even hint at trying to impress her. What was going on? A joke earlier and now a blatant case of social climbing. He'd be telling her next that he was a drinking chum of A. A. Gill. She shuddered at the thought.

He lowered his menu and contemplated her. 'You're going to have to get your act together, Jessica,' he said sternly. 'Now that you're back in England you'll have no excuse for being out of touch.'

Her act of out-of-touchness was her deliberate way of showing up other people's hoity-toity pretentiousness. And anyway she had never been out of touch with England. The *Sunday Times* had always been available to her in Corfu and her mother had regularly sent her videos of all the best in TV drama, though she had begun to question Anna's taste when tapes of *Star Trek: The Next Generation* had arrived in the post. 'Why should I have to get my act together?' she asked Piers. She was being bold now. Well, why not? If she was being given the old heave-ho, she might just as well go out fighting to the last.

He didn't answer her. Instead he caught the eye of a passing waitress and began ordering his lunch. When he'd finished he looked pointedly at Jessica. So did the waitress.

'I'll have the duck whatsit on a bed of asparagus, followed by the pan-fried chicken liver with rosti, and I want the liver cooked. I don't want to cut into it and find lumps of strawberry jelly.' She slapped the menu down on the table and leant back in her chair. She was really getting into the part now: recalcitrant and thoroughly obnoxious.

'In that case we'll have a bottle of red wine,' Piers said, ignoring her performance and making her feel like a naughty child. 'I think the 1994 St Chinian will be suitable.'

When they were alone he said, 'How's the new house?'

Now this was going too far. Piers making small talk. No, really. This had to stop. 'Piers,' she said, 'would you please get to the point?'

'The point?'

'Yes. Just why on earth have you dragged me all the way down here?'

He smiled. Well, it was almost a smile; a slight lifting of the corners of his mouth. For a split second he looked almost handsome. Jessica had never before considered Piers as a good-looking man, but she decided that if he could only get the hang of this smiling thing he would stand a chance of being half decent; marriage material even. To her knowledge – Stella being her main source of information – Piers had never been married and at the age of forty-seven he gave the impression of having no desire to do so. Jessica would put money on him not being gay, though why she felt so strongly on this score she had no idea. Perhaps it was his brusqueness that precluded this possibility. Not that all gay men had to go around gushing like Julian Clarey.

Their wine arrived and Piers instructed the waitress to leave them to it. He poured out a large glass for Jessica and one for himself.

'I think this is what the clever-arsed folk would call a champagne moment,' he said, raising his glass, 'but you know me well enough to know that I'm not a champagne person, or clever-arsed for that matter, so this will do well enough instead. Come on, raise your glass.'

Jessica did as she was told, but viewed Piers suspiciously. He was up to something. A spot of softening up before delivering the blow perhaps?

'To your next contract,' he said. 'Congratulations.'

'My what?'

'You heard. Go on, drink up.'

She took a sip, then a gulp. Followed by an even larger mouthful. 'So why didn't you tell me this on the phone?'

He leant back in his chair. 'I wanted to tell you in person. I think the occasion merits such treatment. Nothing's definite and it's all down to you to make the final decision, but how do you feel about switching horses?'

'I think you'd better explain.'

Their first course arrived and while they flapped napkins open, sprinkled salt and pepper and poured out more wine, Piers explained. 'As you know, now that you've delivered *A Carefree Life* you've fulfilled your contract which means –'

'Which means I'm now out of contract.'

'Precisely. And I think you've outgrown where you are.'

'How do you work that out?'

96

'I've had an offer from another publisher who's prepared to pay a substantial amount of money for you.'

Jessica reached for her wineglass. 'How much? And which publisher?'

'One question at a time.'

She gulped her wine and tried to stop her knees from shaking under the table. It was all turning out so differently from how she'd imagined, and the combination of shock and relief was transforming her into a jittery mess. She planted both feet firmly on the ground in the hope it would keep her legs from moving. But it didn't work. They carried on banging away like pistons.

'You're being offered a two-book contract,' she heard Piers say. But suddenly he stopped and stared at her. 'Jessica,' he said, 'are you playing footsie with me?'

'Certainly not!' she squeaked. And with enormous will-power she forced her legs to be still.

He carried on, but with a curious expression on his face. 'As I was saying, it's a two-book contract and three times what you're currently being paid.'

Jessica drained her glass and goggled. The cutlery on the table began to rattle as her legs started up again.

Piers refilled her glass and said, 'Got anything to say?'

'Um . . . supposing I don't like my new editor?'

Piers rolled his eyes. 'For this kind of money, Jessica, I'd make an effort to get on with Genghis Khan.'

'But I like where I am.'

'In that case you'll have to accept their lower offer.'

'Which is?'

'A two-book contract and only twice what you're currently getting.'

Jessica considered what Piers had just told her. It was difficult to take it in. One minute she was worrying about her mortgage and the next she was feeling like Barbara Taylor Bradford. 'Even if I take the lower offer, it's still a lot of money, isn't it? I mean, it's oodles more than I ever thought I'd get paid. Squillions more in fact.'

'Such a precise command of the English language you have when it comes to money, Jessica. But it's only what an author of mine deserves. How's your duck by the way?'

They left the restaurant a little after three and took a cab back to the office. Jessica had been too shocked and excited to eat a thing and had drunk far more than was good for her. She tried to sit upright in the back of the cab, but somehow she kept slipping to one side. At one point she ended up with her head on Piers's shoulder. In a more sober state she would sooner have put it inside a tandoori oven.

They sat in his office and Stella was instructed to bring them coffee. And lots of it.

'I'm not drunk,' she told Piers as she sank into a chair.

'And I'm the Archbishop of Canterbury,' he said drily.

She giggled and found she couldn't stop. She laughed and laughed until tears were rolling down her cheeks. He came over and passed her his handkerchief.

'Thank you,' she said, pressing the hanky to her face. The square of crisp linen smelt of aftershave. *Piers wore aftershave?* Why hadn't she noticed that before? She tried to picture him at home in his bachelor bathroom splashing about with bottles of Givenchy or Chanel for Men. But it was no good. All she could imagine was Piers shaving in his office, too busy to bother with anything as trivial as men's toiletries.

She looked up at him as he stood leaning against his desk, his hands placed either side of him. She suspected that he was having a crack at smiling again, that mouth of his was definitely slightly more curved than it had been a few moments ago. She suddenly wondered what he was like in bed. Underneath that stern façade was there a passionate man who was dynamite between the sheets? Never mind the bedroom, how about the office, spread-eagled across the desk? The thought that she would like to find out had the effect of instantly sobering her up. *Arrgh! She'd actually just considered the possibility of having sex with Piers!*

She reached for the cup of coffee Stella had brought in some time ago and quickly drank it, even though it was nearly cold.

'Fully recovered now?' Piers asked, regrouping to the other side of his desk.

'Er . . . yes, thank you,' she said. She tried to make her voice sound sure and businesslike, and made an even bigger effort to sit up straight. 'Sorry about that, it's the shock. You know, the excitement of it all.'

He stared at her, his head slightly tilted to one side.

He knows, she thought. He knows what I was just thinking. She squirmed in her seat.

'So,' he said slowly, 'what's your decision?'

She cleared her throat. 'Um . . . I don't know.'

He tutted. Sentiment, his expression said. Nothing but woolly-minded sentiment. 'I'm sure I don't need to remind you that you have to think of your long-term future.'

'I know all that, but it's not just the money,' she said lamely, 'it's the personal side of the working relationship that counts as well. Cara and I get on. I might not like my new editor.'

'I thought we'd already covered that.'

She frowned.

He held up his hands. 'Okay. If you don't want to make the move that's fine by me. It's entirely your decision.'

Jessica needed some time on her own to work things out. So she went to the toilet to make up her mind. It was a ridiculous thing to do, but after ten minutes of deliberation she decided that if the loo flushed perfectly first go she would stay where she was. If it took two yanks of the handle, as it normally did whenever she used a strange toilet, then she would take the money and run. She held her breath and gave the loo handle an almighty shove – Frank Bruno couldn't have put more into it.

She went back to Piers. 'I'm staying with Cara and the team,' she said firmly, but not looking him in the eye – her decision to accept a lower offer meant that Piers had just lost out financially as well.

He made no comment, but offered her another cup of coffee and insisted on personally taking her back to Euston for her train.

'It's to be the red-carpet treatment from now on, is it?' she said, as they walked along the station platform, 'now that I'm one of your big earners.'

'I've always treated you well, Jessica.'

She came to a stop. 'Piers, you've never once walked me to my train and as far as I'm concerned you've treated me abominably ever since I've known you. You take a tenth of anything I earn and make me feel like shit.'

He raised an eyebrow. 'Good to know that I'm so good at my job. And if you really want to know why I'm escorting you to your train it's because in your current state of mind I wouldn't trust you to find the end of your nose.'

Chapter Fifteen

Jessica found herself a seat in a relatively uncrowded compartment. She hoped that there wasn't a clone of Porky lurking somewhere in the carriage.

As the train pulled out of the station she closed her eyes. Her head was beginning to ache again. What was needed was a quick forty winks.

But a nap didn't work and by the time they reached Rugby she knew she was in for a migraine. The dull ache had spread to the right side of her head and was throbbing with all the intensity of a pneumatic drill. She kept her eyes shut to stop the pain caused by the blinding overhead light and when the train stopped at Crewe she went and stood in the corridor by an open window, hoping that the cool evening air would help.

But it didn't and twenty minutes later, when the train finally pulled into Cholmford Station, Jessica walked like a zombie along the deserted platform. The station was unmanned and there was no sign of a phone. She was completely alone. She cursed herself for not having arranged for a taxi to pick her up. There was nothing else for it but to walk.

She staggered along the empty lanes for almost a mile, her head feeling as though it were going to explode. She felt so desperately ill that she was tempted to lie down in the road and wait for a passing car to run her over and put her out of her misery – if only there were any cars about. She had reached the stage now where the migraine was making her feel sick and light-headed. She reckoned that her mother's house was only a mile away so she struggled on. But it was no good. She couldn't go another step. There was a gap in the hedgerow and seeing that there was a small stump of a tree hidden in the long grass of the verge, she sat down and tried to breathe slowly and deeply. All around her it was very quiet. It wasn't yet dark, but the light was fading fast. She had never felt so isolated. A perfect night for a murder, she thought. No one to hear her screams. No one to appear on the *Six O'Clock News* as a key witness. She was just cursing her mother for living in the most remote spot in the whole of Cheshire when she heard the sound of a car coming along the lane.

'Oh please, God,' she said, seeing the headlights and getting to her feet, 'let it be someone prepared to help a damsel in distress.' She stood in the middle of the road determined that the driver would have no choice but to stop for her. She didn't give a thought to her safety – the person behind the wheel could be the mad axeman of Cholmford on the look-out for his latest victim for all she cared. He could chop her up into convenient bite-sized pieces and it would be fine by her – she'd even hold herself steady so that he could get make a better job of it – because at least then her head would stop hurting. Perhaps she could insist that he start by chopping her head off first.

Josh slowed down. He switched off Michael Nyman's *The Draughtsman's Contract* and as he approached the strange figure in the road he recognised who it was. It was his neighbour from number four. He got out of the Shogun and went to her. She didn't look at all well. She was very pale and her eyes were unfocused. She was shivering, too.

'Please,' she said, 'whoever you are, can you give me a lift to Cholmford Hall Mews? And if you are a mad axeman, do you think you could treat yourself to a night off?'

He smiled. 'Okay, but just this once.' He helped her into the car.

She didn't speak for the next hundred yards, then suddenly she blurted out, 'Stop!'

He slammed on the brakes and before he could get out of the car to offer his assistance she was on the roadside bent over a clump of stinging nettles.

After a few moments she got back into the car. He handed her the box of tissues he kept in the glove compartment. 'I'm not drunk,' she murmured, 'if that's what you're thinking. I've got a migraine, it always gets me like this. I'm sorry.'

'Let me know if you need to stop again,' he said.

'Don't worry, I will.' She put her head back against the head-rest and closed her eyes. She looked really ill now. He wondered if she had recognised who he was yet.

In all, they stopped three times. When they finally reached Cholmford Hall Mews, Josh parked as close to number four as he could. He went round to her side of the car and opened the door. 'Okay?' he said. 'You're home. Have you got your keys?'

She stepped down, took a couple of paces and lurched forward, almost knocking Josh clean off his feet as she fainted against him.

Regaining his balance, he decided the best thing he could do was to push her back into the car and take her over to his place. It didn't seem fair to leave her all alone.

She came to just as he started up the engine. 'I thought I'd already got out of the car,' she said drowsily.

'You did, but you also fainted.' He drove across the courtyard.

'Oh dear, I'm making a nuisance of myself, aren't I?' she said in a small voice. 'Where are we going?'

He pulled on the handbrake. 'My house. I don't think you should be on your own. And don't worry, I promise you, hand on heart, I've taken the evening off from axe murdering.'

She looked at him for the first time. 'I've just realised who you are. You're my rude neighbour, aren't you?'

Josh frowned at this description of himself.

'Right,' he said, when they were inside the house. 'What do you normally do when you have a bad migraine like this?'

She leant back against the wall, light-headed and dizzy. 'Bed, hot-water bottle and complete darkness.'

'Okay, can you manage the stairs?' It was strange asking somebody else this question. Usually it was asked of him. They made slow progress and Josh was glad that his neighbour was unable to go any faster, at least it meant he could keep up with her.

At the top of the stairs he led her to the spare room. The bed wasn't made up, but he opened a cupboard and pulled out a duvet. He threw it on the bed, followed by a couple of pillows. He also found a hot-water bottle. 'I'll be back in a minute with this,' he said.

Downstairs in the kitchen he boiled a kettle, found a bucket – just in case – from under the sink in the utility room, filled the hot-water bottle and grabbing a box of tissues from the window-sill he slowly made his way back up the stairs. He tapped lightly on the door and went in. She was already in bed, fully dressed, judging by the lone pair of shoes on the floor. She was very nearly asleep. He handed her the hot-water bottle and put the other things on the floor beside her.

'I'll leave you to it,' he whispered, 'just give me a shout if you need anything.'

She nodded and he crept quietly away.

Jessica opened her eyes, but then immediately closed them. She didn't want to wake up. She wanted to stay where she was in Gavin's arms. They had been making love on the hot sand beneath a cloudless sky – it had been like *From Here to Eternity*, but in colour and without the messy crashing waves. But try as she might to recapture the dream, she couldn't, it was gone.

And so was her migraine.

She opened her eyes again and remembered where she was – her neighbour's spare room. She peeped under the duvet. She was fully dressed. Well, that was okay then. She looked at her watch and saw that she'd been asleep for just over an hour. She sat up slowly. Very slowly. If she moved too quickly at this stage the blinding pain would come back. She shifted the pillows behind her shoulders and looked about her, taking in the room in the semi-darkness. For a man who had just moved house there was very little sign of him having done so. All was neat and tidy. Apart from there not being any curtains up at the window.

She could make out the sound of music coming from downstairs. It was a familiar opera, but one she couldn't remember the name of. It irritated her that she couldn't recall its title. Puccini, she decided. It was definitely Puccini. But which opera?

After ten minutes of sitting quietly she ventured out of bed. She stood up and found that the dizziness had gone, as had the nausea. She felt a bit embarrassed going downstairs. It wasn't every day that she ended up sleeping in the house of a man whom she barely knew and who had taken on more than his fair share of neighbourly kindness.

She found him in the sitting-room, bent over a mound of paperwork. From an impressive-looking hi-fi system in the corner of the room Puccini was still doing his stuff.

'Hi,' he said, when he saw that she was there. He put down his work, took off his glasses and got to his feet. 'How are you feeling?'

'Like I've been beaten over the head with a frying pan,' she said, squinting against the light.

'Is it too much for you? I'll turn it off if you like and just leave a lamp on.'

She nodded her thanks and watched him move across the room. He seemed to be limping much more than she remembered when she'd first seen him.

He caught her looking at his leg. 'It's an old skiing injury,' he said hurriedly, 'it comes and goes. Please, sit down.'

She hesitated. 'I really ought to go. You've done so much to help me, the least I can do is leave you in peace.'

'Nonsense. I'll make you a drink. What would you like?'

'Tea would be great.' She was glad that he wasn't making her feel that she should be off straight away and while he was out of the room she settled herself in a chair as far away from the lamp as possible.

Whoever her neighbour was he had good taste. The room, though sparsely furnished, was comfortable and homely. The chair she was sitting in matched the leather sofa, which was black and well worn and had a couple of terracotta-coloured cushions placed at each end. In front of it was a glass-topped coffee table that her neighbour had been working at, and on the floor was a large rectangular black-and-red rug that had Rothko stamped all over it. The other pieces of furniture were all modern in design and appeared to be made of beechwood; they contrasted stylishly with the wrought-iron lamps. There were several Italianate architectural prints in gilt frames covering the walls and either side of the fireplace were hundreds of books crammed into the built-in shelves that went right up to the ceiling. Jessica was pleased to conclude that her Good Samaritan was a man who liked to read.

Unlike Gavin.

She was sure that the last book Gavin had read was *Noddy Gets Into Trouble.*

It was a shame that she was still feeling so groggy as she would have loved to have prowled round the room and explored her neighbour's belongings.

'Have you managed to take any pain-killers, yet?' he asked, coming back with two large mugs and a packet of something under his arm.

'No,' she said, 'and that was the problem. I didn't have any with me.'

He put the mugs on the glass-topped table and handed her the packet he'd been carrying. 'Try those,' he said, sitting down on the sofa, 'they usually do the trick for me.'

'You get migraines as well?'

'Not so much these days.' Which was true. He might have a lot else going wrong with him, but hey, the migraines had eased up. Fair exchange was no robbery, as they say.

Jessica read the back of the packet, popped two tablets out of the foil packaging and swallowed them down with a gulp of tea. 'This is really kind of you,' she said. 'I don't know what I would have done if you hadn't come along.'

'It's no problem.' He smiled.

And what a smile, thought Jessica. Here's a man who could teach Piers a thing or two.

'My name's Josh, by the way,' he said, leaning back into the soft leather of the sofa and straightening his long legs, 'Josh Crawford.'

'And I'm Jessica Lloyd and I can assure you I don't normally go around throwing up in the bushes for an evening's entertainment.'

He smiled again.

Wow! When the sex appeal was being handed out this guy must have been first in the queue.

'You know, I've always meant to apologise to you,' he said.

'What on earth for?'

'For that day when I barged my way into your house for my keys. I had no idea the show house had changed.'

'Oh that. Forget it. And if it makes you feel any better my mother thought you were rather dishy. That's her phraseology, not mine.'

'And what did you think?'

'I thought you were exceptionally rude.'

He lowered his gaze, surprised at her candour. 'Then I have to hope that my rescue of you tonight has in some way made up for my appalling behaviour that day.'

Jessica smiled. 'Put like that, I have no choice but to agree fully with my mother's description of you.'

He looked up and saw from her face that she was gently making fun of him. 'Good,' he said, entering into the spirit of the conversation. 'So this mother of yours, who has such impeccable taste in men, does she live nearby?'

Jessica laughed. 'Yes, very close by. We passed her house on the way here. I would have pointed it out to you, only I was otherwise engaged. It's the one just by the canal bridge.'

He raised an eyebrow. 'There? It's a lovely house. Great situation as well.'

'Everyone says that.'

'And is that where you grew up?'

Jessica nodded and as she finished her tea the music on the hi-fi came to an end. It seemed the right time to leave. 'I really should go now,' she said, stretching forward to put her empty mug on the table.

'Must you?' he asked. It had been a while since Josh had enjoyed the company of a woman in this way and he was reluctant for the evening to come to an end.

'It's quite late,' she said, 'I'd hate to outstay my welcome.' Much as she thought she ought to be making a move, Jessica was more than happy to stay and chat. Having decided that her rude neighbour wasn't at all the uncouth monster she'd thought he was, she was keen to find out a little more about him.

'You're more than welcome to stay,' he said. 'In fact, I'd rather you did, it would stop me from working.'

Jessica glanced at the open files at the far end of the table. 'Okay,' she said, 'it's a deal.'

'Good. Would you like something to eat?'

'No thanks, but another cup of tea would be good.'

She watched him limp out of the room, then she too got up. She went over to the CD player and inspected the two tall beechwood columns of CDs. There was practically every taste in music accounted for: Northern Soul, Choral, Reggae, Frank Sinatra – *Frank Sinatra?* – Rock, Classical and Blues. She then checked the CD that they'd been listening to and found that she had been wrong. It hadn't been Puccini at all. It had been Verdi's *La Traviata*.

When Josh came back into the room, she said, 'Can we have this on again, please?'

'Sure.' He put their mugs on the table and came over and pressed the start button. They were standing very close, so close that even in the half-light Jessica could see the intense dark hue to his brown eyes as he looked at her. She could also see how dilated his pupils were. *Talk about the stuff of romantic fiction!* She cleared her throat – unnecessarily – and moved away, back to the chair in which she'd been sitting.

'So where have you been today?' he asked, also resuming his earlier position. 'You look too smartly dressed to have been out rambling.'

She cast her eyes over her sleep-crumpled suit – her one and only suit. 'I'd been down to London,' she said.

'For pleasure or for business?'

'Could London ever be for pleasure?'

'Depends on your viewpoint.'

'Well this was definitely for business and I'm afraid to say I behaved very badly at one point.'

'Oh?'

'I was given some fantastically brilliant news, having expected the reverse, and the shock of it made me drink too much over lunch, which I couldn't eat, and I very nearly made a pass at my agent, so that tells you how bad I was.' She groaned and hung her head, recalling her behaviour in the taxi and in Piers's office.

He laughed. 'There's a lot of information packed into that one sentence. Any hope of you disentangling it for me?'

She looked up and smiled. 'It'll have to be another time. I'm too tired now.'

'Well, when you've drunk your tea I'll be the perfect gentleman and see you safely across the courtyard.'

'I wouldn't want to put you to all that bother, not with your dodgy leg.' As soon as her words were out, Jessica knew she'd said the wrong thing. It was as if a cloud as black as the shirt he was wearing passed over Josh's face. 'You'll have to go easy on the skiing in future,' she said, trying to make light of the situation. 'Bones, ligaments, muscles, they're all tricky blighters, they take for ever to mend.'

'Yes,' he said flatly. 'I guess you're right.'

When Jessica had gone, Josh turned up the volume on the CD player and the final act of *La Traviata* filled the sitting-room. He threw himself on to the sofa.

He was angry.

Not with Jessica – she couldn't have had any idea that what she'd said would have meant anything to him. No, he was furious with himself. Why did he let these things get to him? Why couldn't he just brush it off? It was a chance remark. Nothing more. They were getting on fine until he'd acted like an idiot.

And there was another thing. Why had he lied? *Skiing injury! It comes and goes!* Too bloody right it does. Just what the hell had he thought he was doing?

Apart from wanting to make a good impression on Jessica.

Apart from wanting her to view him as a whole man.

Apart from convincing her that he wasn't some weak, uninspiring invalid.

Oh, to hell with it! What was the point anyway?

In spite of his anger he couldn't help but smile at the memory of the pair of them over by the hi-fi. There'd been a split second when he had thought of kissing Jessica. In the old days he wouldn't have hesitated. He would have swooped in on her and steered her towards the sofa.

He got up and went in search of something to drink. He found some Scotch in the dining-room, poured himself a large glassful and took it back to the sitting-room.

Like in the old days, he repeated to himself. The good old days before . . . before everything had started going wrong. Before he'd started having trouble with his balance. Before his legs had begun to feel like lead. And before that humiliating night in Hong Kong when he'd fallen down a short flight of stairs and everyone had thought he was drunk.

He took another swig of Scotch.

His last girl-friend had run a mile when she'd found out that she was dating a guy who was likely to end up in a wheelchair.

Well, lucky old her that she could run a bloody mile. Good bloody riddance!

Chapter Sixteen

It was Saturday afternoon. The sun was high and very hot, and as it shone through the window it beckoned Tony to leave the confines of his study, where he was checking through that month's sales figures, and go outside.

It was a tempting thought and one he was inclined to take up as it would give him a welcome break from Amanda endlessly rushing about the house getting it ready for that evening's dinner party. She had dusted, cleaned and polished from the minute she had got out of bed and, for no good reason that he could understand, she seemed intent on ruthlessly cleansing the entire house from top to bottom. She was now vacuuming the hall and as she approached the study he experienced the sensation of his breath being sucked out of his body.

A walk with Hattie was definitely what he needed. He switched off his computer, stood up and turned to confront the turbo-powered monster making its way into his study.

'Why don't you take Hattie for a walk?' Amanda shouted above the din. She seemed to Tony in that moment just as much a turbo-powered monster as the machine she was wielding. 'I'm sure she'd like that.'

'Good idea,' he said, thoroughly irritated that Amanda had suggested what was already in his mind.

Hattie ran on ahead, while he strolled behind at a more leisurely pace. They took the path leading away from the development and began walking through the long grass, and as the distance between them and the house grew he thought how strange it was to be on his own with Hattie with Amanda's blessing. It was an unusual occurrence. Invariably Amanda wanted him to spend more time with her.

He knew that she had found it hard adjusting to her role as stepmother, but there had been times in the past few months – though not this week – when he had found himself impossibly torn between his wife and his daughter. Maybe it was to be expected. Perhaps a second wife had more to be insecure about than a first.

With an unknown act to follow, and if the relationship was to work, it was more than likely that the new partner needed, *and deserved*, a much greater depth of love and reassurance than the previous wife. If this was true, and Tony suspected it was, then he knew with certainty that he was unable to offer Amanda what she needed most from him.

When they reached the cool shade of the copse of trees Hattie said, 'Shall we climb a tree?'

They found a suitable candidate: a small oak with a branch that was just low enough for Tony to hoist Hattie up on to it. She began moving along the thick branch to a hollow spot nearer the trunk of the tree and waited for him to join her. He jumped, caught hold of the bough and hauled himself up.

'It's great, isn't it?' Hattie said, squeezing herself close to him. 'We can see for miles. Look, there's our house, right over there.'

He stared to where she was pointing and dangled his legs beneath him. It was years since he'd climbed anything other than the corporate ladder and being here with Hattie brought back happy carefree memories from his own childhood. Days when the biggest dilemma he had had to face was whether there was time to play another game of tag in the street with his friends before his mother would call him in for tea. Now he was head to head with perhaps the biggest dilemma of his life – how to carry on with his marriage.

He had reached this depressing conclusion while driving home from work last night. He had had a lousy day, having delivered the news to three of his most experienced salesmen that they were no longer required by Arc. Throughout each session he had cursed Bradley Hurst for his short-sightedness. Letting go of good men like Dave, Alan and Richard didn't make sense. Not when they would eventually end up working for their main rivals, taking with them years of accrued knowledge and invaluable experience.

Dave had been gracious enough to say, 'No personal ill feelings, Tony. I know it's not your fault. It's the way things are done.'

But both Alan and Richard had been furious, particularly Alan, and with good reason, as his wife was expecting their third child any day. 'You're nothing but a yes man, Tony,' he'd snarled across the desk. 'And don't think we don't know how chummy you are with that bastard Hurst. Each time he comes over and gives you the latest edict you're practically kissing his arse to keep in with him.'

The insults had escalated until Tony had insisted that Alan get out of his office, which he did, leaving Tony in no doubt that Alan held him directly responsible for the loss of his job. And when driving home late last night, having the roads practically to himself, Tony had been filled with the desire to jack it all in. He'd had enough of being in a no-win situation at work. He hadn't slogged his guts out ever since leaving school to be on the receiving end of such dog's abuse.

At the entrance to the avenue of chestnut trees he had stopped his Porsche and wondered what the hell he was doing at Arc Computers. Was this really the life he had imagined for himself? And as he'd sat in the car in the gathering dark, he couldn't figure out which depressed him more, his job or his loveless marriage.

'Daddy?'

He turned and faced Hattie. He could see from her expression in the dappled sunlight that she must have been trying to attract his attention for some time.

'I'm sorry. What did you say?'

'Why do you look so sad, Daddy? Is it Mummy, do you still miss her?'

His heart twisted. 'Yes,' he said honestly. And he truly did. Every time he looked at his daughter's face he was reminded of Eve.

'Are you missing her now?'

'A little,' he confessed. The truth was that a part of him – that bit he kept from the rest of the world, including Hattie – missed Eve every day. It now occurred to him that since her death his life had lacked direction. With Eve, he had seemed set on a particular course – a shared course – and one that he'd been keen to follow. But now none of those life goals seemed important. Everything seemed shallow and trivial and uninteresting. Work. Marriage. Even the new house that he and Amanda had been so keen to buy. Though if he was honest it had been Amanda who had settled on Cholmford Hall Mews. She had hated moving into the house that he and Hattie lived in and had started going round the various estate agents in the area picking up details on all manner of properties. But then at least she'd been straight with him and said how she felt about sharing the home that he and Eve had created. Not that he would have been so insensitive as to have expected Amanda to slip neatly into Eve's shoes.

He wondered now about Amanda's sudden change of heart. Or whatever it was that had happened to her these past few days. Ever since that night out with the Hursts she had been acting differently. It was as if she had turned over a new leaf and was going out of her way to please him. It was callous of him, but he couldn't help likening her to a Stepford Wife. He'd noticed too that she was trying harder to get along with Hattie and of that he realised he should be glad. But deep down he knew that whatever Amanda was doing, without a monumental change of heart within himself it was pointless.

'It's like we've run away, isn't it?' Hattie said, looking up into his face. 'Nobody knows we're here. We could just stay here in this tree for ever and ever.'

And ever – he echoed in his head. He smiled and gave her a hug, and pulled out a packet of Opal Fruits from his back pocket. 'I sneaked them from the tin in the cupboard in the kitchen,' he confessed. He offered her the first one.

She chewed noisily on the strawberry-flavoured sweet, making great sucking noises. When she'd finished she said, 'When Kate came to baby-sit she told me that there was a pond here somewhere. Shall we see if we can find it? Maybe we could go for a paddle.'

'If you like.'

They climbed down from the tree, Tony first and then Hattie. She slipped with a light thud into his waiting arms. As they walked further into the copse, Tony had to acknowledge that his daughter's mention of Kate was stirring up yet more disquieting thoughts in him – innermost thoughts that so far he'd been unable to formulate or, more truthfully, hadn't had the courage to express with any clarity for fear of what he might discover about himself. Was it possible that whatever it was he felt for Kate was because his life was in such a mess? Were chaos and turmoil making him behave irrationally? Was his troubled mind causing him to imagine himself in love with a woman whom he didn't know? And if all this was true, what was to become of him? Was he one step away from the funny farm?

'Yucky!' said Hattie, pulling a face when they came to the edge of a large pool of murky green water, 'I don't want to paddle in that. What shall we do now?'

'How about a game of hide and seek?'

'Good idea. I'll hide first.'

'All right,' agreed Tony, 'but only on condition that you don't go anywhere near the water. Got that?'

She nodded and scampered away. 'Close your eyes and count down from fifty,' she shouted over her shoulder.

Tony did as she said and as he called out the numbers he had the sinking feeling that he was performing a countdown on his life.

When at last they had exhausted all possible hiding places Tony swung Hattie up on to his shoulders and slowly they made their way home in the hot afternoon sunshine. He was in no hurry to get back – he had no desire to be caught up in Amanda's determined attempts to impress their new neighbours – and if it weren't so hot and Hattie weren't desperate for a drink he'd have willingly stayed out longer. He had enjoyed his afternoon with Hattie and, giving her tired little legs a squeeze as they dangled over his shoulders, he made up his mind that whatever madness he was on the brink of he would spend more time with her.

As they drew level with the front door of number one he caught sight of their immediate neighbour just getting into his Shogun. He hadn't yet had the opportunity to introduce himself and seizing the moment, Tony went over to say hello.

Chapter Seventeen

At long, long last Oscar had fallen asleep.

Alec switched off the cassette player and brought a much needed end to his ordeal. Since leaving Oxford it seemed as if he'd heard the same banal song over and over – if he was forced to hear one more squeaked 'eh-oh' from the Teletubbies he'd throw the wretched tape out of the car window. He glanced sideways at Kate and saw that she was looking at him.

'Has it been very awful for you?' she asked.

'Yes,' he said, but then he smiled and reached out for her hand and squeezed it. 'Only joking. It's hard work, though, isn't it, keeping him entertained the whole time?'

Kate didn't agree, but she wasn't going to risk upsetting Alec by saying so. Their trip down to Oxford had been fun and had helped to heal the damage caused by their argument of Thursday night, but even so, Kate was anxious not to rock the boat and say the wrong thing to Alec.

He couldn't have apologised more for what he'd said to her, but she still felt the sting of his words – You thought *you*'d enjoy it. Never before had she heard Alec's usually soft voice weighted with such coldness and never would she have imagined him capable of wanting to hurt her. But he hadn't meant to hurt her, he'd told her that repeatedly in bed after she'd come back from sitting outside in the dark.

'I don't know what came over me,' he'd said, cradling her in his arms. 'I'm sorry, truly I am.' He had fallen asleep almost immediately, but she had lain awake, for the first time unsure about her future with Alec.

Only a few days ago she had thought she had discovered perfect peace at last, that the sense of belonging she had craved all her life was to be found through Alec. But lying there in the dark emptiness of the night she had begun to worry that this was not the case.

She had slipped out of bed and crept quietly downstairs and while making herself a drink she had wondered if out of need for that most basic of human requirements – to love and to be loved – she had been too hasty and unrealistic in her expectations of Alec. In her ready acceptance of a man she thought could offer her all the love and reassurance she had ever wanted, had she deliberately overlooked the one vital question she should have asked herself before she'd got so inextricably involved with him: had her upbringing led her into a situation that was doomed to fail?

But who was to say what was and what wasn't an acceptable basis for a loving relationship? What did it matter that she loved a man who was old enough to be her father? Surely all that mattered was that she loved him.

And she did love Alec.

So much so, that for him she was willing to sacrifice her desire to have children.

She had always wanted to have a child of her own, but Alec had made it very clear, right from the start of their relationship, that he didn't want any more. 'I'm too old to go through all that again,' he'd told her, 'much too old. I want to be able to enjoy myself with you, not be up in the night chasing bottles and nappies.'

And because she had felt so wonderfully secure, wrapped in his love and affection, she had been confident that she could come to terms with this ultimate sacrifice. But the longing for a child was never far away and Oscar's ever-increasing presence in her life was a poignant reminder of what she was to miss out on.

But perhaps this too was another example of her subconscious searching to resolve her own childhood.

'Penny for them?' Alec suddenly said.

'I was thinking about supper over at number two tonight,' she said. It was her first lie to Alec. Was this the start, then? Was this when they began to cover up their true feelings for fear of hurting or upsetting each other?

'Are we in for a deadly dull evening, do you think?' he asked, interrupting her thoughts once more.

She smiled, determined to put her anxiety aside. 'It would be worse if Jessica weren't going.'

'You seem to have made a good friend there; I'm glad about that.'

'Are you?' Immediately she regretted the words.

Alec took his eyes off the motorway and looked at her. 'What a strange question,' he said. 'Why wouldn't I be pleased?'

She didn't say anything, but Alec knew why she had asked it. And it served him right for playing the part of possessive lover the other night. His behaviour had told her in no uncertain terms that he wanted her all to himself, that he couldn't bear to share her with anyone. He badly wished that Thursday could be erased from their memories, but he knew it couldn't. His complete sense of unworthiness compelled him to go on seeking confirmation from Kate that he hadn't hurt her as much as he knew he had. More than anything he needed to believe that she had forgiven him. 'Are you still upset about the other night?' he asked gently.

But before Kate had a chance to reply a sleepy voice from the back of the car said, 'I need a wee.'

At four o'clock they pulled up outside Ruth and Adam's beautifully proportioned Georgian cottage. It constantly amused Kate that Adam chose to live in such an exquisite home himself, but designed for others some of the oddest houses she'd ever seen.

The sight of a bright-red MR2 on the driveway didn't amuse her, though. It was Melissa's car. And while Alec switched off the engine and unbuckled his seat-belt, she fought back the urge to brush her hair and check her face in the mirror.

Oscar ran on ahead and banged on the front door, while Kate and Alec followed behind, carrying between them an assortment of his luggage, along with his car seat. Ruth opened the door.

'I've been to Oxford,' Oscar announced excitedly. 'Kate took me on a big bus that didn't have a roof and we saw lots of –'

But Ruth wasn't listening. 'There you are at last,' she said, directing her words at Kate. 'Why didn't you phone to say you were going to be so late?'

'I didn't think we were late,' Kate answered.

'Come on, Ruth,' Alec said, oblivious to his daughter's rudeness, 'out of the way so we can off-load this little lot.'

She let them pass. 'No, not there, Dad,' she said, 'you're cluttering up the hall. Take it through to the playroom.'

Kate followed behind Alec, their footsteps echoing on the polished wooden floor. They deposited Oscar's car seat beside a row of boxes containing tidied-away building bricks and puzzles and farm animals. Kate had never seen the room littered with toys and she had the awful feeling that Oscar was rarely allowed to spoil the neatly arranged boxes.

'I don't suppose there's a drink on offer, is there?' Alec prompted.

If there was, Kate didn't want it. She wanted to be off. She didn't feel up to an encounter with Melissa. But Alec was hell-bent on a drink.

'After what I've put up with since yesterday, at the very least I deserve a triple whisky.'

Ruth took them out to the garden. It was beautifully kept, and so it should be, thought Kate, who knew that Ruth had a gardener in twice a week to see to the lawns and borders. She watched Oscar go up to his father and heard him tell him about his trip round Oxford on an open-topped bus, but like Ruth, Adam wasn't paying his son any attention, he was deep in conversation with a smartly dressed man about the same age as Alec. Kate didn't recognise the man and wondered who he was.

Disappointed, Oscar left his father's side and came back to Kate. He tucked his hand inside hers. 'They're not listening to me,' he said, his words reflecting the sadness in his face.

'Not to worry,' she whispered, 'they're just busy at the moment. Who's that man talking to your father?'

'Don't know.' Oscar shrugged miserably. 'I'm going in for a drink.'

For a few minutes Kate found herself standing alone. With a large tumbler of whisky in his hand, Alec had now joined Adam and was being introduced to the stranger.

'Hello Kate,' came a silky voice from behind her. It was Melissa. 'How was Oxford? I thought you were very brave taking Oscar away with you. I bet Alec hated every minute of it. But good for you for trying to turn him into a more participating grandparent. Though to be honest, I think you're wasting your time.'

'Alec thoroughly enjoyed himself,' lied Kate.

'I doubt that very much,' Melissa said with a laugh. 'He couldn't bear Ruth when she was that age, so there's no reason to suppose that Oscar will stand any higher in his estimation. Now if you'll excuse me I must go and have a word with Alec. Poor devil, he looks quite worn-out.'

Kate watched Melissa move away, the heels of her shoes sinking slightly into the soft lawn. Much as she didn't like Alec's ex-wife, Kate had to admit that Melissa was still a very attractive woman. She dressed in what Kate called expensive grown-up clothes and gave off an air of relaxed confidence, which in turn had the effect of making Kate feel plain and gawky, and about fifteen years old. There was an aura of poise and sophistication to Melissa which Kate knew she would never possess and she often wondered what it was that Alec saw in a girl like her, when for so long he had been married to such a beautiful woman.

As Kate watched Melissa move in on Alec, who was now on his own with Adam, she experienced the familiar wave of jealousy whenever she saw them together.

'Hello there.'

She turned to her right and realised that the unknown man, who earlier had been talking to Adam and Alec, was now at her side. At such close range, she decided that he wasn't particularly good-looking – his eyes were too pale and his jaw too square – and that he was one of those slightly overweight middle-aged men who looked as good as he did because of the expensive clothes he wore.

He held out his hand. 'Tim Wilson,' he said.

She shook hands with him. 'And I'm Kate.'

'I know,' he said. 'In fact I know lots about you.'

'You do?'

'You're Alec's girl-friend, aren't you?'

She nodded. 'So who are you?'

'I suppose you'd call me Melissa's boy-friend.'

The surprise on Kate's face must have shown.

'She's not mentioned me before, then?'

Kate shook her head.

He seemed disappointed. 'Well, it's a recent thing.'

Kate was curious and wondered why Melissa hadn't shown off the fact that she had a boy-friend. 'How did you meet?' she asked.

'Oh, the usual; dinner party, eyes across the table. How about you and Alec?'

'Much the same,' she lied.

'And how do you get on with this business of them still seeing one another every day?'

Kate followed his gaze across the garden to where Alec and Melissa were chatting.

'It doesn't bother me at all,' Kate lied again. How many lies was that today? she thought wretchedly.

He eyed her closely. 'It bothers me,' he said flatly, 'it bothers the hell out of me.'

'But Tony,' cried Amanda, 'how could you do this to me? Now the whole meal will be a disaster!'

'Nonsense, just don't give everyone such big helpings.'

Amanda tried desperately hard to keep her anger in check. But it wasn't easy. Not when she had put so much effort into that evening's meal and it had all been ruined by Tony waltzing in with Hattie after their walk saying he'd invited their other neighbour for dinner. She wasn't given to acts of the miraculous involving loaves and fishes, so just what exactly did Tony think she was going to do?

'I'm sorry,' he said, 'I should have thought. What can I do to help?'

At the sound of Tony's words she suddenly thought of her role model. Now what would Errol Hurst do if she were presented with the same situation? How would she react if Bradley were to turn up from work with an unexpected car-load of Japanese clients for supper? Calmly and proficiently capable, that was how Errol would be. There'd be no domestic histrionics. No apportionment of blame. Just a professional willingness to provide her husband with that all-important back-up so necessary in order for him to get on. Errol would be so resourceful she'd probably raid next door's fish tank just so that she could serve a meal of sushi if she thought it would help Bradley's career. Well, anything Errol could do, she could do better.

'Do you want me to go over and explain to him that we haven't got enough food?' Tony suggested. 'I'm sure he'd understand, he seemed a nice enough bloke.'

Amanda stared at Tony and slowly forced a smile to her lips. 'Oh, don't be silly. Of course I can rustle up something. Just leave it to me. And at least now the numbers around the table will be equal.' She turned away from Tony, amazed at how sincere she'd sounded. It almost made her want to laugh.

Tony was amazed too. How could Amanda be so angry one minute and apparently so understanding the next? It was bizarre. Was this a hormonal thing, he wondered, or just a case of schizophrenia?

Chapter Eighteen

At a minute past eight Jessica peeped out of her kitchen window to see if there was any sign of Kate and Alec heading for number two. But there was no sign of anybody and determined that she wasn't going to be the first to arrive she decided to ring her mother for a chat – anything to forestall the inevitable.

She had almost finished dialling the number when she remembered that Anna was still away. Damn, now what? She couldn't just sit here twiddling her thumbs. She caught sight of last Sunday's partially unread copy of the *Sunday Times*. She began idly flicking through it, until she came to the book section. She looked to see who had said what and about whom and, only too thankful that she hadn't written any of the novels that had been given the sniffy literati treatment, turned to the television guide to see what she would be missing that evening.

Mm . . . *Prime Suspect* was on at nine o'clock. Aha! The ideal delaying tactic, right in her lap, setting the new video would take for ever. She'd be drawing her pension before she made it to Amanda's dinner-table. 'Oh, sorry I'm late,' she'd be able to say, 'but videos, aren't they just the worst?' Playing the helpless bimbo would appeal to Amanda's superior air, she suspected.

At seven minutes past eight Josh looked at his watch. He then glanced out of his kitchen window, checking for some sign of movement from across the courtyard. In particular from number four.

When Tony had introduced himself that afternoon and had invited Josh for dinner, he had very nearly refused, but when Tony had said who else would be there he had instantly changed his mind. He'd enjoyed Jessica's company last night and saw no reason to be antisocial and miss out on an opportunity of seeing her again.

At ten minutes past eight Kate slipped out of Alec's arms and said, 'Come on, we'd better get a move on, we're already late.'

He pulled her back down on to the bed and kissed her. 'I wish we didn't have to go.'

'So do I, but I promised Jessica I wouldn't back out at the last minute. So hurry up and get dressed.'

He smiled. 'One more kiss and I'll think about it.'

At twenty-one minutes past eight, and much to Jessica's amazement, she found that she had managed to set the video recorder and with nothing else for it she picked up the box of chocolates for Amanda and made a move.

At twenty-two minutes past eight Josh pulled out a bottle of red wine from the wine rack in the kitchen and decided he might just as well be the first to arrive.

At twenty-three minutes past eight three front doors opened simultaneously and four dinner guests faced each other across the courtyard. Josh waited for the others to join him on his side of the development.

After the necessary introductions had been made, Jessica said to Josh, 'I didn't know you'd been invited.'

'I think I was an afterthought.'

'That makes two of us.'

They fell in step behind Kate and Alec as they led the way. Josh could quite see why his brother had been struck by the sight of Kate, she was stunning, but personally he was more taken with Jessica. She looked so much better than she had last night. Gone were the pale face and the dark-rimmed eyes, and in place was a very attractive woman. She looked great in a tight-fitting lycra top – Crawford's had sold thousands like it last year, as they had the long wrap-around skirt that she was wearing. He noted how it fell open with each step she took and he wondered how such a fantastic pair of legs had slipped his attention last night.

They were greeted by Amanda who, after being handed an assortment of flowers, bottles and chocolates, took them through to the sitting-room. Sparkling white wine with cassis was offered and as the drink was already poured out and waiting for them on a tray Josh took his fluted glass politely, wishing, though, that he'd been given the choice of a beer. He caught Jessica pulling a face at the sight of her drink and they exchanged a small knowing smile.

'Tony will be down in a minute,' Amanda said, handing Alec and

Kate their glasses, 'he's just putting Hattie to bed. Why don't you all sit down?'

Jessica waited to see where Amanda would sit, then chose the sofa which was as far away as she could get from their hostess.

Josh came and joined her. 'How are you feeling?' he asked in a low voice.

'Much better, thanks. You were great last night, by the way, a true hero.'

He smiled. 'Glad to be of service.'

'What's all this, then?' asked Amanda, rudely interrupting Alec, who in answer to her question had just been explaining what business he was in. 'Who's been a hero?'

Jessica considered inventing an outrageous story about herself and Josh, but as she couldn't be sure of her audience, or that Josh would be willing to play along with her, she decided to keep the fiction to a minimum. 'Let's just say that despite the unusual circumstances we found ourselves in last night,' she said, unable to resist leading Amanda on, 'this fine young man behaved as a perfect gentleman.'

She needn't have doubted Josh.

'And it would be far from correct of me to elaborate on what Jessica has told you all,' he said, 'my lips are sealed, a gentleman never betrays a lady.'

Alec and Kate laughed, but Amanda, who was waiting for a full explanation of what was being implied, was distracted by a movement in the doorway. Jessica followed her gaze and saw a small, pretty girl dressed ready for bed. Holding her hand was a good-looking fair-haired man. Tony and Hattie, she assumed.

'Now Hattie, what did I tell you?' Amanda said. Though her words revealed little more than a hint of mild irritation, there was nothing mild about the expression on her face. Jessica could see that she was clearly cross and she remembered what Kate had said about Amanda not being ideal stepmother material.

'Hattie just wanted to come down and meet everybody,' Tony said affably. He brought his daughter further into the room.

'Well, a few seconds won't do any harm, I suppose,' conceded Amanda, 'but then it's straight to bed, young lady,' she added, 'and no nonsense. This is grown-up time.'

'Oh dear.' Jessica laughed. 'On that basis I'd better join Hattie.' The expression on Amanda's face gave Jessica every reason to suspect that she had just made herself public enemy number one.

Not long after Hattie was dispatched to bed the rest of them were ordered into the dining-room. They were told where to sit and what they were eating.

'It's a Gary Rhodes recipe,' Amanda told them in a loud voice, interrupting Tony, who was talking to Kate and Alec at his end of the table. 'I know he's a bit showy and that there's a lot of window dressing to him, but his recipes do actually work. What do you think, Kate?'

Oh Lord, thought Jessica, recognising that Amanda was going to insist that everybody participated in her dinner party, whether they wanted to or not. There would be no skulking behind napkins for any of them.

Kate took a few moments to finish what was in her mouth and politely agreed with Amanda. 'Though I quite like the Two Fat Ladies,' she added.

'Really?' asked Amanda. 'You do surprise me.'

'It's their originality that –'

'Original, I agree, but so unhygienic,' Amanda said dismissively. She then turned from Kate and fixed her attention on Josh. 'And Josh, how about you? Do you like to cook? Or are you one of those terrible *Men Behaving Badly* types in the kitchen?'

Jessica couldn't believe the crassness of the woman. Somebody shove a bread roll into that great big mouth! she wanted to shout across the table. But she was pleased to see that if Josh was at all put out by Amanda's assumption that because he was a single man he was therefore a complete dick-head when it came to feeding himself, he didn't show it.

'I manage pretty well,' he answered smoothly. 'I particularly enjoy Thai cooking.'

Jessica silently applauded Josh for his subtle slap in the chops of their hostess.

But after a long silent pause, the weight of which could have equalled any number of lead balloons, Jessica scooped up the last of her salmon mousse and thought, well, this *is* going splendidly. What fun we're all having. She wondered how Helen Mirren was getting along.

'So tell us about your writing, Jessica,' Amanda said, moving her attention around the table. 'It's not every day we have an author in our midst. I thought of writing a book once.'

Oh, here we go, thought Jessica. If she had a pound for every person who had ever said that to her she'd be up there with Jeffrey Archer.

'But I've never had the time,' Amanda went on. 'I've always been too busy.'

Yeah, yeah, yeah. She'd heard it all before.

'It must be wonderful to be able to earn a living from something as easy as writing.'

Jessica was nearly out of her seat and reaching for a gob-stopping bread roll. *Easy! She'd give her bloody easy!*

'I don't think it's quite as simple as that,' Kate said diplomatically. 'If it were, too busy or not, we'd all be doing it, wouldn't we?'

Jessica gave Kate a grateful look.

'Well, I wouldn't know about that,' Amanda carried on. 'Do you sell many books, Jessica? I saw one in the supermarket yesterday.'

'I get by,' replied Jessica. Tight bitch, she thought, noting that Amanda had said 'saw' and not 'bought'.

'I didn't know you were a writer,' Josh said, seizing a few seconds of conversational lull while Amanda chewed on a piece of cucumber.

'It's not something I go out of my way to advertise,' Jessica said – *was it any wonder when there were people like Amanda in the world?*

'Jessica's an excellent writer,' Kate said generously. 'I've read both her books.'

'So what kind of novels do you write?' Josh asked.

'Romantic comedies,' Jessica replied. 'Probably not your cup of tea; not enough explosions or car chases.'

Alec laughed. 'From what Kate tells me, your sex scenes are pretty explosive.'

'But all done in the best possible taste,' Jessica joked.

'I suppose you must have to do an inordinate amount of research,' Josh said with a playful smile.

'Oh, an inordinate amount of research,' Jessica said, matching his expression.

Josh slowly leant back in his chair. 'You must let me know if there's anything I could help you with in the future,' he said, his eyes still fixed on her.

Jessica's own gaze held firm. She took a long, deliberate sip of her wine. 'And who knows,' she said, 'I might just do that.'

Aghast at the way in which Jessica and Josh were carrying on, Amanda began gathering up the plates and cutlery. She gave Tony a get-up-and-do-something look and he immediately got to his feet and went round the table refilling glasses. He was secretly envious of the way in which Jessica and Josh were flirting with each other. It reminded him of himself and Eve. They had met on a management training course and he had been determined from the moment he'd set eyes on her to get her into bed before the end of the three-day course. By the close of day one, when they'd spent five hours solving what the tutor had called 'Mind Opening Puzzles' they had built up a flirtatious rapport. By day two they were found kissing in the hotel lift and on the final day, when they should have been attending an afternoon talk on 'There's More than One Way to Look at a Problem' they were in his hotel room making love. The memory of such a happy time in his life made him risk a glance in Kate's direction. How he longed for the evening to be over. Sitting in the same room as Kate without being able to talk to her, in the way he wanted, was unbearable.

Even more unbearable was Alec's presence.

What made it so bad was that Tony found himself liking the man. It was beyond him that he could chat so effortlessly to Alec when all the time he was imagining what it would be like to hold Kate in his arms.

'No more wine for me, thanks.'

Tony looked down to see Josh's hand covering his wineglass.

'Sorry,' he said distractedly. 'What can I get you instead?'

'Water would be fine, thanks.'

Josh watched Tony fill his water glass, then he raised his eyes to look at Jessica. She was turned slightly to her left, talking to Alec, but he had the feeling she knew full well that he was staring at her.

Last night when he'd gone to bed and thought about his evening with Jessica, he'd known that he was attracted to her and now, as he viewed her across the table, he realised that for the first time in a long while he was experiencing the urge of wanting a woman. The impulse was so strong that it was outweighing the fear and loss of confidence that had crept over him since his illness had been diagnosed. One of the aspects of MS that appalled him most was the threat of impotence. What if he couldn't perform? What if his useless body let him down? One of the specialists he'd seen at the hospital a few months ago had waved the subject aside when Josh had put it to him. 'You don't need to concern yourself about that now,' the man had said – a man who in Josh's opinion looked like he'd lost interest in sex years ago – 'worry about that when it happens,' the doctor had added. Easy for you to say, Josh had thought angrily.

And since his last girl-friend had done a runner, the subject of sex had become nothing more than a hypothetical conundrum anyway.

But now . . . well now, it was very much on Josh's mind. He had the feeling that it was on Jessica's too. Or was that just wishful thinking?

Jessica was the first to say that she was tired and that she ought to be getting off home. 'It's been a wonderful evening,' she said, faking a yawn. She wasn't lying completely. Excluding Amanda, she'd enjoyed everybody's company once they'd all relaxed. She pushed her empty coffee cup away from her and stood up.

'I hadn't realised it was so late,' Josh said in turn, also getting to his feet. He didn't want Jessica rushing off without him.

Which caused Alec to say that he and Kate had had a long day and that they had better be going as well.

Thanks were made, goodbyes said, and finally the four dinner guests departed. It was past midnight and the dark sky above the courtyard was pricked with bright, twinkling stars. It was very quiet. And very still.

'Well, good-night then,' Alec said to Jessica and Josh, 'it was good to meet you both. If there's anything in the neighbourly department you need, don't hesitate to knock on our door.'

'The same goes for my door,' Jessica said, 'knock any time you need to. See you for coffee during the week, Kate.'

Kate and Alec walked away, arm in arm, their feet crunching noisily on the gravel.

'Well,' said Josh, turning to face Jessica.

'Well indeed,' she repeated.

'I don't suppose you'd fancy a nightcap, would you?'

'I thought you'd never ask.'

Chapter Nineteen

When Jessica awoke the following morning it was very late. It was getting on for lunch-time.

In Corfu she had never slept in. Early morning, before anyone else was about, had been her favourite part of the day. It was so quiet sometimes that she could hear the distant sound of goat bells high up in the hills behind her house. On days like that it was as if she had the island to herself. It was when she worked at her best. She would make a pot of coffee and a plate of toast dripping with butter – not for her the local breakfast of yoghurt and honey and the occasional fig that Helen and Jack relished – and go and sit outside on the terrace. She had never tired of the view and each morning she had lost herself in admiring the tranquil setting. She had often wished that instead of being a novelist she had Helen's skill as an artist. She would have loved to have been able to paint the myriad shades of blue, green and white that for her epitomised where she lived – sand as silvery as the moon; beaches whitened by sun-bleached pebbles; water the colour of pure turquoise; and cypress trees, lush and green, their verdant tips spearing a cloudless sky of china-blue.

Then, once she had had her fix of admiring the view, she would get down to work. The hours would slip by effortlessly as she lost herself in her latest cast of characters who were facing all manner of dramas as a result of her vivid imagination.

Thinking of work reminded Jessica that it was high time she got stuck into her next novel. When she'd had lunch with Piers on Friday he had asked her only once what she had in mind to write next – he'd probably decided not to push her, thinking that it would be unlikely that he'd get any sense out of somebody who was making such a fool of herself.

And he would have been right. He would have got more reason out of the salt and pepper pots on the table than her.

It wasn't often that she let the side down so appallingly, but on that occasion she'd certainly gone all the way. She cringed at the memory and buried her head deep into the pillow. Gavin would have loved seeing her behave so badly and wouldn't have thought twice about using it against her if she'd ever dared to show so much as the merest hint of disapproval over one of his frequent drunken binges.

She turned on to her back and stared up at the hideous lace canopy above the bed and thought of Gavin.

She wondered what he'd be doing right now. Probably he was down on the beach at Avlaki: Ray-Bans on, hair catching the breeze and no doubt putting his breath-taking charm to good use on some keen-to-please female tourist whom he'd met the previous night in a bar in Kassiopi. 'I've never tried sailing before,' the silly girl would have simpered, which was all the opening Gavin would need. 'Then I'll teach you' – his stock reply to anybody stupid enough to give him the opportunity to show off how good he was in and on the water – 'be on the beach for ten thirty tomorrow,' he'd add, 'and I'll take you through the theory, then we'll get down to the exciting stuff. I guarantee you'll be sailing single-handedly by late afternoon and to celebrate your success we'll have a drink afterwards at the nearby taverna.' His technique was persuasive and irresistible.

She ought to know, she'd fallen for it herself.

Since leaving Corfu, Jessica hadn't once deluded herself that Gavin would be pining for her. But she did wonder whether he missed her. Just a little.

She supposed not.

If he had, he might have been in touch with her. But there had been nothing. Not one phone call. Not even a letter.

But then, what could she expect? It had been she who had chosen to end things between them.

It was a strange phenomenon, though, that one could be so involved, so wrapped up in another person, then be so entirely separate.

Mind you, with Gavin it had been a basic physical wrapped-upness rather than any meeting of minds. Jack had often asked her what she saw in Gavin and Helen had laughed at him.

'You imbecile, Jack, the man's an Adonis, what do you think she sees in him?'

Helen had been quite right. The physical attraction between them had been like a white-knuckle ride; no matter how often they made love the thrill was as great as the time before.

But gradually it had dawned on Jessica that a physical thrill was only as good as the moment it took to fulfil itself. She had then begun to want more. And poor Gavin didn't have more to offer. It had been a sad realisation, that. It had also made her feel old. Expectations in one's youth are delightfully low and straightforward, you put up with anything. But age brings with it higher and more complicated expectations from a partner, such as consideration, respect, faithfulness, understanding and, worse still, something as horrifying as a planned future.

Gavin's idea of a planned future was choosing what he was going to eat for lunch.

She sighed and got out of bed. She pushed back the curtains and leant her elbows on the window-sill. It was a glorious morning and beyond her garden, a sun-filled landscape of fields and clumps of trees presented itself to her. It was beautiful. Very different from what she had been used to for the past few years, but just as captivating. She opened the window and leant out over the white-painted sill.

She thought of Josh. He, too, was different from anybody she'd previously known.

It would have been the easiest thing in the world to have carried on their flirting to its natural conclusion last night, but when, after a couple of drinks, things had started hotting up on the sofa she had thought, Whoa! I've been here before and I'm not sure I'm in the market for a casual affair.

She had, of course, only herself to blame. She really shouldn't have encouraged him.

Mutterings of 'I'm sorry, I'm not sure I can do this' had seemed slightly ridiculous when he'd tried to kiss her – and just for the record his technique had been faultless: a subtle inching along the sofa so that their legs were almost touching, a beautifully timed silence, a lowering of his eyes to her lips, a lifting of his hand to her shoulder and then the final tilt of his head – always a heart melter that one – as he moved in for the big finish.

Except she had gone and spoilt things for him.

'My mistake,' he'd said, when he'd felt her resistance. He'd backed away from her as though she had a gun pointed at his head.

They'd then metaphorically dusted themselves down and catching sight of the awkwardness on one another's faces they had suddenly burst out laughing.

'Sorry about that,' he'd said with a grin that had enough sex appeal in it to cause her very nearly to say, oh what the heck, let's go for it, anyway!

'I'm sorry too,' she'd said, 'I've behaved outrageously all evening. It's either the fault of that awful woman Amanda, or . . .'

'Or?'

'Or it's your fault.'

He laughed. 'Fancy another drink?'

They finished a bottle of Southern Comfort and moved on to coffee, and all the time they talked. He told her about the company he and his brother ran – he had talked a lot about Charlie – and about all the travelling the pair of them had done, but he wasn't one of those men who only spoke about himself. He prompted her to speak about her own life, about growing up in Cholmford and what had led her to live such a nomadic life, and what had brought her back home. She told him about her mother and her heart condition. She even told him about Gavin. Then there was her writing. He wanted to know all about that, unlike Gavin who had never been interested in what she did, having dismissed her books as the kind of commercial nonsense anyone could do if they put their mind to it – he and Amanda would get on like a house on fire.

She had felt extremely comfortable in Josh's company, so much so that the time had flown by, and before they knew it it was nearly four in the morning. She had tiptoed her way across the gravel and let herself in, just as the first signs of dawn had begun to filter through the bruised night sky.

'Dirty stop-out,' she said with a smile, now turning away from the bedroom window and going into the bathroom, 'what *will* the neighbours think?'

In the make-do show house of plot number three Sue Fletcher, the negotiator, was tidying up her things. Her work at Cholmford Hall Mews was over. Tomorrow she would start work at a new site. She was going to miss Cholmford, it had been one of her more enjoyable assignments. It was a shame, though, that she hadn't managed to sell the last remaining plot, but she'd had a feeling all along that number three was going to stick. Everybody she had shown round the house had had the same criticisms of it – they didn't like the property being divided by the archway; they didn't like the garden; but mostly they didn't like the price. So now it would be down to an estate agent to do his best, but Sue knew as well as the next person that without a substantial drop in the asking price it would be an uphill struggle to find a buyer.

Still, it wasn't her problem. Her next challenge was an exclusive block of apartments in Altrincham.

Happy that everything was in order, she locked the door behind her for the final time and as she turned round she saw the man from number one driving out through the archway. She returned his smile and wished that all the clients she dealt with were as easy on the eye.

Josh drove like the wind to his parents' house in Prestbury. He parked his car alongside Charlie's and because it was such a hot day he walked slowly round to the back of the house, assuming that everybody would be sitting in the garden.

He was right. His brother, dressed in shorts and a T-shirt, was lolling in a hammock slung between two apple trees and his father was coughing and spluttering over the barbecue, where the coals were sending up great lung-threatening clouds of smoke.

His mother was sitting in her usual sun-lounger and was doing the usual crossword. She looked up when she realised he was there. 'Hello, Joshua,' she said, putting her newspaper down. 'We'd nearly given up on you. I was about to send Charles in to give you a call. We were getting worried.'

He went and kissed her. 'A late night,' he said by way of explanation for turning up unprecedentedly late for their monthly family get-together. He'd also woken up unprecedentedly late. Normally an early riser, he had surfaced just after twelve o'clock and it wasn't until he was munching on a bowl of muesli in the kitchen and thinking about Jessica that he'd caught sight of the calendar hanging beside the telephone on the wall. With a thud of realisation he'd remembered that he was supposed to be washed, dressed, shaved and in Prestbury within the hour. Dumping the half-eaten cereal in the sink, he had gone back upstairs to do something about his appearance. Glad that his body was at least continuing to keep up with him, as he'd stood in the shower, and conscious that he was feeling okay for yet another day, he dared to hope that his MS was entering a period of remission; that the symptoms of his illness were lessening. It had happened before. So why not again?

'Shall I get you a beer?' his father offered.

'That's all right, Dad. I'll go and help myself.'

When he went into the kitchen and pulled open the fridge door he heard footsteps following in behind him. It was Charlie. 'You want one as well?' he asked.

'Please.'

Josh handed him a can. 'I met your wondrous creature last night,' he said.

'And?'

Josh smiled. 'She's really not your type.'

'Hey, I'll be the judge of that.'

'And she's also fairly well partnered up.'

'Shit!'

'Language, Charles.'

'Sorry, Mum,' Charlie said, turning to see their mother coming into the kitchen.

'So how are things?' she asked Josh as she went over to a chopping board beside the sink and picked up a plate of vegetable kebabs.

Josh tried not to over-react. He knew his mother had to ask and that she did her best to put it in such a way as to imply that a general enquiry was being made of him, but in reality the question was much more specific. It was stupid of him, but he'd much prefer his mother to come straight out with, 'So which bit of you isn't working properly today?'

'I'm fine,' he said and, going for a deflection he added, 'and the house is pretty well organised now. You and Dad will have to come over.'

'We'd like that,' she said. 'Now go back into the garden and get some sun on you. You look far too pale and all that black doesn't help. Don't you have any clothes in any other colour these days?'

'She's right,' Charlie said as they went outside and found themselves a couple of chairs away from the smoke, 'you do look pale.'

'If you'd drunk as much as I did last night you'd be pale.'

Charlie raised an eyebrow. 'Tell me all.'

Josh told him about being invited to dinner with his new neighbours.

'So that's how you got to meet my scampering angel,' Charlie interrupted. 'What's the husband like?'

'I never said she was married. She lives with somebody, a guy called Alec.'

Charlie leant forward in his chair. 'Not actually married, eh? So all is not lost. What's he like? A right Smart Alec? Or is he some kind of brainless gladiatorial hunk who's charmed her with his pecs?'

Josh laughed. 'She's a whole lot smarter than that.'

'So come on then, what am I up against?'

'You're not going to believe it. He's got to be about fifty, grey-haired and –'

'You're winding me up!'

'Nope.'

'You mean that fantastic creature has thrown herself at a man nearly twice her age. Why?'

132

Josh shrugged. 'He's a nice bloke, maybe she just goes for the father-figure type. It takes all sorts.'

'Who likes the father-figure type?' asked their father, coming over and seizing the opportunity of his wife's absence from the garden to stand easy from his barbecue duties for a couple of seconds.

'A neighbour of mine whom Charlie has decided he's fallen in love with.'

Their father laughed. 'Missed the boat again, Charles, have you?'

'I wouldn't say that exactly. I reckon I'm a worthy match for a grey-haired has-been any day.'

'Nothing wrong with grey hair,' William Crawford said, running his hand through his own. 'And may I remind you that you're not short of a few threads of silver yourself.'

'Thanks, Dad.'

'William,' called a voice from inside the house, 'those chops, they're burning!'

He hurried back to his sentry post.

'So what are your other neighbours like?' Charlie asked.

'A couple with a young daughter and . . .' he hesitated.

'And?'

'And a writer.'

'Really. What's he like?'

'*She.*'

'Oh. Any good?'

'Not sure about her writing skills, but she's . . .' Josh's voice faltered. How exactly should he describe Jessica? The usual adjectives of striking and attractive somehow didn't seem appropriate. She was more than that. But what? Interesting? Was that how he would describe her? Or how about sententious? She was certainly to the point. She was also extremely funny. But these were hardly the normal descriptions a man would use of a woman whom he had every intention of getting into bed.

'She's what?' prompted Charlie.

Josh smiled. 'Never you mind.'

'Oh, like that, is it?'

'I should be so lucky.' Josh told his brother about Jessica's migraine and his rescue of her. He also told him about last night.

Charlie laughed. 'Well, one thing's for sure, I'll have to take back all I said about no night-life being on offer out there in the sticks. Perhaps your paleness has nothing to do with an over-indulgence of alcohol but an excess of carnal pleasure.'

'I wish.'

'You mean, she was there all that time with you last night and you didn't manage –'

'I was taking the subtle approach.'

'Get away. She didn't fancy you, did she?'

'Course she did.'

'But not enough, evidently.'

They both laughed and drank their beers. Josh listened to his parents battling it out round the hot coals – the chops were done, but the kebabs were not – and felt unaccountably relaxed. Talking to Charlie in this light-hearted way reminded him how it always used to be when they'd teased one another about their sexual prowess. It was one of the things he'd noticed when his illness had been diagnosed; overnight Charlie stopped treating him as the brother he'd always been and had started talking to him like some ancient maiden aunt. The teasing abruptly stopped. So did the mateyness. It was as if it was in bad taste to rib somebody who wasn't a hundred per cent – mocking the afflicted just wasn't on.

'What's her name?' asked Charlie, breaking into Josh's thoughts.

'Who?'

'Don't give me any of that. The woman who turned you down.'

'I told you, she didn't turn me down.'

'If you say so.'

'Her name's Jessica, Jessica Lloyd.'

'Mm . . . nice name. So what kind of writer is she?'

'She writes romantic comedies and according to your darling Kate she writes brilliant sex scenes.'

Charlie held up his hands as though giving thanks to the Lord. 'My darling Kate. How sweet the name doth sound.'

'Put a sock in it, will you? And take my advice. She won't give you a second look. She and Alec are very much a couple.'

Charlie pulled a face. 'Just because you were shunned last night, don't go sour-graping all over me.'

'I didn't say I was shunned.'

'Well what were you then?'

'I was . . . if you must know I was spoken to like I was a normal human being.'

Charlie looked at him closely. 'Meaning what?'

'I mean she didn't talk to me in that does-he-take-sugar-with-it? way so many other people do.'

'Are you getting at me?'

Josh shook his head. 'All I'm saying is that Jessica treated me like a normal bloke because she doesn't know anything to the contrary.'

'She doesn't know about your MS?'

'That's right.'

'But what if –'

'There are no what ifs. I have no intention of telling her about my illness, because at least then I won't have to put up with any crap from her.' His face broke into an expression of intense seriousness. 'She'll treat me as a man, not an invalid. And who knows, I might even get lucky.'

Charlie turned away and looked down the length of the garden, to the old rope swing hanging from the silver birch where he and Josh had played as boys – their mother joked that she still kept the rope swing as a hint that one day she hoped to have grandchildren playing on it.

He thought about what his brother had just said. He had the feeling that Josh liked this Jessica, that he viewed her as being more than just a potential one-night stand. If that was the case, and if Josh really thought there was any chance of a relationship with her, then surely it had to be founded on honesty. Not on deception.

He'd be a fool to think otherwise.

Chapter Twenty

It was Monday lunch-time and at first glance the car-park of the Vicarage looked as if it were full. But driving round to the back of the pub, Kate spied a small space that had been ignored by everybody else and with breath-holding care she squeezed her Mini between an ugly people carrier on her left and a white-painted wooden barrel on her right, which was stocked with a large flowering hydrangea and an abundance of yellow and purple pansies that clashed horribly with the blue of the hydrangea.

She found Caroline perched on a bar stool, pretending to be reading the lunch-time menu on the blackboard to the right of her. In reality, Kate knew better. Caroline was eyeing up a group of noisy businessmen at the far end of the bar. Nothing changes, she thought. 'Hi, Caroline,' she said, tapping her friend on the shoulder.

Caroline whipped round. 'And about time, too. I've been sitting here on my own for ages. It gives a girl a bad name.'

'Sorry, the traffic was terrible, but I'm sure you've been able to amuse yourself in my absence.'

'Definitely not my type,' Caroline said, catching Kate's eyes straying over to the far end of the bar. 'They've done nothing but discuss company cars and Manchester United. What are you drinking?'

'I'll get them,' Kate said, reaching into her bag. 'What would you like?'

'Dry white wine, please.'

Kate attracted the attention of the woman behind the bar and when they'd got their drinks and ordered two prawn salads they went outside to the garden. They chose a table which had an umbrella above it. Kate sat in the shade and Caroline positioned her chair to catch the sun, and pulling off a loose-fitting silk shirt she revealed a skimpy strapless top and a pair of deeply tanned shoulders.

'It must be hell being you,' said Caroline smugly. 'You can keep your dazzling head of red hair and perfect pale skin, I'd sooner be a boring brunette any day and soak up the rays.'

'Well, at least I shan't look like a prune when I'm fifty.'

'Don't give it another thought. I shall have had the very latest in drastic surgery by then. I'll have my face stretched right round to the back of my head. I'll look sensational.'

'You'll look like Bette Davis.'

Caroline laughed. 'My word, but you're frisky today. Now tell me what you've been up to. I want to know everything. How's the big relationship going and is the sex still as good and have you found yourself another job yet?'

There was never any chicanery to Caroline's conversation. 'If I were a stronger person I'd tell you to mind your own business,' Kate said.

Caroline smiled. 'Yeah, but I know that deep down you're just dying to tell me what a wonderful time you're having so that you can rub in what a dreary depressing life I lead. Hey, do you mind moving slightly to the right? There's a drop-dead gorgeous guy sitting over there and he can't see what he's missing out on with you in the way.'

Kate obliged and finding that the sun was now in her eyes she put on her sun-glasses.

'Do you have to do that?' Caroline asked, 'those shades make you look even more glamorous; you look like Julia Roberts. Take them off at once.'

'No,' Kate said firmly, 'now stop treating me like one of the poor pensioners in the library you bully so sadistically and tell me what *you*'ve been up to.'

Caroline raised an eyebrow. 'My, my, Kate, who's been teaching you how to be so assertive?'

'It's you! You've taught me everything I know.'

'So that's it, I'm to be hoisted by my own petard, am I?'

Their lunch arrived and when they were left alone again Caroline said, 'You're looking particularly well. Dare I ask, is that what the love of a good man does for you?'

Kate smiled and reached for her knife and fork. 'You should try it some time.'

'Ouchy-ouch! You're turning into a nasty piece of work, Kate Morris.'

'So there's still no decent man in your life, then?'

Caroline sighed. 'Chance would be a fine thing. Do you know, I'm so desperate I've thought about joining one of those dreadful introduction agencies, you know, the ones you see advertised in the paper all the time.'

Kate held her tongue. She had never confided in Caroline about how she had met Alec and she certainly wasn't about to start now – Caroline was the last person on earth that she'd trust with such a delicate and private piece of information. It still amazed her that she'd had the courage to join the agency in the first place and had done so in secret. She had thought about it for months before finally taking the plunge. It wasn't so much that there had been a lack of boy-friends in her life, it was just that they were all the wrong kind. They were either too serious or not serious enough; too quiet or too noisy; too nervous or over-confident. Having your personality traits matched to those of a like-minded man seemed a good way to cut through all the toe-curling embarrassment of a first date that was obviously going nowhere. But it hadn't been anywhere near as simple as that – there was only so much a computer could come up with – and there followed several disastrous evenings before she'd struck gold with Alec. 'So why don't you join an agency?' she asked Caroline innocently.

'But it's so desperate. I mean, the whole set-up must attract all the wrong kind of men, the flaky ones whose trousers are too short, and who wear grey slip-on shoes and want to unburden themselves on some equally sad woman.'

How tempting it was to prove Caroline wrong. 'But how do you know it would be like that?'

'Believe me, Kate. I just know.'

'Well, perhaps you should give it a try. You never know, you might meet somebody really special. I'm sure it would be worth a go. What have you got to lose?'

Caroline chewed thoughtfully on a prawn. 'Do you really think so?'

I know so, Kate wanted to say, but instead she nodded her head and sipped her fizzy water.

'Anyway, enough about my non-existent love life, tell me about yours. Any sign of the clanging of wedding bells yet?'

'Alec and I are happy enough without getting married.'

Caroline contemplated her friend. 'If you don't mind me saying, that sounded just an itsy-bitsy bit too pat; it also had the distinctive ring of an untruth behind it.'

Kate blushed.

'Doesn't he want to get married?'

'It's not something we talk about.'

Caroline scoffed. 'He's taking you for a ride, girl.'

'He's not,' Kate said indignantly, quick to leap to Alec's defence. 'And why should we change things when we're both happy with what we've got? Everything's perfect between us.'

'Mm . . .' said Caroline. She sounded far from convinced. 'Okay then,' she said, 'you give me no alternative but to test your idea of perfection. Suppose I were to put the question of, let's say, how could you possibly improve on your relationship? And don't give me any bullshit about your lives resembling a day in the life of Adam and Eve before the wily snake made his appearance.'

'That's a silly question.'

'So what if it is, give me an answer.'

Kate didn't want to. She knew what her answer was and she was frightened that hearing herself actually say the words out loud might court disaster for her relationship with Alec.

'Come on,' pressed Caroline. 'It doesn't have to be something monumental. It could be something as simple as changing the colour of his socks. Or guiding him through the tricky transition from Y-fronts to boxers.'

Kate relaxed and smiled.

'Or, of course,' Caroline went on, 'it could be something more earth-shattering like you . . . like you wanting to have a baby and him not being interested because he's done that scene already.'

Don't react, Kate told herself. She's only fishing. She has no way of knowing.

'Well?'

There was no avoiding the question. She would have to come up with something credible in order to make Caroline drop the subject. 'I'd like to be rid of Alec's ex-wife,' she said with a sudden flash of inspiration. It was even true.

'Why?' latched on Caroline, 'is she a problem? He doesn't still have a thing for her, does he?'

'Heavens no!'

'How can you be so sure?'

'Really, Caroline, are you so jealous of me that you want to unravel my relationship with Alec completely?'

Caroline had the grace to look shamefaced. 'Spoil-sport,' she said. 'Come on, eat up and I'll go and fetch us another round of drinks. Same again?'

'Please.'

When Caroline returned she said, 'So if you're going to be boring and not tell me anything about you and Alec, tell me how you're managing financially and what you're doing about getting another job.'

This was much safer ground and Kate pushed her finished plate to one side and said, 'I had a bit saved for a rainy day, so I'm okay for a while, but . . . but I think I'm going for a career move.'

'Oh, sounds interesting. What are you thinking of doing? With your new-found assertiveness you'd make an ideal doctor's receptionist.'

Kate smiled, but thought about what her friend had said. Had she changed? Was she really standing up for herself more these days? 'With all the cutbacks going on I really don't hold out much hope of getting another librarian's job in the immediate area, so the obvious answer is to retrain.'

'Go on.'

'What do you think about teaching?'

Caroline groaned. 'The only kind of teaching I'd consider would be in an all-boys' school with an excessive amount of sixth-form testosterone to drool over. So what age do you see yourself with?'

'Infants.'

Caroline groaned again. 'Well, you always were the only one at the library who could control the little horrors. You should have seen the state Maggie got into on Saturday when we had the first of the summer holiday story-time sessions. I thought she was going to hit this one boy who kept interrupting her. "Please Miss, please Miss," he kept whining. It was only after Maggie had finished the story and all the children stood up that she realised why the pest had been wittering on at her. He'd wanted the loo and had used the carpet in the end. Oh happy days.'

'The poor boy.'

'Poor Maggie, you mean. You know how obsessive she is about hygiene. She's becoming even more of a basket case these days. She's started wearing gloves, saying that the average library book contains more germs than a public lavatory. She reckons the books taken out by men are the worst. She's probably right.'

Kate laughed.

'So what does Alec think about you becoming a schoolmarm?'

'I haven't talked to him about it yet.'

'Why not?'

'Because I only started thinking about it over the weekend.' It was while she had been waiting for Alec to finish talking with Melissa on Saturday afternoon that the idea had begun to take root. Melissa's boy-friend, Tim, had asked her what she did for a living. When she had explained, he'd said, 'I don't recall librarians being as attractive as you.' She had felt the colour rising in her cheeks and had hoped that Melissa hadn't overheard what he'd said.

'So why aren't you still stamping books and telling people to ssh?' he'd asked.

'I was made redundant.'

'I'm sorry. Any idea what you'll do next?'

'I'm not sure, to be honest. Which I know sounds pathetically feeble.'

'Not at all, but what would you most like to do if you had the pick of any job?'

She had thought about this for a few seconds, then, seeing Oscar coming towards her, she had found her answer. 'I like children, so maybe I could do something in that line.'

'Teaching perhaps?'

'Yes,' she'd said, and responding to Oscar's hand searching for hers she'd added, 'I think I'd like that a lot.'

'Hello. Anybody at home?'

'Sorry, Caroline,' Kate said. 'I was miles away then.'

'I could tell. So what are you going to do about this career change? If you act fast now you might be able to join a teacher training course starting this autumn. Why don't you come over to the library and go through all the further education information?'

Kate drove home full of optimism, which made her realise that she must have been feeling the opposite before she'd arrived for lunch.

Since losing her job and moving in with Alec she had perhaps been too quick to put her life on hold. Being content to drift along was all very well, but it couldn't go on that way. She would spend the rest of the summer taking care of Oscar, as she'd promised Ruth, but come the autumn there would be her own life to see to.

It had been good to see Caroline again. One of her friend's greatest strengths was bullying people into sorting out their lives.

She decided to stop off at the supermarket on the way home and buy something special for supper that evening. She felt the need to celebrate the fact that a twinkling of an idea had been turned into a fully fledged decision.

She saw it as an important decision; one that she was convinced was going to make everything right again between her and Alec.

Having a new career to work for would stop her wanting something she couldn't have.

Chapter Twenty-One

Jessica was fooling herself that she was working. Or rather, she was trying to fool herself that she was working.

Sitting with her head bent over a pad of foolscap and sucking pensively on the end of a pencil, she was giving an impressive performance of a writer. Only trouble was, the paper was blank and the pencil, completely unused, was as sharp as a pin.

Her attempt at putting a story-line together was not going well.

In fact, it was going depressingly badly. Not a word had been written since eight o'clock that morning. It was now ten thirty and the great Muse of romantic fiction had yet to get out of bed, apply her make-up, don her heels and make an appearance in Jessica's study.

The worry was, perhaps she never would.

Maybe the goddess who had worked so well for Jessica in the past had deserted her and had stayed behind in Corfu. 'Forget it,' the mythical Greek goddess had said to her many sisters when she'd learnt of Jessica's plans to leave the island, 'I ain't working my butt off in some freezing outpost called England!'

Jessica flung down her pencil. It bounced off the desk, hit the corner of the printer and broke its sharp point clean off.

'Serves you right,' Jessica said with childish satisfaction.

Starting a new novel in the past had never been a problem for Jessica. In fact, she had invariably enjoyed the anticipatory element of staring at a blank piece of paper and waiting for ideas to start to flow. It was at this stage, before she had progressed to working on her laptop, that she had the most fun. So long as she didn't have a single word written she could kid herself that her next novel would be her crowning glory; her *magnum opus*. It would win universal critical acclaim, the like of which had never been heard before – even Germaine Greer and A. S. Byatt would find it amusing, in a deceptively meaningful and thought-provoking way. It would race straight to the No. 1 slot of the *Sunday Times* bestseller list and it would stay there longer than Helen Fielding's *Bridget Jones's Diary*.

Not only that, it would have every known television and film producer champing at the bit to serialise or Merchant Ivory it.

But that was the stuff of dreams. It was not to be taken seriously.

She stood up. It was time for another cup of coffee. Her sixth of the day so far.

Not that she was counting.

Not that she was becoming paranoid.

While she waited in the kitchen for the kettle to boil she thought of her phone call with her editor yesterday afternoon – another timely reminder that she should be getting on with the next novel. Fresh from her holiday, Cara had read A Carefree Life over the weekend and had phoned to say how much she'd enjoyed it. 'It's great, Jessica, definitely your best.'

'Thank you, Piers thought so, too.'

'In that case we must be sitting on the book of the decade!'

They'd both laughed, then Cara had congratulated Jessica on her new two-book contract. 'We're all thrilled here that you're staying with us.'

'You know how it is,' she had joked, 'better the devil you know.'

'We're planning a massive promotional campaign for A Carefree Life,' Cara had gone on to explain, 'and just as soon as the art department have done their stuff I'll let you have a copy of the jacket. Any ideas for the next book?'

'Um . . . I'd rather not say just yet.'

'That's fine, don't worry, Jessica. We can always trust you to come up with something good.'

Thinking of Cara's praise now, as Jessica dunked a digestive biscuit into her coffee while staring out of the kitchen window, she felt riddled with worry – we can always trust you to come up with something good. Well, supposing she couldn't do it this time? Supposing she'd only ever had the three books in her and that anything she wrote now would be contrived, samey and destined for the cut-price four-books-for-a-pound stores to be found in every high street?

And there was so much money involved.

It was a frightening thought to be trusted with such an incredible weight of responsibility. This, of course, was one of the reasons why she'd turned down the more lucrative offer Piers had negotiated – the more the advance, the greater the responsibility.

What a wimp she was!

And what a dreadful and unnerving revelation it was to know that deep down she was as scared as Gavin to take on the mantle of responsibility.

She dunked another digestive into her cup and seeing it disintegrate into her coffee, she decided she needed shaking up.

The best person to do that was her mother. They'd spoken on the phone late last night, not long after Anna had arrived home from her jaunt to North Wales, and Jessica had said that she would see her some time today. Now was as good a time as any.

As she walked along the lane to her mother's cottage Jessica tried not to think about the fruitless morning spent in her study. Think of anything, she told herself, anything so long as it has nothing to do with writing.

So she forced herself to count how many flowers in the hedgerow she recognised. She got the easy ones, the daisies and buttercups and dandelions, and even identified the patches of tufted vetch with its pretty pale-lilac flowers and the covering of groundsel greedily spreading itself along the roadside. But it was no good. No amount of nature-trailing was going to stop her worrying. Just what was she going to write about in her next novel? An idiot's guide to Cheshire's least-trodden pathways?

This whole business of not being able to write was getting her down. It was a new phenomenon to her. She had never experienced the dreaded writer's block before. But now she had. And in spades.

The inspiration for her previous books had come mostly from some of her own experiences – her first novel had featured a young backpacker; her second, *Caught in the Act*, not surprisingly had starred Gavin; and *A Carefree Life* had more than a passing similarity to her own life. Oh, but heaven help her if she was relying on her new situation to throw a shaft of illuminating light on a potential story-line, because so far, Cholmford seemed to be doing its best to keep her permanently in the dark.

Since she'd been living back in Cholmford, she had tried several times to get started, but on each occasion she had failed. And miserably. It was as if she were clean out of ideas. She had blamed it on her new surroundings to begin with, convincing herself, after each failed attempt, that the next day she would crack it. It wasn't even as though she was having trouble in getting chapter one off the ground, it was worse. Much worse. She had no characters. She had no setting. She had no story-line. In short she had a resounding zippo. No wonder she'd nearly throttled Amanda on Saturday night – *It must be wonderful to be able to earn a living from something as easy as writing*. Hah! The horrible woman should try it some time. She should try rolling up her sleeves for a day of creative black-out.

The strange thing was she could say with great authority – enormous authority in fact – what she wasn't going to write next. That was easy. She didn't want to write some thinly disguised copy of a classic. The bookshelves were full of contemporary reworkings of *Jane Eyre, Pride and Prejudice, Emma,* and more recently *Rebecca* had been given the same treatment. She was sick of bright young things always getting their man.

The other kind of novel she didn't want to write was the one about the bored, frumpy housewife, who manages overnight to shed three stone and with little more than a wave of a new mascara wand makes the sexy love interest fall at her feet.

If she was sick of bright young things getting their man, she was equally sick of middle-aged women making good.

Where was the reality?

Where was the nitty-gritty, hard-up-against-the-wall portrayal that all men were bastards and weren't worth the effort?

So, having condemned most of the popular romantic fiction currently on offer, what exactly did that leave her to get her teeth into?

A good juicy murder story?

It would be her own if Piers got wind of the mess she was in.

Oh Lord, what on earth had happened to her? Why was she so thoroughly cynical about love and romance all of a sudden?

She came to an abrupt stop in the road.

Gavin!

That was what was wrong with her. It was all his fault that she couldn't write. He had knocked the stuff of love right out of her and now she couldn't write about it.

'Damn you, Gavin!' she said out loud. A startled sparrow flew out of the undergrowth and disappeared into the safety of a hawthorn tree.

And what's more, she thought as she stomped her way along the road, having stolen her creative Muse, Gavin was very probably having his nautical way with her.

By the time she reached Willow Cottage Jessica's fury was just waiting to unleash itself.

She found her mother heaving a large rock out of the back of her Fiesta.

'Oh hell,' muttered Anna, when she saw the look of fuming anger on her daughter's face. 'I'd hoped to hide this before you arrived.'

'I bet you did!' stormed Jessica, going over to the car and pushing her mother's hands away from the enormous filched lump of North Wales coastline. 'Just what do you think you're doing?'

'I would have thought that was quite obvious.'

Jessica struggled with the rock, then pitched it into the wheelbarrow which her mother had positioned against the car. The barrow shuddered and nearly toppled under the weight of its cargo.

'In heaven's name, couldn't you have found something smaller?'

Anna smiled. 'The others are.'

'Others!' cried Jessica, now following after her mother, who was staggering behind the barrow and pushing it round to the back of the house.

'I'm building a rockery,' Anna said over her shoulder.

'I don't believe this,' Jessica said when they stood looking at a pile of stones. 'You've got enough here to rival Stonehenge.'

'Oh, don't exaggerate.'

'Well if you're not worried about your own suspension, what about the car's? You must have been dragging the boot on the ground the whole way home from George and Emily's.'

'It's my body, my car, I'll do as I please.'

Jessica frowned. Why couldn't her mother behave as she was supposed to? Why couldn't she be happy with a little light weeding and the odd coffee morning to keep her out of mischief? Why this bloody need to kill herself! 'And what was George thinking, letting you do this? I thought I could trust him.'

'Look, Jessica, I know you mean well, but do you think you could ease up a bit? And for your information, George wasn't around when Emily and I loaded the car. So don't go blaming him. Here, just help me tip the barrow to get this rock out.'

Jessica did as her mother asked. 'I'm sorry,' she said, when the stone rolled away from them and joined its compatriots, 'it's just that I can't help but worry about you.' She knew that she'd just taken out her anger and frustration on Anna.

'I know, dear. But honestly, I'm fine. Which is more than I can say for you. Now why don't you sit down for a few moments and tell me what you've been up to while I was away. Oh, and before I forget, George and Emily send their best wishes and they both loved your last book. They want to know when the next one comes out. I said you'd write and tell them yourself.'

Jessica rolled her eyes. 'Letters will be all I'll be good for at the rate I'm going.'

Anna could see that her daughter was unusually upset. 'Come on,' she said, 'sit on the swing and tell me all about it while I prune the roses.' Without waiting for a response from Jessica, she led the way.

The swing had been one of Anna's proudest achievements in the garden. It had been a present for Jessica on her tenth birthday. It was built out of a sturdy combination of wooden sleepers and metal girders, and Anna had trained clusters of baby pink roses to grow over it. Now, after all these years it resembled the prettiest of rose arbours.

Jessica sat on the wooden seat and breathed in the sweet smell of roses; the perfume was as fragrant as she remembered from her childhood. She suddenly felt sad. The time would come when one day, these beautiful roses would be nothing but a memory.

'So what's the problem?' Anna asked, pulling out a pair of secateurs from her skirt pocket and snipping away at the deadheads; she dropped them tidily into a trug on the ground.

Jessica picked up her feet and gently began swinging to and fro, setting off a steady rhythmic creaking. 'I can't write,' she said simply.

Anna carried on with what she was doing. 'You mean you've got writer's block?'

'Something like that.'

'So what are you going to do about it?'

'I wish I knew.'

'Remind me to fetch some oil out here, that swing sounds as fed up as you. Any idea what's caused this block?'

'Promise you won't tut or scoff?'

'Have I ever?'

'Frequently. Especially over Gavin. When you met him for the first time you did nothing but tut and scoff.'

Anna turned and faced her daughter. What Jessica had just said was true. She had never really taken to Gavin. 'Are you saying he's the reason for your writer's block?'

Jessica nodded.

'Dear me,' was all Anna said. She went back to her roses.

'He's made me so cynical about love and romance that I don't think I can write about it as I used to.'

Anna tutted.

'You promised!'

'No I didn't. And the answer is simple. Find somebody new to love. Have a bit of a fling to restore your faith in all things romantic.'

'I can't possibly do that!'

'Whyever not? There's nothing like a casual affair to put the spring back in your step. Now tell me how your house is coming along.'

147

Jessica was amazed at her mother's extraordinary suggestion. Mothers weren't supposed to go around saying things like that! Little did Anna know that Jessica had already had the offer of something to put the spring back in her step, but had turned it down. She wondered, now, why she'd done that. Why had she backed off from Josh Crawford in the way she had? Was it simply that it was too soon after Gavin? Well, chances were she was going to find out. Last night, Josh had called over to invite her to dinner this evening.

'Jessica,' Anna said with a frown, 'I'm getting more attention from that creaking swing than from you. I asked you how your house was.'

'Sorry,' Jessica said, dragging her attention back to her mother. 'It's fine, though I'm not sure how much longer I can put up with some of the décor.'

'Then do something about it.'

'I will.' Jessica smiled. How clearly her mother saw things. If there was something wrong, then Anna's immediate response was to put it right – have a fling, redecorate, whatever. She never wasted any energy complaining about a thing.

'Which room bothers you the most?' Anna asked.

'Um . . . the kitchen probably, it's too slick, too much like an operating theatre.'

'Then let me decorate it for you.'

'What about Stonehenge?'

'I am capable of doing more than two things at once you know.'

'All right,' said Jessica. 'You're on.' At least if her mother was helping her it meant she could keep an eye on what she was getting up to. 'Do you think you could help me with something else?'

'Depends what it is. It's nothing to do with Gavin, is it?'

'No it isn't,' Jessica said crossly. 'I need to buy a car, and I wondered if you'd like to chauffeur me round a few garages and help me choose one?'

'When?'

'This afternoon?'

Anna looked disappointed. 'I wanted to make a start on the rockery.'

'Please.'

'Oh, all right. And don't think for one moment that by putting me off today I shall lose interest and not get around to doing it.'

'Hadn't crossed my mind.'

'Liar.'

Jessica stayed for lunch with Anna and told her about her new publishing contract.

'Does this mean you're going to be fabulously wealthy?'

'Don't be daft. It means there's a lot of hard work ahead of me . . . if only I could get started.'

After lunch they went in search of a car.

'What are you thinking of buying?' Anna asked Jessica as they drove away from Cholmford. 'Something with a decent engine I hope. Will your ill-gotten gains run to something brand new and swanky? I quite fancy being driven around in style. How about a little sports car? We'd look good in that.'

'I was thinking more along the lines of a second-hand runabout.' Even though Jessica knew she was about to start earning what in anyone's book was a decent amount of money, the years of living with little more than a backpack stuffed full of frugal uncertainty had made her unable to splash out too lavishly.

'You're surely not telling me you want a boring old Metro that's been driven by a dull old dear who's never pushed it beyond third gear?'

'It'd be better than your Fiesta that's been used as a skip. Honestly, Mum, the state of this car's disgusting. When was the last time you cleared it out?' She held up a pork pie wrapper that had been stuffed into the space where cassettes were supposed to be stored.

'You're turning into a right old whinge. Where, oh where, did I go wrong with you?'

'You didn't. I'm the voice of reason.'

Anna groaned. 'Now that you've come home, I'm not going to see too much of you, am I?'

'Thanks, Mum. Love you too.'

'One can have too much of a good thing, you know.'

'I'm beginning to see that.'

'Good. Just so long as we know where we stand. Now tell me about your neighbours, what are they like? And more to the point, what's the story behind the good-looking man we saw the day you moved in? Single, married, divorced or gay?'

Jessica laughed. 'I've a good mind not to tell you.'

'You could always walk to the garage.'

'Okay, I give in.' Jessica began by telling her mother about Tony and Amanda, then moved on to Kate and Alec next door. 'I like them, they're nice. They're not married but they're very much in *lurve*. She's a lot younger than him and a real stunner, but one of those who doesn't realise it.'

'You mean, she's stupid?'

'No. There's a naïvety about her that's really quite refreshing. I'd love to use her as a character in a book one day.'

'And what about him? Is he a middle-aged lech?'

'Not at all. He's the kind of man I'd have liked as a father.' She immediately wished she hadn't said that.

'I'm sorry not to have obliged you, Jessica.'

'I didn't mean it like that.'

Anna smiled kindly at her daughter. Years ago, Jessica had always been on at her to find a husband. But what with bringing up a child on her own and running a busy employment agency, the opportunity had never shown itself. Perhaps if it had, Jessica wouldn't now be so overly attentive.

'So,' she said, 'we've covered Mrs Social-Climber and her cute husband, and Mr and Mrs Lovey-Dovey next door, how about our good-looking young man? What have you got to tell me about him? I see that you've kept him till last. Would he be any good at helping you over your writer's block?'

'Honestly, Mum, why don't you just come right out and ask if I fancy sleeping with him?'

'I thought I just had.'

Jessica feigned a look of shock and told Anna all about being rescued after her trip down to London. She went on to give an edited version of the nightcap session following Tony and Amanda's dinner party.

'And?' Anna said when she'd finished.

'And, there isn't anything else to tell.'

'You sure?'

'Kindly remember there are certain things a daughter can't share with her mother.'

'It must have slipped my memory. Didn't I ever tell you that you were adopted?'

Jessica laughed. 'Forget it. I'm not telling you any more about him. So keep your nose out of my private life and your eyes on the road, I'd forgotten what an appalling driver you are.'

She had decided not to tell her mother that she was having dinner with Josh that evening and would keep it that way until she had made up her mind where she stood with him. It was all very well her mother suggesting that she have a fling with one of her neighbours, but how would it be when it was over and she and Josh had to face each other across the courtyard?

And surely Anna was wrong? Rushing headlong into the arms of somebody, for whatever reason, so soon after Gavin didn't seem like the most sensible of ideas.

It sounded like a perfect recipe for disaster.

Chapter Twenty-Two

Josh read through the recipe for Thai salmon parcels one more time and got down to work.

He grated the small stump of fresh ginger, crushed the clove of garlic, squeezed the juice out of two limes, chopped up a spring onion together with some coriander, then put it all in a pyrex bowl. Next he melted a chunk of butter in the microwave, then laid out the first of the sheets of filo pastry. As he began brushing the melted butter over the thin layer of pastry he had to concentrate hard on keeping his right hand moving.

It's fine, he told himself, determined to ignore the pins and needles and stiffness that were building up in his fingers. There's nothing to worry about. It'll pass.

But the cruel voice of Past Experience said otherwise. *If you're struggling to hold a pastry brush now*, it sneered at him, *how do you think you're going to relieve Jessica of her clothing later on tonight? Just think of all those buttons and fastenings to get through.*

He told Past Experience to bugger off and carried on with what he was doing, but the brush slipped out of his hand, rolled off the edge of the island unit and landed on the floor. He picked it up and threw it into the sink, then hunted through the drawer for another. When he found one, he laid a second sheet of filo pastry on top of the first and smeared it with the melted butter.

I'll be fine, he told himself. It's only the one hand that's playing up and anyway, I could always claim I'd hurt it during the day.

How? the gloating voice sneered at him again, *a squash injury perhaps?*

He blotted out what he didn't want to face, just as he had his brother's expression on Sunday afternoon when he'd told him about Jessica. He could tell what Charlie was thinking, but he didn't care.

'I'm not looking for a big relationship that's heavy on commitment,' he'd said to Charlie, when they'd eaten lunch and were tidying the kitchen, while outside in the garden their parents dozed in the sun. 'There's no point anyway. I just want a bit of fun . . . while I still can.'

'But wouldn't you rather have something that's more meaningful?'

'Like I say, there's no point. What can I offer anyone?'

Josh knew that he was being selfish, that what he had in mind that evening was all about himself. Jessica might not have wanted to go to bed with him the other night, but he had every intention of making things turn out differently tonight. And to hell with the consequences.

He finished making the salmon parcels and went through to the dining-room to check there was nothing he'd forgotten. Everything looked in order. He'd set the table earlier when he'd got back from seeing a customer in Stoke and all that remained to be done was to light the candles when Jessica arrived.

In the sitting-room he went over to the flowers he had bought on the way home. They were large creamy white lilies and had been the most impressive-looking flowers in the shop. 'They'll last for days,' the florist had said, 'and the scent's terrific.' Now he wondered if they were a bit too much; the room seemed to be filled with their rich, powerful fragrance. He carefully picked up the vase and carried it away from the mantelpiece and positioned it on a small table beneath the open window where a cool breeze gently blew in. He stood back and stared at the lilies. He didn't know why, but they didn't look right. There was nowhere else to put them so he returned the vase to the mantelpiece. He then fiddled about with the cushions on the sofa and chairs, and straightened the magazines on the coffee table.

Bloody hell, he thought, what was he doing, turning into some neurotic housewife plumping up the cushions?

All the same, he couldn't resist going upstairs and checking the bedroom. He smoothed out the duvet which he had changed earlier, kicked his work shoes under the bed and pulled open his bedside drawer. A new packet of condoms winked back at him and before the malevolent voice that had taunted him in the kitchen had a chance to say anything, he shut the drawer and went and inspected the bathroom. All was clean and tidy. No hairs in the bath plughole and not a sign of any shavings in the basin. Even the towels were hanging straight.

He went back downstairs to the kitchen, where the tantalising smell of garlic and lime was making itself at home. He poured out a glass of wine from the bottle already uncorked in the fridge and congratulated himself. The stage was perfectly set for an evening of seduction. All that was needed was for Jessica to make her appearance.

Jessica was totally unaware of the time.

After an exhausting but successful afternoon spent car hunting with her mother, she had come home and run herself a bath. While lying back in the hot scented water and thinking about the evening ahead, the miraculous had happened – inspiration for her next novel had leapt out at her. What's more, the title had even presented itself.

And amazingly it was all down to her mother. Though heaven forbid that Anna should ever know that the credit was hers!

Not wanting to lose a single precious idea, Jessica had made a fast exit from the bathroom and with only a towel tied around her she had hurried down to the study where, on a creative high, she began throwing together a cast of characters along with a rough outline for a story.

Only when her neck and shoulders started to ache from being hunched over her desk for so long did she wonder what time it was and, remembering that she was supposed to have been getting ready to go out, she went through to the kitchen. The digital clock on the oven unit told her it was twenty to nine. She gasped in horror. She was nearly half an hour late for Josh.

She flew upstairs and threw on the first things to hand – the long wraparound skirt she had worn the other night for supper at Tony and Amanda's and a loose-fitting sleeveless top the colour of ivory, which made her look browner than ever. She slipped a pair of gold hooped ear-rings through her ears, brushed her hair and was downstairs in a matter of seconds, ready to open the front door. It was then that she realised she'd forgotten to put on any knickers. Back up the stairs, she yanked open a drawer and found that she was down to her last pair – they were years old and had seen rather more action than was decent. She wriggled into the worn-out pinky-grey cotton-and-lycra mixture and dashed downstairs again, remembering on her way out of the house to grab the bottle she'd bought for Josh.

When she knocked on his door she was flushed and out of breath.

In contrast, Josh looked like he deserved better than her cobbled-together appearance and antique knickers.

He stood there smiling at her, every inch of him heart-stoppingly, stomach-lurchingly gorgeous. And she was so busy taking him in – every little bit of his clean-cut splendid self, dressed in black jeans and crisp white T-shirt – that she almost missed the kiss being planted on her cheek. She reacted just in time and caught the benefit of his lips brushing against her skin.

'Here, this is for you,' she said. She handed him the bottle of Southern Comfort. 'Seeing as I helped you polish off the last one.'

'Thanks, we'll have a go with this later, perhaps. Come on through to the kitchen, I'm just in the middle of something.'

She followed behind him. Mm . . . nice bum, she found herself thinking. She even thought his limp was attractive and decided that it gave him an interesting air of vulnerability. As they passed what she took to be the downstairs loo, she was aware of a heady nose-clearing cocktail of Pine-O-Fresh toilet cleaner and some kind of air freshener. Bless him. The bachelor boy had been busy.

In the kitchen, she watched him open the oven door and take out a tray of croûtons. Her taste-buds responded to the delicious smell of garlic and olive oil. 'Sorry I'm so late, by the way,' she said.

'I was beginning to wonder whether I was going to be stood up,' he said, closing the oven door with his foot and tipping the perfectly cooked croûtons into a yellow-and-blue pottery bowl. 'I would have been very disappointed.'

'Oh, I wouldn't have done that,' she said, 'standing people up isn't my style.' She had the feeling that they were flirting with one another again.

'Good, I'm glad to hear it. So what's your excuse for being late? And I shall expect something highly imaginative and original from you, no ordinary explanation will do, not from a writer.'

She laughed. 'Well, Crawford – you don't mind if I call you that, do you?'

'If it amuses you, go ahead. Though I'd like to know why.'

'How very tedious of you. But let's just say that a little formality never does any harm. It's a useful device for putting people at their ease.'

He moved across the kitchen and slid the baking tray into the sink. 'An interesting concept, with more than a hint of Oscar Wilde to it.'

'You're not accusing me of plagiarism, are you?'

He turned round and laughed. 'Oh I wouldn't dare. Now, about your excuse for being late.'

'Heavens, you're like a dog with a bone. Would you believe me if I said that burglars broke into my house in the middle of the night and stole all my clocks, thereby leaving me unable to keep track of the time?'

'No. Try again.'

'Localised earthquake?'

'Hopeless.'

'I overslept?'

He shook his head.

'Okay, I admit it, I was with another man having great but meaningless sex.'

He smiled. 'The truth at last. Glass of wine?'

'Thanks.'

He poured out a glass and handed it to her.

'Actually, I'm late because I've at last started work on my next novel.' She told him how depressed she'd been that morning. 'You can't imagine what a relief it is for me to get going again. There were a few nasty moments today when I thought I'd lost it.'

'I'm delighted to hear that you haven't. Am I allowed to know the title?'

She hesitated. Normally she didn't share too much of a new novel with anyone, not until it was firmly in her mind – a new book was like a tiny flickering candle flame, blow too hard on it and it would be completely snuffed out. But she decided to tell him. He would probably think it funny. Well, he would if he knew what her mother had suggested today. 'It's going to be called *A Casual Affair*,' she said, 'what do you think?'

It was his turn to hesitate.

'Don't you like it?' she asked, concerned.

'No. I mean, yes. Yes I do, it's great.' He lowered his gaze and busied his hands with adding the croûtons to the bowl of salad. *A Casual Affair*, he repeated to himself. Well, considering what he had in mind it was perfect.

When they sat down to eat Jessica was impressed. 'You've gone to a lot of trouble, Crawford,' she said mockingly, watching him light the candles on the table. 'Or is this the way you always eat?'

He smiled. 'Only when I want to impress somebody special.'

'Oh,' she said in a coy girlie voice, 'does that make me special?'

He passed her a dish of Jersey Royals that were coated in butter as well as a sprinkling of chopped chives. 'What do you think?'

'I think that you've a manner smooth enough to charm the devil and that I should be very wary of you. And,' she continued, helping herself to a couple of potatoes and adding them to her plate of salmon, 'a man who can cook as well as this is clearly to be viewed with the utmost suspicion. The bottom line, Crawford my boy, is that you're too good to be true. There has to be another side to you that you're keeping under wraps.'

He shook his head. 'See, there's the thing, I'm told that all the time.'

'I can well believe it. Take it from me, this new man stuff of being a whizz in the kitchen will do you no good at all. It only serves to undermine the majority of women and frighten the pants off them.'

He grinned. 'Sounds like justification enough to me. *Bon appetit!*'

The salmon was perfect, as was everything about the meal, and when they'd finished eating Josh told Jessica to go and relax in the sitting-room while he made some coffee.

Alone in the kitchen, he punched a fist in the air. *Yesss!*

Everything was going exactly to plan. They were getting along just fine. All he had to do was get some coffee down Jessica, followed by a couple of glasses of Southern Comfort, then it would be up those stairs. Yes, yes, *yesss!*

The fact that he had hardly any feeling in his right hand did nothing to dampen his confidence and he congratulated himself on his performance over dinner – he'd managed to eat with the fork in his right hand, which didn't need too much manipulative skill, and had used his left for the trickier business of cutting up his food.

And if his luck continued to hold out he was certain he was going to get away with the rest of the evening.

He filled the cafetiere with Sainsbury's Colombian coffee, placed it on the tray with the cups and saucers, along with a box of mint chocolates, and took it through to the sitting-room, where he found Jessica standing in front of the bookcase. She turned to look at him when she heard him come into the room.

'What's the interest in multiple sclerosis?' she asked. She showed him the book in her hands, *Multiple Sclerosis – And How to Get the Better of It*.

He gripped the edges of the tray and carefully moved across the room; all his euphoria instantly gone. He lowered the tray on to the glass-topped table, sank into the sofa and swallowed back his shock. He racked his brain for something convincing to say.

She came over and joined him, the book still in her hands. 'It's an illness I know nothing about,' she said.

'The majority of people don't need to know anything about it,' he said flatly.

'I suppose not. But do you know somebody with MS, then? Is that why you've got this?'

He swallowed and hoped that Charlie would forgive him. 'Yes,' he said, 'my brother Charlie.'

She put down the book on the table. 'Oh, I'm sorry.'

Aware that he could still save the situation, he poured out the coffee with his good hand and began the not so subtle web of lies that he hoped would satisfy Jessica and get him off the hook. 'Charlie's not got it too badly,' he said, trying to sound casual, 'it's just every now and again that he gets caught out, he gets tired easily. But most of the time you'd never know there was anything wrong.'

'When did it start?'

'A few years back. It was quite out of the blue.' He paused, then said, 'Do you think we could drop the subject of my brother?'

'Of course,' she said, 'I'm sorry, I was being nosy.' Jessica had already concluded that Josh and his brother were close, but going by the tone of Josh's voice, it was clear that he was also extremely concerned about Charlie. She felt annoyed with herself for her insensitivity.

'How about some music?' Josh asked, already on his feet and going over to the CD player. 'What do you fancy?'

She was tipsy enough to say 'You,' but sober enough to refrain. 'You choose,' she said.

He put on *The Best of Chris Rea* and 'The Road to Hell' started up. The irony was not lost on him. He went back to the sofa and poured out two glasses of Southern Comfort.

They sat in silence for a while listening to the music and, conscious that they were only a few inches apart, Josh decided it was now or never. It was time to make a move on Jessica. He turned and faced her, and found that she was staring at him. He reached out to her hand on her lap, but was cheated of the touch of her; his fingers were completely numb. He raised his good hand to stroke her face and when she made no attempt to push him away, he kissed her, slowly and lingeringly, and for the first time that night he felt his entire body relax. It was wonderful. He hadn't realised just how uptight he'd been. He gently pushed her along the length of the sofa and began parting the front of her skirt. It was going to be easier than he'd thought.

Dead easy.

He was home and dry.

She was as keen as he was.

But from nowhere he experienced a bolt of self-revulsion; it caught him like a punch in the stomach. He saw what he was doing for what it really was – he was using Jessica as a means to boost his self-esteem. By bedding her, he hoped to chalk up a point of victory over his illness.

And with this clarity of thought came a wave of nausea. He

wanted to put it down to the overpowering smell coming from the lilies on the mantelpiece, but he knew deep down that it was something more. He felt cheap and shabby, and knew he couldn't go through the motions of seducing Jessica in the contrived manner he had planned so exactly. It was all wrong. With a shock he realised that instead of the desire for a mindless easy lay upstairs on the clean sheets, he was overcome with the need for something more.

But what?

Charlie's words came into his head – *Wouldn't you rather have something more meaningful?*

No! he wanted to shout.

No. No. *No!* I'm not capable of anything more. What the hell can I offer anyone in a long-term relationship?

Chapter Twenty-Three

It was the first wet day in over three weeks and as Alec drove past Capesthorne Hall the rain came down even harder. He switched the windscreen wipers on to full and dropped his speed as he joined the queue of cars which stretched back almost two hundred yards from the traffic lights at the junction ahead. It was always busy at this time in the morning and every day as he waited in this same stream of traffic he promised himself to leave the house earlier in order to avoid the rush.

He thought the same now.

But as the wipers tump-tumped across the windscreen he suddenly thought, why? Why should he?

Why should he deprive himself of a few precious minutes at home with Kate just so that he could reach the office at eight thirty instead of eight forty? What possible difference would it make?

None.

None whatsoever. He would still get exactly the same amount of work done. So why bother?

Because the old Alec McLaren had spent a lifetime on the treadmill convinced that the only way to be was to adhere to the puritanical work ethic that his father had drilled into him – a busy mind is a pure mind.

He smiled and not for the first time wondered what his poor father would have made of his relationship with Kate. The old man's verdict would probably have been that Alec hadn't kept himself busy enough. 'Your mind has wandered,' he'd have said, 'and wandered badly into the mire of evil.'

Alec had been terrified of his father as a child and had never attached himself to any of the religious views he propounded, finding the commitment to such an apparently cold and unforgiving deity too austere a concept to consider as having any value or relevance.

He preferred his mother's God. While his father had frightened him with his tales of hell and purgatory, his mother had told him reassuring stories of a merciful God who was more interested in seeing a smile on Alec's face, rather than a grim expression of servitude.

His mother had been a quiet, affectionate woman whom Alec had adored. Being her only child she had spoilt him as much as she dared and, without ever defying her husband or the strict code of conduct by which he expected them all to live, she had managed to ensure that Alec's childhood was a happy one.

He wasn't quite sure that it was something he should admit, or ever explore in any depth, but there were definitely times when Kate reminded him of his mother. Physically the two women were quite different – his mother had been a tiny dark-haired woman – but they both had the same ability to give him a sense of true well-being. Often when he left work and drove home to Kate he experienced the same degree of comfort and anchorage as when he'd been a ten-year-old boy arriving home from school on a cold, wintry afternoon to find his mother pulling a tray of freshly baked oatcakes out of the oven.

If he wanted to offer up a superficial analysis of any of this, he supposed it was possible that he loved Kate as much as he did because, like his mother who had eased the severity of his father's treatment of him, Kate had wiped away the shock and pain of what Melissa had done.

In the end, time had helped him to resolve the difficult relationship with his father. As an adult, Alec had grown to understand, and on occasion almost respect, the strong will and reserved manner that had kept them apart. To this day, though, it saddened Alec that they hadn't been closer. When his father was dying and he and his mother had spent so many hours by his hospital bedside there had still been that impenetrable barrier of stiff formality between them. What would have seemed the most natural thing in the world to have done was to have hugged his father and said that he loved him. But it hadn't happened. Even at so poignant a moment to have shown the slightest flicker of emotion in front of this formidable man was unthinkable. And perhaps that's the way it should have been. It was probably what his father would have wanted. No emotion. Just a quiet acceptance that his life was over.

Except it wasn't.

No life was ever over. It could never be that clear-cut. There was always a legacy that kept the deceased well and truly alive. And in his father's case he had bequeathed Alec a confusion of conflicting attitudes that was hard to shake off. It was frightening just how good a job his father had done, because sure enough, the work-till-you-drop ethic was clearly ingrained in Alec, which was why from time to time he had to force himself to stand firm and veto this edict from the grave.

So, no, he now said as the lights changed to green and he turned left on to the Chelford Road. No, he would not leave the house any earlier to avoid the traffic just so that he could gain an extra ten minutes at his desk.

He reached the office at the same time as Melissa and parked alongside her MR2. She let them into the redbrick building that had once been the local village school. With its distinctive Victorian arched windows, it still looked exactly like a school from the outside, but inside it was completely different, with many of the walls knocked down to open up what had originally been small cramped classrooms into large areas of creative working space. The windows were perfect for letting in plenty of natural light so that the three artists they currently employed could work at their best. Where the light wasn't quite so good, Melissa and Alec had their offices, along with other members of the team who carried out the administrative side of the business.

Many of the people whom they employed had been with them since Thistle Cards had moved to these premises back in 1981. Before those days the business had been little more than a dream, consisting of him and Melissa putting in a full day's work for a small advertising agency where they were both employed as designers, then taking it in turns to look after Ruth or spend an evening inhaling the fumes of turpentine-based ink in a rented basement room beneath Squeaky Clean, a dog parlour that was a local harbouring ground for fleas, ticks and any other ghastly canine parasite you'd care to think of. Alec didn't know which was worse, the stink of the turpentine in that tiny dank room as they worked until gone midnight producing a limited range of cards, or the permanent smell of wet dog seeping through the rotten floorboards above their heads.

'What are you smiling about?' Melissa said, catching the expression on his face as she looked up from sorting through the mail in her hands.

'Sorry,' he said, 'I didn't realise I was. I was just reminiscing.'

She followed him through to his office. 'Reminiscing about anything in particular?'

'I was thinking about Squeaky Clean.'

Melissa shuddered. 'I gave up thinking about those awful days a long time ago. I much prefer to think of the present.'

He sat in his swivel chair and considered what she'd just said. 'In all ways?' he asked.

The question hung in the air while Melissa returned his gaze. She thought about answering it, but decided not to – cheap shots at an ex-husband were two a penny. Instead she said, 'I want to check a few things with you about Birmingham.'

At this time of the year the Birmingham trade fair was their biggest concern. There was a colossal amount of work involved in order to be ready for the September event. But despite the organisational headache both he and Melissa thrived on it. They always had. It was where the bulk of their business was done and where most importantly they found their entrée into the export markets; a third of their money was made in the USA, Japan, Australia and more recently Iceland had been added to their order books. The trade fairs were a fundamental part of the greetings card industry, without them they might just as well pack up and go home.

'What is it?' he asked. 'A problem?'

She sat in the chair opposite him. 'Of course not, stop thinking the worst.'

He was reminded of Kate on Monday evening when he'd got back from work and found her eager to share some news with him. 'Sit down,' she'd said, 'I've got something to tell you, and don't go jumping to conclusions and thinking the worst.'

'What is it?' he'd asked warily. The awful thought had gone through his mind that Kate was about to tell him that she was pregnant. He'd sat awkwardly in the armchair petrified that his expression would betray him. He knew that Kate would love to have a baby and knew too how she would want him to react to such a piece of news. But when she'd told him that she'd decided that she wanted to retrain and become a teacher he had pulled her on to his lap and hugged her.

'That's a brilliant idea,' he'd said, kissing her. 'That's fantastic.'

Thinking now about his relief that Kate wasn't pregnant it struck him how utterly selfish he was. It wasn't a pleasant realisation. In fact, it was a rather unpalatable conclusion that spoke volumes about their relationship. Without doubt he loved Kate more than he'd loved anyone, but it was all too clear that he didn't love her sufficiently to give her complete happiness. Whereas Kate loved him selflessly. Because of her love for him she was prepared to deny herself something she desperately wanted – a family of her own.

What was he prepared to sacrifice for Kate? Good God, he hadn't even had the decency to marry her.

When he and Melissa had finished discussing the Birmingham trade fair Alec phoned Kate. He suddenly wanted to hear her gentle, loving voice. He needed confirmation that he wasn't a complete heel.

Kate put down the phone and went back to pouring out a small mug of Ribena for Oscar.

'Was that Gramps?' he asked from the table where he was busy painting.

'Yes,' she said, handing him his drink.

He put down his paintbrush, taking care to keep it on the newspaper that Kate had partially covered the table with.

'Would you like a rice cake?'

He shook his head.

'A biscuit?'

His face lit up. 'Yes please.'

Kate fetched the biscuit tin from the cupboard and came back and sat next to him. She prised the lid off and offered him the tin. He took a custard cream and began nibbling on one of its corners. He stared at her thoughtfully. 'If you were married to Gramps, would that make you my grandma?'

Kate smiled. 'I don't think so,' she said, amused at the notion of being a grandmother.

'Good,' he said. 'I don't want you to be like Grandma Melissa.'

Much as a good bitching session about Melissa would intrigue her, Kate knew better than to draw Oscar on the subject. 'Grandma Melissa and I are very different,' she said tactfully.

'I don't like her,' he confessed, his eyes lowered. 'She tells me off.'

'Well,' Kate said slowly, 'if you've been naughty then she has every right to tell you off.'

He raised his eyes and looked indignant. 'But I wasn't naughty. I only said that I liked you better than her.'

'Oh, Oscar,' Kate said, 'you mustn't say things like that.'

'Why not?'

'Because ... because you must have hurt Grandma Melissa by saying what you did and that's something you mustn't do, you mustn't go around hurting people. It's not nice.'

'I didn't mean to hurt her,' he said, his face full of concern. 'Mummy says I mustn't tell lies ... I was telling the truth. I only told Grandma Melissa that I liked you better than anyone else. What was wrong with that?'

Nothing, thought Kate, if you were a four-and-a-half-year-old boy. 'Come on,' she said by way of distraction, 'how's this picture coming along?'

Oscar drained his mug of Ribena, set it down next to the jam jar of greeny-grey water and picked up his paintbrush. 'I'm going to do the sky next. Will you help me?'

'If you want. But you go first and I'll do a tiny bit at the end.'

Kate watched Oscar dip his brush into the jar of water and select his colour from the plastic tray of paints. He covered the stumpy bristles in blue and started stroking the brush across the top two inches of his picture. He worked carefully and slowly, and Kate watched his face closely. It was rigid with concentration, his tongue poking out of the corner of his mouth, his smudgy little eyebrows furrowed lest he make a mistake.

This was Oscar's first day with Kate – and Ruth's first day working alongside Adam. She had arrived late, having told Kate on the phone last night to expect her at eight o'clock. She'd eventually turned up at a quarter to nine. 'The roads are a nightmare,' she'd said to Kate, bundling Oscar out of the car as the rain had lashed down on them, 'I can't believe how selfish people are all travelling in separate cars. Haven't they heard of public transport, or car pools for that matter?'

Kate would have liked to suggest that maybe Ruth ought to travel to work with Adam and save yet another car from adding to the congestion, but she hadn't; instead she had taken Oscar's hand and led him through to the kitchen.

'I've brought his jacket and boots so that you can take him for a walk,' Ruth had added, throwing the things down on the floor in the hall, 'he must have at least half an hour of fresh air.' She made him sound like a dog. 'And here are some rice cakes for him to eat instead of biscuits. I don't want you filling him up with rubbish. I'll see you at about six.'

She'd flown out of the house without so much as a kiss for Oscar and together he and Kate had waved goodbye from the doorstep.

'There,' Oscar said, turning to face Kate and handing her the paintbrush. 'I've left you the bit in the corner.'

'Thank you. But tell you what, why don't we put a bright jolly sun in that space? What do you think?'

He turned away and looked out of the kitchen window to the scene of the courtyard that he'd been painting. 'But there isn't a sun today, it's still raining,' he said.

She smiled. 'But we're using our imaginations to do this, aren't we? Let's paint a sun in, then maybe if we're really lucky it might make the rain go away and we could go for a walk.'

'I'll need some clean water.'

She got up and took the jam jar over to the sink. She refilled it and cleaned the brush under the tap. When she went back to Oscar the phone rang.

It was Caroline. 'Hi,' she said, 'have you got a minute?'

'Of course, but not too many, I've got Oscar here with me.'

'Oscar? Who's he? Some gorgeous hunk?'

'Gorgeous, but not a hunk. He's Alec's grandson.'

'Oh, yes, I remember you saying something about a child. But never mind all that. You're not going to believe this, but I've taken your advice.'

'You're right, I don't believe you. You never listen to anything I say, never mind act on it.'

'Well, this time I have. I've joined an introductions agency.' These last two words were whispered into the phone. 'And if you breathe a word about this to anyone I'll kill you. Got that?'

Kate smiled. 'Don't worry, I shan't say a word to anyone. So tell me all about it.'

'I won't bore you with all the details now, but hopefully by this time next week I shall be fixed up with my first date. I just hope it isn't somebody I know. Can you imagine the shame?'

'Well, don't forget, it will be the same for him. He'll be just as embarrassed.'

'That would be impossible.'

'But it's true. The men are bound to feel as awkward as you.' She recalled Alec telling her how anxious he'd been about meeting her. 'I very nearly bottled out,' he'd admitted. 'I parked the car and as I walked to the wine bar I thought I was going to be sick with nerves.'

'So how come you're suddenly such an expert on the matter?' Caroline demanded.

'I'm not,' Kate said quickly, 'I'm just imagining how it must be, that's all.'

'Look, I'm going to have to go now, the place is swarming with creepy old men in macs with nothing better to do than make a nuisance of themselves in the library. First drop of rain in weeks and they bloody well come in here dripping wet umbrellas on the carpet. By the way, when will you be in for that teacher training info?'

'How about first thing next week?'

'Come in on Tuesday morning and we can have lunch afterwards.'

'I might have Oscar with me.'

'He can come so long as you put a muzzle on him. Bye.'

Kate put down the phone and when she looked up she saw two figures hurrying across the courtyard in the rain. Amanda and Hattie.

Oh, heavens, what did Amanda want now?

Chapter Twenty-Four

Amanda removed the heated rollers from her hair and carefully began brushing it. She framed her face with her full bob of hair in the way that she normally wore it. Then she looked critically at herself in the mirror and changed her mind. She decided to go for a completely different look and, sweeping back her hair, she tucked it behind her ears, and before it had a chance to flop forward she quickly fixed it into place with some maximum-hold hair spray. When she'd finished she stared at her reflection and smiled at herself. Not bad, she thought. Not bad at all.

But then, at that precise moment she was feeling particularly pleased with herself anyway.

Not only had she finally decided on the fabric and wallpaper for the sitting-room – and found a decorator who wasn't fully booked up until Christmas – but she had managed to off-load Hattie on to Cholmford's very own equivalent to Maria von Trapp for that evening, leaving her and Tony free to take her mother out to dinner. And if all went well tonight, and there was no reason to suspect that it wouldn't, the outcome would be that her mother would baby-sit Hattie next month, enabling her and Tony to go away for an all-expenses-paid weekend that Arc was putting on.

'It's nothing special,' Tony had said at breakfast that morning, 'it's just the usual Arc "do" to encourage the team.'

Tony might not think that a long weekend spent at Gleneagles was special, but she had other ideas. Compared with what she was used to, three days of pampering would be bliss and she had every intention of indulging herself to the full. The first thing she planned to do, once Tony and his boring colleagues had gone off to the golf course, or whatever it was they were expected to do, was to hit the hotel fitness centre, followed by the beauty salon where she would gratify herself for as long as she wanted. And after three days of being steamed, covered in seaweed, plucked, waxed, massaged and manicured she would emerge a new woman. It would be fantastic. She couldn't wait.

The only thing that could conceivably get in the way of this wonderful weekend was Rita refusing to do her bit.

Downstairs she heard the sound of the doorbell. Good. That meant the ever reliable, ever sweet Kate had arrived.

Tony let Kate in. He took her through to the kitchen where he was in the middle of tidying up Hattie's tea things. 'This is very good of you,' he said, 'I hope you don't think we're taking advantage.'

She smiled and shook her head. 'Of course I don't.'

He tried not to stare at her, but he couldn't help himself and as he watched her push her wonderful hair away from her face he experienced a wave of something he hadn't felt in a long time.

It was a wave of desire.

And not some piddly ebb and flow of desire.

This was a roller.

A breaker.

A torrent.

A ruddy great tidal wave.

To hell with that, it was the Niagara Falls of desire.

He cleared his throat and went back to scraping the remains of Hattie's tea into the bin. Watch it, Tony, he said to himself as he dolloped tomato ketchup on to a half-eaten apple, you're imagining things. Nobody could have that effect on anyone.

Wrong!

Eve had. Eve had bowled him over the second they'd met.

He swallowed. Why was it that every time he was in Kate's company he was reminded of Eve? Was it because she had the same effect on him?

'Hello Kate.' It was Hattie. She was not long out of the bath and as she came into the kitchen Tony could smell the sweetness of her; a combination of bubble bath and talc. He watched her approach Kate and envied the warm hug she received. 'Will you read to me like you did last time?' she asked Kate.

'I should think so,' Kate answered. 'Why don't you go upstairs and choose which books you'd like.'

Hattie smiled. 'I've done that already.'

Tony laughed, went over to Hattie and lifted her up into his arms. 'What a terrible little opportunist you are,' he said, holding her aloft. He kissed her cheek and she kissed him back, smack on the lips, her hands clasped tightly around his neck.

'Will you come up and say good-night to me before you go out?' she asked him, her eyes wide and appealing.

'Try and stop me.' He gently lowered her to the floor. 'Go on, off

169

you go, I'll be up in a minute.' He watched her leave the kitchen, then turned to Kate. 'Would you like a drink?' he asked.

'No thank you,' she said.

'Sure?'

'Yes.'

'How about something to eat?'

She smiled. 'I had a sandwich earlier.'

'Is that all?'

'I'm fine, really.'

'So there's nothing I can offer you?' Bloody hell! What did he sound like? – *So there's nothing I can offer you?* Why didn't he have done with it and start wearing a chunky gold bracelet and a fake tan, and take a crash course in *double entendres* for the intellectually challenged?

'*Kate*,' came a voice from the landing, 'are you coming up now?'

But before Kate could answer, Amanda made her appearance in the kitchen, her high heels clickety-clicking across the tiled floor. 'You really mustn't let Hattie boss you about, Kate,' she said, opening her small leather purse and slipping a tissue inside, then snapping it shut.

Hattie isn't bossing Kate about, Tony wanted to snipe back at Amanda, and without meaning to he ran a critical eye over what his wife was wearing.

She was smartly dressed in a pair of oatmeal-coloured linen trousers with a navy blazer and she had on just the right amount of gold jewellery – she'd got the balance exactly right, any more and she would have looked ostentatious. Her make-up had been carefully applied and enhanced her high cheek-bones, as well as smoothing away the fine lines round her eyes. He sensed that there was something different about her hair, but he couldn't put his finger on what exactly. He also sensed that anyone meeting Amanda for the first time, dressed as she was, would say that she was a most poised and elegant woman, that she was the epitome of a woman in her mid-thirties who knew what she was about – a no-nonsense woman who was completely in control of her life. Which was what had attracted him to her in the first place. He had recognised in her an ability to take charge of his disorganised life. He had seen in her someone to resolve all his problems.

But she hadn't, he now realised, she had only added to them.

He risked a sideways glance at Kate. The contrast between the two women couldn't have been greater. Kate was dressed in faded blue jeans with a tiny sort of misshapen cotton cardigan that was not only low-necked but also so short it didn't quite meet the top of her jeans and revealed about an inch of tantalising waistline. She wore no jewellery and as far as Tony could see, no make-up either. She was delightfully natural and fresh-faced, and standing beside Amanda she made her look overdressed and starchy.

'I'll just go and say good-night to Hattie,' he said, hastily retreating from the kitchen before the expression on his face gave him away. He wasn't imagining it, he told himself as he climbed the stairs. What he felt for Kate was no trick of the mind. His feelings for her were as real as those he'd felt for Eve. So why the bloody hell had fate done this to him? Why had it let him marry the wrong woman, then taunted him with exactly the kind of woman whom he could have loved and been happy with?

Back in the kitchen, Amanda was saying, 'Now you know where everything is. Just help yourself to teas and coffees and anything else you might need. We shan't be that late, about eleven thirty I should think.'

'That's fine,' said Kate, 'please don't worry about the time.'

'I hope Alec doesn't mind you doing this for us.'

'He doesn't mind at all. He's working late tonight anyway, but he might join me when he gets back. Is that okay?'

'Of course.'

Uncomfortable in Amanda's presence and anxious not to prolong their conversation, Kate said, 'I think I'll go up and start reading to Hattie. Have a good evening.'

When she reached Hattie's bedroom door she paused, suddenly unsure whether to go in or not. She felt as if she might be barging in on Hattie and her father. She could hear them talking, their voices low and confiding. She thought about going back downstairs, but as she turned to go the floor betrayed her presence and gave off a loud creak.

'Is that you, Kate?' asked Hattie.

She pushed open the door and went in. Tony was sitting on the bed beside Hattie. He had one of his arms around her shoulders and from nowhere Kate was reminded of what she'd missed out on as a child. She couldn't ever recall being tucked into bed when she'd been little. Her mother had always been too busy arranging her own life to be bothered with sitting on the edge of a bed to kiss her good-night. Even now her mother was too busy to bother about Kate. The only contact between them was a Christmas card enclosing a cheque each year and the occasional birthday card sent from her latest home, which she shared with her third husband in Sydney, Australia. It had been like that for years. Kate didn't hold it against her mother, there was no point, some parents just weren't designed to be parents.

Kate looked at Tony and realised that he was openly staring at her in a way that made her feel unaccountably confused.

The meal was dreadful and the company diabolical.

Bloody Rita was the last person on earth with whom Tony wanted to spend an evening. And as he picked out the artificially red cherries from the enormous slice of black forest gateaux in front of him he found himself wishing that Amanda's father was there with them instead of taking the minutes at the AGM of his local history group – Roy might be one of the most boring men on the planet, in fact he could bore for the entire universe on the subject of ancient burial sites in the area, but his company would at least have had a sedative effect.

Tony forced himself to listen with half an ear to what his wife and mother-in-law were rattling on about. But he had no interest in their conversation – what did he care that some neighbour of Bloody Rita's was applying for planning permission to extend his house? With a more than willing mind he turned his thoughts to Kate.

He was trying to work out how he was ever going to see her alone. He knew he was playing with fire, but he couldn't help himself. He wanted to be with her. He wanted, just once, to be able to touch her, maybe even kiss her. Because perhaps then the spell she had cast on him would be lifted. He was trying to convince himself that what he felt for her had to be little more than infatuation and that no harm would come to either of them if he could just touch her and make the fantasy disappear.

'Isn't that right, Tony?'

'Sorry,' he said, suddenly alert to having been caught out not listening to the conversation.

Amanda frowned at him. 'I was just telling Mum about the important weekend away that Arc have asked us to host.'

It was his turn to frown. It was news to him that they were supposed to be hosting the event. But a kick under the table told him that Amanda was deliberately exaggerating the importance of the weekend in order to enlist her mother's help.

'Yes,' he lied, 'it should be quite an interesting weekend.' Hell's teeth, it would be the usual boring routine of trying to rally the troops – such as they were – to keep them working themselves into the ground in order to please Arc. He couldn't imagine anything worse.

No. That wasn't true. A weekend with Bloody Rita would win hands down.

He didn't know what it was about the woman, but she had an uncanny knack for metaphorically disembowelling him each time they met. He prided himself on getting on with most people, but here was somebody he'd failed to impress. She made it very clear to him that he didn't match her expectations for her only daughter. If he'd been a doctor or a barrister, or even an accountant, he might have given her something to be pleased about, but in her opinion being a sales director was nothing short of making a living out of knocking on doors with a suitcase of polishing cloths to pedal.

It was a class thing, of course. In her eyes he was nothing but a cloth-capped lad in clogs from Rochdale. 'Rochdale?' she'd said in a disappointed tone of voice, at their first meeting when she'd asked 'And from where do you hail?' – *from where do you hail?* – did any normal human being talk like that these days? He had no obvious accent to speak of, but her cross-examination of his upbringing had made him want to return to his roots and stretch out his vowels.

Rita's dislike of him was set in stone from that day on.

Even on the phone she couldn't bring herself to communicate with him more than was necessary. 'Is my daughter there?' would be her opening gambit if he ever picked up the phone when she called – she made no pretence at small talk.

Her generosity was as abundant as her conversation. Her Christmas present to them last year had been a pair of salt and pepper pots. Except they weren't a pair. They didn't match.

A bit like him and Amanda really.

Maybe Bloody Rita had known this right from the outset and had been trying to tell him something.

He tuned in again to what Amanda was saying. It sounded as if she was getting to the crucial bit.

'So we thought that perhaps you might like to help us out.'

'How exactly?' said Bloody Rita, her eyes narrowing, her lips tightening to a point.

How do you think, you stupid woman! Tony wanted to yell across the table.

'With Hattie,' Amanda carried on bravely, 'we wondered whether you could come and look after her for us. There's nobody else we can ask.'

The eyes had almost disappeared, as had the lips, which had been sucked in, in an expression of wary mistrust. 'For how long?' she asked, when a few seconds had passed.

'It'll only be a couple of days.'

Rita stared at her daughter. 'Be more specific, please.'

'From Friday morning through till Sunday evening,' interceded Tony, who could be as specific as the next person when he chose.

'I don't know,' Rita said, without even bothering to look at Tony, 'I haven't brought my diary with me. I'm away on a bowling trip during August.'

'Yes I know,' said Amanda, 'you're going the first weekend, our weekend is the second.'

Tony had to admire Amanda's persistence, but he didn't hold out much hope of Bloody Rita being persuaded into any kind of agreement. He understood her well enough to know that they were a long way from clinching the deal. But to be honest he didn't care. He wasn't fussed about a ra-ra weekend of team bonding, not when he was so disillusioned with the whole show. It had been different last year; company morale had been good and he'd gone to great lengths to organise a nanny to take care of Hattie so that he could join in with the fun, but what would be the point this time? With Bradley Hurst's blood-stained butcher's knife hanging over everybody, what fun would there be for any of them?

On top of all that, he wasn't keen on the idea of Hattie being looked after by Bloody Rita. In fact, the more he thought about it, the less he liked the prospect of his daughter having to put up with this witch of a woman.

'Perhaps we've been too presumptuous,' he heard himself say, 'we shouldn't have put you on the spot like this, Rita. Forget we ever mentioned it.'

He got a sharp kick from Amanda and a look that would have withered the strongest of men. He also received a sceptical lifting of an over-plucked eyebrow from his mother-in-law.

The atmosphere in the car after they'd dropped Rita off at home was deadly. Tony had no intention of speaking. He knew Amanda was cross with him, so it was just a matter of waiting until she'd calmed down enough to spit out the words in the right order.

Inevitably she did. 'What the hell did you think you were doing back there?' she hissed. 'After all the softening up I'd done you just waded in and blew it all away.'

He decided to be honest, which was a dangerous thing to do, but he was past caring. 'I don't want your mother looking after Hattie. If you really want to know, I don't ever want her to take care of my daughter.'

'What!'

'You heard.'

'I don't believe I'm hearing this.'

'You did ask. And you'd better believe it.'

They drove on in silence for a further mile and as they approached the small bridge over the canal Amanda found her voice once more. 'Are you serious, or are you just annoyed with her? I know the pair of you don't exactly get on.'

What an understatement! 'I'm serious. I want Hattie to be with someone who is genuinely fond of her. Your mother clearly isn't. She would only be doing it out of a sense of duty, which is never the right motivation to do anything.' He of all people knew how true that was.

Amanda was stunned. 'Well, that's that then. We shan't be able to go. Unless . . .'

'Unless what?'

'Unless Maria von Trapp would do it.'

'Who?'

'Kate, of course, who else.'

'No,' he said firmly. 'Absolutely not. We've imposed on her enough. You're not to ask her, it wouldn't be fair.'

They remained silent for the remainder of the journey.

Amanda stared out into the blackened fields. She was furious with Tony, but was determined not to be cheated out of her weekend of indulgence; she knew very well that she *would* ask Kate. Probably tomorrow. She would buy some flowers and pop over as she had this morning.

When they reached home they found Kate in the sitting-room reading. She was alone.

'Alec didn't show, then?' Tony said, his spirits lifted by the sight of Kate.

She stood up. 'No, he had some work he wanted to do on the computer at home.'

Amanda flopped into a chair. 'These shoes are killing me,' she said bad-temperedly. She kicked them off and rubbed her aching feet.

'Everything all right with Hattie?' Tony asked.

'No problem. She was fine.'

'Good. That's great. I'll see you out.'

He led her to the hall and as she reached to open the door he did exactly what he'd planned to do while sitting in the restaurant – he placed his hand over hers. 'Here, let me get that for you, it can be awkward at times.'

For a fraction of a second their hands were together and knowing that he had no more than a moment to ensure the final part of his plan was carried out he opened the door, said good-night and quickly kissed her cheek.

– A kiss that was as innocent as a neighbourly debt of gratitude.

– A kiss that was as guilty as a lover's act of adultery.

He watched her cross the courtyard in the darkness and as she let herself into number five she turned and glanced back at him.

He gave her a little wave and knew that he had to touch her again. Once wasn't enough.

But then he'd known it wouldn't be. He'd merely been fooling himself that the fantasy could be disarmed so easily.

Chapter Twenty-Five

Dear Cara,

Synopsis of A Casual Affair

The story so far!

Our heroine, Clare (aged twenty-eight and as feisty as a Tabasco sandwich) is bored with her going-nowhere job with a large insurance company and on the point of handing in her notice when her boss obligingly drops down dead. A replacement is quickly found who turns out to be Miles – thirty-something, attractive-ish but shy, unmarried and, according to the office gossip on the third floor from where he's been plucked, sexually inexperienced, with a preference for putting all his energy into his work rather than chasing women. Clare immediately sees the potential her new boss can offer her and, into scheming overdrive and with designs not just on promotion but on Miles, she decides that a casual affair with him would be as good a way as any to relieve her current boredom and further her career. But attracting Miles's attention proves to be more difficult than she imagined.

Hope this meets with your approval, Cara.

Best wishes,

Copy to Piers Lambert.

Jessica printed three copies of the letter – one for Cara, one for Piers and one for her file – and when she'd signed them and addressed the envelopes she looked out of her study window, over to Josh's house and wondered if she was using the wrong deodorant.

It was now a week since Tuesday night and she had the sneaky feeling that, like Clare's new boss in *A Casual Affair*, Crawford – the slimy toe-rag – was ignoring her; there hadn't been so much as a call or a visit from him.

Well, let him ignore her.

What did she care if he had decided that she was the last person on earth with whom he wanted to spend any time?

Unfortunately – and this was the annoying part – she did care. Oh boy, she cared. Josh Crawford, she had come to the conclusion, with his sexy smile and neat bum, had seemed an ideal antidote to the malaise that Gavin had left her with.

Put like that, it did seem a bit calculating to have viewed Josh in such a way, so perhaps it served her right that things had turned out the way they had. But what the heck, it was all hypothetical now anyway. Clearly Josh wasn't the slightest bit interested in her.

She lowered her gaze from his house and let it rest on the card on her window-sill. It was a familiar picturesque view of the harbour at Kassiopi: fishing boats and pleasure crafts were neatly lined up around the small quay, and in the background shops and tavernas with stripy awnings were bustling with sun-tanned tourists, and above the jumble of pastel-painted buildings the sky was an unbelievable shade of blue.

But then the card itself was pretty unbelievable.

It was from Gavin. And all that was written overleaf, apart from her address, were the words – *Wish you were here, missing you something rotten. Come back!*

Yeah right! And just who did he think he was kidding? had been her initial response to this unexpected communication.

Did he really think that a few scribbled words would have her leaping on the next available flight to Corfu?

Did he truly imagine her sitting in England, sad and lonely, strumming her fingers to the beat of her aching heart?

She looked down and caught sight of her fingers playing over the desk. She snatched up her hand and frowned.

She was not sad.

She was not lonely.

And she certainly wasn't longing for Gavin – any more than he was longing for her.

Not in her wildest dreams did she think it remotely possible that if she were to go back to Corfu she would find a heart-broken Gavin wasting away, yearning for her.

Fat chance of that! More likely she'd find him busy rubbing sun-tan oil all over the sleek, man-made body of Silicone Sal. And if not her, then some other beach babe.

But deep down, somewhere deep in the dark, romantically candle-lit recesses of her childlike gullibility, where she still wanted to believe in fairies and Father Christmas, she also wanted to believe in

Gavin. She wanted him to be missing her, for him to have come crashing to his senses and realise what he'd lost.

At the sound of a car she glanced out of the window and saw Josh's midnight-blue Shogun sweep into the courtyard, followed by a flashy open-top sports car, the engine of which gave off an impressive and satisfying throaty roar as it came to a stop. Very nice, thought Jessica. She watched Josh get out of his car, then the other driver as he emerged from his. He held a briefcase in one hand and a small brown paper carrier bag in the other – which, with its tell-tale splodges of grease, made it look suspiciously like a take-away. Whoever it was who was dining at 1 Cholmford Hall Mews that night, he was slightly shorter than Josh, but equally good-looking and as well-dressed, but in marked contrast to Josh's usual black attire he was wearing a vivid orange-and-green check shirt with a light-coloured suede jacket hanging off one of his shoulders.

The thought of the tasty meal that Josh and his friend were about to tuck into made Jessica leave her study and go in search of something to eat for herself.

She suddenly realised that she was famished and as she began rooting through the near empty fridge for some kind of culinary inspiration – she really must get into the habit of shopping more regularly – she thought of the supper Josh had cooked for her.

He really had gone to a lot of trouble that evening – and not just in the kitchen. In her experience single men rarely reached for the Pine-O-Fresh without there being an ulterior motive behind such an out-of-character activity, namely that of luring a woman upstairs and into their beds.

So why the sudden red light that night?

One minute they had been on the verge of a repeat performance of their *après* Tony and Amanda dinner-party session – except this time she had planned on being a willing participant – and the next Josh had been up on his feet saying it was late and that he had an early start the next day.

It didn't make sense.

Unless it had all been a deliberate ploy to get his own back on her for having messed him around previously. Had he played dirty to prove a point with her? No girl teases Josh Crawford and gets away with it. Had that been his game?

Could he really be that proud and petty?

Charlie was worried about Josh. Which was why when they had

finished work he had suggested that they pick up a take-away and spend the evening together.

Not since Josh's illness had been diagnosed had Charlie seen his brother so low and despondent. There was an awful emptiness to him that concerned Charlie. The past few days had been particularly bad, with Josh seemingly distancing himself from those around him. He had become morose and deeply withdrawn, punctuating his moody silences with a level of cynicism that was cruel and barbed, and aimed at anyone who got in his way.

Yesterday at work, Charlie had found Mo in a full-blown tearful strop. 'I only asked him if he was okay when I took him in a cup of coffee,' she'd told Charlie, 'and he bit my head off. He can make his own coffee in future.'

Charlie knew that not only did Mo have a soft spot for Josh, but that under normal circumstances she wouldn't have thought twice about blasting off at him for treating her in such a way, but since his illness had become general knowledge at work she, like everybody else, had tended to shy away from speaking her mind. 'What's got into him?' she'd asked Charlie, when Josh had gone to Failsworth to check on a lost delivery and had given everybody the chance to come out from hiding for a couple of hours.

'I wish I knew,' he'd said in answer to Mo's question.

More than anything, Charlie wished he knew exactly what was going on inside his brother's head. Which was why he was here now. He had no intention of leaving until he'd got to the bottom of what was making Josh so unbearable at work.

'Another beer?'

Charlie looked up from his lamb korma. 'I'll get them,' he said.

He was almost on his feet when Josh said, 'Sit down. This is my sodding house and if I'm offering you a drink I'll bloody well get it myself. Okay?'

Charlie watched Josh limp across the kitchen and open the fridge. When he came back to the island unit he handed him a can of Budweiser. Charlie took it and experienced the urge to smash the can into his brother's face. Appalled at the level of anger he felt for Josh, he wondered if their lives would ever be the way they used to be. But then they couldn't be, could they? Josh could never be the man he had been. It was unfair and selfish to expect that of him. Charlie wasn't proud of himself for thinking it, but he didn't know how much longer he could put up with his brother's mood-swings.

They continued their meal without speaking, each forking up his food and washing it down with the occasional mouthful of beer.

Charlie couldn't bear it and in the end he pushed his unfinished plate away. 'I've had enough of this,' he said.

Josh raised his eyes. 'I hope you're referring to your meal because if you're about to start on one of your bloody lectures you might just as well leave now. I'm not in the mood.'

'That's just the point. What kind of mood are you in? You seem to be going out of your way to upset everyone.'

Josh gave an indifferent shrug of his shoulders. 'Can't say I'd noticed.'

Charlie silently counted to five before saying in as calm a voice as he could, 'What the hell's got into you, Josh? Why are you acting like this?'

Josh stood up and went over to the window, which looked out over the courtyard. He saw Jessica moving about in her kitchen. He turned away. 'You just don't get it, do you?'

'All I can see is you intent on punishing everyone else for your MS and if you want my honest opinion on that, I think it sucks.'

'Maybe you're right,' Josh said flatly, 'but you should try having all your dreams taken away from you. Imagine . . . imagine wanting something and knowing you couldn't have it . . . that all that was on offer to you was something so second-rate it wasn't worth having.'

Charlie didn't know what to say. Who was he to make a comment on what Josh had just said? He hadn't had his dreams taken away. He didn't know what it felt like. He hoped he never would. 'Are we talking generally or specifically?' he asked.

'What the hell do you think?'

Charlie had no idea. 'Josh, I'm not a mind-reader, so just cut the crap and tell me what's going on.'

Josh came and sat down. He picked up his can of beer and began turning it round in his hands. 'I'm not sure I understand it myself,' he said. He badly wanted to say what he'd been feeling all this week, but each time he tried to put it into words, even to himself, it only served to fuel his anger and bitter frustration. Ever since that evening with Jessica, when the realisation had hit him that he wanted much more from her than he'd bargained for, he'd felt confused, depressed and demoralised. His low sense of self-worth told him that he couldn't expect a woman like Jessica to be the slightest bit interested in him when he had so little to offer. And supposing she did allow herself to become involved with him, when she knew the truth, how long would it last? How long would it be before she decided she wanted to be with a man who wasn't going to become a burden?

He looked up and saw that Charlie was waiting for him to speak.

He suddenly felt sorry for him. Poor Charlie, so keen to help and so clearly out of his depth. Not unlike himself really. 'Do you remember at Mum and Dad's the other Sunday,' he said, 'when you asked me if I wouldn't prefer a relationship that was a touch more meaningful than a one-night stand?'

'Yes,' Charlie said cautiously.

'Well, you were right . . . and that's the problem.'

'Is this to do with your neighbour Jessica?'

Josh nodded and slipping off the stool, began slowly prowling round the kitchen. When his leg started to ache he stopped in front of the window and stared out across the courtyard. Charlie came and joined him.

'So what's the problem?' he asked. He now had a pretty good idea what was going through Josh's mind, but he wanted his brother to go through the process of actually explaining it to him.

'Like I said to you that day, what's the point in me getting into a serious relationship, or even considering one? What could I offer Jessica?'

'Quite a lot, I should think.'

Josh shook his head. 'Maybe a few good years . . . and when my health really starts to deteriorate, what then? I'm hardly the pull of the decade, am I?'

'Isn't that for her to decide?'

'I wouldn't want her pity.'

'Is she the pitying kind?'

Josh considered this. He thought of the way Jessica called him Crawford and accused him of having a manner smooth enough to charm the devil. He also thought of her vibrant face and slightly mocking eyes. There was an energy to her that he found exciting. Each time he had been with her he'd been aware of her vitality and her strength of character. 'No,' he said with a hint of a smile. 'No, she's not the pitying kind.'

'Well then, why not give it a go and see what happens? And if it doesn't work out, I guarantee it's because she catches on to what a pillock you are.'

'You reckon?'

Charlie smiled. 'I reckon. Now, when do I get to meet her?'

It was just gone ten o'clock when Josh watched Charlie's car disappear through the archway and for a few moments he stayed where he was on the doorstep, contemplating his brother's pep talk.

Was Charlie right? Was Jessica worth pursuing?

With an evening's worth of beer inside him he decided that there was no better time to find out. He'd go over now and ask her out to dinner later in the week. What's more, he'd be honest with her and to hell with the consequences. If she didn't like the idea of him being a potential cripple, then tough. Humiliation was something he was going to have to learn to deal with.

He put his front door on the latch and started walking across the courtyard, but with each step he took his confidence began to wane.

He was mad. Mad to think that Jessica would be remotely interested in him. He glanced at his watch. Surely it was too late to call on her? But as he looked up, all set to do a quick turn-about, he saw her gazing at him from her kitchen window. *Hell!* Now what? What excuse could he give for going across to see her?

But there was no time to think of anything, her front door suddenly opened and there she was, staring straight at him. She looked as if she was dressed ready for bed. All she had on was a T-shirt emblazoned with the slogan *Wind Surfers Do It Wet And Standing Up*. It was difficult not to stare at her long legs.

'Hi,' she said, aware of his gaze, 'and what brings you here at this time of night?'

'I . . .' He paused, ran a hand through his hair, shifted a little to the right, then back to the left. 'I was just wondering –'

'You were just passing and wondered if I had any sugar, is that it?'

'Not exactly.'

'Coffee, then?'

He shook his head. Oh shit, why was he so nervous? And where the hell was his alcohol-induced confidence when he needed it?

'Well, Crawford, I know I'm a writer, but I'm running out of lines here; you're going to have to help me out.'

He swallowed. Or rather he would have if his throat hadn't dried up – was it from desire at the sight of Jessica's legs, or just plain nerves? 'I wondered whether you'd like to come for a walk,' he said. *A walk!* He couldn't believe he was hearing himself. Was he completely out of his mind? He'd be suggesting a quick jog around the block next.

She stared at him, then up at the night sky. 'Mm . . .' she said, 'the moon and stars look pretty enough. Why not? Give me a couple of minutes and I'll put something on. Come in while you wait.'

He stood in the hall and listened to Jessica moving about upstairs. He stupidly hoped she wasn't putting on too much. Within minutes she was back with him – the T-shirt had been exchanged for a baggy sweat-shirt and her lovely legs had been covered with a pair of jeans.

'You've put your legs away,' he said, disappointed.

'And you've been ignoring me all this week.' She shut the door behind them and led the way across the courtyard. He struggled to keep up. She turned and faced him. 'Sorry, was I going too fast?'

'Yes,' he admitted, 'and I haven't been ignoring you.'

'So where have you been? I tried several times to thank you for dinner last week, but each time I knocked on your door there was no answer. In the end I shoved a note through your letter-box.'

'I got it, thanks. There was no need, though.'

'Yes there was. You went to a lot of trouble.'

'Not really.'

'Are you going to dispute everything I say?'

He didn't answer and they carried on without speaking. The night was warm and very still, and as they approached the copse, bone-dry twigs crackled noisily beneath their feet and the moon shone down on them, intermittently lighting their way as it filtered its silvery brightness through the leafy branches of the trees. It wasn't long before Josh's leg was giving out on him. He needed to rest and spying a fallen oak, he grabbed Jessica's hand and pulled her towards it.

'So,' she said, sitting beside him on the moss-covered trunk and drawing up a knee to rest her chin on.

'So?'

'So, why are we here, Josh?'

He shrugged. 'I fancied a walk and thought you might like to join me.'

'And is this something you do a lot of, nocturnal wanderings?'

'Not really. I just wanted the opportunity to talk to you.'

'Aha, in that case, I'm all ears.' She lowered her leg and turned to face him, her eyes flashing with that mocking humour he had come to know. 'Fire away.'

He cleared his throat, ready to launch himself into what he had to say. *See, here's the situation: I'm thirty-seven, not unattractive – so I'm told – I'm financially solvent. I have my own home and car, and a more than healthy interest in sex – especially with the right partner. The only downside is that there's a strong possibility that I'll be a dead weight hanging round your neck within a few years. So how about it? How about you and me getting it together? Oh sod it!* He couldn't do it. 'Will you have dinner with me again?'

A slow smile crept over her face. 'Yes. But on one condition.'

'What's that?'

'That you stop messing about and make full use of the romantic opportunity offered here beneath the stars and kiss me. I've waited long enough.'

He laughed out loud, and as his laughter drifted away into the darkness, it was as if all the tension of the past week went with it, as though if he watched closely, he would see the bits of himself he hated and despised being cast into the night sky. If there was one thing he had come to realise in the short time he'd known Jessica it was that when he was with her, she had a fantastic effect on him. Her sense of fun was wonderfully recuperative.

'I'm waiting.'

'Are you coming on to me, Jessica?' he asked with a smile.

'Certainly not. I just want a kiss.'

'And would this be for research purposes?'

'It might be.'

'Well, we'd better get it right, then, hadn't we? What kind of kiss did you have in mind, exactly?'

'Let me see what you've got to offer.'

He gave her a chaste peck on the cheek.

'Sorry, but I don't write that kind of novel. My readers expect a little more from my romantic heroes.'

He moved closer and kissed her lightly on the lips.

'Better, but I was hoping for something a little more melt-in-the-mouth, like the other night.'

'You should have said.' He held her face in his hands and gave her a long, deep kiss. 'Now was that more what you had in mind?'

'I'm not sure,' she said breathlessly. 'Could you run it by me one more time?'

He did, and as their mouths came together, he slipped one of his hands under her sweat-shirt. He felt the tremor in her body as he found her breast and her instant response to his touch exploded within him. With only one thought in his mind, he very gently began pushing her backwards. But he'd forgotten what they were sitting on and the next moment they were lying in a heap on the soft bedding of leaves and ferns the other side of the fallen tree. Their happy laughter filled the dark copse and after they'd disentangled themselves they sat down again.

Jessica rested her head against Josh's shoulder. 'Why did you give me the brush-off at your place last week?' she asked.

He reached out for her hand and wondered what to say. Was this the bit when he told her the truth?

No. No, he couldn't. Not yet. He couldn't face it right now. He didn't want anything to spoil what he was feeling. 'I didn't give you the brush-off,' he lied.

She raised her head and looked at him. Straight at him. 'You did. You couldn't wait to get me out of your house, my feet didn't touch.'

He flinched at the strength of her directness. 'Okay,' he said, 'you're right.' And determined to give at least part of the truth, he tried to explain his actions. 'I wasn't very subtle that night, was I? I'd planned to get you into bed and suddenly I felt ashamed of myself in the way I'd gone about it. It seemed too contrived . . . and I didn't want it to be like that. I'm not sure I really understand it myself, but I suddenly realised that I wanted something more than what I'd intended to make happen . . . and it had to be something that you wanted as well.' He watched her closely while she took in his words. 'I'm sorry,' he added.

She regarded him with a steady gaze. Then she smiled. 'Crawford,' she said, 'you're a man of surprises.'

Aren't I just, he thought. 'Come on,' he said, 'let's go back, it's getting cold.'

When they reached Jessica's house she let them in. 'Would you like a drink?' she asked. 'Wine, coffee, brandy, or . . .' But her voice broke off as Josh, with unexpected force, took her in his arms, pressed her against the wall and kissed her.

'Or tea?' she managed to say when he finally let her come up for air.

'I'm not thirsty,' he whispered.

'Me neither,' she whispered back. 'Josh, why are we whispering?'

He smiled. 'It's supposed to be romantic.'

'I must remember that.'

'Isn't that what romantic heroes get up to? I thought they only spoke in hoarse whispers.'

'Not in my books, they don't.'

'Oh well, never mind . . . Jessica?'

'Yes.'

He looked deep, deep into her eyes and she felt herself go limp with longing. She watched his Adam's apple bob about as he swallowed.

'Do you think there's any chance that –'

'You've stopped whispering,' she interrupted him, 'does that mean the romantic interlude has passed?'

'No, it means we're on to the serious stuff now.'

'Serious stuff?'

'Yes. I'm about to ask if you'd like to go upstairs.'

'To do what?'

'I thought I could slowly undress that beautiful body of yours and make love to you. But only if you wanted me to.'

'I'd need to think about that.'

'Take your time. I'm in no hurry.'

'Would there be much kissing, like just now?'

'Comes as standard.'

'Caresses?'

'Lots.'

'All over?'

'Definitely.'

'Of the light-as-a-butterfly's-wing variety?'

'Lighter.'

'Pounding hearts?'

'Like steam hammers.'

'Gasps of pleasure?'

'Loud enough to wake the neighbours.'

'Bodies as one?'

'A perfect synthesis of intimacy.'

'Soaring high as a bird?'

'Spinning into orbit.'

'The "Hallelujah Chorus"? I would have to insist on that.'

'It's yours, followed by the *1812 Overture*.'

'With cannons?'

'Fireworks as well.'

She smiled. 'You paint a tempting picture.'

'And your answer?'

'Oh, the answer was always going to be yes.'

THE MIDDLE

Chapter Twenty-Six

Kate stared and stared at the small white stick in her hand. What she had suspected since the August Bank Holiday, just over a week ago, was now confirmed. She was pregnant.

Pregnant!

She hugged the secret to her. She hadn't shared with anyone the thought that she might be pregnant; not Caroline, not Jessica, not even Alec.

Definitely not Alec.

But now she would have to. Tonight, Alec would be arriving back from his week away at the Birmingham trade fair. He had wanted her to go down with him, but knowing that Melissa was going to be there, too, she had cried off – staying in the same hotel as Melissa for a whole week was not something she had any desire to do. Instead, she had stayed at home and mentally ticked off the days on the calendar waiting for the first possible opportunity to use the pregnancy test kit that she had already sneaked into the house.

She continued to gaze at the little white stick and despite the sense of foreboding about breaking the news to Alec, a warm feeling of euphoric happiness crept over her. Her greatest wish had been granted. She wanted to leap in the air, clap her hands, even dance a little jig round the kitchen, and she would have done exactly that if the phone hadn't rung. She skipped across to it and snatched up the receiver. 'Hello,' she said, hoping that it was Alec – while he'd been away he had called her at least twice a day.

But it wasn't, it was Melissa. 'Kate, I haven't got long, it's unbelievably busy here, but over breakfast I spoke to Alec and he suggested I talk to you. Have you got your diary to hand?'

'It's in the study, hang on a minute.' Light-headed with happiness, Kate went through to the study. *I'm going to have a baby*, she chanted delightedly to herself. She found the diary Alec always kept on his desk and picked up the phone extension. *I'm going to have a baby!*

'Melissa, are you there?' *I'm going to have a baby.* How wonderful it would be to let the words trip off her tongue.

'Yes, I'm still here. Now flick through to 22 November. It's a Saturday, are you both free?'

A baby! Her very own baby! 'Yes we are.'

'Good. I'm giving a dinner party for Alec that night, seeing as it's a special year for him.'

Kate froze. 'Special,' she repeated. 'What do you mean?'

'Good Lord, Kate, don't tell me you've forgotten that it's Alec's fiftieth birthday on 15 November. Surely you're doing something for him? I deliberately chose the following weekend because I thought you would be organising some kind of party on the actual day.'

Kate was mortified. Alec's fiftieth! How could she have made such an oversight?

'Clearly you had forgotten. Anyway, I must go, Alec and I are having lunch with some Japanese distributors.'

Kate replaced the receiver and sank into the chair in front of the desk. She was devastated, not because she hadn't given Alec's birthday any thought, but because Melissa had. The ex-wife of the man she loved – *the father of her child* – had shown her up, had pipped her to the post good and proper.

And what was more, she hated the idea of *Alec and I are having lunch.*

Breakfast, too.

She should have gone with Alec to the trade fair. He had wanted her to go and she had let him down, preferring instead to stay selfishly at home nursing the possible gestation of her greatest desire.

So now what? What was she to do? Pretend that she'd arranged a party all along? And if so, whom should she invite?

She decided to go next door and see Jessica. She would know what to do.

Throughout the summer, she and Jessica had formed a strong friendship and when her writing wasn't going well they would go for long walks. Some days it was just the two of them, occasionally it would be Oscar. When he was with them they would put a picnic together and Jessica would tell him they were going exploring. She knew the surrounding area well and had taken them on some wonderful walks, but her favourite route was along the banks of the canal. It had become Oscar's favourite place to potter as well, especially if there were any passing boats to watch. Invariably he would be too tired to walk all the way back to the house and they would take it in turns to carry him home.

But it wasn't just during the day that she and Jessica got together. Now and again, they would go out as a foursome; she and Alec, and Jessica and Josh. Only the other week, Alec had commented to Kate that he thought their neighbours made a great couple. Kate thought so too. Jessica's sharp wit, which might have threatened and undermined another man, was always met with an equal measure of mercurial humour from Josh. But there were times when Kate felt there was another side to Josh's character: a more intense facet of his make-up that she suspected was only glimpsed when his guard was down. On one of their recent evenings out together she had noticed that Josh had been unusually quiet and that his normally handsome face had borne an expression of painful weariness. At the time she had put it down to tiredness, knowing that he had just spent a hectic week down in London, but a few days later when they'd all been having a drink at Jessica's she had seen the same exhausted countenance. She wondered if he was working too hard, was maybe under a lot of pressure.

But Josh's problems were not hers to solve. She had enough of her own.

She went back to the kitchen, tidied away the pregnancy test kit and called on Jessica. 'Is it a bad moment?' she asked, when Jessica let her in. She was always wary of disturbing her when she was working.

'Your timing couldn't be better. I'm getting nowhere with chapter eleven so a distraction is perfect. Fancy some fresh air?'

They took the path towards the copse, then set off in a south-easterly direction between recently harvested fields of corn. Though it was September and the midday sun wasn't as high in the cloud-dotted sky as it had been a few weeks ago, it was still warm enough to make Jessica strip off her sweat-shirt and tie it round her waist. 'So what's eating you?' she suddenly asked.

Kate looked up. 'Oh dear, is it that obvious?'

'Sure is. The long face is a dead give-away.'

'I've just let Alec's ex-wife get one over me,' Kate said miserably. 'Go on.'

'And what's worse, it was through my own selfishness. I've been so preoccupied with myself these past weeks I'd forgotten all about Alec's birthday.'

'And Melissa remembered?'

Kate nodded.

'Oh dear, well that certainly sounds like a life-threatening situation. I mean to say, you forgot and she remembered. Wow!

Sorry, but I can't see what the fuss is all about. She was married to the man for goodness knows how long, she's going to have the date permanently etched on her brain.'

'It gets worse. It's his fiftieth.'

'So?'

'It's special. Melissa's doing a dinner party for him to mark the occasion.'

'Mark the occasion, my foot! She wants to rub his nose in the fact that he's getting on.'

'He's not getting on,' Kate said defensively.

'Sorry, I could have put that better, but you know what I mean.'

'I think she's done it to make it look as if I don't care about Alec. That I'm not up to the job.'

Jessica could see the distress in Kate's face and knew that it was real enough, but in all honesty she doubted whether there were many women who would go to so much trouble just to undermine their ex-husband's new partner. Over the summer, she had got to know Kate sufficiently to realise that at times she allowed her insecurity to get the better of her. 'Alec knows how you feel about him and that's all that matters,' she said.

'But it's not enough, is it? It's not just a case of pleasing Alec, I've got to prove myself to Melissa.'

'Oh come on, Kate, think about what you've just said; it's ridiculous.'

'No it's not and I have thought about it – there are times when I think of nothing else. Proving ourselves is what all second wives and girl-friends have to do. We're constantly having to compete with the wretched person we've replaced; it's all part of the bloody awful triangle.'

Jessica had never heard Kate swear before. The mild-mannered Kate whom she knew rarely broke into anything more vitriolic than a sneeze. Clearly something was wrong. 'Ever thought that it might be the other way around?' she suggested.

'You mean Melissa competing with me?' Kate shook her head. 'You've never met her, she's not the type to need to prove herself. She's so confident and together.'

'You sound like you're frightened of her.'

'I'm terrified of her . . . and jealous. I'm convinced that if she ever wanted to make a play for Alec she could do so.'

'And so what if she did? From what I've seen of you and Alec he's potty about you, his eyes barely leave your face and I've noticed how he struggles to keep his hands off you when we've been out together. It's like being with a couple of teenagers.'

Kate blushed. 'But supposing Alec's only infatuated with me, supposing it's not love at all?'

Jessica needed time to think about this. Were Kate and Alec having problems? Was that why Kate was so edgy? And if so, what sort of advice should she be offering?

They had come to the end of the footpath that crossed the open fields and they now had to climb over a stile and join another path, which led down to the canal and would eventually wend its way to Willow Cottage.

'You haven't answered my question,' Kate said, as she stepped over the wooden stile.

'I haven't because I'm trying to work out what's behind this sudden loss of confidence in your relationship. It can't just be that Melissa has decided to treat her ex to a meal; you've told me yourself there are endless family get-togethers, so why is this one any different? You sure there isn't something else that's bothering you?'

Bothering was not the word for it. Kate could hardly believe that only an hour ago she had been thrilled to bits knowing that she was expecting a baby, but then Melissa, straight out of the blue, had phoned and like a bird of prey had swooped down on her and plucked her happiness right out of her hands.

Except she knew in her heart that wasn't really what had happened. Melissa's call had simply tugged on one of the slippery silk ribbons that held her and Alec's relationship together. With startling clarity she now saw that it wasn't, as she'd always thought, Melissa who held the key to her happiness, it was Alec. How would he react when she told him about the baby? If he was only infatuated with her then their relationship was over – he had made it very clear that he wasn't interested in having any more children. Only a man who truly loved her would stick with her in the circumstances.

'I've just found out that I'm pregnant,' she said, 'and I know that Alec is going to hate the idea of being a father again.'

'Ah,' Jessica said, 'well, cheer up, just think, that's one hell of a birthday present Melissa can't give him.'

Kate tried to laugh, but she couldn't. 'I was so happy when I found out, but now I'm frightened how Alec will react when I tell him. He'll be furious. He might even want me to get rid –'

'I doubt that very much,' cut in Jessica. 'Most men hate the idea of babies littering the house, but when confronted with the reality of the fruits of their loins they usually manage to step into the role of proud father without too much persuasion. Mark my words, Alec will be as proud as anything. There's great kudos involved when an older man starts begetting wee ones. There's nothing like an offspring to prove a man's virility.'

Kate looked up hopefully. 'Do you really think so?'

Jessica smiled. 'Not for sure, but it sounds about right, doesn't it?'

They were now walking along the tow-path of the canal. It had rained the day before and the ground, in parts, was damp and slightly soft underfoot. Everything looked lush and green. Tall, upright stems of ragwort leant casually over the bank as if, while nobody was looking, the vibrant yellow flower-heads were trying to catch their reflection in the still water. Red clover speckled the long tufts of grass and the occasional bee staggered from flower to flower with its heavy load of nectar. Seeing a straggly bush of blackberries, Jessica came to a stop and helped herself to a handful of fat juicy berries. 'Mm ... beautiful,' she said, when she'd tasted one. She offered her hand to Kate. 'Eat up, you'll need all the vitamin C you can get from now on.'

'I'm going to need more than vitamin C to get me through the ordeal of telling Alec about the baby,' Kate said despondently. She started to cry. 'Oh dear, you must think me very silly.'

'Nonsense, you're at the mercy of your hormones, you're allowed to cry over the slightest of things, spilt milk even. Dare I ask how it happened? I assume at least one of you was doing something to prevent this happy event ever taking place.'

'I've never liked taking the pill and the idea of a coil makes me cross my legs, so it was down to Alec. I guess something just went wrong.'

'Well, at least he can't accuse you of being deliberately careless, not unless he thinks you're not above sabotage, you know, sticking pins into certain things behind his back.'

Kate wiped her eyes and almost smiled. 'But you do see the problem, don't you? Alec is so against us having a family, he's had one ghastly child and the thought of another like Ruth must terrify him. How do you think Josh would react if you were to tell him you were pregnant?'

Jessica gave a loud snort of laughter. 'Josh and I don't have that kind of relationship.'

Kate frowned. 'You mean you don't ... you don't ...'

'Oh we have sex right enough. No, I just meant that our relationship is very different from what you and Alec have.'

'What do you mean?'

'Good question,' Jessica said thoughtfully. What exactly did she and Josh mean to each other? There was no doubt that they got on well together, more than that, there were times when she felt so close to him it was as if she'd always known him. He was fun to be with and she respected his quick and alert mind. He was urbane and erudite, and had rapidly gained her respect. And since that day in July when they'd gone for a late-night walk in the copse, he had proved to be as good in bed as he was in the kitchen – two qualities, in her opinion, no woman should ever underestimate when choosing a partner. It amused her to think of Josh on that unforgettable night when they'd first made love. He had been so nervous when she'd opened the door to him – she'd seen less nerves in a dentist's waiting-room. His awkwardness had touched her and had made him utterly irresistible, prompting her in the woods to demand a kiss from him. But by the time they'd made it to the bedroom his nervousness had vanished and he'd made love to her with a gentle skill that made Gavin's technique seem more like a Grand Prix driver racing round the track of her body, hell-bent on clocking up as many erogenous zones as possible on his way to the finishing line – which at the time had been breathtakingly exhilarating, but which now appeared to be a little lacking compared with Josh's more loving approach. In short, sex with Gavin had left her wanting more, whereas sex with Josh left her feeling wonderfully content.

And quite apart from any physical compatibility between them, she had come to value Josh's opinion, to such a degree that she had actually allowed him to read a few chapters of *A Casual Affair*, something she had never done in the past with anyone – an unfinished manuscript was such a fragile and vulnerable thing. But Josh had been awarded special status in this respect. The question was, why?

Especially when, just recently, she had begun to feel a little uneasy about their relationship. He rarely invited her over to his house these days, saying that he preferred to come to her, and often he would arrive straight from work and cook them supper while she finished off what she was doing. And whenever they made love – and they did frequently – it was strange, but he never stayed the night.

If she wanted to be objective about his behaviour she would say that Josh was a man who had to compartmentalise his life, as though anything he did with her had to be completely isolated from anything else he chose to do, which probably meant that no matter how close they became, there would always be a part of Josh that would remain shut to her.

But if she wanted to be subjective she would say that Josh was turning out to be just like Gavin – allergic to commitment.

And like Gavin, Josh was showing signs of being unreliable. On several occasions in the past couple of weeks when they had arranged to go out, he had backed out at the last minute. On one particular evening somebody from work, possibly a secretary, had called to say that he was sorry, but he'd been held up in a meeting, which was likely to go on for quite a few hours yet.

It didn't take a fool to wonder if Josh was leading a double life. Heaven forbid, but the situation had the signs of a Gavin and Silicone Sal scenario stamped all over it.

What was it with men? Why did they always have this need to cheat and double-cross?

And why hadn't she kicked Josh into touch yet?

Well, because if she was honest she was intrigued to see how long he thought he could go on fooling her, and so long as she didn't get herself too emotionally involved – whatever that might mean – she was sure that he wouldn't be able to hurt her in the way Gavin had.

And, so much for the lying, cheating wretch in Corfu who was supposedly *missing her something rotten*, she'd not heard another peep out of him since that postcard back in July.

Realising that Kate was still waiting for an answer, she said, 'Josh and I are nothing like you and Alec. Commitment is written all over Alec's face. As the old line goes, Josh and I are just good friends.'

'Do you think it will stay that way?'

Jessica laughed. 'With my track record, yes. I know it's a corny thing to say, but I long for the day when a man will be sufficiently nuts about me to want to spend his every waking moment in my company. The nearest I ever get to being with my ideal man is writing about him. You don't know how lucky you are with Alec.'

But it was the wrong thing to say.

Kate's face crumpled and she started to cry again. 'I know exactly how lucky I am . . . that's why I'm convinced that I'm going to lose him.'

Chapter Twenty-Seven

Josh took off his glasses and flung them down on to the desk. He ran a hand over his face, then rubbed his eyes. He felt dreadful. Like death.

It was only four o'clock and normally he wouldn't dream of leaving work at this time of day, not when he still had so much to get through, but today he would have to – if he left it much later there was a very real danger that he might not be able to drive himself home.

Both his legs felt as though they were on fire; the heat was radiating through his trousers as if he had a fever. It had been going on like this for a few days now, the mornings would start off okay, but by the afternoon the tingling would kick in and the excruciating burning sensation would follow. He'd experienced something similar last year, but nowhere near as bad as this, and certainly not in both legs. Which probably meant his MS was getting a firmer hold on him.

For a short while during the summer he had thought he was on top of the illness. The symptoms had lessened and his energy levels had definitely increased; even his leg had shown signs of loosening up. And certainly his relationship with Jessica had gone a long way to revitalising him, bringing about a resurgence in his confidence as well as a general sense of well-being. For a few wonderful weeks it was as if the clock had been turned back and he was his old self.

But the period of remission – if that was indeed what it was – had been cruelly short-lived. The only warning he got that the holiday was over was a feeling of extreme tiredness creeping over him as he and Charlie had driven back from London after their week at the Earls Court trade show. By the time Charlie had dropped him off at Cholmford his arms and legs had felt heavy and sluggish. He'd gone out that night with Jessica and Kate and Alec, but had been far from good company for them – just trying to join in with the conversation had taken all his concentration. By the time he'd reached the safety of his own house, having fobbed off Jessica with some lame excuse about being tired, he'd crashed out in bed and woken up the following afternoon to find that his co-ordination was all over the place, as was his balance, and when he'd eventually mastered the art of walking upright and without falling over, his feet, which were virtually numb, gave him the sensation that he was walking on thick cotton wool. It had been a grim weekend.

He put his glasses back on and tried to focus his mind on the design specifications for their summer range for the following year. But it was no good. He couldn't concentrate. All he could think of was the agonising pain in his legs and the desire to immerse himself in a bath of icy cold water. He had to get home. He slapped the pile of papers into his briefcase, in the hope of working on them later that night, and got to his feet, then suddenly found himself plunged into darkness.

When he opened his eyes, Charlie was kneeling on the floor beside him. He couldn't see Mo, but he could hear her anxious voice in the background.

'Is he okay? Shall I get a doctor or something?'

He wondered in the confused fog of his mind what a 'something' could possibly be. He tried to sit up, but a hammering immediately set off inside his head. He tentatively touched his left temple where the worst of the hammering seemed to be located and when he looked at his hand it was covered in blood.

'It looks worse than it actually is,' Charlie said at once, handing him his handkerchief. 'Mo, will you go and get the first-aid kit, please?'

When Mo had discreetly shut the door behind her Charlie said, 'What happened?'

'How the hell should I know,' Josh snapped. He pushed Charlie's hands away and got determinedly to his feet. 'One minute I was packing up to go home and the next you're in here acting like Florence frigging Nightingale.'

There was a knock at the door. Mo stepped into the office and handed Charlie the first-aid kit. She tried not to stare at Josh and at the amount of blood trickling down his face. 'I'll put all calls on hold, shall I?' she asked.

'Yes,' said Charlie, 'whoever it is, say we'll get back to them tomorrow.'

When they were alone, Charlie made Josh sit down so that he could assess the damage. 'Like I said, it looks worse than it really is. I don't think you need stitches, but I'm going to put a dressing on it.'

While his brother fussed with antiseptic, squares of lint and plasters, Josh rummaged in the red plastic box for some pain-killers. There was nothing stronger than Paracetamol, so he swallowed four and hoped they might take the edge off not just the pain in his head but the burning sensation in his legs. He tried to reason what could have happened. He must have caught his foot on something and tripped, and head-butted his desk. It was the only logical explanation.

It had to be.

Oh God, please let it be that, he thought desperately. Not blackouts. He couldn't take that. He wouldn't be allowed to drive. It would mean the end of his independence, of everything.

'There,' Charlie said when he'd finished. 'Now what?'

'I want to go home,' Josh said bleakly.

'Okay. I'll drive you.'

Josh felt too awful to argue that he was capable of driving himself. He knew he couldn't, that he was beaten. He even doubted his ability to walk out of his office, never mind make it to the car-park.

They waited until everybody else had gone home, then Charlie helped Josh to the lift and took him down to the ground floor. He went and fetched his car, and brought it round to the front of the building where Josh was waiting for him. They drove out of Manchester, through the rush-hour traffic and down the A34. Neither of them spoke. Josh's head was back against the head-rest, his eyes closed.

When they reached Cholmford Hall Mews, Charlie parked as near to the house as he could. 'Don't try and help me,' Josh said, opening the car door, 'I don't want –'

'Don't be so bloody stupid!'

Too weak to fight back, Josh found himself willingly putting his arm round his brother's neck as he helped him into the house. Just once he looked over his shoulder to see if Jessica had seen him. But there was no sign of her.

Charlie took him through to the sitting-room, where he collapsed, exhausted, on to the sofa. Every bit of him ached, particularly the joints in his legs. The burning sensation had now spread to the rest of his body. He started kicking off his shoes, pulling at his jacket, then the buttons on his shirt.

'What do you need? What can I get you?' Charlie asked, suddenly aware just how ill his brother looked. His face was flushed and tiny beads of sweat were forming on his forehead, his lips were pale and drawn. He looked terrible.

'Run me a bath,' Josh murmured, leaning back on the sofa, his eyes tightly closed, 'a cold one, I'm burning up.'

Charlie went over and touched him. 'Shit!' he said, 'you're right. You sure you haven't got flu?'

'I wish!'

Charlie went upstairs and began running a bath. He stood over it, watching the water gush out from the taps, wishing he could do more for Josh. Perhaps Mo had been right earlier, maybe they should have called a doctor.

When he went back downstairs he found Josh in the kitchen. He was stripped down to his boxer shorts, lying stretched out on the tiled floor, a bag of frozen peas on one knee, a frozen loaf of bread balanced on the other. It was reminiscent of years gone by when at a party they'd both ended up so drunk that they'd crashed out on their friend's kitchen floor, surrounded by a knocked-over vegetable rack. But that had been fun. This was different. This was Josh suffering God knows what.

'It's bliss,' Josh said, when he realised Charlie was there, 'better than sex.'

'You'd better not let Jessica hear you say that.'

'She's a very understanding woman,' Josh said, shifting the bag of peas to his ankle.

'And why, if she's so understanding, haven't you told her about your MS?'

Josh scowled. 'How do you know I haven't?'

'Don't bullshit me! I saw the way you were peering over your shoulder when I helped you into the house. You were terrified she'd see you . . . that she'd see the real you.'

Very slowly, Josh got to his feet. He returned the peas and loaf of bread to the freezer and walked stiffly out of the kitchen, every now and again reaching out to the wall to support himself.

Charlie followed him to the hall and up the stairs. 'Well?' he said, when Josh had immersed himself in the bath. 'Have you told her the truth?'

Josh continued to ignore his brother. He slipped under the cool water. He opened his eyes and through the ripples could make out Charlie's distorted face staring down at him. How easy it would be to finish it all like this one day, he thought. All it would take would be some pills and a bottle of Scotch, and for him to let himself simply sink beneath the surface of what was left of his life.

He closed his eyes and stayed where he was, feeling nothing beyond the stabbing pressure on his lungs. But then he was suddenly being hauled out of the water and Charlie's face, a picture of fury, was glaring at him. 'Don't even think about it, you bastard!' he yelled. 'Just don't even think about it!' There was real anger in his face . . . and tears in his eyes.

Bowing his head in shame, Josh coughed and spluttered as his chest heaved at the sudden intake of oxygen. When his breathing had steadied he said, 'I'm sorry. Let's just say it's been a bad week.'

Charlie grabbed a towel and dried his hands and arms, then settled himself on the loo seat. 'With your fondness for irony, I assume that has to be a colossal understatement.'

Josh rested his head back against the bath. 'Look,' he said wearily, 'I've told you before, I don't have any spare energy to try and help you understand what I'm going through. I've barely enough for myself. I'm just trying to learn to cope with this on my own, that's all. I can't keep dumping on you.'

'Well, you just have, big time. How do you think it makes me feel realising you're going through hell knows what and you won't let me help? You can't go on shutting us all out; me, Mum, Dad . . . even Jessica for that matter.'

'She doesn't need to know,' Josh said sharply.

'Why? What makes you think you have the right to go round operating on some stupid need-to-know basis?'

'She doesn't need to know because . . . because I'm probably going to stop seeing her.'

'What?' Charlie was bewildered. He had yet to meet Jessica, but from what Josh had shared with him he got the impression that she was good for him. Certainly up until the past couple of weeks Josh's mood-swings had levelled out and he'd seemed much better in himself.

'Don't look at me like that,' Josh said, reaching for the plug. He was shivering now and wrapping himself in a large towel he carefully stepped out of the bath, his movements awkward and clumsy. 'Why don't you do something useful like make us some supper? There's a lasagne in the fridge, bung it in the microwave. I'll be down soon.'

On his own, Josh lay on his bed and stared up at the ceiling. His body had miraculously cooled down, but his head still ached. He touched Charlie's dressing. It was sopping wet and fresh blood was beginning to seep out. He breathed in deeply, then exhaled slowly. What was he going to do? And not just about coping with what was happening to him, but with Jessica. Was he really going to stop seeing her?

No, he wasn't. He'd only said that as a knee-jerk reaction to what Charlie was saying.

He had no idea how he'd managed to hide the truth from Jessica for as long as he had. He hated the deception – and himself for what he was doing – and had lost track of the number of lies he'd told her. Not once had she questioned him, not even when he'd let her down. He was ashamed of his selfishness, that by hiding the truth from her he'd tried to ensure their relationship could continue. He covered his face with his hands in an agony of shame, appalled at the depth of his deceit as he recalled the catalogue of lies he'd devised: getting Mo to ring Jessica to say that he was held up in a meeting, when the truth was he'd been having a bad-speech day and had been unable to string more than two words together; backing out of dinner dates at the last minute because some bit of his body had given up on him; and worst of the lot, refusing to spend one single night with her.

That bit of deception seemed particularly hurtful. After making love he would immediately start pulling on his clothes and get ready to leave her. 'Crawford,' she'd said once, 'is my bed not good for anything more than a bonk?' And he had laughed, kissed her good-night and slowly made his way across the courtyard in the dark to the loneliness of his own bed, when all the time he'd wanted to lie next to Jessica and hear the steady rhythm of her breathing and feel the warmth of her arms around him. But he couldn't take the risk of enjoying that particular pleasure because he never knew what he would wake up to. If he had woken beside her and found he was unable to walk properly, or that his speech was slurred, or his hands refused to grip anything, she would have wanted to know what was wrong and the game would have been up.

Not that he saw their relationship as a game, far from it. He was dangerously close to admitting that he cared deeply for Jessica, in a way he'd never experienced before. And to make matters worse, because he'd been so adroit at keeping her at arm's length he had no idea what she really felt for him.

He wished now that he had told her about his MS in the first place. If he'd had the courage at the outset, he wouldn't be in the mess he was in now. But he'd been so terrified of losing her that he'd kept quiet, living each day as it came, hoping that by some miracle there would never be the need to tell her the truth. For he knew that when she did find out the truth it would destroy their relationship. Much as he hated the lies, he had no choice but to carry on with them . . . it was the only way he could be sure of seeing Jessica.

*

In the kitchen, the microwave hummed its tuneless tune, then pinged intrusively. Charlie finished setting the table for supper and went upstairs to see if Josh was ready. He found him asleep on the bed, still wrapped in the damp towel. Carefully, he manoeuvred it away and covered his brother with the duvet.

Downstairs again, he helped himself to a plate of lasagne. It was only when he'd finished eating that he remembered he was supposed to be somewhere else – having dinner with Rachel. Rachel had joined the firm of solicitors below Crawford's a few weeks ago. She wasn't really his type, but these days it seemed he couldn't be choosy. He reached for his jacket hanging on the back of the chair and pulled out his mobile phone.

Rachel wasn't impressed when he made his apologies and explained that something had come up. He didn't blame her, he wasn't exactly chuffed with the way things had worked out either.

But then, nor was Josh, he suspected.

Chapter Twenty-Eight

While preparing supper, Kate could hear Alec running the shower upstairs. He was just back from Birmingham. The M6 had been a nightmare and having contended with roadworks and an accident just north of Stafford, he'd finally made it home an hour and a half later than he'd originally told her to expect him. He'd spoken to her several times on his mobile to warn her that he was held up, as well as wanting to pass the time by talking to her.

'What are you doing now?' he'd asked, when he'd called her twenty minutes after their first conversation.

'Talking to you,' she'd said evasively. She couldn't tell him that she was actually standing in front of the hall mirror, sideways on, foolishly checking to see if there was any discernible change in her shape. She had also been trying to work out how best to break the news to Alec.

As she was now.

There were any number of ways of going about it, but she had yet to decide on the right one.

Darling, she could say, *I've got some news.* But that sounded awful, like some trite piece of sit-com dialogue.

Or there was: *Alec, you'll never believe it but I'm* –

That sounded horribly flippant.

Almost as bad as *Guess what, Alec?*

She carried on chopping up pieces of bacon for the carbonara and flung them into the frying pan. She gave them a half-hearted prod with a wooden spatula. Oh, how she sympathised with poor Mary! What must the poor girl have gone through after the Angel Gabriel had paid his little visit and she'd had to wait for Joseph to appear after a hard day's toiling with his chisels – Joseph, trust me, and doubt me not, but behold, I am with child. Joseph, why dost thou look at me with eyes of disbelieving scorn?

She prodded the bacon again and let out a sigh.

'What's that for?'

She spun round at the sound of Alec's voice and forgetting the wooden spatula in her hand, whacked him smack on the chest with it. She reached for the dishcloth but he caught her hand and raised it to his lips.

'I've missed you so much,' he said. He drew her into his arms. 'Promise you'll come with me to the Harrogate fair in February; a week's too long to be without you.'

'I'll do my best,' she said and slipping out of his arms she quickly turned her attention to the pan of spaghetti that was threatening to boil over.

Alec watched Kate moving about the kitchen. Something was wrong. He could see it in her body; the lovely fluidity of her movements was gone. She looked stiff and awkward, like she did whenever Melissa was in the same room as her.

'Did Melissa ring you?' he asked, knowing full well that she had. He helped himself to a handful of grated cheese from the dish next to the cooker, wondering if his ex-wife, with her blunt way of speaking, had upset Kate in some way. He should have phoned Kate himself and not suggested Melissa speak to her.

'Yes, she did,' Kate said, hoping that she could hide behind the conversation she'd had with Melissa until she'd finally summoned up sufficient courage to tell Alec her news.

But as the evening wore on she realised that she was no nearer to making her confession. They ate their meal in the sitting-room with trays on their laps, while watching a Channel Four programme on the changing face of the British work-force. Kate had no interest in it, but Alec was engrossed, occasionally shaking his head and pointing his fork at the television screen in disagreement. 'It's all hyperbole, jingoistic rhetoric of the day. It's common sense that if you pay a man a decent wage he'll do a better job.' He turned to Kate. 'These idiots don't have a clue . . . Kate, are you okay? You haven't eaten a thing.'

She pushed her untouched meal away from her. 'I'm just tired,' she said, 'take no notice.'

Alec put his tray on the floor, reached for the remote control and switched off a fat-cat industrialist expounding on the lack of motivation in your average Brit. 'Kate,' he said gently, 'I know there's something wrong. Is it . . . are you still upset about not doing the teacher training?'

Kate shook her head guiltily. Guiltily because she had lied to Alec. She had been all set to make her formal application to the college when she had begun to suspect that she was pregnant. She had then decided against the course. There seemed no point, not when she would soon have a baby to take care of. She had told Alec that her application had been turned down by the college because she had missed the last date for enrolment.

'You're not upset about Melissa organising that dinner party, are you?' Alec persisted.

She shook her head again, desperately hoping that the right words would magically pop into her head. But they didn't. Instead she blurted out, 'Would you like me to do a party for your birthday? I didn't go ahead and organise anything because I wanted to know what you'd like to do. Not everyone wants a party, do they? And I know that you don't like a lot of fuss. Oh . . . I'm sorry, Alec, but the truth is I forgot all about your birthday. I'm sorry.'

Alec smiled at her kindly, relieved to know at last what had caused Kate to be so unhappy. 'It's okay,' he said, 'I don't particularly want to be reminded of how old I'm going to be.'

'But you're not old,' Kate said vehemently, 'and I love the way you are.' She suddenly threw her arms around him and hugged him tightly. 'I don't ever want things to change between us.'

'They won't,' he whispered into her ear, 'I won't ever let anything change between us.' Then, pulling back from her, he said, 'And anyway, I've decided what I'm doing for my birthday, I'm taking you away for a romantic weekend. Just the two of us, no family or friends to worry about. Just us.'

Kate buried her face in his neck and clung to him. *Just us.* She couldn't tell him now, not now.

Alec smiled to himself, thinking of his plan to take Kate to Venice, where to mark the occasion of his fiftieth birthday he intended to ask her to marry him, something he should have done months ago. He just hoped she'd say yes.

Chapter Twenty-Nine

Late that night Tony brought the car to a slow and steady stop. He didn't want to jolt Hattie awake. She was fast asleep in the back and had been so since they'd joined the motorway at Exeter. Amanda was also asleep with her head lolling to one side, but as he opened his door and activated the interior light she stirred. She stretched her legs. 'Good,' she said, 'we're home. At last.'

Her words didn't come anywhere near his own thoughts. He was more than glad to be home. Never before had home been such an attraction. Their last-minute booked holiday – a cottage in Devon – had been nothing short of a lifetime in Purgatory and he'd spent most of the week wishing he were back in Cholmford. The thatched cottage that they had rented had been advertised as being idyllically situated, quaint and cosy. It had been none of these things. It had been cramped, damp and dismal, and had made the tiny terraced house in which he'd grown up seem like a palace in comparison. And with the rain that had poured down almost every day they had been forced either to stay indoors and risk cabin fever, or go out and join the other miserable holiday-makers wandering wretchedly around butterfly farms, cheese-making factories and any other lucrative enterprise that had been set up to entertain bored and depressed tourists too bedraggled to fight back and say to hell with your so-called attractions, I'm off! He suspected that if some local had stuck up a sign outside his garage and declared it to be a Museum of Post-War Horticultural Implements, he and hoards of other suicidally depressed holiday-makers would willingly have got in line to stare at a bench of B & Q garden tools. What was it with people on holiday that made them put up with being taken for such a monumental ride?

He'd expected Amanda to be the first to say she wanted none of it, but some perversity must have taken hold of her because she'd actually admitted to enjoying herself. Extraordinary.

He reached into the back of the car for Hattie. He carried her indoors, up to her bedroom where he carefully removed her sandals and snuggled her into bed. He kissed her forehead. In response she turned on to her side. He kissed her again, unable to resist her warm little cheek.

Downstairs, he found Amanda going through the mail that Kate had thoughtfully placed on the breakfast bar for their return. 'Anything urgent?' he asked, thinking of the present he and Hattie had picked out specially for Kate.

It had been Amanda's suggestion that they go away and also her idea that they ask Kate to keep an eye on things in their absence. 'She won't mind watering a few plants,' Amanda had said. 'After all, what else has she to do all day while Alec's at work?'

In return for Kate watering the patio tubs of geraniums and trailing lobelia, Amanda had suggested that they reward her with a half-pound tin of Devonshire cream toffees. But Tony had had other ideas and had gone shopping with Hattie, and between them they had settled on a hand-painted silk scarf for Kate. They found it in a smart little shop selling quality-produced arts and crafts. He didn't tell Amanda how much he'd paid for the scarf and hoped that Hattie wouldn't attach any significance to his using his Barclaycard rather than cash.

It was picturing the smile on Kate's face when she opened the present that had mainly kept him going during the week. There had been other thoughts that had gone through his head as well during the interminable days of rain and boredom, but he had tried to dismiss them as nothing more than the wild imaginings of a desperate man.

Wild imaginings or not, they had come to him in the long empty nights in that poky cottage where he had no escape from Amanda. Initially he'd tried to resist the powerful images in his head of him and Kate together – whichever way he tried to justify it, lying next to Amanda and wishing that she were Kate was wrong – but in the end, and because it was the only way he could get to sleep, he had given in to the fantasy.

And now he was doing it again, but not in that hole of a bedroom that had mould-spotted wallpaper held up in places with drawing-pins and Sellotape, but lying in their own comfortable bed.

Here it felt even more wrong.

This was their marital bed. This wasn't some anonymous cheap plywood divan and damp mattress that a thousand other unfortunate couples had shared.

Guiltily, he turned his thoughts to something altogether less shameful.

It was Hattie's first day at her new school tomorrow and to surprise her he had specially taken an extra day off work to drive her in himself. He wouldn't hang around, he'd just help her find her new classroom and leave quietly. Once that was done, he planned to take the silk scarf over to Kate, when . . . when Alec would be out of the way and Amanda at the supermarket stocking up for the week ahead.

The house was wonderfully quiet and Amanda was revelling in it.

Having taken Hattie to school, Tony was now in the sitting-room reading the newspaper and she was in the kitchen – her lovely, spacious, airy kitchen, at least four times the size of that hateful kitchenette she'd suffered in Devon. She was putting a shopping list together: *Lurpak. Olio Spread. Fromage frais.* But her thoughts soon strayed from Sainsbury's dairy produce to their week in Devon.

It had been an unmitigated disaster. She had never seen Tony so fed-up and she was glad of it. He deserved to be miserable. It served him right for the humiliating weekend he'd put her through last month.

The Arc weekend at Gleneagles – the jolly that she had been so looking forward to – had turned out to be nothing of the kind. There had been none of the manicures and massages that she had imagined, nor any of the elegant dinners enjoying excellent food and interesting company set amid stylish surroundings.

What she'd got instead was a shambles of a doss-house that couldn't provide sufficient hot water for a bath after she'd spent most of each day being drenched and covered in mud – and not the expensive stuff that was so good for the skin.

She shuddered at the memory.

It had been humiliating.

And downright unfair.

Having dumped Hattie on Kate and Alec, much against Tony's wishes but very much in line with Hattie's, they had arrived at the hotel in the depths of the Shropshire countryside, only to find that everyone else had got there at least three hours ahead of them and, judging from their boisterous behaviour, must have settled themselves into the Anne Boleyn bar for most of that time.

The owner of the hotel, not in evidence himself – he was away on holiday in Marbella – was a fan of Henry VIII, and had gone out of his way to share his love of the man with his guests and had named all the rooms accordingly. She and Tony were staying in the Sir Thomas More suite and after they'd unpacked they joined everyone in the bar. Tony introduced her to the other wives, then abandoned her and went and chatted with his colleagues. The women all knew one another and it soon became clear that in the current climate of job insecurity at Arc she was, as Tony's wife, classed as the enemy. One of the wives, a tiny woman with a strong Mancunian accent and the longest nail extensions Amanda had ever seen, asked her which of Agatha Christie's novels she thought most resembled Arc's attitude to its employees. Amanda had said, 'I'm sorry, I've no idea.'

'*Ten Little Niggers*, of course . . . *and then there were none.*'

She had laughed politely, but then realised that she was laughing alone. It wasn't a joke.

Embarrassed, she had struggled through the rest of the evening, picking out ominous curly brown hairs from her coq au vin in the Thomas Cranmer dining-room and trying very hard to ingratiate herself with the two men either side of her. She gave up when one of them, no doubt rendered brain-dead from the amount of beer he'd earlier chucked down his throat and which he was now topping up with Piesporter plonk, kept referring to her as Eve.

'Well, Eve,' he said, 'how's that sweet little daughter of yours that Tony's always on about?' He repeated the question a further five times, despite the looks others were throwing him.

She barely slept that night, due to the Thomas More suite being situated directly above the Anne Boleyn bar, the staff of which couldn't have been acquainted with the phrase 'last orders', and in the morning, as they dressed for breakfast, Tony told her what they would be doing that day.

'What?' she'd cried, looking out of the dirty window at the rain beating down on the weed-infested tennis court, making it resemble a large rectangular pond. 'Orienteering? But I haven't brought any-thing to wear to go tramping through woods.'

'You don't need to worry about that, the hotel specialises in these kinds of activities; they provide boots, waterproofs, everything you could possibly need.'

'The hell they do! I haven't seen anything here that remotely resembles a beauty salon or a personal fitness centre.'

'I did warn you,' he'd said, 'I told you that it wasn't going to be the normal event. In view of the downsizing going on at work, Marty decided that the usual extravagant do at Gleneagles would be inappropriate.'

'And this is appropriate?'

He'd shrugged his shoulders in that pathetic way he did sometimes

– you wouldn't catch a man like Bradley Hurst shrugging his shoulders.

'Why didn't you tell me exactly what it was going to be like?'

'I didn't know anything about it. Marty organised the whole thing. It was to be a surprise.'

It was a surprise all right.

She was put into a group with the woman with the nail extensions, whose name was Wendy, along with Marty – the one who had kept calling her Eve the previous evening.

'Right then, Wend and Mand,' Marty said, rubbing his hands together and obviously deciding that in their group he was the only one qualified to take charge. 'This isn't a race exactly, but I want us to get back to base at least twenty minutes ahead of the others. Remember, there are no winners, only losers. Mand, sweetheart, you ever done this kind of thing before? Any good with a compass?'

They'd finished last, which probably was due to the sit-down row she'd had with Marty. Not that he'd seemed to notice. The man had a skin thicker than tarmac and with about as much sensitivity.

'I'm not going any further,' she'd screamed at him, after she'd slipped in the mud for the third time. The rain was pouring off her ill-fitting sou'wester, cascading into her face and streaking what wasn't already streaked of the make-up she'd applied before Tony had broken the news to her. 'I've been out here in this bloody awful rain for over five hours, I'm not taking another step. I've had enough.' And she'd thrown herself down on the muddy ground and added, 'You'll have to carry me back.'

'Hey, Mand, sweetheart,' Marty had said, adopting a let's-be-reasonable tone of voice and squatting down beside her, 'this is the bit where you have to apply your mind. Your body's tired and is attempting a mental coup of your brain, you've gotta step right in there and put a stop to it.'

'Balls!'

Wendy had laughed out loud. 'That's what I like to hear, a bit of plain speaking.'

'And you can shut up as well!'

Wendy ignored her. 'When the going gets tough, it's time for a bevvy.' She leant against a tree, pulled out a hip flask from a pocket and began swigging on it. The forethought of the woman had incensed Amanda even more.

The weekend didn't get any better and by the time they were safely heading for home Amanda had promised herself that, if it was the last thing she would do, it would be to teach Tony a lesson. Of course he'd known what Marty would organise. Wasn't it his job to know what was going on?

So when they'd arrived in Devon last weekend, to find that the cottage they'd booked through the small ads in the *Sunday Times* was little more than a thatched coal shed, she had been delighted. The expression on Tony's face as they'd let themselves in was one to savour.

'It's disgusting,' he'd said, after taking one look at the grimy sofa and coffee-cup-ringed table in the sitting-room that measured less than their *en suite* bathroom. 'We can't stay here. The place stinks.'

'Oh, do you think so?' she'd said, 'I think it's rather quaint.'

As the days slowly went by and the rain came down, she could see that Tony was becoming more and more depressed. Now you know what it feels like, she thought maliciously. This is nothing compared with what you put me through in Shropshire.

Amanda looked down at her shopping list. She hadn't got very far with it.

Which was how she felt about her marriage. Her attempts back in June to try and inject some kind of purpose into her life with Tony had fallen foul of the realisation that Tony was never going to be another Bradley Hurst. He didn't have the killer instinct. All he seemed to care about was Hattie.

Was Hattie happy?

Would Hattie cope with her new school?

Of course she would. That girl, with her uncanny knack for manipulating people, was one of life's great survivors. Just look at the way she could get Kate drooling over her. And as for the way she wound Tony round her little finger, well, that was plain sickening – a day off work just to take her to school! Pathetic. Surely he had more important things to be doing. Bradley Hurst hadn't got to where he was by fussing over a devious child.

She finished her shopping list and as she underlined the last entry, she forced herself to swallow the unpalatable truth that the way things were going between her and Tony, their marriage was heading for a fall. What had seemed at the outset to be a marriage of happy convenience on both sides was now proving to be a battleground of silent dissatisfaction. She had accepted for some time that Hattie resented her, and equally so, she resented Hattie. But now she was beginning to feel the same for Tony.

In fact, she felt little else for him.

*

214

Tony thought Amanda would never go off to the supermarket. How long did it take to put a shopping list together, for heaven's sake?

He checked himself one more time in the hall mirror. His hair was newly washed, he was wearing fresh clean clothes – he'd spent ages deciding what to put on – and had poured enough aftershave all over himself to knock 'em dead in John o'Groats.

But was it enough to make an impression on Kate?

Well, it was time to find out.

He locked up the house, straightened his collar, cleared his throat and strode across the courtyard. He knocked lightly – in view of what was on his mind, anything louder would have been a flagrant announcement of his intentions.

He waited for her to come to the door.

And waited.

He knocked again, this time slightly louder.

Still no answer.

He looked over his shoulder at the staring windows behind him. His guilt was so palpable he was convinced that if anyone was watching him they would know exactly what he was up to. He was about to give up and accept that maybe Kate was out when he heard a movement from within.

Very slowly the door opened and Kate appeared. She was crying. More than that, her whole body was shaking as tears streamed down her pale face. Something terrible must have happened.

Overcome with concern at the sight of her distress, Tony stepped over the threshold, took her in his arms and closed the door behind him.

Chapter Thirty

Jessica was in her study where she was trying to heighten the tension between Clare and Miles. She'd got to the tricky bit in the middle of her first draft of *A Casual Affair*, the bit where there had to be some kind of romantic action going on between her two main characters, and if Clare didn't get Miles to surrender to her charms in the next few pages then the reader was going to get bored and give up on the book – and on Jessica Lloyd.

Jessica knew as well as the next novelist that a loyal reader is the best friend an author can have and that they should always be treated with respect. As Piers had once said to her, 'To short-change a loyal reader is an act of gross stupidity, Jessica. Take care that you're never foolish enough to make that mistake.' It was as basic as knowing that every story had to have a beginning, a middle and an end.

So come on, she told herself as she stared at the blank screen in front of her, it was time for Clare to get tough with Miles. So far Clare had been pussy-footing about with him – casually dropping hints over the photocopier along the lines of there being more to her than met the eye was never going to crash through Miles's shy reserve. She was going to have to come up with something infinitely more to the point, like ... like cornering him in his office and grabbing him by his insurance bonds.

Jessica laughed, suddenly recollecting the scene in Piers's office when her vivid imagination had run riot and had wondered what it would be like to have its wicked way with her agent across his desk.

Mm ... she wondered. What if ... what if Clare tries that?

And what if Miles responds? Unbridled passion across the spread-sheets would certainly hot up the pace.

She started tapping away at the laptop, the scenario in her mind rapidly taking shape.

'Jessica,' came a voice from somewhere beyond the study.

'Yes,' answered Jessica absent-mindedly. In her ability totally to absorb herself in her writing she had forgotten that Anna was spending the day with her and that she was making a start on redecorating the kitchen.

'Isn't it about time for a coffee break?'

Clare and Miles's big moment was put on hold as Jessica left the study and went and joined her mother in the kitchen. Anna was half-way up a pair of aluminium step-ladders and was stripping wallpaper from around the window that faced the courtyard. Jessica watched her pull at a piece of wallpaper; it came away in one long, satisfying piece. She made some coffee and they sat at the kitchen table. It was covered with colour charts and several back issues of *Ideal Home*, which Anna had brought with her to help Jessica choose a new look for her kitchen. Between them they had decided on 'clotted cream' for the walls and 'summer blue' for the skirting and kitchen cupboards – Anna had assured her that sanding down the expensive units and repainting them would be simplicity itself. 'I've seen them doing it on the television, it looks straightforward enough. We'll change the doorknobs as well while we're about it.' Jessica had had no idea how expert at DIY her mother had become. She watched her now as she picked over the biscuit tin hunting for one of the few remaining chocolate bickies.

She was enjoying having her mother around. Since the rockery argument, when Anna had made her feelings about her independence very clear, she had managed to curb the desire to watch over her too zealously. It wasn't always easy, as Anna at times seemed to have a death-wish. She'd recently taken up going to the local swimming baths first thing in the morning and after she'd been boasting about the number of lengths she could notch up in an hour Jessica occasionally made the effort to join her so that she could keep a surreptitious eye on her and make sure she didn't overdo it, especially as her mother had recently bought a black Speedo costume, an obscene-looking rubber hat and a pair of goggles.

Breaking into her thoughts, Anna said, 'I should have the rest of the wallpaper off by tomorrow, then I can make a start on rubbing down the units.'

'There's no need to rush things.'

'No point in not.'

That was the trouble, thought Jessica. Every minute counted to Anna, not a single second was to be wasted. She doubted whether she would ever view life in the same way. It wasn't that Jessica was idle, well, she didn't think she was, it was more a case of having lived such a happy-go-lucky existence for so many years – Corfiotes were not people to rush things – that she tended to take a more relaxed approach to getting things done. Her mother on the other hand was a human dynamo and didn't know how to slow down.

'So how's the writing going?' Anna asked, digging around in the biscuit tin again.

'Not bad, I was having trouble getting the main character and her love interest together, but just before you called me through I found a way round the problem.'

Anna raised her eyes from the biscuit that she was dunking in her coffee. 'And how's Josh? I've not heard you mention him recently.'

Jessica laughed. 'So subtle, Mother dear. I don't know how you do it.'

'Well? How is he?'

'Good question, I haven't seen him for a few days.'

'How many days?'

'Over a week.'

'Mm . . . that doesn't sound good.'

'Thanks!'

'You must face up to these things, Jessica. If he were seriously interested in you he'd be banging that front door down and pulling you by the hair across to his place and . . . well, I think I can safely leave the rest to you. I wonder if he'd consider a more mature woman?'

'Forget it, there's mature and there's downright gone off.'

But Jessica knew that her mother was right. The way Josh had vanished from her life so suddenly hardly gave a girl cause to hope. And yes, she was well aware that she could quite easily go over and see him herself. Or for that matter, she could phone him. But that wasn't the point. It was *she* who had phoned him last, it was now down to him to make the next move. No way in the world was she going to go crawling to him. Her begging days were over. Fool that she'd been, she'd done enough of that with Gavin.

From his bed, Josh gazed out of the window, across the fields and towards the distant lumpy shapes of the Peak District. It didn't seem that long ago since he and Charlie used to go off to Derbyshire for walking weekends – weekends which usually had a habit of turning into long-distance pub crawls. But wallowing in memories never did him any good.

He pushed back the duvet, slowly slid his legs out of the bed and placed his feet firmly on the floor. So far so good. Then, holding his breath, he stood up. That was good, too. Okay, now it was time to move. Still holding his breath, he took a couple of paces.

Yesss! He was mobile.

When he'd lain on the bed last night, his head aching from where he'd struck it at work, the rest of his body had felt as though it would never move again. It was a huge relief to him now to know that this was not the case.

Spurred on, he shuffled over to the wardrobe and knowing there was no chance of him making it in to work that day, he pulled out a pair of black jeans. He considered a shirt, but thought of the buttons and instantly dismissed the idea – his fingers had all the dexterity of a bunch of bananas. He chose a T-shirt instead. Next it was over to the chest of drawers for some socks and boxer shorts, followed by the staggering journey right across the bedroom to the adjoining bathroom. He was exhausted by the time he reached it and leant against the basin for support. But at least he'd made it. By shit he'd made it!

He didn't bother with shaving, but once he'd washed and dressed he stood at the top of the stairs and geared himself up for what today, for him, was his very own equivalent to the downward climb of the north face of the Eiger.

As he'd suspected, when he finally entered the kitchen Charlie was already there and was making breakfast. He'd known that his brother would stay the night, that he would never have left him alone. He was grateful, touched by Charlie's concern, but too much of him was angry at the circumstances in which he found himself to be able to thank him in the way he ought.

'You look better than you did last night,' was Charlie's only comment when he saw him.

'Thanks. So do you.'

They ate in the kitchen. Josh would have liked to have had breakfast outside on the patio in the warm morning sun, but the thought of traversing the entire length of the hall, sitting-room and the two steps down to reach the garden made him settle for where they were.

'I thought I'd hang around here for the day,' Charlie said, 'if that's okay with you?'

Josh shrugged. 'Sure.'

'I've phoned Mo and explained we won't be in. I thought if you were feeling up to it we could go for a pub lunch later on?'

'And maybe a walk afterwards?' The sarcasm in Josh's voice made Charlie throw down his knife.

'Sod it, Josh! I'm just trying to help, that's all.'

Josh buried his head in his hands. 'I know,' he said, 'I know.' He looked up. 'I can't help myself at times. It's like there's more anger in me than I know what to do with. I'm . . . I'm sorry.'

'Will you promise me one thing,' Charlie said, his face suddenly earnest. 'What went through your mind in the bath last night . . . you . . . you wouldn't ever . . .'

'What, top myself?'

Charlie nodded.

'I don't think that's a promise I can make . . . or perhaps anyone is capable of making. The dark demons of the mind leap out on you when you're least expecting them, a bit like Jehovah's Witnesses really.'

'That's hardly the reassuring response I need, though.'

'Yeah, well, right now it's the best I can do.'

'But you've got so much going for you.'

'Have I?' Josh's voice was expressionless.

'Yes!' Charlie was defiantly adamant. 'There are so many people who care about you and apart from anything else, how the hell would I run the business on my own?'

'You'd manage.' Again the same flat voice.

'But I don't want to run it alone, I want you there with me, or . . . or there'd be no point.'

Josh turned away. He couldn't cope with Charlie's honesty. 'Look, can we drop this?' he muttered. 'It's really not helping either of us.'

'And what about Jessica?' Charlie had the bit between his teeth now.

Josh looked up sharply. 'What about her?'

'Last night you said you weren't going to carry on seeing her. Why? Isn't she someone who'd be worth living for?'

'Don't you think I haven't thought of that!' Josh rounded on him.

'Then stop bloody well pissing about and do something. Go over there and tell her the truth. Give her time to think about it and start treating her with the respect she deserves instead of palming her off with all those lies you've been dishing out. Yes, Mo told me about the phone call you asked her to make. I dread to think what else you've been up to.'

Josh stared angrily at his brother. 'Have you quite finished?'

'No!' Charlie retorted, 'no, I haven't.' But as he tried to think of what else he wanted verbally to throw at his brother, he realised that his fury at Josh's stubbornness had suddenly rendered him impotent. He could think of nothing else to say. Nothing that would be of any help. He stood up. 'This is no good,' he said, 'I can't cope with you when you're like this. I'll be at work if you need me.'

Unable to get to his feet fast enough to go after his brother, Josh listened to the sound of the front door shutting, then the unmistakable rumble of Charlie's TVR starting up.

He slowly lowered his head into his hands, saddened beyond measure that he continually treated Charlie so badly.

Chapter Thirty-One

Acting as a shoulder to cry on wasn't exactly what Tony had had in mind when he'd knocked on Kate's door half an hour ago, but it was all he could do in the circumstances.

She had stopped crying now, but was still sitting hunched on the bottom step of the stairs – she'd been there since she'd let him in. In front of her was a half-empty box of Kleenex, beside it, a pile of soggy screwed-up tissues. His present for her was lying unopened on the hall table next to the phone, which she kept glancing at. She was doing so now. 'When he's calmed down, he'll ring, won't he?' she said, her bloodshot eyes filling with tears once more as she hugged her knees to her.

'Maybe,' Tony said softly beside her. From what Kate had told him it seemed pretty unlikely that Alec would call for a few hours yet. 'He needs time to cool off,' he added. He had to admit, though, that Alec's reaction to Kate telling him that she was pregnant did seem a bit extreme. He remembered how he had felt when Eve had told him she was expecting Hattie. It had come as a complete surprise to them both as they hadn't planned on having children so soon. But his reaction had been one of amazement rather than shock. 'How come?' had been his first astonished words. 'Because you've impregnated my body with your sperm, dummy,' had been Eve's response, followed by a smile that had shown him how pleased she was. They had gone out for a meal to celebrate and later they'd made love. 'It won't harm the baby, will it?' he'd asked afterwards, suddenly concerned. She'd laughed and rolled on top of him. 'Honestly,' she'd said, 'men, they know nothing!'

'It takes time for a man to adjust to the idea of being a father,' he said kindly to Kate. He slipped his hand over hers and squeezed it. 'It took me a while really to get to grips with the idea of Eve being pregnant. I was frightened that a baby might come between us. Men can be very insecure when it comes to sharing the woman they love.'

Kate looked down at Tony's hand holding her own. He had nice hands, she suddenly thought. 'How long did it take for you to come round?'

The truthful answer was less than a few days, but the truth wouldn't help Kate right now. 'A couple of weeks,' he lied. 'It might even have been longer.'

'But Alec might never come round to the idea,' she said, staring into the middle distance. In her mind's eye she could see Alec's face earlier that morning; first the shock in it, then the disappointment and finally the anger.

Over breakfast she had summoned up the courage to tell him about the baby. He had been listening to Sue MacGregor and John Humphrys bringing to the nation's attention that inflation was up – or was it down? – and that as a result home-owners would be worse off, but investors would be happier. And I don't give a damn, she'd thought as she'd got up from the table and switched off the radio and faced Alec. She didn't wrap her announcement in any kind of fancy packaging. She simply stood before him and in a matter-of-fact voice that was vaguely reminiscent of Sue MacGregor reading the news she said, 'Alec, I'm pregnant. I know this isn't what you wanted, but I'm afraid it's definitely something I want.'

His eyes were what she noticed first – they suddenly seemed to grow larger; it was the shock, she supposed. Then it was his hands that caught her attention; they stopped what they were doing and came to rest either side of his plate of half-buttered toast, the palms face down as though feeling for some levitational force that was about to start making the table bounce about.

Very slowly he had begun to move. He stood up. Then he spoke. 'You knew I didn't want this. You knew.' The disappointment in his voice was heart-breaking.

But worse was to come when he walked out of the kitchen. He paused in the doorway, turned back to her and said, 'You've used me. Ruth said you would. She warned me, but I wouldn't listen.'

And that was the anger. Scalding, accusative anger, as though she had planned the whole thing.

Within seconds he was gone, the door closing quietly behind him – Alec wasn't a dramatic man, slamming the door would have been too hackneyed. She watched him get into his car and drive away to work.

To Melissa.

She had started to cry then, tears of sobbing heartache that she had been storing up over the weekend. Or was it longer? Had she always known that it would end like this?

It was while she was trying to pull herself together, at the same time clearing up the breakfast things, that she had heard the sound of knocking. At first she'd ignored it. She didn't want to see anybody. But then she'd wondered if it was Jessica and realising that she was the only other person who knew her predicament and that she might be able to help her, she went to the door. But it had been Tony. The details of what happened next were hazy, but she could remember the sense of relief as he'd held her – she hated crying alone and to be able to cry while somebody held her somehow made the hurt seem slightly more bearable. He'd sat with her on the stairs, handed her tissues and listened while she told him what had happened.

'It's over,' she now whispered. 'I know it is. Alec thinks I've done this deliberately.'

Tony put his arm around her shoulders. How easy it would be to manipulate the situation to his own advantage, he thought, to write off Alec and claim Kate for his own. But he couldn't. Kate's distress touched him too much even to consider what had earlier been in his mind. 'Come on,' he said gently, 'let's get you somewhere more comfortable to sit.'

They went into the sitting-room. Kate curled herself up in one of the armchairs in the bay window. He took the chair opposite. He handed her the present which he'd picked up from the hall table. 'Here,' he said, hoping it would provide a temporary diversion, 'open this, it's a thank-you for looking after the house while we were away.'

She carefully unwrapped the layers of cream tissue paper. 'It's beautiful,' she exclaimed, when she saw what was inside, 'but I don't deserve it, I only watered a few plants.'

'Nonsense, of course you deserve it. Hattie and I chose it together. Are the colours okay? We hoped all those different shades of pale green would suit you.' He was conscious that he was speaking too quickly. He so wanted her to like the present.

She nodded and lovingly stroked the silk scarf. 'It's perfect. Thank you. And will you thank Hattie for me? How is she?'

Brief as the diversion might be, Tony was glad that the scarf had brought about a respite in Kate's unhappiness. 'She's fine. Or rather she was when I left her a few hours ago. It's her first day at her new school. I think I was the more nervous of the two of us when it was time to say goodbye. Do you think you'd be up to a visit later when she comes home? She'd love to see you. Children are wonderful for taking your mind off things.' He saw immediately the pained expression on her face. 'I'm sorry,' he said, 'that was insensitive of me.'

She blinked away the threat of fresh tears. 'I've always wanted children,' she said wistfully. 'I'd love a little Hattie of my own . . . you're very lucky.'

'Yes,' he said softly, 'I know I am.' Then before he could stop himself, he added, 'But it didn't always seem that way, not when . . . not when Eve died.' He clenched his hands in his lap. 'I've never told anyone this before, but . . . but I would have willingly swapped them over.' He leapt to his feet. 'Oh God, what does that make me sound like?' He leant against the window, resting his hands on the sill and, needing time to compose himself, he stared through the glass, concentrating his gaze on the jutting shape of Bosley Cloud in the far-away distance.

After a few seconds he slowly turned round and faced Kate. 'I didn't mean that I wanted Hattie dead, it wasn't like that, I just wanted Eve. I wanted her so desperately . . . I would have done anything to have her alive again.' But as he spoke those last terrible words he felt his composure going again. He had to fight hard to overcome the terrible pain that always threatened to engulf him when he thought of Eve's senseless death. 'I've no idea why I'm telling you all this,' he said, his voice low and shaky, 'but I love Hattie more than I thought possible. Maybe it's guilt. Maybe I'm overcompensating for what I once felt.' He cleared his throat and willed himself to finish what he'd started. 'And as a result I know I've made the biggest mistake of my life. I made the error of thinking that Hattie needed a mother more than . . . more than I needed a woman I could love.'

They stared at one another, the room suddenly still with a taut silence.

'I thought so,' Kate said at last.

He was stunned. He sat down again. 'Is it that obvious?'

She didn't answer his question, but said simply, 'What will you do?'

He shook his head and let out his breath. 'I've no idea.'

Chapter Thirty-Two

Alec wasn't interested in what Susan Ashton from the warehouse in Oxford had to say. It didn't bother him that the hand-finishing on one of the Christmas card lines was taking longer than originally estimated; for all he cared Susan could have phoned with the news that the entire factory had burnt down and there were no survivors.

All he could think of was Kate.

Why, oh why had this happened?

They'd been fine as they were. Now everything would be different. All the plans he'd had in mind were ruined. There'd be no more romantic dinners together. And there'd certainly be no chance of any romantic weekends away. In fact, experience told him that there'd be no bloody romance at all.

He could remember all too vividly what it had been like when Ruth was born; the whole house had been given over to her. It was the smell he'd disliked most; whichever way he turned there was the smell of drying nappies, sour milk and sickly talcum powder. There was no escape from it.

He'd become a stranger in his own home, unable to walk into any room for fear of disturbing Ruth who might be sleeping there in her Moses basket – it had always seemed absurd to him that such a tiny being not only possessed its own mini-empire within hours of its birth, but was actually given the power to rule and dominate it.

But the trouble had started way before Ruth's arrival in the world: it had begun when Melissa discovered that she was pregnant. Pregnancy hadn't suited her and from day one it had made her tired and crotchety, and she'd been in bed by eight thirty most nights, with sex clearly no longer a viable proposition. After Ruth was born he'd waited patiently for Melissa to wave the green flag. But there was still no sign of affection between them. By the time Ruth was five months old he was beginning to lose hope of them ever having any kind of sex life again. If he gave so much as a hint that he desired her in bed, Melissa would turn away from him. It was only after she had stopped breast-feeding that things improved. But it was never the same.

It had always been his opinion that it was Ruth's conception that had created the first crack in their marriage.

And exactly the same would happen between him and Kate. A child would come between them. He just knew it.

Kate would, of course, deny that anything would change between them, but he knew better. It was all down to nature. Nature dictated that a woman behaved differently the moment she became pregnant. She didn't realise what was going on herself, but very gradually all her thoughts became wrapped up in that small being that was fast taking her over, allowing no room for anything else in her life, or anyone else for that matter. And when the baby was actually born, nature stepped in to ensure it survived by putting its needs first and foremost in its mother's brain. There was no room for any other thought, all nature allowed the mother to think of was providing nourishment, warmth and a safe environment for her child.

And that was another thing nature did – the child was never *their* child, it was only ever *her* child.

Ruth had never been his. His initial clumsy attempts at bathing or dressing her had been mocked and devalued, and had reduced him to the position of onlooker, where his services were only required in the middle of the night when Melissa was too exhausted to soothe a teething Ruth.

He could imagine Kate saying she would never be like Melissa, that she would never make the same mistakes, but in his heart he suspected that she would be worse – she was so very desperate for a child of her own that she probably wouldn't let him have a single look-in. He would be squeezed out. Surplus to requirements.

It had been just like that when Hattie had stayed with them that weekend last month. Kate had spent nearly all her time entertaining the child. Thinking that he mustn't let his jealousy get the better of him he had left her to it and spent most of Saturday and Sunday at work.

'So what do you want me to do, Alec? Give it one more try?'

Susan's insistent voice at the other end of the line forced Alec back to what she was saying. 'I'm sorry,' he said curtly, 'I've got to go. Speak to Melissa about the problem.'

He replaced the receiver and sank back into his chair. Almost immediately the phone rang again. He snatched it up. 'I'm busy,' he barked at the receptionist who'd put the call through. 'I don't want to be disturbed.'

Was there to be no peace for him?

The answer was obviously no, as at that moment his door opened and in walked the very last person with whom he wanted to speak. Hell, she'd love every minute of this, he thought. He watched Melissa drop a batch of sample cards on his desk and for the first time since Tim had arrived on the scene he experienced a wave of angry jealousy about the relationship she had with him. How simple it must be for the pair of them, he thought enviously, there was no danger of a pregnancy to bugger things up because very conveniently Melissa had had a hysterectomy six years ago. And unable to stomach the idea of her gloating, he stood up quickly and pulled on his jacket. 'Whatever it is, it'll have to wait,' he said. He moved towards the door. 'I'm going for an early lunch.'

Melissa stared after him. Something was wrong. Very wrong. In all the years she had known Alec she had only twice seen such a distraught look on his face – when his mother had died and when she'd told him she wanted a divorce. She had never forgotten that sad, wounded expression. She had hurt him so badly and it had taken all her strength to carry out what she had instigated. He had never known how near she'd come to changing her mind that night.

But it had been the right thing to do. She had never since doubted the decision she'd made. She and Alec got on much better as friends and business partners than they had as husband and wife. She still loved him – she always had – and that was perhaps why she had divorced him; if they'd stayed together they might have ended up hating each other and she'd never have wanted that; it had been a case of being cruel to be kind. It had been difficult at times, though, she'd had to adopt a tough veneer to convince Alec that she no longer cared for him in the way she once had. In the early days after she'd moved out, when he'd taken to drinking the lonely evenings away, she'd had to fight back the urge to comfort him. Instead, she had put on what she called her tough bitch act and bossed him about, ordering him to pull himself together. Little did he know that she had spent many a lonesome night worrying about him.

Still, that was all in the past. She now had Tim and Alec seemed to have found genuine happiness with Kate.

Alec was driving much too fast for his car to cope with the country lanes and after coming within an inch of his life on a tight bend and almost smashing his Saab into the back of a tractor he lowered his speed.

He had been driving recklessly and mindlessly for the past hour, but now as he approached the village of Swettenham he decided he needed a break, as well as something to eat. He headed towards the Swettenham Arms. The car-park was large and not very full, and he easily found himself a space.

Inside the pub he was met by the comforting smell of real ale. He ordered a pint of bitter and a steak and kidney pudding, and took his drink over to the only available table. It was in the window, where not so long ago he and Kate had sat. They had been celebrating some kind of anniversary – five months of knowing one another, or was it six? Whatever it was, happiness and contentment had flowed between them as they'd sat wrapped in each other's love that warm, sunny spring afternoon. There had been a small vase on the wooden table containing a single carnation which he had taken out and tucked into her hair – a silly, sentimental gesture which had made them both laugh, as well as the couple sitting close by.

There was no flower on the table today, just a solitary squashed chip left over from somebody else's lunch.

He drank his beer and when his food arrived he found he wasn't hungry. He managed to force a mouthful of boiled potato down but gave up after a feeling of nausea spread over him.

Eating wasn't going to solve his problem. Nor was drinking. He looked reproachfully at the almost empty glass in his hand. He'd already been down that particular road when Melissa had left him. It hadn't worked then. It wouldn't work now.

So what was the answer?

Go home and talk to Kate?

But what good would that do? Talking would only lead to one of them compromising. And again, what good would that do?

If it was he who compromised there was a danger he would always hold it against Kate, that the slightest disagreement between them would be blown out of proportion because he would feel he'd conceded so much to her already.

And if it was she who compromised – could he really expect her to have an abortion? – then he would never be able to look her in the eye again for fear of seeing the most profound bitter regret in her face. And worse would come – her bitterness would turn to pure hatred for what he'd made her do.

Either way, they couldn't win.

He drained his beer, pushed his uneaten lunch away and made himself accept that because of his selfish love for Kate he had almost certainly lost her. There could be no hope for their relationship now.

*

Caroline was full of fighting talk. 'The bastard! How dare he say that to you? It's he who's used you.'

'Caroline,' hissed Kate, 'keep your voice down, people are looking.'

'Let them,' Caroline said even louder, staring defiantly round at the faces now glancing their way. 'Let them know what a pig he's been.'

'Caroline, if you don't shut up I'll walk out of here.'

Caroline stared at her friend, mystified. 'Well I must say, you seem to be taking this very calmly. Don't you feel angry at the way he's treating you?'

'I'm too confused and upset to feel angry,' Kate said. 'Now please, can we order what we're going to eat and talk rationally.'

When Tony had left her that morning – having made sure that she was over the worst of the tears – she had phoned Caroline to see if she was free for lunch. She had been in luck: Caroline was enjoying a few days off work. The really good thing about her friendship with Caroline was that she never failed to focus Kate's thoughts and make her feel level-headed, and as she'd driven to the wine bar in Knutsford to meet her she had known that within minutes of listening to her friend's over-the-top reaction to her news she would feel composed and empowered.

A good-looking waiter came and took their order, and when he walked away, after Caroline had tried a bit of small talk with him, she said, 'Now, Kate, he's much more what you should have gone after, not some old duffer who's not prepared to take on his responsibilities.'

Kate frowned. 'Alec is not an old duffer, Caroline, how many times do I have to tell you, he's only forty-nine?'

Caroline snorted. 'Whatever you say. So what are you going to do?'

'I think that depends on what Alec is going to do.'

'Well, as to that, I think you'll find he's had his bit of fun, now he'll be off. Mark my words, he'll have you out of that house before you've had your first antenatal appointment. He'll have some kind of legal document drawn up, stating he knows he's the father and here's the dosh for the next X years, then it'll be a case of it's been nice knowing you, ta ta.'

'He might change his mind,' Kate said, ignoring her friend's damning indictment of Alec, and determined to give him the benefit of the doubt she added, 'Tony says lots of men over-react when they hear they're going to be a father.'

Caroline looked up, interested. 'Who's Tony?'

'He's a neighbour and he . . .'

'And he what?'

'He came over this morning when I was doing my hysterical bit. He was very kind.'

'Was he indeed?' smirked Caroline.

'Don't be ridiculous,' said Kate, but despite herself she couldn't prevent her face from colouring as she thought of Tony. She recalled his hand on hers and the way he'd comforted her. When he'd started talking about his problems she had felt so sorry for him that for a few minutes she had forgotten her own worries and had been concerned only for a man who in the midst of his troubles had shown her such kindness. It was strange that without having acknowledged it to herself she had known all along that Tony wasn't happy with Amanda. Or maybe it wasn't strange; after all, Amanda wasn't a particularly lovable person. There was a coldness to her that was at odds with Tony's naturally warm personality. Perhaps anybody who got to know Tony and Amanda as a couple would quickly realise that he couldn't possibly have married her for love. Equally so, she suspected, they would guess that Amanda's readiness to marry Tony had also had very little to do with love.

'So what's he like?' asked Caroline.

Kate smiled. 'You're impossible, you really are.'

'Answer the question. I want to know what kind of men you're keeping in with. Tell me all.'

'There's nothing to tell.'

'Not much, there isn't. You've gone the colour of my nail varnish.'

Kate gave in. 'He's quite tall.'

'How tall?'

'Five foot ten-ish.'

'Hair?'

'Yes.'

'Don't get clever. What colour?'

'Fair-ish.'

'Eyes?'

'Blue-ish.'

'Age?'

'Mid-thirties-ish.'

'And I suppose if I were to ask what kind of car he drove you'd say it was fast-ish. Are you being deliberately vague?'

Kate smiled. 'He drives a Porsche and it's silvery grey –'

'Don't tell me,' interrupted Caroline, 'it's silvery grey-*ish*.'

They both laughed.

'Well, with or without the babe-catching machine he sounds distinctly eligible. How would he feel about taking on somebody else's child?'

'He's married and has one of his own. So end of story.'

'There's always something to spoil it, isn't there? Oh, good, here's lunch.'

After the waiter had left them alone again, Kate said, 'Caroline, I want to talk seriously with you now.'

'Do you have to? I was just beginning to enjoy myself.'

'I want to ask a favour of you. If Alec . . . if I do have to move out, can I come and stay with you, just until I've got myself sorted?'

Caroline inwardly groaned. The picture of her lovely little house messed up with crate-loads of Pampers and sicked-on Babygros did not appeal, but realising that her attitude was sympathising with the enemy – namely Alec – she said cheerfully, 'Of course you can, so long as we have an understanding; if I'm lucky enough to bring a man back to the house you're to keep out of sight, one look at you and they won't be interested in me. Hey, you're not about to start blubbing, are you?'

Kate swallowed and blinked away the threat of tears. 'I'm just really grateful, that's all. It probably won't come to it. Alec and I will sort everything out, but if I do need a place to go to, it's nice to know there is one.' And, keen to change the subject, she said, 'Tell me how the dating's going.'

Caroline knew that she was one of the least sensitive people around – she knew this because Kate was always quick to tell her that it was the case – but today she could see only too clearly that Kate needed her to distract her and she was more than ready to comply with her friend's wishes. 'You won't believe some of the dorks I've met,' she said. 'It beggars belief that there are so many weirdos out there. There was this one guy who wittered on for hours about his collection of purple ceramic dragons. Well, it would have been for hours if I hadn't pretended to feel violently ill and excused myself. There was one guy who kept going on about all his previous girl-friends. And there was another who was a Buddy Holly freak; he turned up in a fifties suit with those hideous specs and asked if I minded being called Peggy Sue for the evening. I just did a runner, straight out the door, down the high street and to my car. I went home and drooled over my George Clooney scrapbook with a cup of hot chocolate. It's a nightmare, a total nightmare. They sound sane enough on the phone, but believe me they all turn out as dorky as Woody Allen and with twice as many hang-ups.'

'But you must have met at least one decent man,' said Kate.

'If I did, I must have missed him among all the dross.'

They carried on eating for a while, then Kate said in a low voice, 'I've a confession to make.'

'You do fancy that Tony guy? I knew it!'

'I wish I'd never mentioned him now,' Kate said crossly. 'I was going to tell you that it was through an agency that I met Alec.'

Caroline lowered her knife and fork and stared at Kate, then gradually a small, wry smile appeared on her lips. 'Well,' she said, raising her glass of wine, 'I rest my case, m'lud, not a decent man among the lot of them.'

It was late afternoon when Kate drove through the archway of Cholmford Hall Mews. The first thing she saw was Alec's car parked outside the house. She was tempted to reverse straight back out through the arch, but several hours of being in Caroline's company had prepared her for the inevitable confrontation with Alec. 'I will not fall apart,' she told herself firmly as she parked alongside his Saab. 'I am in control of the situation,' she went on, as she locked her car door, 'I will hold my ground.'

She let herself into the house.

He was in the study, bent over his desk, flicking through some letters he must have brought home with him from work. He turned round when she entered the room.

'I think we should get this over with,' she said, her hands gripping her keys behind her back.

'You're right,' he said. He followed her through to the kitchen.

Why was it that so many of life's big decisions were made in the kitchen? Kate wondered as they stood facing each other, the table between them acting like a barrier. So this is it, she thought. This is really it. This is when I make my choice and stand by it. She marvelled at how calm she felt. I've aged about ten years today, she reflected.

All his emotions petrified, Alec stared down at his shoes. He was waiting for Kate to speak. He didn't think he had the courage to go first. But when she didn't say anything he slowly raised his eyes. Not directly at her, but to the window, then to the fridge where Kate had stuck one of Oscar's paintings – it was a picture of him and Kate holding hands, beneath their feet was a thin green strip of grass and above their heads a wobbly stripe of blue sky, and written in pencil in Oscar's four-and-a-half-year-old shaky handwriting were the words, *Grampa Alec and Kate.*

'I'm sorry,' he blurted out, unable to take the silence a moment longer. But still he didn't look at her. He kept his eyes on Oscar's picture – Kate with her impossibly long, matchstick-thin legs and he with a round barrel of a stomach and tiny stumps for legs. 'I'm sorry,' he repeated.

'What are you sorry for, Alec?' she said.

He tore his gaze away from Oscar's artwork and looked at her. The late afternoon sun was pouring in through the window and her hair was glowing a vibrant shade of golden chestnut. It was tied up with a silk scarf he didn't recognise and the colours in the fabric brought out the exquisite shade of green in her eyes – large, sad eyes that were fixed on him. He thought he'd never seen her look more beautiful. And as he thought this, the awful strain and horror of the day suddenly lifted from him and he knew what he had to do.

He went to her, wrapped her in his arms, needing to undo all the harm he'd done – desperate for her forgiveness. 'Oh, Kate,' he whispered, 'I didn't mean what I said this morning. It was the shock. Just give me time to adjust and I promise everything will be all right. I promise.'

Chapter Thirty-Three

By Monday evening Josh was feeling a lot better. The burning sensation that had plagued him for most of the previous week had gradually receded over the weekend and other than coping with the usual stiffness in his leg he had felt relatively normal today.

He'd gone in to work for a couple of hours that morning and, after making his peace with Charlie and sorting out a few things that had been left pending since Thursday, he'd come home after lunch with his briefcase stuffed full of faxes to deal with, from their suppliers in Hong Kong. He'd decided – before Charlie had had a chance to suggest it – to take things easy on his first day back.

He'd spent most of the weekend taking it easy. In fact, he'd slept through the best part of it, finding it difficult to stay awake for much of the time. He hated to admit it, but maybe in the future he ought to take more notice of his body. Perhaps if he hadn't struggled on trying to ignore the pain in his legs last week he wouldn't have ended up so exhausted . . . or head-butting his desk. He was now fully convinced that what he'd experienced in his office on Thursday afternoon hadn't been the start of him suffering from black-outs, but had been a one-off case of him collapsing through exhaustion. His body had simply had enough.

The only disturbance to his weekend of recovery was a call on Saturday morning from his mother – he suspected that Charlie had been at work in the background and had prompted her to ring him.

'Everything all right for Sunday lunch next week?' she'd asked. 'You'll be able to make it, won't you?' He had heard the tense wariness in her voice, knowing that she was torn between wanting to rush over and make sure he was all right – but knowing that it would be the last thing he'd want – and pretending that she knew nothing of his latest MS attack.

'Yes, as far as I can tell,' he'd replied, feeling genuinely sorry for her. Ever since he had lost his temper with his mother, the day after he'd been diagnosed as having multiple sclerosis and when he'd felt smothered by everyone's concern, she had been wary of him. She had been so hurt by his lashing out at her that she had never wanted to repeat the episode and had tiptoed round him, scared of saying the wrong thing. He kept meaning to talk to her about it, but somehow the right moment had never presented itself.

Their conversation hadn't lasted long. But using as much tact as she could, she had asked him how he was and in a by-the-way tone of voice had added that Charlie had spoken to her, and in order to circumvent the painful process of her drawing out the grisly details from him he'd said, 'I'm fine, Mum, please don't worry. I'll see you next week. I'll be there as usual.'

As he'd put down the phone he'd made himself promise to find time to speak to his mother, to talk to her properly.

Now as he finished dealing with the last of the faxes that he'd brought home with him he took off his glasses and sat back in his chair. He gazed across the courtyard, through the sash window of his study, and wondered if now was the right time to stop hiding from Jessica and talk to her. He didn't hold out much hope that she'd want to say very much to him, though. It was ages since they'd last spoken – it was when she'd called him and he'd been feeling rotten, and the resulting conversation had been as lively and interesting as a party political broadcast. No wonder she hadn't bothered to ring him again.

He turned away from the window and looked at the bookshelf to the left of his desk. There, in pride of place between a framed photograph of him and Charlie on the slopes at Val d'Isère and another of the pair of them up at Victoria Peak in Hong Kong, were copies of Jessica's books. He'd read them both and much to his surprise – he'd never read a romantic comedy in his life before – had laughed out loud. Her style of writing was incisive, pacey and sardonic – just as she was herself – and he was conscious that given his behaviour towards her of late, she could make short work of him if she so chose. God knows, she was entitled.

He returned his attention to looking out of the window and twirling his glasses round in his hand, and thinking just how much he'd missed Jessica's company he caught sight of her in the room directly opposite. She had just walked into her study.

Without giving himself time to change his mind he leaned forwards, picked up the phone and dialled her number from the piece of paper he had propped against the halogen desk lamp – a piece of paper that had stared reproachfully at him for nearly two weeks now.

He watched her pick up her phone. 'Hi,' he said, 'it's Josh.'

There was a pause, then the sound of her voice. 'Mm . . . now let me see, would that be Josh Reynolds the painter chappie, or that other well-known Josh, the man who led the Israelites to the Promised Land?'

'Neither. It's Josh the pain in the bum who hasn't spoken to you for . . . for quite a while.'

'Oh, that one. Well I have a sketchy picture of him in my mind, but you'll have to help me out, he's little more than a vague memory these days.'

'If you look out of your window you might catch a glimpse of something that could help.'

There was a slight pause. 'Good heavens, there's a mad man out there waving back at me. Fancy that. But hang on, I think you're right, there is something familiar about him. It's beginning to come to me now.'

'How are you, Jessica? I've missed you.'

'Have you?'

'Yes.'

'Really?'

'Really.'

'Like hell you have!'

'But it's true, I have.'

'So why haven't you been in touch?'

'I've been busy.'

'Crawford, save me the bull. Get off the phone and get your butt over here and make your apologies in person.'

'I . . . I can't.'

'Why not?'

'Because . . . because I'm just getting over flu.' Oh hell! He was off again. More lies.

'Why didn't you let me know you'd been ill? I could have come over and made broth, and mopped your brow for you and stood prettily at the end of your bed.'

'Nice idea, but I'm afraid I make a lousy patient.'

'Believe me, most men make lousy patients. So why are you ringing me?'

'I'd like to see you.'

'I'm not sure I want to see you.'

'Jessica, I said I'm sorry. I've been busy, work's been crazy –'

'And don't forget how ill you've been with the flu.'

'Can I see you tomorrow evening?'

'You sure you'll be well enough?'

'I'll make sure I am.'

'Okay. Be here for half past seven. And Crawford –'

'Yes?'

'No excuses this time, okay?'

'As if.'

Josh spent most of Tuesday praying that he'd make it through the day. If something went wrong with him and he didn't get to Jessica's that evening she was never going to believe another word he said.

And as it was the truth he wanted to speak tonight, it was important that nothing prevented him from seeing her.

Speaking to Jessica on the phone yesterday evening, it couldn't have been further from his mind to own up to her about his MS. When she'd suggested he call on her there and then, he'd suddenly lost his nerve and had been terrified that he might get half-way across the courtyard and keel over. So rather than take the risk, he'd backed out and given her some crap about recovering from flu.

How pathetic.

And how cowardly.

It was after he'd put down the phone and he'd made himself some supper that he'd known that he couldn't go on as he was. It was time to come clean with Jessica. He would rather she knew the truth about him than have her condemn him as a complete shyster.

At half past five he gathered up his things and switched off the lights in his office. Out in the reception area Mo was chatting to Charlie. When she saw Josh she handed him a small card. It was an invitation.

'It's my birthday on Friday, I'm having a party, will you come?'

'Of course he will,' Charlie said.

'I'm not sure,' Josh said hesitantly.

'Oh, please,' said Mo. Reluctantly she added, 'You can bring Jessica if you want. Charlie's going to try and persuade Rachel to come.'

'I'll think about it.'

'You're an ungracious bugger,' Charlie said as he and Josh walked to their cars. 'You could have just said yes to Mo.'

'I don't like making promises I might not be able to keep.'

Charlie let it go. He was tired of reasoning with his brother. 'Doing anything tonight?'

'Yes. I'm seeing Jessica. I'm . . . I'm going to tell her.'

Charlie came to a stop. 'About your MS?'

Josh nodded.

Charlie wasn't sure what to say. If he said anything glib like: 'It'll be fine, don't worry,' it would be an insult to Josh's intelligence. And though he himself had urged his brother on many occasions to be honest with Jessica, he didn't for one minute underestimate the risk Josh was taking. His last girl-friend's sudden departure from his life was proof enough that love didn't always conquer all.

'Good luck,' was all he could think to say. 'Give me a ring if . . . well, you know.'

'What, if things don't turn out well?'

However Josh had thought the evening might turn out, he couldn't have predicated the way it did.

He called on Jessica, spot on seven thirty as she'd instructed, but when she didn't let him into the house as he'd expected, his plan of quietly explaining things to her immediately went on hold.

She led him towards her car and said, 'Get in and don't argue. It's time for you to loosen up. You're going to sit for two whole hours in my company whether you want to or not, and what's more, you're going to do it in the dark and you're going to laugh. I might even let you have some popcorn if you're good.'

The film was billed as a knockabout comedy with Steve Martin playing a love-struck oil tycoon.

'This really isn't my kind of thing,' Josh said petulantly as they took up their seats in the crowded cinema.

'Yeah, I know, this is far too unsophisticated for you, isn't it. But then, that's your trouble, you've let yourself go. You're old before your time and have forgotten how to enjoy yourself. Now, why don't you sit back and let the child within come out to play?'

'I'd rather be an adult at home playing with you.'

'Ssh! The film's about to start. Have some popcorn. And don't look like that, sulking won't get you anywhere with me.'

When the credits began to roll at the end of the film, to the sound of Aretha Franklin singing 'What Now My Love', they joined the stream of people queuing for the exit and left the cinema. It was dark outside and soft rain was beginning to fall.

Jessica unlocked the car and they climbed in. 'Well,' she said, 'it wasn't such a bad film, was it? I distinctly heard you laughing back there.'

'I was laughing to please you,' he conceded.

She threw him a look and for the first time noticed the cut to his temple. 'You've hurt yourself,' she said. 'How did you do that?'

He hesitated. Was this the opening he needed? Was this the

perfectly timed moment for him to tell her the truth? That he suffered from MS and it had got the better of him last week at work. 'It's nothing,' he said, turning away from her, 'nothing at all.'

Jessica started up the engine, drove out of the car-park and, as she waited for the traffic lights on the main road to change, she said, 'Josh?'

'Yes?'

'I don't believe you.'

'What don't you believe?'

'That you would want to please me.'

There was an awkward pause between them.

'Well, you're wrong,' Josh said at last. 'Nothing would give me more pleasure than to please you, only –'

'*But* alert! *But* alert!' Jessica said, shifting into first gear and moving off. 'As clear as daylight I sense one looming large on the horizon.'

He frowned and reached out and gently stroked her neck, just in the bit where he knew she liked it. 'The *but* is I don't think I'm up to the task.'

'And if that isn't the sound of a man back-pedalling his way out of a relationship I don't know what is. You'd better take your hand away or we'll smash into the car in front.'

Josh did as she said and decided to wait until they were home before telling her what he had to say. He wanted to be able to see her face when she realised the truth about him, to read her expression. It was crucial.

When they finally drew up alongside her house, Jessica snatched on the handbrake and switched off the engine. Without looking at him and keeping her eyes straight ahead she suddenly said, 'Is there somebody else? Because if there is, do us both a favour and tell me. All I want to know is where I stand. I don't think I'm being unreasonable.'

Oh hell! she thought, I'm sounding like a paranoid middle-aged wife. Any minute and I'll be telling him to consider the children and the effect it will have on them. But much as she disliked the sound of the words coming out of her mouth, she knew that now that she had started, in true *Mastermind* fashion, she was going to bloody well finish and have her say. He was going to get the full force of her anger for the way he'd treated her. In fact, he was probably going to get Gavin's share as well!

'If there is somebody else I think I have the right to be told,' she went on. 'One minute you're there in my life and the next you're not.

I'm not a possessive woman, I just don't like being mucked about. I had enough of that with Gavin and I'm not about to start accepting that kind of situation all over again. And of course, if it's the perennial problem of a man being scared of commitment, then –'

'I'm not scared of commitment,' he interrupted her, magically stemming the flow of her anger, 'at least not in the way you mean.' She felt a hand on her shoulder and he slowly turned her round. 'And there's no one else,' he said firmly. 'I'm appalled that you should think there is. Now be quiet long enough for me to kiss you. And when I've done that, can we go inside? There's something I want to discuss with you.'

She swallowed back her relief. *There wasn't anybody else! Oh, thank you, God!*

'So what do you want to talk about? Devolution? Unification? Or global warming?'

Oh, heaven help her, she was rambling again. What was it about him tonight that was making her so nervous?

He shook his head. 'Nothing as trivial as that.'

Another swallow. 'Oh. Something serious then? In that case it must be the escalating cost of the Millennium Dome.'

'More serious than that.'

'Come off it, nothing's more serious than the greatest white elephant this side of Lord Irvine's pad. Not unless you . . . but surely you can't mean the Charles and Camilla conundrum. We're not going to discuss that, are we?'

Somebody stop me!

'For pity's sake, Jessica, shut up.' He silenced her with a long kiss. 'Now please, can we go inside before I lose my nerve?'

Chapter Thirty-Four

The house was in darkness as Jessica unlocked the front door and let them in.

'*What now my love,*' she sang happily, à la Ms Franklin – there was nothing like a good kiss to calm the nerves. She switched on the hall light. '*Now that you've left me –*'

'Please don't sing that,' Josh said abruptly.

'Why?' She laughed. 'Don't you like my singing?'

He followed her into the half-decorated kitchen and watched her throw her bag and keys on to the table. 'It's not that,' he said.

She came towards him and put her arms around his shoulders. 'What, then?'

'It's the lyrics, they're too sentimental . . . too melancholic.' They were also too close for comfort. Particularly the lines that came next – *How can I live through another day watching my dreams turning into ashes and all of my hopes into bits of clay* – and with what he was about to say to Jessica and her possible reaction, these were sentiments he didn't want to hear.

She smiled. 'There's nothing wrong with a good dose of schmaltzy melancholy, it's good for the heart.'

He didn't return her smile and as he stared down into her eyes Jessica was shocked to realise how changed he was since she'd last seen him. The youthful, handsome face that had come to be so familiar to her was gone and in its place was the expression of a deeply troubled man. He looked pale. His eyes were sad and sombre, and conveyed an impression of intense dread within him, and as her body rested against his she sensed that he was tense and unyielding. 'What did you want to talk to me about?' she asked nervously, suddenly concluding that the change that had come over him had to be connected with what he wanted to discuss with her. Immediately she'd reached this conclusion her mind began stacking up a set of possible explanations for his apprehension – he had lied earlier in the car about not seeing anyone else, or worse . . .

But what could be worse?

What terrible revelation did he have to throw at her that was causing him so much consternation? Come off it, his face didn't so much betray consternation as downright fear.

Oh, my grandfathers, she thought. What was the current nightmare for anyone not in a long-term relationship? What was the spectre at the feast when it came to sex these days?

She slowly released herself from his arms and stepped away from him. No wonder he'd been absent from her life recently. He'd probably been ill . . . and not with flu. 'You've got AIDS, haven't you?'

A mixture of horror and incredulous disbelief swept over Josh's face, but before he had a chance to speak the phone rang. It made them both jump.

'I'm letting it ring until you answer me,' Jessica whispered. She was motionless with shock. Rigid with fear. *If he had AIDS then so might she.* Above the insistent shrill of the phone she racked her brain, trying to think if they'd ever had unprotected sex. But they'd always been careful. Even the first time they'd made love, when Josh had been unprepared for the way the night had turned out, she had managed to produce a remnant of her old love life. They had joked about it and pretended to blow the dust away from the small packet. 'Well?' she demanded of him. 'What have you got to say?'

'Please, Jessica, stop being so dramatic and just answer the bloody phone.'

'No! Not until you've told me the truth.'

He shook his head, and went over and picked up the receiver. A few seconds passed before he put it down. 'Jessica,' he said, his face even more anxious than it had been before. 'It's your mother, she's had an accident.'

'Not serious!' Jessica roared at Josh as he sat in the passenger seat of her car once more. 'How the bloody hell do you know it's not serious?'

'Because she said so,' he said calmly. 'She said that she was okay and that you weren't to worry or think the worst.' When he'd answered the phone in Jessica's kitchen, Josh had been surprised to hear a faint voice at the other end of the line saying, 'I've no idea to whom I'm speaking, but don't whatever you do put Jessica on. Just tell her that her mother has had a slight accident and if she'd like to pop over, I'm at home. Be sure to explain that I'm okay and that it's nothing serious.'

He could see now why Jessica's mother had specifically asked not to speak to her daughter. Frantic with worry, Jessica had just rocketed her car through the archway of the development and with her foot jammed down on the accelerator they were speeding along the avenue of chestnut trees.

It was raining harder than when they'd driven back from the cinema and Josh watched her fumble for the switch for the windscreen wipers. 'Some lights might be a good idea,' he suggested.

Jessica flashed him a look of fury. 'Nothing to worry about, my foot,' she muttered while flicking on the headlights. 'Let me tell you, my mother was taken into hospital for what she said was a routine operation and that there was nothing for me to worry about. When I arrived at the hospital I discovered that she was having a triple heart bypass operation. I've since learnt to ignore anything she says.'

'Perhaps you shouldn't. Perhaps it isn't fair to treat her like Cassandra.'

'Like who?'

'Cassandra, the Greek prophetess who was cursed never to be believed.'

'I don't believe I'm hearing this. My mother could well be dying and you're giving me a lecture on Greek mythology? She's my concern, so if I want to worry about her, I bloody well will.'

'Fine, if that's the way you want it.'

'I do. It's exactly how I want it.'

'And by the way, I don't have AIDS, so you needn't worry about that as well. I haven't infected you with anything.'

'Right now I couldn't give a damn whether you have or not,' she fired back. 'All I care about is what in heaven's name my mother's done to herself.' She gripped the steering wheel knowing that she was behaving atrociously, that Josh didn't deserve this, but so long as she was able to take out her anger on somebody it meant that she was just about in control of the situation.

She pulled up in front of Willow Cottage and before Josh had even climbed out of the car was letting herself into the house with the key that she'd insisted Anna give her some weeks ago. She called out to her mother.

'I'm up here,' came a faint reply.

Jessica took the stairs two at a time.

She found Anna on the floor in her bedroom. A pair of step-ladders and the contents of an upturned box of tools lay all around her, as well as the phone from the bedside table.

'I'm sorry, Jessica, but I'm afraid I've broken it.' Her mother nodded towards a decapitated china statue that Jessica had given her when she was a child, the head of which had rolled across the room and now lay with its nose tucked into the carpet pile in front of the dressing-table. 'I caught it with my foot on the window-sill,' Anna added, as though this made everything clear. 'I think I may also have broken my arm,' she said as Jessica crouched beside her, 'and my ribs don't feel so good. Oh, you must be Josh.'

Josh came into the room. 'Hi,' he said with an easy smile and, joining them on the floor, he started to pick up the scattered tools, 'you look like you've been busy.'

'I do my best,' Anna said. She returned his smile and passed him a screwdriver that was clutched in her hand.

'Any chance of making it to the bed?'

'Well you're a fast one, I must say. But I'm not sure Jessica would approve. She looks furious as it is.'

'Of course I'm furious,' exploded Jessica, her anxiety now given rein to turn into full-blown angry relief. 'How many times have I told you to be careful? How could you do this!'

Anna smiled at Josh. 'How long do you give her before she says I told you so?'

'And I'd have every right to say that. This is serious, Mum, you could have killed yourself.'

'What, and missed the opportunity to meet this delightful young man?' Anna said with a wink at Josh. 'No fear.'

Jessica looked even more enraged and opened her mouth to remonstrate further, but Josh intervened. 'Jessica,' he said firmly, 'this isn't helping. Now, Mrs Lloyd, do you think you can manage the stairs? From what I can see of your wrist it most certainly is broken and I think we should drive you straight to a hospital.'

Tony was in no mood to speak to Bloody Rita. He didn't make any effort to be polite to her, but handed the phone over to Amanda and went upstairs for a shower. He'd had a tedious day that had got him nowhere. Bradley-Dewhurst-the-Butcher's-Boy had set up a tele-conference late in the afternoon and it had served no purpose other than to delay everybody from getting off home.

On his way to the bathroom he hovered outside Hattie's door. He pushed it open a crack, just to see if she was asleep.

'Is that you, Daddy?'

He smiled and went in. 'Come on, you little pixie, you should have been fast asleep hours ago.'

'I can't get to sleep.'

He smoothed out the rumpled duvet, then sat on the edge of the bed. 'And why's that?' He was instantly worried that maybe her new school was bothering her. He knew that Hattie was by nature a confident child, but it was a dangerous thing to overestimate her ability to accept change. It seemed pretty unlikely, however, that there was anything wrong at school as only yesterday her teacher had told Amanda how well Hattie was fitting in.

'You're not worried about anything, are you?' he asked.

She nodded.

He stroked her hair. 'Is it school?'

She shook her head.

'What, then?'

She pulled him down to her and whispered into his ear, 'It's Grandma Rita.'

'What about Grandma Rita?' he whispered back.

'Amanda says she might be coming to stay with us.'

Tony sat upright. 'That's news to me,' he said.

'Amanda said you wouldn't mind.'

'And when did Amanda discuss this with you?'

'In the car coming home from school. She said it was a surprise, though. It's not a very nice surprise, is it?'

Tony smiled.

'Does she have to come?'

'We'll see. Now off to sleep with you.' He kissed her forehead, then squeezed her hand.

'You won't tell Amanda I said anything, will you? I think she might be cross with me.'

'Of course not. Now go to sleep.'

He was almost out of the room when she sat up and said, 'Daddy, what's a boarding-school?'

He frowned and came back to the bed. 'What do you mean?'

'I heard Amanda talking to Grandma Rita on the phone about something called a boarding-school.'

'Did you indeed?'

'Would I like it?'

He shook his head. 'No,' he said grimly, 'no, you wouldn't. And nor would I.'

'Amanda told Grandma Rita that it would be best for me.'

'Well, she's wrong. Very, very wrong.'

'So what is a boarding-school?'

'It's not something you ever need to think about. Now, it really is time for you to go to sleep. Good-night.' He kissed her again and wondered at the ruthlessness of his wife, that she could plot and scheme about his daughter's future behind his back.

Later, when Tony came out of the shower, he found Amanda in their bedroom sorting through a large plastic laundry basket of ironing. She was a meticulous ironer, everything was steamed and pressed, even his socks. 'How's your mother?' he fished.

'Fine. She sends her love.'

Like hell she does! Bloody Rita would no more send him her love than she would dance naked through the streets of Alderley Edge where she lived. 'That's nice of her,' he said, totally convinced that Hattie must have been right and that Amanda was now switching on to 'softening-up mode' before announcing that Rita was coming to stay. 'We haven't seen her for a while,' he added, 'what's she been up to?' – *something sweet and innocent like evenings out with the Ku-Klux-Klan?*

'Oh, just the usual; bridge and bowling. The bowling club's hoping to go off on tour again.'

'Sounds good.' *Especially if it were a six-month tour of Australia! The further away the better.*

He didn't trust himself to cross-examine Amanda about the boarding-school issue and so got into bed. Well, she could forget that little scheme. He would never allow it to happen.

He closed his eyes and listened to Amanda moving about the room, tidying away clothes into cupboards and drawers. He wondered what Kate was doing. He had no way of knowing what had happened to her since he'd seen her yesterday morning. He didn't know whether she and Alec had resolved things between them, or if Alec was still refusing to accept his child. He hadn't mentioned any of this to Amanda – the thought of her gossiping about Kate was too much for him. He hoped, though, that if Kate needed any help she would feel able to come to him. He'd given her his work number, just in case, and throughout today he had stupidly hoped it was her each time his phone had rung. What kind of help he thought he'd be able to give he wasn't sure. Possibly what he wanted to offer Kate would only complicate matters.

And what exactly was he offering?

He was a married man with a child; the sort of man who would never have imagined himself capable of cheating on his wife. But that was exactly what he'd planned to do, wasn't it? When he'd gone to see Kate yesterday morning he had knocked on her door with the sole expectation of tempting her into an affair with him.

And given half a chance he still would.

He turned on to his side and pulled the duvet up over his head. He wanted the world to disappear.

No, that wasn't true.

He just wanted Amanda and Alec to disappear.

Chapter Thirty-Five

A Casual Affair was getting nowhere – Clare and Miles had spent the past week locked in one another's arms and as passionate embraces went, theirs was proving to be the longest in history.

Following Anna's accident on Tuesday night, Jessica had moved into Willow Cottage to look after her mother. She had brought Clare and Miles along with her on her laptop, but much as she cared about their will-they-won't-they relationship, she had found she didn't have a spare minute to devote to them, or if she were honest, the inclination. Her heart just wasn't in it. She was too preoccupied with her mother.

She had thought that Anna's wilfulness would be dramatically reduced by having an arm in a sling, but if anything, the plaster cast was proving a challenge to her obstinate mother – she had even threatened Jessica with it.

'Ask me one more time if I'm comfortable, Jessica, and I shall bring this wretched cast down on your head.'

It wasn't an easy situation, but as Jessica prodded another log into place in the grate with a pair of old brass tongs, she knew that it was down to her to make her mother see sense and keep her from straying from the safe confines of her armchair by the fire.

She put down the tongs and glanced out of the window. The weather, she reflected, was as jittery as she was. Yesterday had been clear and bright, with a warm September sun drying away the early-morning dew and mist, but today a north-easterly wind had chilled the air and there was no sign of the sun as it hid behind the thick banks of grey clouds that threw down the occasional downpour. It was a cold, wet, miserable day. It felt more like winter than autumn and just before lunch Jessica had lit the fire in the sitting-room and insisted Anna sit beside it. But Anna hadn't wanted to and had accused Jessica of treating her like a child. 'That's because you're behaving like one,' Jessica had retorted, 'now please, do as I say.'

Jessica moved away from the fire. She sat in the chair opposite her mother and began pouring out their tea.

It was Friday afternoon and so far they'd been cooped up together at Willow Cottage for three whole days. Jessica didn't know how much longer she could cope. She was exhausted and irritable with worry. The thought that Anna's accident could have ended so differently was never far from her mind. But it hadn't been fatal, she had to keep reminding herself; a broken arm and a cracked rib weren't life-threatening; her mother would be all right. She leant forward and placed a cup of tea on the little table beside her mother's chair.

Anna put down the magazine Jessica had bought for her, which she wasn't really reading, and added it to the pile that had been thoughtfully placed within arm's reach. 'Thank you,' she said, wishing that she actually meant the words. She felt as grateful to Jessica as a blind man would if somebody had helpfully switched on the light for him. She really didn't know how much more of her daughter she could put up with.

What she regretted most about her little mishap – which had happened while she had been trying to fix a window lock in her bedroom – was that it had brought out the worst in both herself and Jessica. In her desire to help, Jessica had turned into a monstrous gaoler and she herself had become a dispirited prisoner with only one aim in her life: to escape.

She raised her cup to her lips, stared across the mahogany table in front of the fire and looked at her daughter's unhappy face. She looked ragged and worn-out. Clearly the situation was doing neither of them any good. They resembled a middle-aged couple who'd been together for a thousand years and now had nothing to say to one another. You saw them all the time, glum-faced people mindlessly stirring cups of over-brewed tea in British Home Stores restaurants all over the country.

Something had to be done.

And soon.

'You know, I'm beginning to feel much better,' Anna said brightly. The immediate look of scorn on Jessica's face silenced her from trying her luck with suggesting that she could now manage on her own and wasn't it time Jessica went back to her own home?

She stared forlornly out of the window at her deserted garden. How she longed to roll up her sleeves and get her hands dirty. It was most frustrating, especially when there was so much to do. Plums were dropping like manna from heaven from the fruit trees; the stakes and ties for the dahlias needed checking in case the wind got up; the roses were in need of deadheading and it was more than two weeks since she'd last sprayed them for mildew, and goodness only knew what the greenfly were up to while her back was turned. And there were all those dwarf daffodil and tulip bulbs waiting to be planted in the rockery she'd built earlier in the summer. Dermot was all very well, and the lad did his best, but it was her garden and nobody loved it as she did.

If only Jessica were green-fingered, at least then there might have been a chance of her putting something of her over-zealous caring energy into looking after the garden instead of plaguing her.

No, that wasn't fair, she thought, Jessica was only doing what she thought was best.

'Are you sure you shouldn't be working?' Anna tried again – the prisoner had her eye on the imaginary set of keys dangling from her gaoler's belt.

Jessica lowered her cup and looked at her mother. 'You're more important,' she said simply.

The keys were once again moved out of the prisoner's grasp.

'But what about your deadline? You know how much you worry about delivering a manuscript on time.' Desperate now, the prisoner was considering a swift blow to the gaoler's Achilles heel – Jessica's obsession with meeting her publisher's deadline.

'That's not for ages, not until next year, and anyway I can give Piers and Cara a ring, they'll understand.'

Anna frowned, then a tiny idea took hold. An idea that made her realise that she had hit upon a means of tunnelling her way out of her prison cell . . . and all she would need was a sneaky peep at Jessica's address book. But how could she get Jessica out of the way long enough to do that?

Her question was answered sooner than she'd thought possible when the sound of the doorbell broke the dreadful silence that had cloaked the house since her well-meaning daughter had moved in.

Jessica put down her cup and quickly went to answer it. Anna listened to find out who it was – if only it could be a passing member of the SAS expertly trained in dealing with hostage situations. It was a few seconds before she recognised the voice: Josh. A smile spread over her face. Her immediate thought was to leap out of her chair and invite him in, thereby providing a distraction so that she could slip upstairs to Jessica's room and snoop through her things for the precious address book. But she knew it was more than her life was worth even to move from the chair and anyway, if she were painfully honest, the only leaping she was capable of doing was a leap of the imagination.

'If that's Josh, don't keep him on the doorstep, bring him in,' she called out to Jessica. 'It'll be nice to have a visitor' – *yes, it would break the suffocating monotony.*

'Hello, Mrs Lloyd,' Josh said when Jessica brought him into the sitting-room. He held out a pot of white chrysanthemums. 'I saw these on the way home from work and thought you might like them. How are you feeling?'

'Please, you must call me Anna, and I'm feeling much better, thank you.'

Jessica tutted loudly and took the flowers from Josh. She placed them on the oak dresser, alongside the half-eaten box of Thornton's Continental chocolates that Josh had brought earlier in the week. 'She'd be a darn sight better if she kept still for two minutes,' she scolded.

Anna winked at Josh and he smiled back at her.

'Jessica, why don't you make a fresh pot of tea? I'm sure Josh must be thirsty.'

Jessica looked at Josh, her expression clearly indicating that she expected him to refuse any such hospitality.

'That would be great,' he said.

Anna smiled triumphantly and watched her gaoler pick up the tray from the table and retreat from the room. When they were alone she carefully leant forward and whispered to Josh, 'You've got to help me, she's driving me mad.'

'Earl Grey or ordinary?'

Anna jerked her head towards the doorway where Jessica was standing with a grim scowl on her face.

'Ordinary will be fine,' Josh said smoothly. 'What's the problem?' he asked, when he and Anna were sure they were alone.

'She won't leave me be, not even for a few minutes. It's not so much a case of mother's little helper as mother's little tormentor.'

He laughed.

'I'm serious, Josh, she's turned into a monster. I can't do anything without her fussing. She watches me the whole time.'

'So what do you want me to do?'

'I need you to get her out of the house for a few minutes, take her for a walk, anything, so long as it gives me an opportunity to make a call to somebody who'll come to my rescue. Will you do that?'

'I'll try, though I'm not sure it'll work. I'm not exactly her favourite person at the moment.'

'Mm . . . I noticed that the other day when you called. What have you done? You've not two-timed her, have you? She's not very keen on men who do that.'

He shook his head. 'No, nothing like that.'

'What, then?'

Josh hesitated. 'I've . . . I've hidden something from her, something important which I was about to explain to her on the night of your accident.'

'How intriguing. What is it? Are you really a world-famous drug baron lying low here in Cholmford?'

'Who's a drug baron lying low?' asked Jessica, coming in with a tray and banging it down on the table between Josh and her mother.

'Nobody,' Josh answered, sitting back in his chair. He watched Jessica drop on to the sofa. She looked tired and there was no denying the coldness she was displaying towards him. She had been the same when he'd called on Wednesday on his way home after work. Ostensibly he'd dropped in to see how her mother was, but mainly because he wanted a chance to talk to Jessica. She had made it impossible for him to do so, busying herself in the kitchen with cooking supper for herself and Anna. Even when he'd started to say that he wanted to finish the conversation they'd started on Tuesday night she had pushed past him saying that she didn't have time to listen. She had been close to crying and, sensing that his presence was adding to her distress and the apparent antagonism between them, he had said goodbye and left. He couldn't help feeling confused. It was as if she were blaming him for her mother's accident.

He'd called again today, fool that he was, because he had decided to ask Jessica if she'd go with him to Mo's party that evening. He didn't hold out much hope that she'd say yes, and if the look on her face as she poured out his tea was anything to go by he'd be lucky to escape without having his ears boxed.

'Thank you,' he said when she handed him his cup. 'How's the book going?' He hoped the question would place him on firmer ground than he'd been on previously. He soon found it did no such thing.

'Hah!' she said scornfully, 'as if I've got time for writing.'

He exchanged the briefest of looks with Anna and wondered how he could now suggest that Jessica had time for an evening out. Feet first seemed the only way. He took a fortifying sip of his tea and said, 'I know it's short notice, but I don't suppose you'd like to come to a party with me tonight, would you?'

Anna marvelled at Josh. In the face of her daughter's open hostility towards him the man had real courage. She held her breath and waited for Jessica's reply.

It came in the form of a tut of derision. 'How can you expect me to leave Anna all alone?'

'Oh, what nonsense,' Anna chipped in smartly – *just think of it, a whole evening to herself!* 'I think it's a wonderful idea and just what you need to perk you up.'

'Perk me up?' Jessica said indignantly. 'Who says I need perking up?'

'Not perking up *per se*,' Anna said quickly, 'but it'll give you something to think about other than worrying over me.' *Oh what bliss, to be allowed to settle down to an evening of telly without being interrupted by Jessica continually suggesting that what she really needed was an early night. She'd stretch out on the sofa with a great big martini, at the same time plundering Josh's box of chocolates.* 'I really think you should go,' she added wishfully.

'I'm sure you do,' muttered Jessica, 'so that you can get up to heaven knows what mischief in my absence. I wouldn't put it past you to knock up a quick loft extension while I'm out.'

Anna feigned horror at such an idea. 'Cross my heart and hope to die, I wouldn't get in to any mischief. I've learnt my lesson.'

'And I promise not to keep you out too late, Jessica,' Josh said. He turned to Anna. 'I'll make sure she's back in time to help you into bed.'

'Well, that all seems to be arranged to everybody's satisfaction then,' Anna said happily, secretly hoping that Josh wouldn't stick to his bargain too literally. It was Friday night and there was bound to be a good late-night film on one of the channels.

Jessica stared suspiciously at Anna, then at Josh. 'Yes,' she said slowly, 'it does seem to be arranged to your satisfaction, doesn't it? Anyone would think you'd cooked this up between the pair of you.'

At eight o'clock Josh returned to Willow Cottage. As Jessica climbed into the Shogun he felt the coolness of her manner towards him increase. Once he'd negotiated the narrow bridge over the canal and was driving along the dark lane he said, 'Your mother will be fine, and if there is any problem she's got the number for my mobile.'

'I know that,' Jessica said stiffly.

Without a word Josh suddenly brought the car to a stop. He switched off the engine, turned and faced Jessica. 'Okay,' he said, 'what's this all about? What terrible thing have I done that's caused you to be so cold and rude? You were warmer to me that night when you thought I was the mad axeman of Cholmford.'

Jessica refused to look at him. She didn't say anything either.

'Look, Jessica, a few days ago you were a different woman. Then you were sexy and sarky and made me laugh, now ... well, now you're moody and miserable; what's got into you?'

'I would have thought it was perfectly obvious. I've got more important things on my mind than providing you with a non-stop twenty-four-hour programme of entertainment. And for your information, unless used with care, alliteration is best avoided.'

He smiled. 'I'll bear that in mind in the future.'

'Good. You do that.'

'Any more advice for me?'

'Yes. You can stop encouraging my mother to flirt with you. She doesn't need a toy boy and I'd hate to read about her in the *Sun*. I can see the headlines now: *Senior Citizen in Sleazy Sex Scandal!*'

'I thought you said alliteration was best avoided.'

She turned and looked at him and he saw that there was a glimmer of a smile on her face, and hoping that maybe he had broken the ice between them he reached out and touched her hands in her lap. 'You love your mother very much, don't you?'

The unexpected frankness of his words cut through Jessica's defences and the pain of the past few days rose up and engulfed her. From nowhere a tiny tear appeared in the corner of her left eye. She lowered her head and bit her lip to stop it from betraying the fact that she was so close to crying. She felt angry with herself. Angry, because crying wasn't something she went in for. It was an emotion she had managed without for as long as she could remember. Crying equalled weakness and she wasn't weak. She was strong, always had been. Just like her mother. It was what had held them together when her father died. 'I need you to be strong,' her mother had said that night after the funeral. It was her only real memory of the day; her mother sitting on the edge of her bed, holding her hand, telling her everything would be all right, they just had to be strong.

She heard Josh unbuckle his seat-belt and when he moved nearer and held her in his arms she knew she couldn't hold back the tears any longer.

'I love her so much,' she sobbed into his shoulder, 'and I'm terrified of losing her. I haven't been a good daughter to her, I've never been there for her.'

He held her tenderly and gently stroked her hair.

'I'm all she's got,' Jessica continued, 'it's down to me to take care of her.'

'But you are.'

She pulled away from him and fumbled for a tissue in her bag. 'No, I'm not,' she said, 'I'm making it worse for her. I'm no good at this saintly caring stuff, I know I'm not.'

'You just need to relax, that's all.'

'But how? I try, but I end up behaving like some ghastly fifties-style matron and bossing Mum about, and biting everyone else's head off . . . you included.'

'Me in particular,' he said.

She smiled. 'I'm sorry. I've been horrible to you, haven't I?'

'Yes,' he agreed.

'I was particularly horrid to you the other night, I'm sorry that I shouted and said all those things. What was it you wanted to talk to me about?'

He ran his hand through her hair and let it linger on the nape of her neck. *Now, tell her now,* he willed himself. *Go on. Just say it. Get it over and done with. Just open your mouth and say, Jessica, I've got MS and I'm sorry that I've lied to you.* 'It'll keep,' he said. He'd tell her tomorrow. Tomorrow, when she wasn't so upset about her mother. He slowly moved away from her, then turned the key in the ignition. 'What you need is a party to cheer you up,' he said.

'Don't you mean to perk me up?'

'That too.'

But once again Josh was to find that the best-laid plans have a habit of going entirely their own way.

Chapter Thirty-Six

Back at Willow Cottage, Anna was busy putting her own plan into operation.

Earlier, while Jessica had been in the bathroom getting ready to go out, she had sneaked into her daughter's bedroom and had found what she needed. She was now tapping the number from Jessica's address book into the phone, hardly daring to hope that it would be answered.

It was, almost immediately, which gave her no time to consider what she was going to say.

'Yes,' barked out a cross voice at the other end of the line.

'Good-evening, is that Piers Lambert?'

'Of course it is, who else would be answering my private line at this time of night?'

'My word, you're just as Jessica described you.'

'I beg your pardon? Who is this?'

'My name is Anna Lloyd, I'm Jessica's mother.'

'Are you indeed? And what precisely can I do for you?'

Anna told him.

Mo shared a large Victorian house in Rusholme with two female engineering students, a hairdresser – who frequently carried out ground-breaking experiments on Mo's hair, often with hair-raising results – and a night-club bouncer. Josh had been to the house just once before. He'd driven Mo home from work one day when she'd been ill and had come away thinking that its colourful inhabitants made the characters of *This Life* look like wooden extras from *Crossroads*.

There was nowhere to park directly outside Mo's place, but further up the road there was a parking space between an electric-blue VW Beetle and a wreck of a Fiat Panda. Josh squeezed his Shogun into the space and noticed his brother's car across the road where it was parked in front of a house that looked like it had been burnt out; all the windows were boarded up. He wondered if Charlie had persuaded Rachel to come. It probably wasn't Rachel's kind of party. She struck Josh as being more of a canapé-and-spritzer party-goer.

'Am I going to feel very old and out of it here?' Jessica broke into his thoughts. 'You did say Mo was only twenty-five. Won't all her friends be horribly young and trendy?'

Josh smiled. 'Horribly young and trendy.'

Jessica groaned. 'I knew it. It'll be wall-to-wall global hip-hop, oversized jeans with crotches dragging on the floor, drugs in your face and everyone punctuating their sentences with the word shag.'

Josh smiled again and got out of the car. When Jessica joined him on the pavement and he'd activated the alarm, he said, 'You wouldn't be judging others by your own twenty-something behaviour, would you?'

'Certainly not. When I was Mo's age I needed a clear head to chase all those hunks up and down the slopes of Colorado.'

He put his arm around her. 'I'm not sure I like the sound of that.'

She looked up at him with a smile. 'Why's that?'

He returned her gaze. 'Why do you think?'

'I must be particularly dense tonight, I need it spelling out for me.'

'I've always believed that actions speak louder than words.' And manoeuvring her back against the side of the car, Josh pressed his body against hers and kissed her for the longest of moments. 'Now does that give you any kind of a clue?' he asked.

'It was a bit cryptic in places.'

He kissed her again. Longer and deeper. 'We don't have to go to this party,' he said, after they'd been disturbed by an elderly woman passing with her dog, 'we could go back to your place and –'

She laughed. 'Crawford, get your desire in check and lead me on to the party.'

The hum and thud of a thousand decibels spilled out across the untidy front garden as the door was opened to them by a young black man who was wearing a Jimi Hendrix hairdo and a magenta-coloured velvet suit. He ushered them through the house to a large kitchen where a crowd of people were gathered round a selection of bottles that could have stocked a small off-licence.

'Help yourself, man,' Jimi Hendrix said to Josh. He left them to it.

'What do you fancy?' Josh asked Jessica.

'Some kind of white wine would be nice . . . *man*.'

Josh smiled and began opening a new bottle of wine – he'd heard enough morning-after stories from Mo to know that it wouldn't be wise to trust any of the opened bottles. When he'd poured out two plastic cups of plonk, he said, 'Come on, let's go and find the birthday girl.'

They found her outside in the long thin back garden, where some of the trees and bushes had been decorated with fairy lights. There were flaming torches pushed into the ground and candles flickering on all the window-sills of the house. Mo was easy to spot and Josh burst out laughing when he saw her. She was bouncing on a trampoline and showing off a pair of frilly patriotic knickers to a delighted crowd of onlookers. She saw Josh and waved at him mid-bounce. He waved back and caught sight of his brother in the crowd gathered round the trampoline, and surprise, surprise, there didn't seem to be any sign of Rachel. Holding Jessica by the arm, he took her over to meet Charlie.

'At long last we meet,' Charlie said warmly, 'I've heard a lot about you.'

'Not as much as I've heard about you.' Jessica laughed, realising that this was the good-looking man she'd seen with the suspected take-away and the flashy sports car. As brothers went, the resemblance wasn't that strong between them. If she had to guess which was the elder, she'd say it was Charlie. She wondered if he was envious of Josh's youthful looks and the complete absence of grey from his thick dark-brown hair – Charlie's, she noticed, was speckled with grey and was showing signs of receding.

'What's with the trampoline?' asked Josh.

'It's a present from her parents,' Charlie said, 'apparently she always wanted a trampoline as a child, but it's only now that they thought they could trust her with one.'

'How wrong could they be.' Josh smiled.

Jessica turned her attention back to Mo. She'd been joined on the trampoline by a beautiful-looking Asian man, with a long plait of silky black hair swishing behind him like the tail of a frisky pony.

'Who's the guy with her?' asked Jessica.

'That's Sid,' Josh said, 'he's our designer. His parents are from Hong Kong and he's invaluable on any of our buying trips to the Far East.'

'He's also mad about Mo,' Charlie added.

'They look like they'd make a great couple,' Jessica said as she observed the antics going on in front of her.

'And so they would, but unfortunately Mo carries the torch of love for somebody –'

'Give it a rest, Charlie,' Josh interrupted. 'Jessica doesn't want to hear about that.' And draining his plastic cup he said, 'Anyone for another drink?'

'No thanks,' Jessica said – she'd barely touched hers.

'If you're going that way, you can get me something non-alcoholic.' Charlie handed Josh his empty cup.

'So who's Mo carrying a torch for?' Jessica asked Charlie, as soon as Josh was out of earshot.

'Yonder brother, of course.'

Jessica raised an eyebrow. 'And he's never . . . you know . . .'

'Good Lord, no. Mo's been with us since she was seventeen. I guess we both look on her as a kid sister.'

'Which she probably hates.'

'If she does, she's never shown it.'

'But then, as we all know, men are not the most perceptive or sensitive of beings.'

'So how's your mother?'

Jessica laughed out loud. 'Now you're scaring me. In that one simple question you hope to prove that not only do you and Josh communicate with one another, but that you can be sensitive enough to a complete stranger to enquire after a relative's well-being. I like it, the Crawford brothers are the exception to the rule, they have finer feelings just like women.'

'So, how *is* your mother?' Charlie pursued, entertained by Jessica's forthright manner.

Jessica frowned. 'I don't know is the honest answer. She's got a broken arm and a cracked rib, and tries to make out that she's as fit as a fiddle. If she had her way, she'd dispense with her cast and sling, wrap a bit of sticking plaster round her wrist, pull on her gardening gloves and dig up half of Cheshire.'

'Poor you. It's not easy caring for people, is it?'

'You're not kidding,' but then, catching the reflective tone in Charlie's voice and remembering what Josh had told her about his brother, she said, 'I'm sure you'd be easy to look after.'

He gave her a puzzled look. 'Let's hope I'm never in that situation.'

'Ooh, my legs feel all wobbly, like I've been on a boat.' It was Mo and she was breathless and perspiring from all the bouncing. She reached out to Charlie to steady herself.

'Happy birthday,' he said, propping her up and kissing her cheek.

'Where's Josh?'

'Doing what he's best at, fetching drinks. This is Jessica, by the way.'

'Hi,' Jessica said. As Mo turned to face her she was conscious that the young girl was sizing her up. Jessica was surprised how antagonistic she felt towards Mo. When Charlie had said that Mo had a bit of a thing for Josh, her stomach had done silly things like lurch about. It had reminded her of days gone by when she had discovered Gavin had been seeing other women. She glanced around her, suddenly wanting Josh back by her side, where she could see him . . . where she could keep an eye on him.

She saw him making his way through the crowd of guests and

260

experienced a wave of relief. No, it wasn't relief, it was something else. But what? She stared at his limping figure as he approached and tried to assimilate what her response to the sight of him really meant. Could the combination of that handsome face and those intense brown eyes really be held responsible for making her feel so extraordinarily weak at the knees? Could that tall slim body truly hold so much attraction for her? Could the thought of those hands that were so gentle and instinctive when they caressed her body actually cause her mouth to go so dry? And while they were on the subject, that mouth of his had a charm all of its own. As kissers went, he was the best. Definitely in a class of his own. When God had been handing out the attributes guaranteed to make a man physically irresistible to a woman, he'd given Josh the top-drawer stuff. There'd been no stinting. Josh, my lad, God would have said when he'd seen what he'd created, with you I am well pleased.

Jessica smiled to herself and suddenly realised that she'd stopped breathing, that her throat was tight with desire. She gulped back her wine, draining the plastic cup in one go. And as she did, she found herself admitting that it wasn't a mere physical desire that she felt for Josh. It was much more. And it scared her.

'Hello, Mo,' he said, when he finally drew level. He handed Charlie his drink, then put his hand in his jacket pocket. He pulled out a small package. 'Happy birthday, it's from Charlie and me.'

Mo's face broke into a smile as her eager fingers slipped off the wrapping paper to reveal a box. She opened it hurriedly and lifted away a layer of cotton wool. 'It's beautiful,' she cried, holding up a silver bangle. 'I love it! Thank you so much.' She kissed Charlie without thinking, but approached Josh more shyly.

Once again Jessica's stomach gave a sharp involuntary lurch.

At eleven o'clock, when it was too chilly to stay outside in the garden – unless you were prepared to keep warm by flinging yourself about on the trampoline – Jessica and Josh went inside, to a room that on his previous visit Josh was convinced had been the sitting-room. Now it was empty of most of its furniture, the lights had been lowered and people were dancing to boppy music blaring from two enormous loudspeakers.

'We ought to be thinking about going,' Josh said. The last thing he needed was Jessica wanting him to dance with her. He'd been standing for most of the night and his leg was good for nothing now; his knee ached and every now and again a stab of pain seared through him. 'I did promise your mother I wouldn't get you home too late,' he added.

'Oh,' said Jessica, disappointed. 'Couldn't we have one quick boogie?' She'd drunk just enough wine to think that maybe her mother could manage a short while longer without her.

Josh hesitated. 'I . . . I'm not very good at dancing.'

Jessica laughed. 'You don't have to be.' And when the record abruptly changed to a slow, smoochy number she said, 'Come on, I actually recognise this, it's Elton John, isn't it?'

'George Michael, you idiot.'

'I knew that.' She took his hands and pulled him towards the other couples.

He held her close as they came together and hoped that she wouldn't notice the lack of movement on his part.

'You feel tense,' she remarked.

'Just tired,' he said and, looking for a way to distract her, he asked, 'Any chance of a kiss?'

'Only the one?'

'Quality, not quantity, that's what I always say.'

'Here goes then.'

And by the time they'd kissed their way through 'You Have Been Loved', Jessica no longer felt scared by her earlier realisation.

After all, what possible harm could she come to by falling in love with Josh Crawford?

While Josh looked for Mo to say goodbye, Jessica went in search of the bathroom. There were numerous bodies to pick her way over as she climbed the stairs and when she reached the landing she found Mo all alone and slumped on the floor. She looked ghastly and was holding a wet flannel to her forehead. 'I don't think Bacardi should be so vigorously shaken,' she moaned.

'Can I get you anything?' Jessica asked, crouching beside her. Suddenly Mo didn't seem like a rival any more. In fact, she seemed more like a poor sick child.

'It was probably the pizza I had afterwards that did it,' Mo whimpered. 'Anchovies don't agree with me. I never learn. The five triple vodkas and Cokes was pushing it a bit, I guess.'

Jessica tried not to laugh. 'Do you think some cold water might be in order?'

Mo groaned. 'Death. That's what I need. Nothing heroic, mind. Just a small affair, me and the grim reaper, face to face. I'd go quietly, I'd be no trouble.'

'And what about the funeral? Any ideas on that?'

'Yes. I want a Princess Di do, lots of flowers and fuss. And I'd like Josh to follow the coffin if that's okay with you.'

'I'm sure he'd oblige.'

Mo lowered the flannel from her face and looked at Jessica. 'You're a lucky bitch. I'd give anything to be in your shoes. You will take care of him, won't you?'

Jessica frowned. 'He doesn't seem to be the sort who needs taking care of.'

Mo tried to smile knowingly, but it came out as a sickly grimace. She returned the wet flannel to her forehead and groaned. 'He pretends he doesn't, but really he does. It's what makes him so bloody moody at times. But then you must have noticed that, one minute he's up and the next he's down.'

Jessica shook her head. 'I'm not sure what you're talking about.'

'It's what MS does to you. And before you jump to the wrong conclusion, I don't love him out of sympathy, I loved him way before his illness was diagnosed. I just hope you're not going to dump him like the last girl-friend did. Oh, bugger, I'm going to be sick again.'

Jessica watched Mo stagger into the bathroom just in time. She slowly went back downstairs and with each body she climbed over she asked herself a question.

Why had he lied?

Why had he wanted to keep it from her?

Was this what he had been trying to talk to her about?

And if it was, why had he turned it into such a big deal?

And what the hell was multiple sclerosis anyway?

She suddenly felt angry, as if Josh had been cheating on her.

When she reached the bottom of the stairs she found him waiting for her by the front door. Charlie was with him.

'We couldn't find Mo,' Josh said, when he saw her, 'somebody said she wasn't feeling well.'

'I've just been talking to her,' Jessica said coolly. 'In fact, we had a surprisingly interesting conversation. Revealing is perhaps the word I'd use. Josh, why did you make me believe that your brother suffered from multiple sclerosis? Why didn't you tell me the truth?'

Chapter Thirty-Seven

Somebody had turned up the volume of the music and above the sonic-boom effect of Oasis's 'Roll With It' coming at them down the narrow length of the hallway Charlie said, 'I think this is best sorted out between the pair of you.' And without another word, or a backward glance, he opened the front door and shot out into the night.

'Well?' said Jessica, 'I'm waiting for an explanation.'

Josh leant against the wall behind him and lowered his head. 'Not here,' was all he said.

They drove in brooding silence through the streets of Rusholme and only when they joined the A34 did Josh say anything. 'I'll explain it all when we get home.' His face was dark and sombre. He passed her his mobile phone. 'Perhaps you'd better ring your mother and check that she's okay and tell her that you'll be later than you thought.'

When they reached Cholmford Hall Mews, he parked alongside his house and let them in. He went straight to the kitchen where he poured out two large glasses of Southern Comfort. He added some ice and passed one to Jessica. He took her through to the sitting-room. 'Sit down,' he said, gesturing towards the sofa. He didn't join her, but walked stiffly over to a chair and sank gratefully into it, all his energy now gone. He knocked back half his drink in one quick mouthful. 'So what's your first question?' he said, his eyes fixed firmly on the glass in his hand.

Jessica stared thoughtfully across the room at him. 'I'm not sure,' she said. As they'd driven away from the party she'd had all sorts of questions in mind to fire at Josh, but his uncommunicative manner in the car had made it very clear to her that he didn't want to talk to her then and she'd respected his wishes. But now that she was being given the opportunity to speak she found that she couldn't. It was the sight of his obvious discomfort that was unnerving her. He looked so downcast. So defeated. She'd never seen him like this before.

'Don't you want to know why I concealed it from you?' he asked.

'I would have thought you were dying to know that.' There was a hardness to his voice that made his question sound like an accusation. He still didn't look at her.

'Again I'm not sure,' she said. 'I don't understand why you've turned your illness into such a big deal.'

Now he did look up and straight at her. 'Because for me it is a big deal. Don't you know *anything* about MS?'

She shook her head. 'I told you that the night of my migraine attack, don't you remember –?'

'Yes,' he snapped loudly, 'I remember that perfectly well, there's nothing wrong with my memory. I'm not that far gone.' He lowered his eyes and ran a hand through his hair. 'I'm sorry, I didn't mean to . . .' He drained his glass and banged it down on the table in front of him. 'I'm really sorry, Jessica. This is so bloody important to me and I just seem to be making a hash of it.'

She gave him a tiny smile of encouragement. 'Why don't you tell me why you felt the need to hide your illness from me? When we've dealt with that you can explain what MS is. How does that sound?'

He let out his breath, surprised how reasonable she was being. 'How about another drink?'

'Just get on with it,' she said gently.

He ran a hand over his chin. 'Okay, here goes. But first, I want you to know that I did try telling you . . . it was the night your mother had her accident.'

'I guessed that.'

'I'd spent the best part of the day planning what to say.' He paused, then got to his feet. 'It's no good, I definitely need another drink. You sure you won't join me?'

She shook her head. When he came back into the room he sat down again and she watched him nervously turn the glass round in his hands. The room was so quiet she could hear the cubes of ice chinking against the sides of the glass. She wanted to prompt him, but knew she mustn't – whatever it was he had to say, he had to say it in his own time.

At last he spoke. 'The reason I felt so compelled to hide my MS from you,' he said in a low voice, 'is because my last girl-friend beat a hasty retreat the moment I explained it to her and . . . and I thought that so long as you didn't know there was anything wrong with me I could carry on seeing you.'

'And is that what you expect me to do now,' she asked quietly, 'to run off at the double?'

He shrugged. 'Maybe not right away, but in time, yes.'

'Then you have a very poor opinion of people, Josh. What gives you the right to put a ceiling on my feelings for you?'

He looked up. 'But you said yourself that you don't know anything about MS. You don't know the implications.'

'We'll get on to that in a minute. But first I want to know how far your deception went. Did it include avoiding me at times?'

He nodded guiltily. 'More times than I care to think of.'

She smiled, relieved. 'And there was I convinced that you were doing a Gavin on me.'

'Believe me, Jessica, that would have taken more energy than I possess . . . and even if I had the energy I would never do that to you.'

She went to him and knelt on the floor at his feet. She rested her head against his legs.

'Can I ask *you* a question now?' he asked.

'Of course.'

'When you came down the stairs at Mo's and you said that you'd just been talking to her, you seemed angry. Were you?'

She turned and looked at him. 'I was furious, if you must know, I was spitting bricks.'

'Why?'

'The situation reminded me of Gavin. I know it sounds crazy, but from where I was standing I'd suddenly found out something about you and it was like discovering you'd been lying and cheating on me.'

He stroked her hair. 'I'm so very sorry.'

'Don't be.' She lifted his hand from her head and gently squeezed it within her own. 'Now I want you to tell me what's wrong with you. And no glossing over anything. I want the truth. Tell me everything.'

He sighed. 'Where do I start?'

'In true story-telling tradition, try the beginning.'

'Okay. I have what is known as relapsing-remitting multiple sclerosis.' His voice sounded flat and uninteresting, as if he were reading from a script. 'Which means the symptoms I experience come and go as they please. I have no control over them, I'm at the mercy of whatever my body decides to chuck at me.'

'Such as?'

He let go of her hand and stroked her hair again. 'You name it,' he said. 'The most obvious and frequent symptom I have is the lack of mobility in my leg, which seems to be getting steadily worse . . . I'm afraid I blatantly lied about that, by the way.'

She smiled cautiously. 'Not a heroic skiing injury then?'

''Fraid not.' He then went on to describe the catalogue of

symptoms he'd experienced over the past few years; the slurred speech, the numbness, the tingling, the acute fatigue, the lack of control over his limbs and the most frightening of the lot, the momentary loss of sight in one of his eyes.

When he finished Jessica said, 'But what about a cure?'

He shook his head. 'Nothing. Not even a wonder drug that puts the illness on hold.'

She frowned. 'How bloody unfair! And how bloody awful for you.'

'It isn't always awful,' he said, surprised to hear himself admitting this, 'the symptoms vary in severity, there are some good days.'

'And today?'

He smiled. 'Today's been okay, which was why I plucked up the courage to ask you to come to Mo's party.'

She thought about this. 'Does that mean I've only ever seen you on your good days?'

He nodded. 'Apart from when I moved in and burst in on you and your mother. My speech was all over the place, I could barely get the words out.'

Jessica recalled the day with shame, seeing now his apparently ill-mannered behaviour in a completely different light. 'I'm sorry I thought you'd been rude and even sorrier that I told you so to your face. That was terrible of me.'

'Forget it,' he said lightly. 'You weren't to know. And anyway, that's nothing compared with what I've done to you. I can't begin to think what you must have thought of me each time I deserted you after we'd made love. I hated doing that.'

'I hated it as well. What were you so frightened of?'

'Of the morning . . . of you waking to the truth about me and discovering that I wasn't the man you thought I was.'

'And I suppose you didn't really have flu the other week.'

'No. I . . . I'd been feeling particularly ill that week and I collapsed at work . . . Charlie had to bring me home.'

She looked up at him, full of concern. 'Oh, Josh, I wish you'd told me, I could have helped. I could have been there for you.'

'It's bad enough having to face up to MS oneself without admitting to other people what's going on. Half the time I don't even tell Charlie what's happening, I'm afraid I make his life hell.'

'He strikes me as being able to cope.'

'I'm not sure at times whether he is,' Josh said reflectively, 'he's had to put up with a lot of crap from me. My parents too. Even Mo.'

Jessica smiled. 'Talking of Mo, you do realise that she's completely and utterly in love with you, don't you?'

He didn't answer her. Instead he pulled her on to his lap. 'But more to the point,' he said, 'do you realise that I've gone and let myself fall in love with you?'

'Hang on a moment,' she said with a nervous little laugh, 'it's me who's supposed to write the romantic lines.'

'I'm not kidding, Jessica. God help you, but it's the truth.'

'I'm delighted to hear it, because I reached the same decision about you earlier this evening.'

'You did? My God! When?'

'When I thought that Mo might be a threat, I was so mad with jealousy I could have torn the sweet girl limb from limb.'

He laughed happily and held her close. He couldn't believe the way the evening had turned out. 'I don't suppose there's any chance of you staying the night with me, is there?'

'Mm . . . that's a tempting offer, Crawford.' And relaxing into his embrace, she settled herself in for a good long kiss. But suddenly she sat bolt upright. 'I've forgotten all about my mother! What time is it?'

He looked at his watch. 'One o'clock.'

'*What!*' She sprang out of his lap.

'Calm down. If there'd been a problem she would have phoned. Now let me get my keys and I'll drive you back.'

'You sure you're safe to drive,' she asked when they were outside and he was locking his front door. 'You haven't had too much to drink, have you?'

'I'm fine,' he said. He opened her side of the car and just as she was about to climb in he took her in his arms. 'I'm claiming my good-night kiss now,' he said, 'I might not get another chance.'

Chapter Thirty-Eight

Jessica started buttering a piece of toast for her mother. She spread the low-fat butter substitute evenly, right to the darkened edges of the crusts, then added some of Anna's home-made whisky-spiked marmalade; this too was pressed into place with careful precision, ensuring an equal distribution of finely shredded orange peel. And all the time she was doing this Jessica was thinking of Josh.

Last night he had shared with her two vital pieces of information: first, that he suffered from some illness which he'd gone to great lengths to hide from her, and second . . . and second, that he loved her.

He actually loved her.

Amazing!

Getting anybody to fall in love with her in the past had always been such a mighty uphill struggle – in fact, she doubted whether it had ever happened. Certainly Gavin had never loved her.

But Josh did!

And she loved him.

Oh, yes. She loved him right enough. Falling in love with Josh Crawford had been effortless, it had been as easy, as the silly cliché goes, as falling off a log – just like they had that night in the copse.

In a funny way it almost seemed unfair that it had been so easy to fall in love with Josh and he with her, when for more than a year she had tried to make Gavin do the same – or at least care for her exclusively. But it had never happened. It was strange that so much hard work had gone into that particular relationship and it had all gone to waste.

It was very confusing.

As was Josh's illness.

She wasn't quite sure what to make of it. She knew that Josh had found last night an ordeal and that he'd done his best to explain what multiple sclerosis was all about, but when she'd woken up this morning she had realised that not once had he referred to the future.

What was his future?

Would he stay as he was?

Or was he likely to get worse?

And if so, what did that mean precisely?

And could MS be life-threatening?

Oh God! Why didn't she know? Why was she so ignorant?

And another thing. Why hadn't she sensed that there was something wrong with Josh? How blind and insensitive could a person be? For goodness sake, she was a writer, she was supposed to be a keen observer of her fellow human beings.

How damning it was to realise that she had been so shallow. Always, always, her response to Josh had been to consider the effect he had on her. How could she have viewed him in such a two-dimensional manner?

The answer, she suspected, lay in her relationship with Gavin. Determined never to allow another man to hurt her again she had probably been so preoccupied with self-protection that she had become introverted and unaware of those around her, only thinking what the consequences of anything would be to herself.

How selfish she had been.

Which was what she'd felt last night after Josh had dropped her off. When she had found Anna stretched out on the sofa, fast asleep with a throw-over covering her, she had been appalled. The fire had all but gone out and the faintly glowing embers had stared back at her accusingly as though reprimanding her for having neglected her mother that evening. Guilt had overwhelmed her. How could she have left Anna for so long? How could she have abandoned her mother when she needed her most? What kind of daughter was she that could behave so reprehensibly?

She cut the piece of toast diagonally in half and passed it across the table.

'A work of art,' Anna said, having spent the last five minutes watching her daughter closely, 'thank you.'

It was patently clear to Anna that Jessica had something on her mind. But then for that matter so did she.

Although it was only eight thirty, Anna was willing the phone to ring; it was making her jumpy with nervous expectation. Piers Lambert had said he'd help and ridiculously she was sitting at the breakfast table waiting for him instantly to come to her aid. She had imagined him late last night bursting into action like some mighty Cape Crusader bringing forth with the dawn some way of getting Jessica off her back.

'What do you suggest?' had been his immediate response on the phone, when she'd told him what was going on.

'I don't know, that's why I'm ringing you.'

'You must have had some idea in mind or you wouldn't have called me.'

Jessica had told Anna many times that her agent was direct to the point of rudeness, but she was still taken by surprise at the severity of his manner which, instead of irritating her as she might have expected, did the opposite, it instilled within her a sense of hope – here was somebody who really would get her daughter to step in line and keep her there.

'I want you to crack the whip over Jessica,' Anna had said, 'make her believe that she's got to get on with writing this novel. Can't you make out that the deadline has been brought forward and that she's got to get back to work?'

'That wouldn't be for me to tell Jessica, that would have to come from her publishers. And I'm afraid Jessica's publishers aren't going to start switching round launch dates just to suit you.'

'But surely there must be something you can do.'

'When did she last do any writing?'

'Over a week ago.'

'That's not very long. I think you're exaggerating the case.'

'Look, Mr Lambert, my arm's going to be in plaster for at least another five weeks, maybe longer. Can she afford to take that much time off?'

'Mm . . . perhaps you're right. Leave it with me. Good-night.'

Abrupt and to the point Piers Lambert certainly seemed to be, and Anna wished whole-heartedly that his actions would be as forceful and as effective as his behaviour implied.

Tony knew that he was becoming openly hostile towards Bloody Rita – any day now and he'd be lobbing ruddy great grenades at her. He didn't know what it was about her that got his back up most, her haughtiness, or her coldness towards him. He deliberately banged the phone down on the kitchen worktop so as to give his mother-in-law's eardrums a damn good jolt. He called out to Amanda. 'It's your mum,' he yelled at the top of his voice, knowing that such a breach of etiquette would have Bloody Rita blanching into her *Daily Mail* – it could have been worse, he could have referred to her as *mam*.

When Amanda appeared in the kitchen he said, 'I'm off out with Hattie to her ballet lesson, see you about a quarter past eleven.' He was tempted to hang about and eavesdrop on his wife's conversation

– he still didn't know what she and her mother were up to – but with Hattie hovering at the front door dressed in her little pink leotard and white tights and her ballet shoes in her hands there was no time for loitering with intent. The thought crossed his mind that it wouldn't be a bad idea to make enquiries into obtaining a few bits and pieces of surveillance equipment, just some useful devices for tapping phones, that kind of thing. He smiled to himself, imagining what might follow if he went down that particular road of madness – he'd end up in a false beard and nose, darting about the streets in a raincoat shadowing Amanda. The idea was so ridiculous it cheered him and patting his daughter's head he said, 'Come on, Hattie, let's hit the road for *Swan Lake*.'

The hall was full of tiny girls, their hair swept back from their gleaming foreheads, their tummies and bottoms sticking out as they held on to the bar in breathless concentration as they bent their knees over their toes. When the music from a bulky ghetto blaster came to a stop, the girls relaxed, curtsied to their teacher and chanted '*Mercy M'dame*', then they stampeded to the back of the hall and their waiting parents, who were on hand with life-saving cartons of juice, bags of crisps and KitKats. Tony gave Hattie a quick kiss and watched her rush away on accentuated tiptoe to join her group – it was her second ever lesson and she was still in the first flourish of enthusiasm for a new-found hobby. He then slipped out of the hall and headed towards the newsagent's in the main street of Holmes Chapel.

The sun was shining and the sky was clear and bright, and it struck Tony as being the most perfect of September mornings. There was that satisfying feeling that the early chill in the air would be long gone by lunch-time and the rest of the day would be warm enough to sit outside with a glass of wine and the newspaper.

Or cut the grass, as Amanda would expect him to do.

He kept meaning to have a word with Josh, who had done the sensible thing and acquired himself a gardener. A gardener was definitely what Tony needed, somebody to take care of the grass and flower beds, leaving him free to plan his future.

In the newsagent's he bought a copy of the *Daily Mail* for Amanda – like mother like daughter – and *The Times* for himself. And while he was there, he couldn't resist scanning the shelves for a magazine aimed at the average man in the street interested in pursuing an innocent hobby of domestic espionage. Surely among the multitudinous and divers selection of magazines on offer there had to be at least one for a dim-witted husband wanting to know what his wife and mother-in-law were up to?

He paid for his papers and went back out on to the street, and weighing up whether he could be bothered to nip into the hardware store for some picture hooks that Amanda had been on at him to get, he suddenly caught sight of a flash of copper hair. It was Kate and she was walking towards the church on the opposite side of the road. Before he could stop himself he was calling out her name. 'Kate!'

She didn't hear him.

He stepped out into the road and immediately leapt back on to the pavement as a car hooted bad-temperedly at him. It was then that she noticed him. He waved over to her and when a flurry of cars had passed, he crossed the road and joined her. 'Hi,' he said. It seemed ages since their last conversation when so much had passed between them.

'Hello,' she said shyly. 'How are you?'

He nodded. 'Okay. How about you?'

'I'm fine.'

'And Alec?'

'Trying to say all the right things.' She lowered her eyes as if regretting what she'd just said.

'He'll come round. It'll be all right in the end.' Tony was surprised how sincere and genuine his voice sounded. Deep down, he didn't want Alec to 'come round'. He wanted him to be a bastard. He wanted Alec to play the Victorian baddie and be booed off the stage, so that he, wonderful, kind, considerate Tony, the young hero, could sweep the badly treated heroine off her feet and give everyone the happy ending they wanted. 'So where are you off to?' he asked, shocked at his shallowness.

She hesitated.

'Sorry, I didn't mean to pry.'

She smiled. 'No. I was just going to sit in St Luke's for a few minutes.'

He looked at the austere sandstone church behind them. He hadn't been inside a church since Eve's funeral, not since that dreadful day when he'd sat in the front pew and silently railed against a supposedly omnipotent and loving God, while all about him people prayed and sang hymns of thanksgiving and everlasting life. For him, though, it had been unthinkable to thank anybody who had seen fit to take away the woman he loved. 'Why?' he asked. 'Why do you want to go in there?'

She looked at him curiously. 'Because it usually makes me feel better.'

This was even more unfathomable to Tony. 'Better?' he repeated.

'Yes,' she said simply. 'It's the sense of peace I come away with.'

'Oh.' A sense of peace was the last thing he'd come away with after Eve's funeral service. He didn't know what else to say, so looked along the street at the determined shoppers buzzing in and out of the shops. He was surprised to feel Kate's hand on his arm and even more so to feel her guiding him towards the studded oak door.

He stood in the half-light and swallowed. It wasn't the same church he'd sat in before, but to all intents and purposes it was identical. The pervading smell of age, polish and snuffed-out candles was the same. As was the morgue-like temperature. His body stiffened as feelings of remorse and anger crept over him. Kate began to move away. He quickly followed. He didn't want to be alone. She slipped into a pew and he sat alongside her. He tried to remind himself of the warm sunshine outside, of Hattie happily prancing about in her leotard, anything so long as he didn't have to be reminded of that awful day. He fiddled with the newspapers in his hands, then glanced at Kate, unsure what was expected of him if she was going to apply herself to meaningful contemplation. But instead of finding her deep in prayer he noticed that she was observing him. And closely. 'What is it?' he whispered. 'Why are you staring at me like that?'

'I was looking at the anger in your face,' she said gently.

He turned away. But then found himself face to face with the image of a tortured Christ on the cross in the stained-glass window above the altar. To the right of this was a wooden plaque honouring local men killed in the First World War. Was there no way of getting away from all the senseless suffering in the world?

'I don't think this is a good idea,' he said. 'I ought to be going, Hattie will be waiting for me.' He stumbled out of the pew and hurried towards the escape route. Outside on the pavement he blinked in the bright sunlight and caught his breath. To his horror he realised he was shaking. He breathed out deeply, willing his emotions back into line. But it was no good, it was too reminiscent of the worst day of his life. When the service had finished he'd started shaking and had broken down and wept. He could still remember the reaction from those around him. The older members of the families had frozen in their seats, unprepared and ill-equipped to cope with such a display of loss of control. It had been his closest friends who had comforted him, bundling him out of the church and taking him to the nearest pub for a stiff drink before driving on to the crematorium.

And a stiff drink was what he could do with right now.

The sound of the church door creaking behind him made him turn.

It was Kate. 'Are you okay?' she asked, her face full of anxious concern.

'Sorry about that,' he said, his breathing now back under control. 'You don't fancy a drink, do you?'

'It's a bit early for the pub to be open,' she said, gazing along the street in the direction of the Red Lion, 'you'll probably only get morning coffee served at this time of the day. And didn't you say that Hattie was waiting for you?'

He banged his head with the newspapers in his hands. 'Yeah, of course, stupid me. I'll see you, then.'

'Yes,' she said.

Neither of them made any attempt to move.

'You are okay, aren't you?' she asked again.

'Yes. No. No, I'm not. You have a strange and wonderful effect on me, Kate. You make me remember Eve . . . and you make me want to do crazy things like kiss you.' Which he did, suddenly and intensely. It was the first time since he'd been without Eve that he'd kissed a woman and meant it. His brain told him to stop. It was madness. The consequences could be disastrous. But his heart pounded out a different message.

Chapter Thirty-Nine

Kate drove home in a state of heart-quickening confusion. She was not in the habit of kissing men so freely. But what made it worse was that deep down she had known Tony was going to do it . . . and that she was going to let him.

Ever since Monday morning she had found it difficult to shake off the effect of not just Tony's kindness towards her, but the desperate sadness of his circumstances, which he had conveyed to her so poignantly during their conversation. When he had spoken of his first wife she had wanted to console him, to show him the compassion he had shown her, but she had been wary of doing so, fearful of the consequences, knowing that in that precise moment they were both dangerously vulnerable; made weak and defenceless by their wretchedness – a heavy heart could be implicitly treacherous.

Later, and over lunch when Caroline had questioned her about Tony, she had refused to allow herself to be drawn into giving anything more than a superficial physical description of him, but inwardly she had been thinking of the soft blue eyes that had been unable to mask his misery; of the hand that had held hers; of the thoughtfully chosen gift; and of the expression on his face that night in Hattie's bedroom when she'd interrupted him chatting with his daughter.

His countenance had puzzled her at the time because she had been unable to define it.

But now she could.

Oh yes, she now knew exactly what it had meant. His actions a few minutes ago had defined it perfectly.

And what of her actions?

How exactly could they be categorised?

And how could she be attracted to Tony when she was carrying Alec's child? It went against everything she'd ever thought herself capable of.

She sped along the road away from Holmes Chapel, as though hoping to distance herself from what had just taken place. It was only a kiss, she told herself. A single kiss, that was all. It was hardly a breach of faith.

Except it was, she knew very well it was.

Afterwards Tony had said, 'I should probably apologise for doing that, but I'm not going to, I meant every second of it. When can I see you?'

Flustered, she had checked the busy street to see if anyone was watching them. But the Saturday-morning shoppers had all seemed safely occupied with their own tasks in hand and with a shake of her head she'd murmured, 'I don't know.' She had then fled to the car-park and had driven away without risking a backward glance.

When can I see you?

The words echoed inside her head as she entered the village of Cholmford. And just as she'd known that Tony would kiss her that morning, she was certain he would do so again and that she would let him . . . that she would want him to.

'Did you get the flowers?' Alec asked Kate when she let herself in.

She stared back at him, mystified.

'You know, the flowers for Ruth,' he said.

The flowers! She'd forgotten all about them. They had been one of the reasons for her visit to Holmes Chapel, she was supposed to pick up something nice from the florist to take to Ruth's for lunch that day. 'I um . . . I forgot,' she said truthfully.

Alec smiled at her. 'The hormones have started blatting the little grey cells, have they?'

'Something like that,' she said uneasily, wondering if she could ever legitimately lay the responsibility of that morning's breach of faith on her mixed-up hormones.

'Don't look so worried, we'll get something on the way. Did you remember the dry-cleaning?'

'Yes,' she said with relief – thank goodness she had dropped off Alec's suit before she'd decided to cross the road to go into St Luke's.

Since moving to the area she had often visited the small sandstone church, finding herself drawn to the building that quietly dominated the square in the centre of the village. This morning she had felt the pull of its tranquil sanctuary even more keenly and had gone there in search of a few minutes of calm repose. She had wanted to think about Alec and his apparent acceptance of their child.

'Did they say when it would be ready?' he asked.

'Sorry,' she said, 'when will what be ready?'

He smiled indulgently. 'Your memory really is going, isn't it? I was asking about the dry-cleaning.'

'Oh, that. It'll be ready on Tuesday.'

'That's fine. Do you fancy some coffee? I've put the kettle on. It's such a lovely day I thought we could sit on the patio. We won't get many more chances like this. A few more weeks and it'll be autumn for real.'

'I'll have tea, please, I've gone right off coffee.' She left Alec in the kitchen and disappeared out into the garden, where she hoped to pull herself together. The sight and sound of Alec acting as he always did was too much for her. She wanted him to treat her horribly, at least then she could justify what she had done that morning. How could he treat her so courteously when she was considering . . . she swallowed hard and tried to force herself to put into words exactly what she was considering.

But she couldn't.

Alec drove them to Ruth and Adam's for lunch, stopping on the way at a petrol station to pick up a bunch of rather tired-looking carnations. 'Not as elegantly wrapped as we might have wanted,' he joked when he got back in the car, 'but it'll give Ruth something to be picky about. I swear that girl gets worse. Sometimes I'm ashamed to admit that she's my own.'

Ruth certainly seemed to be on top picky form when she opened the door to them. 'You're early,' she said, clearly annoyed by this lack of thought on their part.

'Hello to you too,' Alec said cheerily, 'have some flowers. And don't worry about us, we won't get in your way, in fact we'll hide in the car if you'd prefer.'

'Dad, you know perfectly well that sarcasm is the lowest form –'

'Of wit,' he finished for her. 'Yes, I know that and don't you just love it? Now point me in the direction of a good bottle of wine and I'll leave you well alone. Hello, Oscar, my fine young man, and how are you?'

Oscar came towards them.

'Shake hands, Oscar,' his mother said.

Oscar extended an awkward hand.

'Other one,' Ruth said sharply.

Kate intervened and stooped down to the little boy. 'I'd rather have a hug.'

Ruth tutted and led the way through to the kitchen. 'Adam!' she called out indiscriminately to some other part of the house, 'Dad and Kate are here, come and entertain them, I've got far too much to do.'

Melissa and Tim arrived late, which caused Ruth further distress. She was so preoccupied with the inconvenience thrust upon her – the pork was overdone and the potatoes were past eating – that she was blind to what was glaringly obvious to the rest of them: Tim and Melissa must have just had an almighty blazing row. Their faces were set like stone, they looked charged and ready to go off at the slightest provocation.

'It's Tim's fault we're so late,' Melissa said as Adam handed her a glass of wine, 'I told him to be ready at twelve, but would he listen?'

'And I told you first thing that I had some important phone calls to make.' Tim's voice was taut with anger, his eyes narrow and threatening.

But by the time they took their seats at the dining-room table the mood had calmed down. Whatever storm had rocked their boat, it seemed to have been lulled. Melissa was now talking about some elderly distant relative in Aberdeen who had recently married his octogenarian neighbour; a woman whom he'd known for the past fifty-five years.

'It was only a small Registry Office do,' Melissa was saying, 'that's why none of us was invited.'

'Can't say that I'd have wanted to go,' Ruth said, pulling a face and passing the first plate of carved meat to her mother. 'Just imagine all those zimmer frames cluttering up the place, to say nothing of the disgusting smell of old age. Oscar, put that book down, it's time to eat.'

'What a kindly view of the elderly you have, Ruth,' Alec said light-heartedly, 'I feel wonderfully reassured by it and can just see you selflessly taking care of me in my dotage. I look forward to that day.'

Ruth passed a plate to Kate. 'Thankfully, I shan't be called upon for that duty; you'll have Kate to swill out your false teeth and change your incontinence pads.'

All trace of the humour that had been on Alec's face was suddenly gone. Kate decided to put Ruth in her place. 'Well,' she said in a clear voice and looking straight at Ruth, 'who knows, Alec might even now end up fathering a child who would *want* to take good care of him if the situation arose.'

Ruth let out a scornful laugh. 'Well, that's the most ridiculous thing I've ever heard. Dad's well passed all that, thank God. Oscar, here's your plate.' past

His normal composure quickly restored, Alec gave Kate a grateful smile. Earlier in the week he had specifically asked Kate not to tell anyone in his family about the baby. 'I want to be the one who tells them and in my own time,' he'd said to her, but with a certain amount of malicious delight coming to the fore, he concluded that now was as good a time as any to break the news. Indeed, his anger at Ruth's thoughtless words convinced him there could be no better opportunity. 'Actually,' he said, raising his glass of Côte du Rhône and gazing at it intently, then twirling it round in his hand and giving off an air of easy nonchalance, 'you couldn't be more wrong, Ruth. It gives me great pleasure to tell you that Kate and I are expecting our first child.'

The silence was stupendous.

As was the expression on Ruth's face.

It was Tim who was the first to congratulate them. 'Well done, both of you,' he said, then, looking pointedly at Melissa, he added, 'and wouldn't it be a laugh if Melissa and I were to follow suit?' Melissa's eyes glittered back at him. Undaunted, he raised his glass, 'To Alec and Kate's baby, may it be the first of many!'

Half-hearted voices around the table joined in, but Kate sensed that the mood was as congratulatory as a deathbed scene.

'Are you sure?' Ruth said when the initial shock had died away.

Alec laughed. 'Well of course we are. Kate's done one of those tests from the chemist.'

Ruth laughed nastily. 'Those do-it-yourself kits aren't all they're cracked up to be,' she said dismissively, 'they can't be relied upon.'

'I've also been to the doctor,' Kate said with quiet authority as she helped Oscar to some carrots, 'and it's confirmed, it's official.'

'Oh, well, in that case you must be pregnant.'

'You don't sound very pleased, Ruth,' Alec said mischievously, at the same time holding back his surprise that Kate had been to the doctor without telling him, 'don't you like the idea of having a baby brother or sister?' He was enjoying himself now. He knew exactly how his daughter viewed him. Well, this would certainly show her.

'And why would you think that?' Ruth responded directly.

Her tight, scathing voice made Alec hesitate. They were suddenly heading into dangerous territory; sibling rivalry wasn't just for the young, it could kick in at any age. He looked at Melissa, hoping that she might diffuse the situation – she'd always been able to calm Ruth in moments of high drama – but all he got from her was an expression that clearly said, 'You've got yourself into this mess, you're on your own.'

'What kind of baby will it be?' asked Oscar, who was chasing a roast potato with his knife and fork – it was so overcooked it was taking all his concentration just to keep it from jumping off the plate.

'A perfect one,' answered Alec, quick as a flash, glad of his grandson's diversion.

Melissa groaned at the other end of the table. 'Not even being a father all over again gives you the right to start talking like that.'

'We'll have to wait and see whether it's a boy or a girl, Oscar,' Kate said. She was trying to work out why she wasn't delighted with Alec for telling his family about the baby, especially as he'd described it as their *first*.

Then it struck her what was wrong. Alec was using her pregnancy as a weapon against his charmless daughter.

Perhaps Melissa as well.

The thought chilled her.

No child of hers was ever going to be used as a weapon. She now wondered if Alec had only accepted the baby because he saw it as a way of scoring points over Ruth and his ex-wife.

Chapter Forty

By early Saturday evening Anna had come to terms with the knowledge that Piers was not going to come to her aid until at least Monday morning, so meanwhile there was nothing for it but to put up with Jessica's infuriating ministrations.

The only phone call they'd received was from Josh. He'd called not long after breakfast and as a consequence Jessica was now thrashing about in the kitchen putting together an unspeakably disgusting supper for the three of them to endure that evening.

When she'd heard her daughter talking to Josh on the phone she'd called out, 'Why don't you invite him for supper tonight?' She liked Josh. The truth was, she was quite taken with him and having his company at Willow Cottage did at least provide her with a welcome break from Jessica's new-found despotic behaviour. It was a shame, though, that her selfishness meant that poor Josh had to stomach one of Jessica's meals.

It was after his phone call that Jessica had explained to her why she had stayed out so late last night. 'I just don't see why he kept it from me,' Jessica had said.

But Anna could quite understand Josh's reasons for keeping quiet. 'The trouble with any serious illness or disability,' she'd told Jessica, 'is that it has a nasty habit of stripping away a person's dignity and that's what that young man is terrified of. He's intelligent and good-looking, and wants to be treated accordingly. He doesn't want shoulder-patting sympathy, no matter how well meant.'

They had then reached for the up-to-date *Family Medical Journal* that Anna had recently purchased from her book club and flicked through it looking for multiple sclerosis.

'*MS is an attack on the central nervous system, i.e. the brain and spinal cord*,' the opening paragraph began. It then went on to talk about something called myelin sheaths being destroyed and exposed nerve fibres preventing impulses from the brain being correctly transmitted. The author of the text wrote in matter-of-fact terms of the twenty per cent of extreme cases of MS sufferers who become so seriously disabled that they end up wheelchair-bound.

When they'd finished reading, Jessica had returned the book to the shelf with a worried expression on her face.

'Best not let on to Josh that we've been researching the subject,' Anna had said. 'And remember,' she'd added firmly, 'he's the same Josh you've come to know these past few months. You haven't treated him as a sick man up to this point, so there's no reason why you should start now.'

'I know that,' Jessica had said.

But Anna wasn't convinced that Jessica did. And hearing the sound of the doorbell and her daughter going to answer it, she sincerely hoped that she would heed her advice.

Josh arrived bearing almost more gifts than he could carry. He came into the sitting-room and Anna tried hard not to notice his limp – previously she'd never given it a second look, but now like a car accident on the motorway it was hard not to take her eyes off the stiffness of his leg and how it affected his gait.

'A fresh supply of chocolates for you,' he said, coming slowly over to where Anna was sitting and offering her a large flat box, 'I thought you might have finished the others by now.'

'Thank you,' she said with a smile, 'how thoughtful and intuitive of you.'

Then he turned to Jessica and handed her a beautifully arranged bouquet of red roses. He kissed her cheek. 'For being so understanding last night,' he whispered into her ear. 'And lastly, but by no means least, something for all of us, a bottle of wine.'

Jessica smiled and took that from him as well. 'Brilliant,' she said, 'it'll go a long way to disguising the awful meal I'm about to make you both eat.'

'Would you like some help?' he asked.

Anna laughed. 'Good idea, Josh. Jessica's told me what an excellent cook you are, why don't you go and see what culinary disaster she's got in store for us? I'm afraid my influence when she was growing up failed to bring out the slightest chance of any cookery expertise in her.'

'I'm sure it won't be that bad,' Josh said, already moving towards the kitchen with Jessica.

'Oh no,' she said to him, 'I'm not having you poking and prying into what I've been slaving over all afternoon and besides, you need to sit down.'

Anna bit her lip. Wrong thing to say, she wanted to shout across the room. She saw it in Josh's face only too plainly. But not in Jessica's. Oh dear, she thought, poor Josh.

When Jessica left the room, Josh came and sat by the fire with Anna. He stared into the burning logs and frowned, his face suddenly pensive, but at the same time painfully vulnerable.

Anna's heart went out to him. She decided to be honest with him. 'Jessica mentioned to me this morning what you told her last night,' she said.

He looked up morosely, his eyes dark and angry. 'What, that I love her, or that I'm a chronic invalid?'

Anna smiled kindly. 'She doesn't see you like that, Josh. Just give her time to understand. And by the way, love wasn't discussed, but I'm delighted that's the way you feel about my daughter. Now why don't you go and join her in the kitchen and help with the supper? At least then I might feel confident that we'll eat something slightly more appetising than wet newspaper.'

That night in bed, Tony lay next to Amanda unable to sleep. Like watching the winning goal in a Cup Final match being replayed over and over in slow motion he was reliving the moment when he'd kissed Kate.

And when *she*'d kissed him.

That it hadn't been a one-sided affair had surprised and delighted him. She hadn't pushed him away as he'd expected. There had been no slap in the face. No enraged 'How dare you!' or 'What the hell do you think you're doing?'. None of that, just one long delicious moment of pleasure.

She had willingly kissed him, and kissed him with more passion than he'd dared to hope for. He had no idea when he would get the chance to see her alone again, but somehow he knew he would make it happen.

He got out of bed and went downstairs and looked out of the kitchen window across the moonlit courtyard. Number five was in darkness. Kate and Alec must have gone to bed. He turned away. He didn't want to imagine Kate in bed with Alec, couldn't bear the idea of another man's comforting arms around her.

So this is when the pain starts, he thought miserably.

As though he hadn't suffered enough already.

Kate wasn't lying in bed with Alec's comforting arms around her. She was staring out of the window and looking towards the copse of trees, remembering the evening she had gone there in tears when she and Alec had had their first argument. It seemed that ever since that night things had gone wrong between them.

They had very nearly argued again this afternoon when they'd driven back from Ruth and Adam's. It was only her guilt over Tony that had stopped her from challenging Alec about the way he'd announced to his family that she was pregnant. She recalled Jessica's words when she'd said that sometimes when a man became a father late in life there was an element of kudos to be revelled in. Was that what Alec was doing? Was he now hell-bent on proving his virility to Ruth and Melissa by flaunting his unborn child? She touched her stomach protectively, frightened that Alec might love their baby for all the wrong reasons.

But who was she to say what was the correct way to love a child? No two people experienced love in the same manner and anyway, it was generally agreed that fathers and mothers loved their children quite differently.

She sighed and a small misty patch of condensation appeared on the glass in front of her. She wiped it away with her fingers and wished it would be as simple to wipe away the sense of disappointment that had been steadily growing within her.

She was loved by a wonderful man and was pregnant – not so long ago this would have been all she would have wanted in life. But it was like wishing for a certain Christmas present for months and months, then opening it up on Christmas morning only to discover that it was no longer what you wanted.

So what did she want?

She turned and looked at Alec asleep in bed. He looked so peaceful, so at ease with himself. Tears pricked at her eyes and she swallowed back the painful truth that she no longer wanted Alec.

Chapter Forty-One

On Monday afternoon, just as the first of Ricki Lake's guests was within a whisker of being confronted with her worst fear in the hope of overcoming it, the phone rang – Anna's worst fear was that her lovely home would never be her own again, that Jessica would sell her house at Cholmford Hall Mews and make herself a permanent fixture at Willow Cottage.

She pointed the remote control at the television and turned down the sound on Ricki's over-excited audience, who were all now screaming and squirming as a large hairy spider was being presented to a visibly sweating, goggle-eyed Kansas mother of six, who in the interest of entertainment was giving a credible performance of a woman going to her death on national television – *you saw it here first, folks!* Out in the hall, Anna could hear Jessica speaking into the phone. From the tone of her voice it didn't sound like Josh. Was it Piers at last? She held her breath and listened in. She also quietly prayed for a small miracle.

'How on earth did you know that I was here, Piers?' Jessica asked.

'It's my job, Jessica, to know where and what you're doing. Haven't I always told you I'm supposed to make your life easier. A shame you couldn't do the same for me. I've been trying your house for days, only to get your maddening squeaky voice telling me you'll get right back to me. And as you haven't had the courtesy to do that, I've been forced into ringing this number which you gave me before you left Corfu.'

'Oh,' said Jessica, taken aback at such a long speech from Piers. Had she given him her mother's number? She couldn't remember ever doing so.

'Oh, indeed,' he said. 'So how's *A Casual Affair*?'

'Um . . .' Piers always made Jessica feel as if she were back at school when he started enquiring about her writing. The second he so much as hinted at wanting a progress report she was back in the classroom, explaining to Mr Hang'em-High-Delaney why she hadn't handed in her history essay on the Battle of Naseby. 'It's on hold for a while,' she said meekly. She took the wise precaution of backing away from the receiver.

'On hold!' roared Piers predictably. 'So that's how it is from now on, is it, Jessica? Suddenly you're earning real money and you're acting like a prima donna. You'll be expecting me to come up there and sort out your shopping next. Or maybe you've ideas of becoming another Barbra Streisand and will be wanting me to put rose petals down the loo for you!'

'I'd rather you cleaned it for me.'

'I bet you would. Now get on and explain what the hell you're playing at.'

'I've got personal problems,' she said – a comment like that to Hang'em-High-Delaney would have had him responding with *You certainly have, it's called scraping yourself off the floor after I've finished with you.* Or, *Miss Lloyd, I have no wish to know about your personal hygiene problems, kindly deal with them and get on with your work.*

'Haven't we all,' said Piers drily.

Which struck Jessica as odd. Piers wasn't the sort to have personal problems, he didn't fit the category at all; to have personal problems one had to have some kind of emotional sensitivity.

'My mother's had an accident,' she said, trying to sound as though she were in the driving seat of the conversation, 'and I'm taking care of her.' Frankly, though, it sounded too much like *Please Sir, the dog chewed up my history book.* 'She's broken her arm and cracked a rib,' she added, just in case Piers needed convincing. *Convincing!* What was she thinking of? What on earth was the matter with her? Why did she let Piers reduce her to this trembling, pathetic state? But it was a familiar question and one that she had never cared to explore too deeply. Delving into her private Pandora's box of lunacy was not a pastime she was keen to pursue. In her opinion it was best simply to nail the lid down on all that jolly psycho-babble and conclude that fathers who died before their daughters had had a chance to become an expensive millstone round their necks, had a lot to answer for.

'I'm sorry to hear about your mother,' Piers said, jolting her out of her thoughts, 'but I'm not sure I see how that prevents you from getting on with *A Casual Affair.*'

Because, you unfeeling soulless man, I can't think straight. Because all my energy's going into worrying about my mother. Surely even a Neanderthal simpleton like you can grasp that small but significant piece of information! And on top of all that I've gone and fallen in love with a man who has some bloody awful incurable disease.

Which was the stark reality of the situation in which she now found herself.

While out food shopping on Saturday afternoon and wondering what on earth she could cook for Josh that evening, she had taken a detour from the supermarket, headed for the nearest bookshop and bought their one and only book on the subject of MS. 'We don't get a lot of call for it,' the woman behind the till had said as she wiped the dust off the small paperback. 'I had an aunt who had MS,' she continued, handing over Jessica's change, 'or maybe it was ME, I get them confused. Anyhow, whatever it was, she died. Her blood got too thick, or was it too thin? She was only young.' Which choice comments had thoroughly depressed Jessica as she'd driven back to Cholmford. It was only late that night after Josh had gone home – having bravely forced down her watery, tasteless shepherd's pie, the lumps in the mashed potato being the only substance to the meal – that she had had an opportunity to open the book. It didn't make for soothing bedtime reading. When she reached the chapter on Sexual Difficulties she had switched off the light. She didn't want to think about that. Sex with Josh was great. Better than great, it was the best she'd ever known. It was chandelier-swingingly fantastic. But would it stay that way?

'Jessica?'

'I'm sorry, Piers, what were you saying?'

'I asked why you weren't getting on with what you're paid to do?'

Jessica muttered something about Anna needing a lot of attention.

'So what am I supposed to tell Cara?'

'Nothing, I'll talk to her.'

'All this is very unprofessional, Jessica, you do realise that, don't you? Especially as I've gone to a lot of trouble to get you a slot on telly, but obviously I can see that it's now out of the question. I'll call the producer back and tell him you're unavailable.'

'Hang on a moment, what slot on telly?'

Having just signed the last two letters that Stella was waiting for, Piers pushed them towards her hovering figure in the doorway of his office and, leaning back in his chair and satisfied that Jessica had taken the bait, he began reeling her in. 'It's not much,' he said airily, 'but it would have coincided nicely with the launch of your next hardback. Cara was delighted when I told her about it this morning.'

'So tell *me* about it.'

'It's one of those new daytime life-style programmes. You know the kind of thing, yesterday's bimbos now all grown up and presenting an hour of uplifting crap. The flavour is feel-good-anything's-possible. The idea was that you would be featured as a young independent woman, attractive and well-travelled, who can rattle off the odd novel while enjoying life to the full. You were supposed to be inspirational.'

Jessica liked the sound of herself. She said modestly, 'I'm not sure about the attractive bit.'

Piers ignored this and reeled her in a few more turns. 'It would be a shame to turn it down, but I can quite see that you wouldn't have the time to fit it in. After all, they'd want to come up and spend an entire day filming with you. It would be very time-consuming.'

'When were they thinking of?'

'They've a busy schedule, Jessica, they said they could only fit you in next week, it's then or never. But don't worry, I'll make the necessary apologetic noises and –'

'It's rather a good opportunity, isn't it? I'd hate to let Cara and the team down.'

Piers had her almost out of the water now; he'd never known an author turn down an opportunity to go on television. 'But like you said, you've got a lot on your plate, they'll understand.'

Jessica was already choosing a new outfit to wear for the programme, something smart, understated, classy, probably black. *boring.* She'd go to Wilmslow and treat herself. 'No,' she said decisively, 'I've got to be professional about this. Tell them I'll do it.'

Piers snapped forward in his seat, triumphant. 'So long as you're sure,' he said, affecting a casual manner and then going in for the kill. 'Now before I forget, Cara mentioned something about your next book being brought out earlier than originally agreed.'

'How much earlier?'

'May.'

'*What!*'

'You heard, Jessica. Cara said she'll ring you about it. My advice is to crack on.'

He put down the phone, pleased with himself. Jessica had always been one of his most compliant authors. She'd never given him any trouble. Not like some. One author actually expected him to make theatre and restaurant reservations whenever he was up in town. It was the older ones who were the worst; they imagined themselves to be still living in an age when writers were revered as demi-gods. They hadn't sussed that these days nobody gave a monkey's arse for their art-form and that publishers were only interested in profit margins and bestseller lists. Most of the time his job swung between appeasing the appalling egos and vanity of his authors and the ruthless commercialism of their publishers.

And relying on Jessica's vanity had paid off. He had never doubted his ability to get her back to work, but even he hadn't been prepared for the face of good fortune to smile on him so benevolently.

Dinner on Saturday night with an old friend who two years ago had left the murky waters of the publishing industry for the equally shark-infested ones of the BBC had provided him with just the carrot he needed to get Jessica off her backside, or rather on to it and back at her laptop. Max had described the new show he was producing and said they'd been let down by an author and did he have a client – a female client – who had led an ordinary but verging on the interesting life. 'We don't want the bizarre or the surreal. Everybody's sick of publishing success stories achieved on the strength of the writer's dubious background. Ex-prostitutes turned born-again missionaries are out. So are tarnished politicians. We want an ordinary woman to whom the viewer can relate, or even aspire to. Know anyone of that ilk?'

This spectacular piece of good luck was then followed by Cara phoning him first thing that morning to explain that several of their lead titles for next year had been switched about and Jessica's was being brought forward, and did he think it would be a problem for her?

And so what if it was? The amount she was being paid she could bloody well pull her finger out. Not that he'd said as much to Cara. 'I'll put it to Jessica,' he'd told her, 'but you're expecting a lot, that's three months' working time you're cutting from her schedule. She'll expect something in return, like an extra push from the publicity department.'

He clasped his hands behind his head and leant back in his chair. Not a bad day's work all in all. And it would probably please Jessica's mother into the bargain, leaving her to enjoy her broken bones in peace.

But enough of the quiet reflection, there was still work to do. He bent forward in his seat and pulled the telephone towards him. His next task was to deal with a recalcitrant mystery writer suffering from writer's block and a monumental drink problem, who was already two months late for his deadline.

If Anna hadn't had a broken wrist she would have clapped her hands delightedly. Piers had come through for her! She tried hard not to look too pleased and stared solemnly at her daughter. 'So what you're saying is that they're bringing your book out that much earlier, which means you've got to finish it sooner. That's rough on you, isn't it?' She hoped there was enough sympathy in her voice.

'But kind of convenient for you, wouldn't you say?' Jessica said. 'You're thinking, yippee, Jessica won't have time to take care of me now, aren't you?'

'Nonsense, you know how much I've enjoyed having you here – why, it's what's kept me going these long dreary days.'

'Hah! You hate having me around.'

Anna smiled. 'On a permanent basis, yes. A lot of you goes a long way when you're trying to be nice, Jessica; you're a bit like saccharin.'

'Thanks for the recommendation, I'm flattered.'

'In the circumstances, it's the best I can do. When are you leaving?'

Jessica frowned. 'I'm not,' she said stubbornly. 'You need looking after. There are things you can't manage.'

'Such as?'

'A whole load.' Jessica looked helplessly about her. 'For a start, you can't clear out the ashes from the fire and re-lay it, and you certainly can't bring in the logs –'

'Only because you haven't let me. If I take it slowly –'

'No. It's out of the question.' Jessica began pacing the room. 'I can't leave you all alone, I shall have to work from here. I'll set myself up in the dining-room. Just because Cara has changed the goalposts it doesn't mean that I have to leave you.'

Disappointment made Anna want to cry. 'But Jessica, you're driving me mad,' she shouted angrily. 'I want some time on my own, why do you think I never remarried? Why do you think I've always lived in Cholmford where there aren't any neighbours to pester me? Can't you get it into your thick head? *I like being alone.*'

Jessica came to a stop behind the sofa. She rested her hands on the back of it and stared at her mother, amazed at her outburst.

'We've got to reach a compromise,' Anna said more calmly, but wondering whether it was physically possible to throttle her daughter with one hand.

Jessica continued to stare at her mother. Then very slowly she moved across the room and sat in the chair opposite her. 'You're right,' she said. Her voice suddenly sounded dragged down with resignation. 'It's just that I don't know how to compromise where you're concerned; you've done so much for me all my life.'

'I was only doing my job,' Anna said lightly, 'and I'm not sure I've done that much for you.'

'But you have. And now that it's my turn to look after you, you won't let me. You're not being fair.'

Anna smiled. 'When I really need your help I'll let you know. Let's just accept that now isn't that time.'

Jessica frowned, far from convinced that this was the case. She thought of her mother's angry outburst a few moments ago. 'Did you really mean what you just said, about not remarrying because you wanted to be on your own?'

'Absolutely. I've always enjoyed my freedom. Granted it's probably what's made me selfish and difficult to get on with, but it's my life and I'll live it exactly how I want to.'

'So you want me out?'

'Yes, please.'

'But what if something happens?'

'Why don't we do what Josh suggested?'

'What was that?'

'We'll get me a mobile phone and that way, should something go wrong, you know, like I collapse in the bathroom, I'll be able to call you at the flick of a switch.'

'Knowing you, you'll leave the wretched thing somewhere and forget where you've put it.'

'Do you mind! I'm not as daft as all that.'

'Or you'll run the batteries down and for that crucial phone call you won't be able to ring me.'

'Your over-active imagination is running away with you, dear.'

'Don't call me dear, it makes me deeply suspicious. Gavin started calling me *dear* and *darling* before I found out about Silicone Sal. And I don't care what you say, I should sleep here with you every night.'

Anna sighed. 'No,' she said firmly. 'You can pop in for a short while every day, just to make sure I haven't pegged out, but that's as far as it goes. Anyway, wouldn't you rather spend more time with Josh?'

Jessica opened her mouth to refute this, but found she couldn't. The truth was she did want to see more of Josh. Lots more of him. And now that he had nothing to hide from her they could actually spend a whole night together.

Seeing the hesitation in her daughter's face and knowing that the last of her resolve had been weakened, Anna pressed on: 'And as Piers has just told you, you have to concentrate on your writing. He and Cara are relying on you. Now tell me again about the BBC coming to film us.'

'*Us?* It's me, your young, attractive, independent daughter they're interested in,' Jessica said, aware that a feeling very much like relief was creeping over her.

'Really? I didn't know I had one of those. But they'll want to film a snippet or two of where you grew up, won't they?' Anna was thinking about getting the garden into shape ready for the cameras. She and Dermot could sweep up the leaves that were already beginning to fall and they could put them in a neat, tidy pile ready for a bonfire on the day the film crew came; bonfires with a thin trail of smoke hanging in the damp autumn air always looked so atmospheric on the television, she thought. What fun it would be.

Chapter Forty-Two

Mo had spent most of the day in hiding. As soon as she'd caught sight of Josh entering the building earlier that morning she'd made herself scarce by disappearing to the loo. She even conned Sid into taking Josh's coffee to him. Sid knew all about what had happened at the party because after she'd finally made it back downstairs he'd told her what had gone on between Josh and Jessica. 'You're in it deep, Mo,' he'd said, 'about as deep as it gets. The look on the guy's face was awesome. I've never seen anything like it.'

'Oh shit,' she'd cried, realising with horror what she'd done, 'oh shit, oh shit, oh *shit*!'

'Yeah, that's the stuff you're knee-deep in,' Sid had said and, taking her through to the kitchen and pushing everyone out of the way, he'd started making her several gallons of black coffee.

'I don't need that,' she'd wailed hysterically. 'What you've just told me is sobering enough.'

'You're going to drink it,' he'd insisted.

Between forcing down several mugs of Turkish-strength coffee she'd kept saying, 'But I thought she knew. I really thought he must have told her. How was I to know he hadn't?'

'Come on,' Sid had said when she'd refused to drink any more, 'come and dance with me. You need cheering up.'

'No I don't,' she'd said miserably.

'Yes you do and while we dance we can work out what you're going to say to Josh on Monday morning.'

And here they were, half past five on Monday afternoon and still she hadn't plucked up the courage to speak to Josh. Sid had been great to her all day and had taken her out for a sandwich at lunch-time to try and calm her down. She knew that he fancied her and really he was quite cute, with that cool hair of his, and maybe she ought to think about him more seriously . . . now that Josh was probably never going to speak to her again.

She bent down beneath the reception desk and began getting her stuff ready to go home. She slipped a bundle of essay notes into her bag, along with a magazine, both of which she'd been too sick with nerves to so much as glance at during the day. When she stood upright she let out a sudden gasp – Josh was standing straight in front of her.

'Got time for a chat?' he asked.

There was no avoiding him now and with a leaden step she followed him slowly to his office, aware that everybody was staring at them – word had soon gone round that she'd blown her future with Crawford's. She was conscious, too, of the chunky heels of her knee-high PVC boots reverberating loudly on the wooden floor as if beating out a painfully slow death march. It made her remember what she'd said to Jessica about wanting Josh to follow behind her coffin when she was dead. Yes, she thought, he'd follow it all right and then stamp on her grave afterwards. How he must hate her. And with every right. She had committed the one act guaranteed to get up his nose: she had gossiped about his illness behind his back.

As she entered Josh's office she caught sight of Sid giving her an encouraging smile over the top of his computer. Then the door closed ominously behind her.

'How are you feeling?' Josh asked.

She watched him loosen his tie and undo the top button of his Paul Smith shirt; it was one of her favourites and it was attractively crumpled from its day's work. And as he rolled up his sleeves and leant back against his desk she thought, *God, I fancy him.* She then thought, *Jeez, girl, pull yourself together! This is no time for lust. This is the moment you get fired. You're history, kid. You're outta here.* 'I'm fine,' she muttered, suddenly remembering that Josh had asked her a question.

'You sure?'

She gave a little nod and twisted her hands nervously behind her back. Her fingers touched the silver bangle Josh and Charlie had given her. How she wished she could turn the clock back to that lovely precious moment in the garden when she'd opened their present.

He went and sat down and, still regarding her, removed his glasses and added them to a pile of sample T-shirts. 'I haven't been able to thank you for Friday evening,' he said. 'Whenever I went to look for you I couldn't find you.'

She swallowed and wished he'd just get on with it. Why put her through all this agony? Did he want her to suffer? And hadn't she suffered enough all weekend, dreading coming in to work? She moved a little nearer to his desk. It was time to get it over and done with. 'Look,' she said, 'I'm really sorry about the other night. I'd had too much to drink and I was feeling wretched and I shot my big mouth off and I'm really –'

'Yes,' he interrupted, 'Jessica said you weren't well when she spoke to you.'

'I am sorry, honestly.'

He looked at her fondly. 'In a way you did me a favour.'

It was a few seconds before Mo registered that there was a hint of a smile playing at the corners of his tempting mouth. 'A favour?' she repeated.

'Yes, but I don't particularly want to go into that now.' He picked up his glasses and began fiddling with them. The hint of a smile was gone.

'Does that mean you're not going to sack me?'

He frowned. 'Why would I want to do that?'

'Because . . . because of what I told Jessica,' Mo said, wishing he wouldn't frown – didn't he know that it made him even more attractive?

He shook his head tiredly. 'Forget it. At the moment what really concerns me is that you've spent the day hiding from me.'

She lowered her eyes.

'And don't look like that, I'm not a tyrant.'

She didn't know what to say, so she stood staring blankly down at her shiny boots. After a while she said, 'Can I go now? I think I'm going to cry.'

He stood up and went to her.

'It must be the relief,' she sniffed. 'You and Charlie have always been so good to me and then I go and do the worst possible thing to upset you.'

'Come on, Mo,' he said gently, 'I've told you it's all right. It was all my fault anyway, it's me who should be sorry for putting you in such a difficult position.'

She looked up at him. 'Do you really mean that?'

He nodded.

'You're not just saying it to make me feel better?'

'Come on,' he said, 'stop giving yourself such a hard time.'

She managed a small smile.

'Now go home and cheer yourself up on that trampoline of yours. Or better still, make Sid's day and get him to take you out for a drink.'

When he was alone Josh dialled the number for Willow Cottage.

He wanted to see if he could make his own day by seeing Jessica that evening.

It was some time before the phone was answered and when it was he was surprised to hear Anna's voice at the other end of the line. 'Hello, Josh,' she said, 'if it's Jessica you want, she's not here, she's gone to one of those late-night-opening stores to buy me a mobile phone, just like you suggested. She's moving back to her own place, isn't that wonderful news?'

'I guess so,' he said, 'you sure you'll be okay?'

'Now don't you start, Josh. I thought if there was one person I could rely on it would be you.'

'Point taken. But . . .' He hesitated. Would Anna accept his help? he wondered.

'But what?' she asked.

'I was just thinking if there was ever something you needed and you didn't want Jessica concerned you could always give me a ring, you know that, don't you?'

'That's very kind of you, Josh, and I promise to bear it in mind.'

When he'd finished his call with Anna, Josh caught sight of Mo through his open office door. She had her large Moschino bag slung over her shoulder and was chatting to Sid while he switched off his computer. Josh smiled, hoping that Mo might at last transfer the affection she had for him to poor patient Sid. He put on his glasses and returned his attention to what he'd been dealing with before he'd finally tracked down Mo. But it was no good. He couldn't concentrate. He couldn't shake off the uncomfortable image of himself that Mo had left him with. Did she really think him capable of sacking her, just like that?

First thing that morning when they were going through the post Charlie had said, 'Go easy on Mo, won't you, she looks sick with worry.'

But he'd had no intention of laying into Mo for what she'd done. It was his own fault that it had happened. He should never have played such a potentially dangerous game. It had been unfair of him to expect Mo to be a mind-reader. How was she supposed to know that he hadn't told Jessica the truth?

'How'd it go?'

He looked up to see his brother peering round the door.

'What, when I finally got to speak to Mo?'

Charlie came in. 'Precisely that.'

'She's fine, it's all sorted.'

'Thank heavens.'

'She thought I was going to fire her,' Josh said, a troubled expression on his face.

'So did everybody else.'

'But that's crazy. Why? Why would I do that?'

Charlie shrugged.

'I'm not some wacko jackboot bully.'

But you give a damned good impression of one at times, thought Charlie. 'If you say so,' he said tactfully. 'Any chance of cadging a meal off you tonight?' he added. 'I'm getting bored of solitary take-aways.'

'Sorry, I'm hoping to see Jessica.'

'Oh.'

'How about you and Rachel?'

Charlie shook his head. 'Nothing doing there. Looks like I failed at the first gate . . . unlike you and Jessica.'

Josh leant back in his chair and slowly tapped a pencil on the keyboard by his hand. 'I wouldn't say it's going to be plain sailing from now on,' he said thoughtfully.

'Why do you say that? When I phoned you on Saturday, you said it was all straight between the two of you, that you'd explained everything and she was okay. Sounded to me like she'd taken it pretty well. Better than you could have hoped for in the circumstances.'

'I know. It's just . . .' He let go of the pencil and flicked it across the desk. 'I can't get it out of my head that she's going to over-react.'

'What do you mean?'

He told Charlie about the way Jessica had been driving her mother round the bend with her constant fussing. 'And she started doing it with me on Saturday when I had supper with them. She wouldn't let me help with anything because, to use her words, "*you need to sit down*". She kept watching me, as if she was worried I'd collapse any second.'

'Well maybe *you*'re over-reacting,' Charlie said. 'Personally I thought Jessica was great when I met her at Mo's; I just hope you don't go and ruin things by acting like a real lulu. Give her time.'

'Yeah, that's what her mother said.'

Charlie smiled. 'So if nothing else, it sounds like you're well in with the future mother-in-law.'

Tony was doing a Reggie Perrin, he was imagining his mother-in-law as a hippopotamus. It was a pleasing picture and took his mind off

Bradley-Dewhurst-the-Butcher's-Boy who was jawing into the phone about last month's spectacularly good sales figures.

'I just want you to know how much we appreciate what you're doing, Tony. You've really turned things around.'

'There's no reason why this month shouldn't be as good, or the next,' Tony said, wrenching his mind away from Bloody Rita half submerged in a pool of mud. He decided to go on the attack. 'Do we really need to go through with the downsizing we discussed when you were over here?'

'Sure we do, Tony. I know it's tough for those men, but I'm certain I don't have to convince you that these are tough times for us all, we gotta do all we can to concentrate the focus –'

Tony drifted back to the pool of mud. Except now there were two enormous wallowing hippos: Bradley Hurst had joined Bloody Rita.

Later he drove home listening to Dire Straits' *Love Over Gold*. Away from the office he allowed himself the treat of letting his thoughts linger on Kate. There had to be a way of seeing her. But how could he do that when Alec was usually around most evenings? Not to mention the continuous presence of Amanda. Could he suggest that she take up a hobby? Cake icing or something equally fascinating. Anything. Just so long as it got her out of the house one evening a week. But there was still Alec to deal with. Admittedly he was away on business sometimes, but those occasions seemed to be pretty few and far between. He had wanted to ring Kate at home today, but each time he'd got out her number somebody had come into his office. Tomorrow he would definitely do it. He'd get to work early and ring her before anyone else arrived. But not too early, or Alec would still be there.

He wondered if he could prompt Amanda to invite Alec and Kate to dinner.

No!

That was not a good idea.

It would be awful. How did he think he could sit for an entire evening in the same room as Kate without actually touching her?

But a dinner party was exactly what was on Amanda's mind, which was odd because it shouldn't have been, not really.

At nine thirty that morning her mother had arrived on the doorstep and had set the strangest of days in motion. 'There's something you should know,' she'd said, taking off her coat and handing it to Amanda. 'You'd better prepare yourself for a shock. Tony's having an affair.'

But shock is relative and while Amanda wasn't exactly consigning her mother's early-morning revelation to the level of mild irritation caused by a snagged nail, she was not sufficiently shocked to be rendered speechless. She led her mother through to the sitting-room, waited for her to sit down, then said very calmly, 'Are you quite sure?'

'Quite sure. Your father was driving through Holmes Chapel on Saturday morning and he saw Tony kissing her in broad daylight. Bold as you like. The street full of people and the pair of them wrapped in –'

'Yes,' Amanda cut in quickly. 'I think I get the picture.' She was surprised how hurt she felt. Then she realised it wasn't hurt she was experiencing, but anger. She was furious. Tony's betrayal had jeopardised everything. If their marriage could be likened to a business partnership – and it was a fair analogy in her opinion – she had just discovered her co-managing director with his hands in the till, wilfully destroying the company's future. Clamping down on her anger and determining to put it to good use at a later date she said, 'Is Daddy absolutely sure it was Tony?'

'I know he's not the most observant of men, Amanda, but credit him with sufficient sense to recognise his own son-in-law.'

'So why didn't you tell me sooner?'

'Your father didn't want to upset you. He didn't even tell me until late last night. You know what a coward he can be.'

Amanda didn't say anything for a few minutes. Nor did Rita. Amanda went over to the window and looked out to the garden and at the fields beyond. She thought back to Saturday morning. What had they been doing? Or more to the point, what had Tony been doing? Then she remembered – Tony had taken Hattie to her ballet class. It must have been then. While his daughter was tripping the light fantastic he was with somebody. But who?

Unable to take the silence any longer, or restrain herself from blurting out what she'd obviously wanted to say from the moment she'd arrived, Rita said, 'I warned you. I warned you on your wedding day, but would you listen? I told you that you hadn't put enough thought into what you were doing.'

Amanda turned back to her mother. 'This is not the time for a lesson in I-told-you-so. Did Daddy say what the woman looked like?'

'Yes, but I hardly think that's the point right now. We need to discuss what you're going to do. We need to –'

'Please, I want to know.' A sixth sense told Amanda that she knew exactly who Tony had been with.

'Why? Do you think it's somebody you might know? Somebody from the office? Some slip of a secretary who's been making eyes at him?'

Amanda shook her head. 'No. Not somebody from work. Somebody closer to home.' *Very close to home.*

'Your father mentioned something about a lot of red hair.'

Yes! Who else but sweet Kate? That vision of innocent loveliness. Dear, sweet Kate.

Being a practical woman with no time or need for emotional outpourings – what possible use would such a waste of energy be to anyone? – Amanda quickly got rid of her mother, then set her mind to what to do next. She was determined to salvage as much as she could from her marriage and by late afternoon she had worked out a plan of strategy. A whacking great divorce settlement was her objective, but before that she would have some fun . . . and at Tony's expense.

A little dinner party was required.

She would suggest that they invite Alec and Kate to dinner during the week. It would be better, she knew, and much more convenient no doubt for everyone concerned to wait until the weekend, but she really didn't think she could hold out that long – and what the hell did she care for anyone else's convenience anyway? It would be rather amusing to watch the happy lovers passing the salt to one another, maybe even to catch a glimpse of eyes meeting and fingers touching. Perhaps she might drop a few hints, subtle hints, but sharp enough to make them fidget in their seats.

Did she know? they'd ask themselves guiltily.

How did she know?

Oh, yes, she would make them sweat.

She would make them suffer.

Then, when she was sure that she had her own future neatly buttoned up, she would pounce on them.

Chapter Forty-Three

By Friday afternoon Jessica was well into her stride with *A Casual Affair*; another five or six chapters and the first draft would be in the bag.

Since she'd returned to Cholmford Hall Mews – straight after breakfast on Tuesday morning and very much at her mother's insistence – she had set to on her laptop with a vengeance, rattling the keys for hours on end, only pausing for breath to make herself drinks, go to the loo and phone Anna, just as she'd promised she would. But it didn't seem to be improving matters between them.

'You're doing it again, Jessica,' Anna had shouted at her on Wednesday. 'You've phoned me a total of twelve times since you left. Now get on with your work and leave me alone. I'm fine and am doing nothing more energetic than turning the pages of my newspaper.'

'I don't believe you,' Jessica had said, 'you're probably back up that blasted ladder fixing something or other. Prove to me that you're in the sitting-room, put the telly on.'

'I can't do that, because I'm in the bathroom.'

'What are you doing in there?' Jessica had asked suspiciously, 're-tiling?'

'Goodbye, Jessica. Speak to you soon, no doubt.'

Her frustration with her mother was making her vent her feelings on her characters in *A Casual Affair*. Miles was getting it in the neck from Clare, who was wondering if the shy, handsome Miles was worth all the trouble. Jessica knew better than anyone that happy endings were her speciality, but in her current frame of mind she was tempted to split Clare and Miles asunder and be damned. Let Clare be a woman empowered by her own actions. Let her discover that she needed a man as much as she needed . . . as much as she needed a recalcitrant mother.

Damn her mother!

No. She didn't mean that. She loved Anna and wanted desperately to help her. But how to go about it was the thing. How did all these caring and compassionate doctors and nurses get the strength to do what they did? Or maybe they'd never come up against somebody as stubborn as Anna?

She returned her attention to chapter thirty-two and when she was satisfied with its ending she set the printer in motion and looked out of the window. After a short while she saw Josh's Shogun drive into the courtyard.

She smiled. And there was somebody else she loved.

But like the love she felt for her mother, her feelings for Josh were beginning to be made all the more poignant by her anxiety for him. Over the past few days she had noticed a change in him. He was quieter. More tired as well. And, at times, slightly introverted. From what she had come to understand of MS from the book she'd bought, it was possible that these were signs that a relapse was on the cards. But amateur armchair diagnosis was a dangerous occupation and not one that she ought to risk.

It was just gone seven o'clock and the light was already fading outside and with her desk lamp switched on she knew that Josh would be able to see her clearly through her study window. He parked his car and as he locked it he looked over and waved at her. She waved back and he started towards her house.

She watched his progress with concern. Even in the half-light she could see that he was exhausted. His steps were slow and awkward, and greatly exaggerated; his briefcase gave the impression of being much too heavy for him to carry. He looked wrung-out. Her heart ached for him. She went to the door to let him in. 'Good day at the office, darling?' she said mockingly, taking his case from his hand and kissing him. She felt the burnt-out heaviness in his body as he leant against her, but there was nothing burnt-out in the way he kissed her.

'Do we have to go to Tony and Amanda's this evening?' he asked, holding her tight.

'Why, are you too tired?'

He pulled away from her. 'No, I just don't feel like it.'

Conscious that she'd said the wrong thing, she offered him a drink. 'I've just finished work, so your timing is perfect. I'm having a glass of wine, just to put me in the right frame of mind for tonight.'

'I'll have the same,' he said, following her into the kitchen, 'I need something to dull the effect of Amanda. Are you sure we can't lie low and simply not turn up?'

Jessica smiled. 'She'd come and get us; there'd be nowhere for us to hide. And anyway, I promised Kate we'd go. Safety in numbers, etc. The poor girl's terrified of Amanda.'

'Whereas we just loathe the dreadful woman.'

'Something like that.'

Jessica pulled a bottle of wine out of the fridge, but before she had a chance to do anything with it the phone rang. She handed Josh the bottle and said, 'Corkscrew's in the right-hand drawer next to the cooker, glasses are in the dishwasher.'

She took the call in the study and was stunned to hear Helen's voice. 'Helen!' she yelped loudly.

'Is that horror or delight that's making you squeal like a pig?'

'Delight, of course, where are you?'

'Would you believe in Huddersfield?'

'No!'

'Yes. We're over for our usual health and dental checks. Any chance of seeing you?'

'Still not trusting the Corfiotes with your body, then?'

'Oh, I trust the Corfiotes with my body, just not the bones of me. Anyway, when can Jack and I come to see you?'

'How about tomorrow? You could come for lunch and spend the rest of the day here.'

'That'll be fine. I'll hand you over to Jack and you can give him directions.'

After a brief conversation with Jack, Jessica went back into the kitchen, happy at the prospect of seeing her old friends again, but she was met with a crash and the sound of breaking glass.

'Bugger it!' Josh muttered under his breath, then seeing Jessica in the doorway he said, 'It slipped out of my hands.' He stooped down to the floor and started picking up the pieces.

'Not to worry, butter-fingers,' she said brightly. 'Here, let me do that.' She made to push him out of the way.

'Leave it,' he snapped back at her. 'I'm quite capable of clearing it up.'

She looked at him, stung by the fierceness in his voice. 'I know you are, I just . . . I just don't want you cutting yourself, that's all.'

He got to his feet. 'Meaning I'm more likely to cut myself than you, is that it?'

'Don't be silly,' she said, forcing a lightness into her words. But his face told her he wasn't taken in and he walked away. She wanted to shout at his retreating figure, to tell him he was being unreasonable. But she didn't trust herself. On top of her mother, Josh acting like a sulky child was the last thing she needed. She cleared up the mess, found another bottle of wine, opened it and when she'd calmed down sufficiently took two glasses through to the sitting-room where she found Josh in the dark staring out into the twilight. She switched on a lamp and cautiously approached him by the window.

He turned round. 'I'm sorry,' he said.

'I'm sorry too.' She passed him his wine. He took it from her awkwardly and catching sight of his hand she suddenly realised why he'd dropped the bottle. His fingers were cruelly distorted and were curled into the palm of his hand.

Shocked, she raised her eyes to his and saw the angry frustration in his face. 'Will we be doing a lot of that?'

'What?' he asked. He knew what Jessica had just been staring at and, uncomfortable with her unspoken concern, switched the glass of wine from his right to his left hand.

'Apologising to one another,' she said.

He shrugged. 'Probably.'

They sat down. 'You need to be more honest with me, Josh,' she said. 'If you had told me that you couldn't open –'

'Believe me,' he cut in, 'it's not as simple as that.'

She put down her glass and took his hand in hers. She stroked it gently. 'What does it feel like right now?' she asked.

He tried to remove his hand from her lap, but she wouldn't let him. 'Tell me,' she said, 'please, I want to know. Does it hurt?'

'A bit.'

'Does this make it worse?'

He shook his head and let out his breath, wanting to be able to admit that what she was doing was good, that it helped. But he couldn't. Instead he said, 'What I hate most is that it makes me so bloody clumsy.'

'And bad-tempered?' she ventured.

'That too.'

She continued stroking the back of his hand, then turned it over and began caressing the palm. Very slowly he flexed and straightened his fingers, and one by one, she stroked those as well, but then like a flower closing at night his hand gradually curled back into the rigid position of before, except now her own hand was held firmly within his.

Kate wished she'd been honest with Amanda earlier in the week. 'No, Amanda,' she should have said, 'Alec and I can't come for dinner on Friday night because your husband is the most physically attractive man I've ever met and I'm worried that if I sit in the same room as him I shall burn up with desire for him.'

Powerful stuff.

Shocking, too.

Was it her hormones again? Or was this what love was really like?

With Alec she had always felt safe. Safe and reassured. Comforted. Protected.

But Tony had a different effect on her. The thought of him made her bold. Tacky though it sounded, he made her want to throw caution to the wind.

And she was certainly doing that!

He had phoned her on Tuesday morning, not long after Ruth had dropped off Oscar, and at the sound of his voice she had experienced a rush of something wonderfully exhilarating flow through her.

'Are you alone?' he'd asked.

'No,' she'd said.

'Is Alec still with you?'

'No. I've got Oscar here with me.'

'Who's Oscar?'

'He's Alec's grandson, I look after him during the week.'

'Does that mean I can't see you for lunch?'

Her heart had pounded. 'No. He goes to nursery school in the afternoons.'

'Tomorrow?'

'I could be free from just after one.'

'Where shall we meet?'

'Somewhere a million miles away from here.'

'It's a bit short notice for lunch on Mars.'

In the end they had decided to meet at John Lewis's in Cheadle. It wasn't a very likely venue for a romantic assignation, but it was at least safe; if they were seen, they could pretend they'd simply bumped into each other while shopping.

'I know you don't approve of what we're doing,' he'd said, as they'd roamed the display shelves of china looking for all the world like a normal married couple, 'and I'm not sure that I do either, all I know is that I have to see you.'

She'd echoed his words, but added what she hoped was a well-grounded warning: 'It'll only last a short while. It's probably a case of caprice. It'll pass and you'll return to Amanda and I'll go back to my life with Alec.'

'I don't believe that for a minute,' he'd said.

In her heart, nor did she.

Nor did she think she had the strength to carry off tonight. Surely the moment she and Tony looked at each other everyone in the room would realise what was going on between them?

She finished dressing and went downstairs to Alec, who had already changed out of his work suit and was wearing a peach-coloured shirt with chinos. He looked younger than his approaching fiftieth birthday.

He looked up from his newspaper when he saw her and gave an appreciative whistle. 'Very nice,' he said, taking in the new dress she'd bought when Tony had left her to go back to his office, 'pregnancy obviously suits you, you look lovely. A regular glowing beauty.'

She turned away guiltily, convinced that it wasn't her pregnancy that was making her glow, but the thought of spending an evening with Tony.

Tony still couldn't believe what was happening. It was like some crazy nightmare from which he couldn't wake himself. There was something horribly different about Amanda. He wished he knew what had got into her. From the minute she'd suggested this dinner party she'd been acting strangely. He'd tried his damnedest to dissuade her from going ahead, but she'd have none of it.

It was on Tuesday evening – the day that he'd seen Kate – that Amanda had announced she was inviting the neighbours to supper again. He'd been horrified and had said the first thing that came into his head, 'I shan't be able to make it, I'm working late that night.'

'But you don't know which night I'm talking about,' she'd said in response, 'and anyway I've checked with your secretary and you're definitely free on Friday evening. I've spoken to everybody else, they're all available. I had a lovely long chat with Alec on the phone, he's such a pleasant man. Did you know that Kate was pregnant? I had no idea. Alec sounded as if he was really looking forward to being a father again.'

'That's not what I'd heard.' Which had been a silly slip on his part, for Amanda had seized on it straight away, probably hoping for some nice juicy gossip to mull over.

'What do you mean?' she'd said.

'Oh nothing, it's just that I'm sure I remember Alec saying that he wasn't keen on having any more children.'

He'd phoned Kate the following morning to see what her reaction was. Half of him wanted her to say that she'd back out at the last minute claiming that she wasn't well, but that was tempting fate and he didn't want her to be ill. The other half of him wanted her to be there, at least that way they would see one another. Her thoughts had been the same as his.

And here they all were. Apart from Alec, who seemed to be as easygoing as ever, the rest of them appeared to be on edge.

Josh and Jessica were certainly quieter than usual, with Josh looking well below par. He'd dropped his fork earlier, as well as knocking over a glass, and he was making slow progress with his meal. He'd also noticed Jessica occasionally casting anxious glances in his direction. Perhaps he was coming down with something.

And, as ever, Kate was looking radiantly beautiful, but again, like Josh and Jessica, she was quiet and only added to the conversation when prompted by Amanda.

As for Amanda, well quite frankly, if he didn't know better he would say that each time she darted out to the kitchen she was having a snort of something. She seemed totally wired and was freaking the hell out of him.

At the other end of the table he suddenly heard her asking Kate when she thought she and Alec would get married. He froze. What would Kate say?

'Because you will, won't you,' Amanda persisted, 'especially now that you're pregnant, such a *sweet* couple as yourselves should do the right thing and tie the knot. I've never seen a couple more in love, isn't that right, Tony?'

'Apart from you and me,' he said silkily.

'Ah, ah, ah.' Amanda's laugh was high-pitched and chilling. 'He's full of talk, just listen to him. But back to you, Kate, you haven't answered my question.'

'I'm . . . I'm not really sure,' Kate said hesitantly.

Alec intervened, aware of Kate's discomfort opposite him. 'Maybe that's for me to decide,' he said jovially.

Jessica laughed. 'Dangerous words, Alec, in this day and age of equality. There's no reason why Kate shouldn't pop the question.'

Amanda turned to Josh. 'And how would you feel, Josh, if Jessica proposed to you, pleased or emasculated?'

Josh swallowed his wine and looked thoughtfully across the table. He contemplated Jessica's face through the flickering candle-light. Her eyes were dark and compelling and so very sure, and she was smiling at him in that challenging way she did. 'I'd be pleased,' he said softly, 'and . . . and I'd say yes.'

The room suddenly went very quiet as Jessica and Josh continued to stare at each other.

Until Amanda, who Tony was convinced had all the sensitivity of a rhinoceros – no, second thoughts, make that a hippopotamus along with her mother and Bradley Hurst – jumped up from the table and said, 'Time for cheese, and why don't we be terribly sophisticated and change seats and swap partners, so to speak.'

Tony stared at her. 'What?' he demanded. He'd have been less surprised if she'd suggested a game of strip poker.

'It's what people do at dinner parties,' she said, 'it makes for better interaction between guests.' She ignored his look of bewilderment and began clearing up the dishes. When she came to Josh's she said, 'You've hardly touched your profiteroles, we can't have you wasting away, you'll have to get Jessica to help feed you in the future and teach you not to be so clumsy.'

Jessica had never wilfully struck another person, not if you discounted the incident at infant school when she hit a girl over the head with her satchel, but she was very tempted to leap up from her chair and smash Josh's bowl into Amanda's face. She'd grind it so hard into that artful countenance that the glaze would come clean off the dish. How dare she speak to Josh in that condescending manner.

But if Josh was riled by what the dinner-party hostess from hell had said he gave no outward sign of it. Jessica was proud of him. As they'd walked across the courtyard earlier that evening he had told her that he didn't want any of their neighbours knowing about his MS. 'Can you imagine what that dreadful woman would say to me?' he'd said, 'she'd probably tell me it's all in my mind and advise me to pull myself together.'

Amanda finished gathering up the dishes, took them through to the kitchen and quietly marvelled at herself. The look on Tony's face when she was asking Kate about getting married, oh, it was priceless. Absolutely priceless.

The shock.

The horror.

The jealousy!

It had all been there in his expression. What a slow-witted fool to have given himself away so easily.

Oh, yes, the evening was definitely a success. And it wasn't over yet. Not by a long way.

She had no idea whether that sharp-tongued Jessica and old limping misery guts knew about Tony and Kate, but she had decided to invite them tonight to find out. She wished she hadn't bothered. Witnessing that excruciating little scene between the pair of them just now had been enough to make her violently sick.

But then, if that didn't make her sick, odds on Kate would. Sitting there like Little Miss Dumb Muffet, convincing everyone that she was the last word in angelic sweetness, was too much. What an act! It would serve the bitch right if she walked straight back into the dining-room and announced that she knew what was going on. 'So Kate,' she could say, 'just who exactly is your baby's father? Alec or Tony? Or maybe you've sampled Josh as well?' That would sure as hell take the smug look off Jessica's face.

It was a tempting thought to stir things up so agreeably, but she wasn't ready yet for such a direct confrontation. She had a much better plan in mind. Since her mother had put her so clearly in the picture she had had plenty of time to consider her options. When her anger had eventually subsided she had wondered – for all of a split second – about doing a Hillary Clinton and turning a blind eye to what Tony was up to; it was one way of ensuring the reins of power stayed firmly within her own grip. But it wasn't in her nature to play the part of forgiving wife and besides, Tony simply wasn't worth it.

What intrigued her most was how she had guessed right away who the 'other woman' was. Funny, that. Without realising it she must have absorbed the connection Tony had made with Kate. And since her subconscious had been forced into a state of acknowledgement she had come face to face with what could only be described as incriminating evidence. Tony's Barclaycard statement, showing the cost of that silk scarf he'd insisted on buying Kate in Devon, was a dead give-away. No wonder he had kicked up such a fuss about a tin of toffees. A bit of overcooked sugar was never going to be good enough to impress a lover. But perhaps the real hard evidence of their affair was the fact that Kate was expecting a baby. Truth would certainly tell on that score.

Hearing a sudden burst of laughter coming from the dining-room, Amanda picked up the plate of cheese that she'd put together earlier along with a basket of oatmeal and Bath Oliver biscuits and went back into the fray for some more fun. 'Well, look at this,' she said, 'you've all moved and yet somehow the shuffling hasn't quite worked. Jessica and Josh are fine, I'll allow that, but Kate, why don't you change places with Alec and sit next to Tony, yes, that's a much better idea. There now, let's see how that improves our intercourse.' She laughed, 'No *double entendre* intended.'

'None taken,' Tony said sharply. Had she been doing a line of Jif out there in the kitchen, or what? And so what if she had? He was past caring. So long as she left him to enjoy the illicit sensation of sitting in such close proximity to Kate, she could do as she pleased.

He was now so near her that he hardly dared to move for fear of actually touching her and, the way he was feeling, if he did touch even the tiniest bit of her he was in danger of turning into a freak case of spontaneous combustion.

'Now Jessica,' Amanda said as she passed her the plate of cheese, 'why don't you tell us how your latest book is coming along.'

Jessica helped herself to a piece of Stilton. 'Sorry, Amanda, I'm afraid I can't oblige you. I *never* discuss my work while it's still in progress.'

'How boring. But tell me, do you often write about infidelity?'

'I –'

'Something stuck in your throat, Tony? Kate, you'd better pass Tony that bottle of water, he looks ready to choke to death. Sorry, Jessica, carry on, you were saying...'

'I was just going to say that I covered the subject quite extensively in *Caught in the Act.*'

'Really. You'll have to lend me a copy.'

'And that's something else I never do. You'll have to buy your own, I need the royalties.'

Amanda gave Jessica a hard stare.

In return Jessica yawned and looked pointedly at her watch.

Chapter Forty-Four

When Jessica opened her eyes she felt unaccountably guilty. Then she realised why. She had just been dreaming of Gavin.

She'd been lying in bed with him. Well, more than that, but she didn't want to think about having sex with a man she no longer loved.

She turned over and immediately Gavin was gone and he was replaced with the man she did love.

Josh.

She gazed at his face – a face that at times could be vulnerably sensitive and open, but at other times closed and drawn. She lovingly traced the outline of his jaw with her finger, down his neck, then to his bare chest. She'd never been into hairy men and Josh's sprinkling of fine hair was just perfect. He stirred slightly at her touch, but not enough to wake, and watching him shift position she thought of what he'd said at Tony and Amanda's last night – '*I'd say yes.*'

Would he indeed?

She couldn't have written the scene any better herself. It had been a few seconds of pure magic. The look in his eyes had been so utterly spellbinding that she could have thrown herself down on one knee there and then. But Amanda had put paid to any chance of that.

Honestly, the woman had no soul.

But there again sensitivity was hardly a phenomenon that Amanda was best friends with, it seemed.

Jessica could handle Amanda's snotty comments about her writing – she'd get even one day with her by using her as a character in a future novel – but her manner towards Josh was altogether another matter. The thoughtlessness of the woman had made Jessica want to take her by the throat and shake her till her teeth rattled and her eyes popped out. It was only out of respect for Josh's amazing ability to ignore Amanda that she had restrained herself and kept her anger in check.

When they'd left the scene of what had been the most extraordinary of evenings, Josh had come back with her and they'd gone straight to bed. He was knackered and it was just beginning to dawn on Jessica what life must be like for him. He'd slowly climbed the stairs, collapsed into bed and had fallen asleep almost immediately, leaving her with no opportunity to enquire about tantalising little details such as what he had really meant by '*I'd say yes.*'

But more important, would *she* ever want to pop the question?

Too soon to tell, she told herself. They hadn't known one another long enough.

So how long would it take?

And did his illness have anything to do with her hesitation?

Now look here, what is this? she asked herself defensively, of course Josh's MS had nothing to do with her hesitation. Why, that would make her an *ist* of some kind and she'd never been prejudiced against anything in her life.

No, the truth was they were still in the early stages of their relationship and only time would tell if they had a future together.

Sure, she wrote about people falling madly in love and knowing within a few chapters that they were made for one another, but that was fiction. Real life wasn't like that. Real people took ages dithering about trying to decide whether they would be able to put up with one another for the next five minutes, never mind the next fifty years. And if they weren't doing that they were wondering if it wouldn't be a bad idea to wait and see if somebody better came along.

Well, didn't they?

Wasn't that what Gavin had been doing?

Damn, now she was back to Gavin.

So why exactly had she been dreaming of him?

That was easy – no Freudian worries on that score! – his presence in her subconscious was all down to her seeing Jack and Helen today and their imminent visit had stirred up all sorts of memories.

Thinking about Jack and Helen's impending arrival had her carefully slipping out of bed and tiptoeing downstairs. They would be here in four hours and she really ought to do something about getting the house into some sort of order.

She also needed to think what she could give them to eat.

She opened the fridge for inspiration.

Mm . . . not too promising.

The freezer was no greater source of creativity either. Not unless she could get away with serving a deep pan pizza followed by a Magnum – one between them all.

Hell! Now she'd have to go to the supermarket. She groaned. Food shopping and cooking were her two most hated chores in the world.

She'd rather spend a fortnight cleaning out an Egyptian public toilet. Okay. Maybe she was exaggerating, make that a week, but who in their right mind enjoyed spending their time browsing along aisle upon aisle searching for yet another way to satiate their stomach? What was happening to them all? Were they turning into a nation of Belly Worshippers? *Oh Great Belly God, unto whom all shopping lists be prepared, receive this miserable sacrifice, a trial special offer of a lime and coriander quorn curry.* There were times when she seriously longed for the simplicity of the small family-run supermarkets in Kassiopi. The less choice, the easier the task. And she was all for an easy life.

She made herself a cup of tea and sat down with a cookery book – her only cookery book and one which Anna had given her years ago. So what was it to be? Could she be crass enough to make moussaka for Jack and Helen? Or should she be equally silly and cook them roast beef and Yorkshire pudding?

No. Helen was mad enough as it was.

Roast lamb, then. That was easy to do, surely? She could do new potatoes, they wouldn't take too much fiddling about with. But hang on, she was now entering the danger zone of being a hypocrite. It was late September and she was considering new potatoes because the very supermarket she had just condemned for offering too much choice would indeed supply this out-of-season vegetable. Stick to your principles, she told herself. Roast potatoes would have to do instead, a little more work involved, but worth it all the same. And they'd have runner beans and courgettes, they were very much in season.

Her brief shopping list completed, she drank her tea, then poured herself another, as well as one for Josh. She took the mugs upstairs. As she slipped back into bed he awoke.

'Hi,' she said. She bent down to him and kissed the top of his head. 'I've brought you some tea.'

He sat up slowly. 'What time is it?'

'Time I was scurrying around with the Hoover. Jack and Helen will be here at one.'

He glanced at his watch. 'Plenty of time.'

She passed him his mug.

He reached out for it, but then hesitated. She looked at his hand, it was tightly clenched, much worse than last night. 'Still bad?' she asked.

'Yep.' He took the cup with his other hand. 'What time do you want me out of here?'

'Sorry?'

'Well, you won't want me around when your friends are here.'

'Says who?'

'I just assumed.'

'You assumed wrong, Crawford. I'd like you to meet them. I ought to invite Mum for lunch as well, she always got on with Jack and Helen when she used to come and stay.'

'In that case, would you like me to cook for you?'

'Would the Pope like us all to be Catholics?'

He smiled. 'I'll take that as a yes, shall I?'

'A resounding yes.'

'What do you fancy?'

'Apart from you?'

'I think you'll find I won't fit in the oven, Jessica.'

'Spoil-sport. I thought of having a crack at roast lamb, but you're the chef, you decide. Tell me what you want and I'll go shopping for it.'

'That's okay, we'll go together.'

'Wouldn't you rather stay here and . . .?' Her voice trailed away.

'What?' he said, regarding her levelly. 'Rest? Is that what you were going to say?'

'Heavens no. I was going to get you on cleaning duty.'

He let it go. He could see it wasn't easy for Jessica. 'I'd prefer to go shopping,' he said, 'you can be in charge of the cleaning.'

'There,' Jessica said, coming into the kitchen, her hands full of dusters, empty coffee mugs and several weeks' worth of the *Sunday Times* rounded up from all corners of the house, 'I defy anyone to find so much as a speck of dust in this place. Mm . . . that smells good.'

'It's the garlic and rosemary with the lamb,' Josh said, glancing up from the chopping board where he was slowly working his way through a mound of carrots, potatoes, courgettes and baby turnips.

'And what fate awaits them?' she asked, coming over to take a closer look at what he was doing.

'They'll be roasted in olive oil with sprigs of thyme.'

'Delicious. You're a man in a million, Crawford. Anything I can do to help?'

He watched her throw the old newspapers into the bin, store the cleaning things in the cupboard under the sink and wash her hands. He tried hard to overcome his natural desire to struggle on, but though the fingers in his right hand were beginning to straighten he knew they didn't have the strength or the dexterity to enable him to get through the pile of vegetables in front of him. 'You could help with the chopping, if you want.'

Jessica dried her hands and came back to him. She wanted to say, 'Now that wasn't too difficult, was it?' But she didn't dare. She guessed that what had just passed between them was a tiny milestone. Josh had actually swallowed a minuscule piece of his pride. But would it be something he would be prepared to keep on doing?

'Now show me how you want them,' she said, 'big chunks or little chunks?'

'Medium-sized chunks.'

'You would.' She began chopping.

'No, not like that, make the shapes more even or some will be cooked while others will still be raw.'

'Show me then, clever dick.'

He stood behind her and placed his hands over hers. 'Here, this is how you do it.'

His breath tickled her neck and as his warm body pressed against hers she thought of the film *Ghost* and the bit when Demi Moore gets an extra pair of helping hands during her late-night pottery session. She started to giggle.

'What's so funny?' he asked.

'It's you, you're distracting me.'

He nibbled her ear and she laughed some more. 'Stop it,' she said, 'or I'll have one of your fingers off.'

He took the knife from her, put it down and turned her round to face him. She gazed into his eyes and saw that they were dark with desire. It suddenly seemed the perfect time to ask him what he'd meant last night by '*I'd say yes*'.

'Josh,' she said, 'you know at Tony and Amanda's when you –' But she got no further. The sound of a car coming slowly into the courtyard announced the untimely arrival of Jack and Helen.

'I must say you're looking extremely well,' Jack said as he helped himself to another glass of wine from the bottle he and Helen had brought with them.

They were in the kitchen and Jessica was doing her best to finish chopping all the vegetables that Josh had left her in charge of while he went to fetch Anna.

'No guesses for why that's the case,' Helen said with a smile. 'You never mentioned anything in your letters about a new man in your life, not that you've written much to us.' She put on an air of hurt.

Jessica laughed. 'If I spent all my free time writing letters to you I wouldn't have had the opportunity to catch myself such a fine-looking man, now would I?'

'How right you are,' Helen agreed, 'they don't come much finer. So why isn't he already snapped up?'

'Same reason as me I suppose,' Jessica said with a smug smile, 'he's been waiting for that special person.'

Helen stuck her fingers in her mouth. 'Please, somebody pass me the bucket.'

Jack smiled at Jessica. 'She's becoming very cynical in her old age. Ready for some wine yet?'

'Yes,' Jessica said. She flung down the vegetable knife and took the proffered glass. 'Though what Josh wants to do next with this little lot is anybody's guess.'

Helen's eyes opened wide. 'Don't tell me he can cook as well?'

Jessica gave Helen another smug smile. 'He sure can. This is *his* meal.'

Helen gave Jack one of her look-learn-and-take-note looks. Then she said, 'Well, I suppose that really does put the tin lid on Gavin's chances.'

'Helen,' warned Jack in a low voice, 'definitely not the time.'

'What?' asked Jessica, noticing the exchange between her friends.

'Oh, nothing,' said Helen. She reached over to pinch a piece of raw carrot.

'Come on, you're holding back on me. What is it? Jack, you tell me.'

But Jack ignored Jessica. He stared awkwardly at his shoes.

Helen crunched on the carrot. 'Oh, what the hell? It's not much, it's just that we promised Gavin while we were over that we'd try and put a word in for him.'

Jessica gaped. 'What kind of word?'

'Look, Jessica, he's really sorry for what he did.'

'*Hah!*'

'No, let me finish. A more contrite man you could never hope to come across. Silicone Sal is way out of the picture and Gavin . . .'

'And Gavin what?' Jessica prompted her friend.

'And Gavin wanted us to see if there was any chance of a reconciliation.'

'You make it sound as if we were married.'

'Perhaps if you hadn't gone rushing off in such a sulk you might have been.'

'Helen, I don't believe you. He was two-timing me. Probably three-timing if the truth be known. And you know jolly well I didn't leave Corfu because of him.'

'Just as you say, Jessica, but as I said, Gavin's old ways are behind him, he wants to make up with you. He wants to –'

'Well, you can tell him he's too late. Whatever he thinks he's offering, it wouldn't be enough.'

'And what would be enough?'

Jessica picked up the small vegetable knife and drove it through the heart of a piece of potato. 'I want commitment. I want to be really needed. I want to feel that I belong to that person and that he belongs to me . . . that he couldn't live without me.'

Helen banged her empty glass of wine down on the work surface. 'Oh, for heaven's sake, Jessica, that's the stuff of fiction!'

'I don't care. It's what I want. I'm simply not interested in anything less.'

Chapter Forty-Five

Alec had long since gone to work and Kate was alone. She lay on their bed and waited for the feeling of nausea to pass. She closed her eyes and concentrated her mind on what she had resolved to do later that day; what she had concluded at five o'clock that morning as being the only way to resolve matters.

Unable to sleep, she had left Alec slumbering soundly and gone downstairs to the sitting-room where she had sat in one of the armchairs in the bay window and watched the dawn break. Staring out at the dramatically changing sky with its swathes of cobalt-blue darkness giving way to bursts of soft pink light, a diffraction of clarity had suddenly cut through her own confused darkness and with it came the knowledge that today she would bring about an end to the muddle that she had created of her life. It was time to be honest with Alec. She couldn't go on treating him so badly. It wasn't fair. She had to tell him that whatever it was that had brought them together in the first place was not enough to keep them together. She wouldn't tell him about Tony, there was no need for that. Tony wasn't the reason she was leaving him. He had been a symptom of their failing relationship. He was not the cause.

But it wasn't just Alec who had to be told the truth. There was Tony as well.

After that dreadful night last week at Tony and Amanda's, when she came away convinced that Amanda was on to them – all that talk of infidelity and swapping partners had to be for a reason – she had known that what she was doing was wrong. She had gone to bed that night shocked and ashamed. Her duplicity appalled her. All those lies she had told. She hated the woman she had let herself become.

She had no idea how Tony was going to react when she told him she wouldn't be seeing him again, but he had to realise that her leaving Alec didn't mean that she was simply making the way clear to be with him. Tony was a married man. No matter what his feelings were for Kate, or hers for him, he had a wife who could not be ignored.

And like Tony, she too had her own responsibility; that of doing the right thing for the baby she was carrying. She wanted her child's tiny fragile beginnings to be founded on love and honesty. Not on deception. Not on depravity. She didn't want her child to have a mother who could be found culpable of wrecking another person's marriage.

She opened her eyes. The nausea of morning sickness still hadn't passed. But she couldn't stay lying on the bed all day, she was meeting Tony in less than an hour. She got to her feet, determined to ignore her threatening stomach, and went downstairs. As she glanced at her reflection in the hall mirror she caught sight of her pale, tired face in the glass. Guilt, she told herself. Guilt and shame. It serves you right.

As arranged, Kate met Tony in the car-park of a pub neither of them had been to before – anonymity was, after all, the essence of a perfect assignation.

The first thing Tony said was, 'Are you okay? You look as white as a sheet.'

'I'm fine,' she said, though she knew she wasn't. It's nerves, she told herself. Nerves at what she had to tell Tony.

Though the day was warm, the inside of the pub was dismally cold, so they ordered their drinks and chose a small table in an alcove a few feet away from a gently smouldering log fire where a large, thickset man of indefinable age was jammed into a chair that looked much too small for him. He had tufts of hair sticking out from under a woolly hat and he was nursing a near empty pint glass in a pair of big, strong hands. He nodded at them. 'A fair day, wouldn't you say?'

'Very fair,' Tony responded with a smile.

'Set to continue, I heard this morning on the radio.'

'That's good.'

The man shifted in his seat. 'Well, it's good and it's not good. A splash more rain would do no harm. No harm at all. In fact, we could do a lot worse than have a bloody great lashing.'

Kate inwardly groaned. How could this happen? How could they have ended up, today of all days, with the pub bore chuntering on to them about the weather? She raised her eyes and met Tony's. She could see he was trying not to laugh and her response to his smiling face was to think how much she would miss seeing him. She pushed this dangerous thought aside. She mustn't weaken. Not now.

320

'Shall I order us something to eat?' he asked.

She shook her head. She felt too sick to eat.

'The ploughman's not up to much,' the pub bore interjected. 'Too much wet green stuff on the plate for my liking. I shouldn't bother with the trout neither. It's never fresh. Nor's the salmon.'

'Kate, are you sure you're all right?'

'Chicken curry's not bad.'

'Kate?'

'Take my word for it, your best bet is the chicken curry.'

Tony's patience was wearing thin. He flashed a look of annoyance at the man in the hope of shutting him up. He turned his attention back to Kate. 'What is it?' he whispered. 'You look dreadful.'

'I'm not sure,' she answered faintly. She rose slowly to her feet. 'I'll be a few minutes.'

He watched her cross the carpeted floor and remembered how Eve had suffered with morning sickness. But even Eve had never looked as ghastly as Kate did just now. He drank from his glass of mineral water and thought about what he had planned to tell Kate over their lunch.

After Amanda's bizarre behaviour on Friday night he had spent the weekend facing up to the truth that he'd been pushed as far as he was ever going to be pushed. He wanted a divorce. He would be generous to Amanda. More than generous. He would give her everything she wanted. He had the feeling, though, that she wouldn't be slow in defining the parameters of a settlement heavily weighted in her favour, but just so long as she gave him his freedom she could demand as much as she wanted. It would be difficult coping with Hattie on his own again, but he would find a way round the problem. He would have to. Whichever way he looked at it, the situation would be preferable to the madness he'd experienced of late.

And perhaps, just perhaps, his freedom would give him the opportunity to offer Kate something more worthwhile than he was currently able to give her.

'Looks like your lady friend has legged it,' the pub bore said. He gave off a throaty laugh. 'Maybe she got wind of the kitchen and thought better of having lunch here.'

Tony forced a smile to his lips. He glanced down at his watch. He'd been on his own for nearly twenty minutes. He began to worry. He was just wondering what he should do when a woman approached him.

'Are you Tony?' she asked.

'Yes.'

'Your girl-friend told me to tell you that she's waiting for you outside. I think you need to get her to a doctor. She doesn't look at all well.'

Tony raced out of the pub. He found Kate leaning against his car. 'It's the baby,' she whispered, her eyes wide and frightened, 'I think I'm losing it.'

He drove to the nearest hospital. He knew next to nothing about miscarriages, but instinct told him that there would be no chance of saving Kate's child.

While he waited to be told what was happening, he phoned directory enquiries for Alec's work number. When he got through to Thistle Cards he left a message explaining where Kate was. No matter what he felt for Kate, or Alec for that matter, it was only right that Alec should know what was going on; he was the father after all.

A few seconds after Tony had finished his call a nurse came and told him what he'd already suspected. He sat by the side of Kate's bed and held her hand. But she wouldn't speak to him.

'I've left a message for Alec,' he told her, 'I expect he'll be here soon.'

She nodded dumbly.

'Do you want me to stay?'

She shook her head and closed her eyes. Tears trickled down her pale cheeks and splashed on to the crisp white pillowcase. She turned from him and let go of his hand.

He walked quietly away.

He couldn't face going back to the office.

Not yet.

He needed to be on his own, so he drove up the A34 and headed towards the motorway. There was surprisingly little traffic and at the speed he was driving Greater Manchester was soon behind him, while ahead the first sighting of open moorland drew him further on. Seeing the sign for junction 21 he pulled in behind a large haulage wagon. He drove through the familiar roads of Milnrow and when he came to Hollingworth Lake he stopped. Other than a shiny red Nissan Micra, whose elderly occupants were enjoying the view and a flask of something hot, he was alone.

He had often come here as a boy. On a Saturday morning he and his friends would cycle over from Rochdale. It seemed quite a distance now, but in those days he hadn't given the journey a second thought. His mum would put together a parcel of jam sandwiches for him and his mates, and the minute they reached the lake they'd eat the sandwiches while throwing stones into the water. They got told off once by a fierce old lady who came out of her house and accused them of frightening the ducks. They'd called her Old Ma Quackers after that.

How big they thought they were.

And how smart.

They presumed so much.

Little did they know how bloody complicated life could be.

He stared at the rippling surface of the lake and thought of Kate and the loss of her badly wanted child. And because he knew that her loss would be so great to her he was convinced that she was going to shut him out.

If she hadn't already.

He wished now that he'd had the opportunity at the pub to explain to Kate that he was going to ask Amanda for a divorce. If she'd known that she might not have turned away from him in the hospital.

His solitary musings were brought to an abrupt end by the sudden trill of his mobile.

It was Vicki, his secretary. 'Tony, where on earth are you? You're supposed to be in a meeting in ten minutes.'

Damn! He'd forgotten all about that. 'Cancel it,' he said.

'Any reason I can give?'

'No.'

'I've also got a message from your wife,' Vicki went on. 'She says she can't collect Hattie from school today.'

'*What!*'

'I'm sorry, Tony, that's the message.'

'Didn't she give any reason? Any explanation?'

'It seems to be the day for people not wanting to explain things,' she said archly. 'Will you be in later?'

'No. I'll see you tomorrow.'

He looked at his watch. Hattie would be coming out of school in thirty minutes. He phoned home to see what was wrong with Amanda. There was no answer. Next he phoned school and asked them to keep Hattie there until he arrived.

He drove faster than he ought, zigzagging his speeding Porsche through the lanes of traffic and all the time wondering what the hell Amanda was up to.

When he and Hattie finally made it home, the answer was waiting for him.

Amanda had gone.

And so had all their furniture.

'Have we been burgled?' asked Hattie, taking a step closer to her father and reaching for his hand as they stood in the middle of the empty sitting-room. Everything had vanished, the furniture, the hi-fi, the television, the video, the pictures from the walls, the knick-knacks, even the pot plants.

Tony finished reading Amanda's letter, which he had found on the floor of their empty bedroom. He screwed it into a tight hard ball and threw it down at his feet – at least she'd left the carpets!

'No, we haven't been burgled,' he said, suddenly realising that his daughter needed his reassurance. He scooped her up in his arms and smiled. Then he threw back his head and laughed. It echoed horribly in the bare room. Seeing Hattie's uncertain little face, he hugged her tightly and kissed her. 'I'm starving,' he said, 'let's go into town and have ourselves a McDonald's.'

'Really?'

'You bet! You can have whatever you want. Gherkins, fries, the lot.'

'Won't Amanda be cross?'

'Amanda will never *ever* know.'

Tony might have felt that for the first time in months he could breathe properly as he sat in the ultra-clean air-conditioned environment of McDonald's, but he was well aware that there was no getting away from the fact that the swift kick in the groin that Amanda had given him – much as it pleased him in the long term – had precipitated his number-one problem: looking after Hattie.

He stared at his daughter across the small table and for a brief moment she took her lips away from the thick gunky milkshake that she was sucking up with a straw. She didn't seem at all put out by what he had just told her in the car. 'Amanda's decided that she doesn't want to be with us any more,' he had explained, which had been a more elegant way of putting what Amanda had written in her letter.

I've taken only what I think I deserve [the letter had begun]. *You can try and fight me if you want, but really I wouldn't advise it. I'm divorcing you on the grounds of adultery – I know all about you and Kate – and you shan't be hearing from me again, except through my solicitor. I'd just like you to know that marrying you was the biggest mistake I ever made.*

'But why did she take all the furniture?' Hattie had asked, adding quite reasonably, 'it doesn't seem fair.'

'Maybe she liked it a lot,' he'd said. With hindsight, if he'd thought it would have got rid of Amanda sooner he'd have given it to her long ago. He couldn't deny that she had a perfect right to be bitter, she had after all discovered that he was on the verge of having a full-blown affair with Kate – in truth, what had passed between him and Kate could not technically be described as adultery, but nevertheless, the intent was there; if the circumstances had been right he didn't doubt for a single moment that he would have taken Kate to bed. Just thinking about it made him long for her.

He wondered how she was. He hoped that Alec was taking good care of her. He felt no jealousy or animosity towards Alec, only a wish that he would be able to comfort Kate when she needed it most.

'Your chips are getting cold,' Hattie said, pointing at him with one of her own. She tickled the end of his nose with it.

He smiled and resumed eating, marvelling at his daughter. She really didn't have a care in the world.

Just like him as a child when he'd thrown stones into the water at Hollingworth Lake and laughed at Old Ma Quackers behind her back.

By six thirty that evening Kate had swapped one bed for another. She was back at home, with Alec fussing around her, straightening and smoothing the duvet, patting her hands, fiddling with her pillows.

She didn't need to be in bed, but Alec had insisted. 'I'm not listening to you, Kate,' he'd said when he'd brought her home from the hospital and she'd told him she wanted to be in the sitting-room, 'I'm in charge and I want you to go to bed and rest.'

And how did he think she could rest if he was going to spend all his time fussing over her?

She knew what he was doing. He was busying himself so that she couldn't see the relief in his face. But she could hear it in his voice. With each gentle and cajoling word he spoke she could hear how relieved he was that she was no longer pregnant.

'We'll go away,' he was saying, as once again he smoothed and patted the duvet, 'just the two of us, to a nice quiet little hotel, where you can be pampered and thoroughly spoilt.'

Did he have to say *just the two of us*?

'I'll take you to that wonderful hotel in Bath I told you about. We'll go for long country walks and in the evening we'll sit by a log fire and drink champagne. Do you like the sound of that?'

No, she didn't like the sound of it. She had no desire to go anywhere. But she wished Alec would go away, that he would leave her alone.

But still he rambled on about all the wonderful things they would do together.

'We'll have a four-poster bed and a jacuzzi the size of a small swimming pool, you'll love it.'

Was there no way to stop him?

Yes. Yes, there was.

'Alec,' she said finally, staring him straight in the eye, 'I'm very sorry . . . and I wish there were a better way to put this, but I think we both know in our hearts that it's over between us.'

Chapter Forty-Six

Josh recognised Tony's car straight away, as well as Hattie's small figure sitting in the back. Within seconds Tony saw Josh in his rear-view mirror and held up his hand in acknowledgement. They drove the remaining distance to Cholmford Hall Mews in convoy and when Josh had parked in front of his house he went over to Tony to thank him for the other night, not out of any genuine desire to pass on his thanks to Amanda, but out of a sense of solidarity – hell, the man needed some kind of support for putting up with such a weird wife.

'How's it going?' he asked when he drew level with Tony and Hattie.

'Come in and see for yourself.'

Inside, Josh stared round at the empty walls. 'What the –?'

'Amanda's left us,' Hattie said with a big smile on her face. She then went upstairs to her bedroom.

'She's cleared me out,' Tony said, when they were alone. 'Fancy a drink to celebrate?'

Confounded, Josh watched Tony take out a bottle of Scotch from one of the kitchen cupboards. 'She left you that, then?' he said.

'Yes, she left me the cheap and nasty booze and took the decent stuff.' He poured two generous measures into a matching pair of plastic cups that were decorated with Walt Disney characters. 'Sorry about the lack of crystal ware,' he said, passing a cup to Josh, 'but she took that as well, china too, but credit where credit's due, she left all of Hattie's things.'

'I hate to pry, Tony, but did she give a reason why? Did you have any kind of clue that this was on the cards?'

'She found out that I was seeing Kate.'

If Josh had been stunned a few moments ago, he was even more taken aback now. He took a large gulp of Scotch. 'You and Kate,' he said, astonished, 'you mean you were –?'

Tony nodded. 'Though nothing had actually happened between us.' He explained about him and Kate. He then told Josh about Kate losing the baby that afternoon. 'I think she's going to push me away. Guilt will make her want to blame somebody for what happened and I guess I'm the obvious target.'

'It's been quite a day for you,' Josh said, 'I don't know what to say. Were you the father?'

Tony looked shocked. 'No. Absolutely not. I told you, nothing really happened between us.'

'And does Alec know about you and Kate?'

'I don't think so. But then I didn't think Amanda knew. But she obviously did.'

Josh looked round at the empty kitchen. 'Obviously,' he repeated. 'So what happens next?'

Tony drained his cup. 'Next is my big problem. I'm going to have to organise a child-minder to take care of Hattie after school each day.' He ran his hand through his hair. 'Though at such short notice I don't hold out much hope of getting fixed up this week. I'll just have to take the time off work.'

'Isn't there anyone you can ask for help? Grandparents?'

'All dead.'

'What about the other mothers at Hattie's school?'

'She's only been there a short while. I couldn't tell you who any of her friends are, never mind their mothers' names.'

Josh thought for a moment. 'How about Jessica? You could ask her, just until you've got yourself properly sorted.'

Jessica and Josh gave Tony a wave and drove through the archway.

They'd both just spent the past hour giving Tony a hand. This was after he and Josh had called on Jessica to tell her what had happened and to enlist her services for collecting Hattie from school. 'Do you mind?' Tony had asked. 'I hate to land this on you.'

'It's not a problem,' Jessica had said. 'But what can we do right now for you? If you've not got a stick of furniture you'd better borrow some of mine.'

And though Tony had said he and Hattie would be fine, Jessica had insisted and between the three of them they'd carted Jessica's barely used dining-table and three chairs over to Tony's and from Josh's house they'd put together a basic selection of crockery. When Jessica had pointed out that Tony didn't have a bed to sleep on he'd refused her offer of dragging one of her mattresses across the courtyard and said that he could make do with an old camp-bed he had in the garage.

Which was what they'd just left him searching for. Amanda might have stripped the house from top to bottom, save for Hattie's bedroom, but she'd either forgotten the things in the garage or had felt kind-hearted enough to let Tony keep the lawn-mower, step-ladders and Boy Scout odds and ends of camping gear – somehow Jessica didn't think Amanda would have much use for an old tent and box of billycans; she didn't strike one as being happy-camper material.

'You didn't mind me suggesting to Tony that you might look after Hattie, did you?' Josh asked Jessica as they drove through the avenue of chestnut trees.

'No. Not at all. Why do you ask?'

'You just seemed . . . well, a bit quiet at Tony's.'

'I think the word you're searching for is gobsmacked. I still can't believe the Kate and Tony thing. I knew Kate was worried about Alec's reaction to being a father again, but I honestly thought they'd sort that out between them and everything would be sweet. Did you have any idea what was going on?'

'Not a clue. Do you think that's what Friday night was all about?'

'Almost certainly. Amanda must have known what was going on and decided to put Tony and Kate through their paces. All that stuff about *when are you and Alec getting married?*' – she mimicked Amanda's voice with unerring accuracy – 'it was just a ploy for twisting the knife in Tony's back and making Kate squirm.'

'But how on earth did Amanda get all the stuff out of the house without any of us seeing?'

'If you think about it that wasn't too tricky. She knew you and Alec would be at work and if you remember back to Friday night she asked both Kate and me what we'd be doing this week. I thought at the time it was odd that she asked specifically about today.'

'You're right, she did rather press the point. Kate said something about seeing a friend for lunch –'

'Who turned out to be Tony.'

'And you said you were going shopping in Wilmslow. I suppose that's what you were up to,' he said with a grin.

She smiled. 'Crawford, you've rumbled me. Guilty as charged. Lock me up and throw away the key.' But suddenly her smile was gone. '*Bloody hell!*'

'What? What is it?'

Jessica slammed on the brakes and brought the car to a shuddering halt just before the brow of the bridge over the canal. 'Look! Just look at that! What the hell does she think she's doing?'

Josh followed Jessica's gaze. In the semi-darkness, sweeping the steps that led from the garden of Willow Cottage down to the tow-path, was Anna. He smiled to himself. Poor woman, she must have thought she was safe from Jessica's ever-watchful eye, having had her daily visit from her daughter a couple of hours ago.

But before Josh could say anything, Jessica was out of the car and running towards the gate of Willow Cottage. She stormed over to her mother and even from where he was Josh could hear her shouting at Anna.

'What do you think you're doing?' she yelled. 'Have you gone completely mad? I thought I'd told you to take it easy.'

Josh opened his door and slowly limped after Jessica. It had been a long day and his leg had given him nothing but trouble for most of it; to-ing and fro-ing to Tony's hadn't helped either. By the time he had managed to drag his worn-out body after Jessica, who was now snatching the broom out of Anna's grasp, he could scarcely feel the ground beneath his left foot. He was ill prepared to put up with one of Jessica's bossy moods. 'Jessica!' he shouted, 'for God's sake, leave your mother alone.' In the dusky lull of early evening his voice bounced off the still water of the canal, ringing out harsh and discordant.

Jessica stared back at him and for a split second he thought she was going to hit him with the broom. To be on the safe side of self-preservation he took it from her and propped it against Anna's wheelbarrow.

'This is none of your business,' she hissed, her eyes wide with astonished anger.

'Oh, stop being such a bloody pain and give your mother some space.' He turned to Anna. 'Shall we go inside for a moment, just the two of us? I said just the two of us, Jessica,' he added firmly, when she started to move with them.

When he and Anna reached the cottage and they stepped into the kitchen his leg finally gave way and he staggered and fell back against the door.

'Josh!' cried Anna, 'are you all right?' She fetched him a chair. 'What can I do?'

'Nothing,' he gasped. He sat down and rubbed at the numb, aching pain in his knee. 'Please . . . don't fuss.'

'I wouldn't dream of it, not when we're such good allies.'

He managed a small smile.

'You looked very cross out there with Jessica,' Anna said, as she hovered anxiously round him, 'you won't hold it against her, will you?'

He stared at her. 'What do you mean?'

'I mean, don't judge her too harshly. Her loss of temper is her way of showing how much she cares.'

'I know that,' he said solemnly, 'I just can't bear to see her treating you as though you don't have any say in what you do . . . it's too close to home.'

She touched his shoulder and gently squeezed it. 'Don't worry about me, Josh. I can handle Jessica. I'm up to speed with her tantrums.'

'Good. So tell me where your mobile phone is.'

She turned away guiltily.

He sighed. 'Come on, Anna. The deal was Jessica leaves you alone so that you can get up to whatever you want, but you have your mobile permanently with you. Remember, it was my idea for you to have a phone. If something serious ever happened to you and you weren't able to call for help, Jessica would never forgive me. And that's certainly something I can do without.'

'It's over there,' Anna admitted sheepishly. She pointed to the cluttered window-sill. 'I keep forgetting about it. It's not a habit with me yet.'

Josh suddenly tilted his head towards the back door. 'Quick,' he said, 'she's coming, put the damn thing in your sling.'

Anna moved nimbly across the kitchen. She was just in time.

'Well?' said Jessica, coming into the kitchen and casting her eyes first on Josh, then on Anna.

'Well what, dear?' Anna asked innocently.

'I've told you before, don't call me dear or darling, it makes me incredibly suspicious. What have you two been up to in here?'

With the greatest of effort, Josh got stiffly to his feet. 'It's all been taken care of, Jessica,' he said. 'Anna had only been outside for a few minutes and she had her phone with her anyway, so if there had been a problem she would have been fine. Isn't that right, Anna?'

Anna smiled and obligingly pulled out the corroborative evidence from her sling. 'See,' she said.

Jessica scowled. She wasn't convinced that anything was fine. How dare Josh railroad her in that appalling fashion. Who did he think he was? Taking care of Anna was her responsibility, not his. What right did he think he had to barge his way in like that?

'Off somewhere nice?' Anna asked, keen to change the subject and aware now that Jessica wasn't cross only with her but also with Josh.

'I'm taking Jessica to meet my parents,' he said.

'Oh,' said Anna, 'well, don't let me keep you.' Given her

331

daughter's mood, heaven help Mr and Mrs Crawford, she thought as she waved them off.

Jessica was all set to be furious with Josh after her mother had closed the front door on them, but as soon as she saw how difficult it was for him to walk her anger changed to concern. 'Josh, we shouldn't be going anywhere but home. You said earlier that your leg was a bit stiff and that I ought to drive, but look at you, you can barely walk.'

'Like I really need to be told that, Jessica. Now shut up and give me your arm.'

She helped him to the car. 'Now what?' she asked when she'd settled him in his seat. 'Home?'

'No,' he said, 'to my parents as originally planned. And please don't think you can boss me about as you do your mother.'

Jessica didn't trust herself to retaliate and wanting to make the right impression on Josh's parents, she concentrated on improving her temper. Think of something nice, she told herself as she switched on the engine. She immediately thought of Corfu; of swimming in the crystal-clear water below her little house and of enjoying a perfect sunset while having drinks on the terrace with Helen and Jack. She then recalled Helen and Jack's visit at the weekend. Despite the conversation about Gavin – and not for a single minute did she believe a word of what Helen had said on that particular subject – the day had gone really well. Helen had been on fine form and had started flirting with Josh. To her surprise, and no doubt delight, Josh had flirted back and before he knew where he was Anna had joined in and was declaring him a dirty dog. 'I don't mind sharing you with my daughter,' she'd said, 'but sharing you with a married woman is going too far!' In the end she and Jack had left Josh to defend himself against Anna and Helen, and had disappeared to the kitchen to tidy up.

'My advice is to forget about Gavin,' Jack had said when they were both stacking the dishwasher. 'Josh is by far the better bet.'

'Thanks, Jack,' she'd said, 'I think so too.' She'd given him a big kiss, only to be caught in the act by Helen who had gone straight back into the sitting-room to tell Josh that she was now a free agent and did he fancy a life in the sun with an older woman? He'd told her he'd be five minutes packing his bag, but could Anna join them?

It had been a day of fun and laughter.

Unlike now, thought Jessica miserably. Just what kind of evening lay ahead?

Before setting eyes on Jessica, William and Constance Crawford had long since made up their minds about the woman their younger son was seeing. They very much liked the sound of her. Charlie was, of course, responsible for influencing his parents in this way, for he had told them in considerable detail what he thought about Josh's latest girl-friend. He was at the house when Josh and Jessica arrived and it was he who greeted them at the door. He saw immediately the state his brother was in and did his best not to react.

'Hi,' he said to Jessica. He kissed her cheek. 'All ready to be put under the spotlight?' he asked with a smile.

He took them through to the sitting-room where William and Constance were standing either side of the fireplace. Constance came forward first. She gave Josh a motherly kiss, chided him lightly for looking tired and offered her hand to Jessica. 'I'm Constance and this is my husband William. Ignore most of what he says, it comes of not knowing the right thing to say.'

Jessica shook hands with Constance and instantly felt at ease. She guessed that Josh's mother was younger than Anna, probably in her early sixties. There was an enviable air of charm and grace about her. She was quite tall and was clearly a woman who knew how to dress. Though Jessica was no expert and didn't know one designer outfit from another, she surmised that the stylish taupe-coloured shift dress Constance was wearing was no knock-down high street bargain. The cream cardigan draped over her shoulders was probably cashmere and the buttons were exquisite mother-of-pearl beauties. Her softly greying hair was elegantly pushed away from her face and seemed to be held in place by nothing more elaborate than sheer will-power. Jessica wondered why she could never get her hair to behave like that.

She then shook hands with William and was immediately aware of the similarity between the two Crawford boys – it was as if their father were the missing link between the pair of them. He was a handsome man and must have been as drop-dead gorgeous as his two sons when he was their age. He insisted that Jessica sit next to him and she didn't refuse.

From across the room, where he was pouring drinks, Charlie winked at her. 'The oldies are having sherry,' he said, 'but what would you like, Jessica?'

'I'll have the same, please.'

He brought the drinks over and handed them round.

Then he turned to Josh, who so far hadn't uttered a word. He was slumped in a chair with his head tilted back. He looked shattered, with deep shadows now showing under his eyes, which were tightly closed. 'Beer, Josh?' asked Charlie.

He opened his eyes and nodded.

'Would you rather sit on the sofa, Joshua?' asked Constance.

He looked at her as if considering her words. 'Why?' was all he said.

Constance turned nervously to her husband, then back to Josh. 'I . . . I just thought that maybe you'd be more comfortable there,' she said in a small voice.

'I'm fine where I am,' he said.

But it was obvious he wasn't and after he'd taken a sip of his beer he put it down and closed his eyes again.

'Well, Jessica, we hear that you're a writer.'

Jessica smiled at William, recognising that with or without Josh's contribution, there was an accepted amount of small talk to get through.

She did her best. So did Charlie. And between them they held the evening together. Every now and then she would look over to Josh and will him to feel better. She also stole a glance or two at the many framed family photographs that adorned the furniture around the large, beautifully decorated room. Constance and William Crawford were rightly proud of their offspring and every stage of their development was there to be seen; from toothless baby grins to formal school portraits to grown men. On a small pedestal table beside Jessica was a lone picture. It was of Josh. She put him at about seventeen or eighteen. He was wearing a baggy sweat-shirt and a pair of John Lennon sun-glasses, and looked every inch like a young baby-faced pop star. His hair was much the same as it was now, thick and swept back – and held in place, she now realised, by the same force that Constance applied to hers. He looked just as attractive at that young age as he did now and Jessica knew that if she'd known him then, as a silly, giggling teenager at school, she would have been madly in love with him – his name would have been scribbled all over her books.

As the conversation continued, Jessica could see that both Constance and William were trying hard not to stare at their younger son, though their concern was clearly visible in their anxious faces. And the question that came into her mind was how did they cope with seeing Josh like this? Jessica had no idea what it felt like to be a mother and she could only guess what it was to experience that strong bond of love between parent and child. She didn't doubt for a minute that more than anything Constance was looking at her son, wanting to wrap him in her love and wish away all his pain.

Because as a lover that was certainly what Jessica wanted to do. In the past couple of weeks since she had been allowed to see the real Josh, her love for him had turned fierce and protective, breathtakingly so at times – that monstrous Amanda had been lucky to have survived the other night when she had been so rude to Josh.

Until recently she'd never been aware of what a temper she had, but what with Anna, and now Josh, to worry over, she realised that it was something she was going to have to get the better of.

Josh had been right in the car when he'd warned her not to boss him as she did her mother. It frightened her that he had been so right. But what scared her more was that she had no way of knowing how to stop it. She also knew that if she didn't find a way, and soon, it was probably what was going to come between them.

Alec was determined to convince himself that what Kate had told him a few hours ago was brought on by the shock of her miscarriage.

He was downstairs in his study, the door shut, the lights out, with a near empty bottle of Glenlivet for company. He poured another glass and told himself yet again what he needed to hear. Kate was just upset and confused. Tomorrow she'd wake up and say that she was sorry, that she hadn't meant any of what she'd said. And he would tell her that he understood and that it was behind them.

He drained his glass and pushed it away from him. He could go on telling himself this until he was blue in the face, but deep down he knew what Kate had said was perfectly true.

She had seen right through him. Of course he hadn't really accepted the baby she was carrying as a child he would love and nurture.

Yes, he was relieved that it was over and was that really such a sin? Was it so bad of him to want a partner all to himself?

Damn it! He was going to be fifty in a few weeks' time, what the hell did he want with fatherhood all over again?

He poured himself another drink, swallowed it down in one, lowered his head on to the desk and fell into a heavy drunken sleep.

Kate was awake by five o'clock and by half past six she had packed the bulk of her clothes into two large suitcases. The rest of her things she would have to come back for at a later date.

She sat on the edge of the bed and wondered what to do next. She wanted to go right away, to get this part over with as painlessly as she could, but she didn't want to leave Alec without saying goodbye. To creep away without a final word would be too cruel. She couldn't do that to him; he deserved better.

She crept quietly downstairs, unsure where Alec had slept the night. As she walked past the study she heard a noise. She took her courage in both hands and opened the door. The small room stank of stale alcohol. Alec was on his feet and was opening the sash window above his desk. He turned and stared at her. He looked dreadful: eyes horribly bloodshot, face mottled with a ghastly grey pallor.

'Shall I make us both some coffee?' she asked.

'I'll do it,' he said.

She bit her lip. Even at their parting he was still being the same considerate Alec.

They sat in the kitchen, in their usual seats, directly opposite each other. Kate was reminded of the morning she had told him she was pregnant.

'I don't suppose there's any point in asking you to change your mind, is there?'

'I'm sorry,' she said, 'I really am.'

He nodded. 'So am I.'

'You've always been so wonderful to me, Alec, I'll always –'

'No,' he said, holding up his hand to stop her. 'Please don't, this is bad enough without you telling me something like you love me, but you're not *in* love with me.'

She caught her breath and watched him blink away his tears. He couldn't have put it better. For that was exactly what she felt for him. She wanted to reach across the table and take his hand, but she knew that would only add insult to injury.

'Where will you go?' he asked gruffly.

'To Caroline.'

'Of course.' He looked up at her. 'She never really approved of me, did she?'

'No.' There was no point in lying to him.

They finished their coffee in silence. She made to get up and said, 'I think I'll get going now. I need to call for a taxi.'

He shook his head. 'A last request from a condemned man,' he said.

She frowned. 'You're not a condemned man, Alec.'

'I'll be the judge of that.'

She slipped back into her chair. 'What, then?'

'I don't actually want to see you go, wait until I've gone to work . . . please.'

Chapter Forty-Seven

Jessica was not the most organised of people and this morning was proving to be more than usually chaotic. It was the day the BBC were coming to make their film and in an hour's time the luvvies would be arriving, and if she didn't get a move on she would appear on daytime telly with nothing but a towel and a look of panic to cover her modesty.

After an early start she'd washed and dried her hair, and after several attempts at trying to persuade it into something a little more stylish than it was used to she'd given up and let it have its own way. Which meant she looked no different from the way she normally did: a mess!

She now tried to decide what to wear. Spread out on the bed were a variety of clothes, along with more packets of tights than she'd possessed in the whole of her life. On one pillow was a selection of opaque tights, they varied in their opaqueness, ranging from so thick they were bullet proof, down to merely wind resistant. They came in black or barely black; matt or shiny. On the adjacent pillow was a selection of sheer tights in all the different shades of black currently available on the market, as well as barley, beige and natural for that *au naturel* look.

It was a bewildering choice.

If it had been for any other occasion Jessica would simply have bought the first available pair, but because today was important she was doing her best to look the part of a successful novelist – whatever that looked like when it was at home. Prior to her visit to Wilmslow, she'd had the quaint notion that tights were just tights – living in Corfu, she hadn't had much call for them: in summer her legs were always bare and in winter they were covered by jeans. But after yesterday she had come to realise just how wrong she'd been; during her absence from England the buying of the silly things had apparently become an exact science. There were probably obscure universities offering postgraduate courses on the subject.

She hadn't expected to derive any pleasure from her shopping trip, but she had hoped to experience, at the very least, an element of cheap satisfaction. After all, it wasn't everybody who was out that day to spruce themselves up for their fifteen minutes of fame on telly. But as was so often the way with any of her expectations, she was wildly off beam. Cheap satisfaction was not to be had. Only the expensive brand was on offer.

She'd favoured a smart black no-nonsense suit when she'd entered the posh clothes department at Hooper's, but had instantly been pounced upon by an eager assistant who had other ideas and had tried to steer her towards a display of acid-green outfits. After she'd managed to give the girl the slip she made a beeline for the undertaker's rail of funereal black.

The prices were enough to make Jessica drop down dead from shock, but the little voice of temptation inside her head said, *Go on, treat yourself, it is in the line of work, after all.* Trouble came when she couldn't choose between trousers or a skirt. Both fitted her like a dream. Temptation whispered that further television appearances might follow and a second outfit would come in handy. Then it was downstairs to the shoe department. And naturally what went with the trousers didn't go with the skirt. Two pairs of shoes later, with the voice of reason asking her if she was feeling all right and wouldn't she like to sit down, she pressed on to the hosiery department. In the end it was just easiest to take as many pairs as she could carry and choose what to wear at home.

Except it wasn't. She was no nearer deciding what to put on this morning than she'd been yesterday.

She should have asked Josh for his opinion. He had such good taste when it came to clothes, but then he would, wouldn't he, it was his trade. She suspected, though, that in the rag trade or not, he would always have had a knack for making the most of his appearance. It didn't matter what he wore – black jeans and a T-shirt, or one of his trendy suits like the one he'd had on at Mo's party with the little stand-up collar – he always looked as if he'd just been posing for the front cover of GQ. She wondered if he was ever disappointed in her abysmal lack of interest in her clothes. If so, he'd never shown it. She looked at the stuff on the bed and wondered whether he'd approve of her choice. It was a shame it was too late to ask him for his advice – she'd heard his Shogun driving out through the courtyard over half an hour ago.

But seeking Josh's guidance on something as trivial as what she should wear seemed in very poor taste after last night. Poor Josh, he must have been in such agony at his parents'.

As the evening had drawn on and she had seen the pain in Josh's face intensify she had twice very nearly suggested that perhaps they should be going, but each time she had opened her mouth to say something she had stopped herself, frightened that her concern to get Josh home would annoy him. She noticed that while she was being careful not to cause Josh any annoyance, so too were his parents. Charlie as well. At no stage in the evening did anybody ask him how he was. Nobody offered to help him as he struggled to his feet when he decided it was time to go. Nobody said anything when he stumbled in the hall. And it wasn't because they didn't care. It was clear that they all cared very deeply about Josh, but they were simply taking their lead from him – if he didn't want to talk about how he felt, then it wasn't their place to refer to it either.

So was that how it was to be?

Was a long-term relationship with Josh going to comprise nervously tiptoeing around him for fear of upsetting him?

And was that really what she wanted? Surely, after being messed about by Gavin, what she needed was an uncomplicated relationship that would allow her to be herself. She thought of Gavin and what Helen had told her. Could he really have changed? And if he had, why hadn't he let her know this himself?

Wondering if Gavin had changed made her remember the first time she'd caught sight of him. She'd been on the beach with Helen, who for once was quiet, as she concentrated hard on the painting she was working on. Very slowly, a small sailing boat had come into view and as the craft had neared the shore Jessica could make out a head of sun-bleached blond hair and a magnificent bronzed body. Helen had seen him too. 'Jessica,' she'd said, 'you're drooling, put your tongue away.'

They'd watched him jump out of the small boat and pull it up on to the hot white sand. There was nobody else on the beach so it was only to be expected that a conversation would ensue. He came over, pushed his sun-glasses up on to his head and took a closer look at what Helen was painting. 'Very nice,' he said. And then as if they'd been expecting him, he settled himself on the sand next to Jessica. 'My name's Gavin, do you fancy a turn around the bay so that we can get better acquainted?'

God, but he'd been sweet. His carefree manner had made it so easy for her to fall for him.

But then everything about Gavin was carefree. Just as her own life had once been. She was shocked to realise that there was a tiny bit of her that was hungry for that way of life again. Since coming back to

Cholmford everything she had anything to do with seemed to be so intense – her mother, her writing, and Josh.

Most of all Josh.

There was an intensity to him that Jessica doubted she was capable of handling.

This doubt about Josh had crept over her last night when she had driven them home from Prestbury. He had made it very clear as they approached Cholmford that he wanted to be alone and she had parked outside his house, as close to his front door as was possible, and had helped him inside by offering her arm as support. She had stayed with him for just a few awkward minutes, frightened of doing or saying the wrong thing – having seen his anger once already that evening she had no desire to provoke a repeat performance. She had gone home confused and uncertain as to what she felt for Josh. She had then phoned her mother to check that she was all right.

And to apologise. 'I'm sorry,' she'd said. 'I went at you a bit, didn't I?'

'You most certainly did,' Anna had replied. 'How's Josh and how was your evening?'

'Mixed. I'll tell you about it another time. I'm going to bed now.'

'Yes, you'll want your beauty sleep for the big day tomorrow. You will come and fetch me, won't you? I don't want to miss out on all the fun.'

The sound of the doorbell downstairs jolted Jessica out of her thoughts. She tightened the towel around her and hurried to see who it was, praying like mad that the luvvies hadn't arrived early.

But it wasn't the film crew, it was Kate.

Jessica stared at Kate's pale face and the two suitcases either side of her. 'Oh dear,' she said, weighing up the situation at once. She stood back so that Kate could come in. 'Life has suddenly become very complicated for us all, hasn't it?'

'It's all gone wrong between Alec and me,' Kate said. 'I've left him.'

'I know. Or rather I thought that's what would happen.'

'You did?'

'Josh and I spoke to Tony last night,' Jessica said simply. 'I'm sorry about the baby.'

Kate swallowed nervously. 'You must think I'm terrible,' she said, 'and that I've behaved very badly towards Alec.'

'I don't think anything of the kind,' Jessica said firmly. She could see that Kate was close to tears, that she was wrung out with punishing herself. 'Why don't you come upstairs and talk to me while I get ready for the film crew, they'll be here any minute.'

'Oh dear, I'd forgotten all about that. I'd better let you get on, you don't want me holding you up.'

'Oh no, you don't.' And taking Kate by the arm Jessica led her upstairs. 'I need your help. Someone has to tell me what to wear.'

And while Kate made helpful suggestions, Jessica gently probed about yesterday's events.

'It was all so fast,' Kate said quietly, 'one minute I was pregnant and the next I knew I wasn't. It wasn't particularly painful . . . the real pain was knowing that I couldn't do anything to stop it. I felt so helpless.' She reached for a tissue by the side of the bed and wiped her eyes.

Jessica came over and hugged her. 'I've no idea what you've been through, Kate, so I shan't trot out a load of platitudes, but why don't you stay here for the day?'

'Won't I be in the way?'

'Probably. But it'll be a laugh and it will take your mind off things.'

Kate thought about this. She had planned to go to Caroline's and spend the day alone until her friend came home from work. But she suspected that being by herself would only make her more miserable than she already was – solitude would make her think of Alec . . . and the baby. She quickly dispelled this last thought from her mind, telling herself that she hadn't been pregnant long enough to warrant such a feeling of loss. But there was no denying what she felt. Physically her body was already recovering from what had happened yesterday – apart from feeling tired and a little weak, it seemed to be getting on with life as if there had never been a tiny baby growing within it – but her emotions were less inclined to carry on as normal and like a tearful child she wanted to shout, *It isn't fair, give me back my baby.*

When she had left the hospital she had been amazed at the ordinariness of the proceedings. The doctor and nurse who had dealt with her had both been kind, but at the same time matter of fact. But then they had to be, she supposed, they must see hundreds of women like her all the time. The doctor had described her miscarriage as being without complication. 'But just to be on the safe side,' she'd added, 'see your GP in a few days' time if you're worried about anything, it's possible that you might need a D & C if the bleeding continues for too long.'

And that was it. It was all over. She was no longer pregnant. It was as if she'd experienced nothing worse than a bad period. She looked up and saw that Jessica was waiting for her to say something. 'Okay,' she said, 'I'll spend the day here, just so long as you're sure I won't be a nuisance.'

'Great.' Jessica smiled. 'Now at least I won't have to worry about making endless cups of coffee for the luvvies; you can do it. Oh, but heavens, listen to me bossing you about. You probably need to spend time with your feet up.'

Kate shook her head. 'I'm okay. In fact I'd rather be busy.'

'Are you sure?'

'Very sure.'

'In that case, I don't suppose you'd do me a real favour and fetch my mother, would you?'

'I'm sorry but I haven't got my car.'

'No problem, you can use mine. Where is yours, by the way?'

'It's still at the pub where Tony and I were having lunch yesterday.'

'Ah,' said Jessica, 'was that where you were when you realised something was wrong?'

Kate nodded and turned, shamefaced, to look out of the window.

'Are you really sure you're doing the right thing in leaving Alec, Kate?'

Kate returned her attention to Jessica. 'I do love Alec, but not in the way . . . not in the way Tony makes me feel about him.'

'Which is?'

Kate lowered her eyes and fiddled with one of Jessica's ear-rings that lay on the bed. 'I'm not sure you'd understand.'

'Try me.'

'I suppose the difference between them is that Alec makes me feel like a young girl, whereas Tony makes me –'

'Feel like a woman?'

Kate coloured. 'Am I that transparent?'

'No.' Jessica smiled. 'I just have above-average intelligence.'

Kate smiled too. Then she said, 'I'm not leaving Alec because of Tony. Or rather, I'm not leaving him *for* Tony.'

'Did you know that Amanda left him yesterday?'

Kate looked startled. 'What?'

Jessica came and joined Kate on the bed. 'The Wicked Witch of the West must have known all about you and Tony, and some time during the day she cleared out the house.'

'I don't believe it.'

'She did. She took the lot, well, everything except Hattie's things and the stuff in the garage.'

'I don't believe it.'

'You're repeating yourself, Kate.'

'But how could she do that? And to Tony of all people.'

'I hate to state the obvious, but I would imagine her motive had something to do with him taking time out of the marriage to see you.'

Kate was horrified. What had she done? By allowing herself to become involved with Tony she had not only wrecked her relationship with Alec, but Tony's marriage. How many more people had she hurt?

As if reading her mind, Jessica said, 'You mustn't take all the blame for what Amanda has done. Tony knew the risk he was taking. I get the feeling he isn't exactly devastated by what's happened.'

Kate thought about this. If Tony's marriage was over, didn't that change things? No, she told herself firmly. She mustn't think of that. She must stop thinking of herself. 'But what about Hattie?' she said, suddenly realising that the little girl had also been affected by her reckless behaviour. 'Who's going to look after her?'

'Tell me about it! I've been roped in to picking her up from school this afternoon, though goodness knows how I'll manage if the filming hasn't finished in time.' Jessica turned her head. 'I can hear a car. It's them and I'm still not ready.' She leapt off the bed and rushed to the window. 'Oh,' she said, relieved, 'it's a taxi. Did you order one?'

'Lord yes! I'd better go down and say I don't need it for now.'

By lunch-time it appeared that the film crew had moved in permanently with Jessica. Bits of her furniture had been shoved aside and replaced with several enormous tripods bearing powerful lights. There seemed to be a ridiculous number of shiny metal cases dotted about the ground floor of the house from which had emerged an even more ridiculous amount of electricity cable and paraphernalia.

The most worrying object for Jessica was what Rodney, the producer of the programme, called a monitor. It was this that he kept his critical eye glued to throughout the proceedings. He was obviously a man who loved his work because he kept wanting to go over the same thing again and again. He was also getting along far too well with Anna for Jessica's liking – the two of them were acting like a regular pair of old buddies.

Kate was busy in the kitchen making drinks and sandwiches for the workers, and Anna and Rodney and his assistant, a young girl called Mel, were crouched over the monitor screen in the study where they and the rest of the film crew were crammed in like sardines. 'Look, Anna,' cried an animated Rodney as he replayed the last bit of the interview they'd just spent two hours filming, 'do you see how Jessica's eyes were darting about when she answered that question? That'll be dreadful on television, she'll look like Marty Feldman. We'll definitely have to redo that bit.'

Mel made a note on her clipboard and Anna said, 'She always does that with her eyes when she's nervous, she did it when she was a little girl whenever I caught her doing something she ought not to have been doing. She does it when she's cross sometimes.'

'Thanks, Mum,' Jessica said, getting up from the chair in which she'd been sitting for the duration of the interview.

The cameraman smiled at her knowingly and the sound man took off his headphones and said, 'Parents, who'd have 'em?'

'Who indeed?'

They ate their lunch in the kitchen while Rodney and Mel discussed the next few scenes they wanted to film. There was a difference of opinion, though. Mel was all in favour of showing an arty-farty Jessica wandering lonely as a cloud through the surrounding woods and fields, but Rodney had been seduced by Anna. 'I think we ought to show the viewer where it all started. Let's have a couple of scenes where Jessica grew up, maybe even have her mother in a shot or two.'

'Oh, do you really think so?' said a delighted Anna.

Jessica rolled her eyes. Then she remembered Marty Feldman.

Rodney was enraptured with Willow Cottage. 'It's perfect,' he crooned, 'just look at the wonderful reflections in the water from those willow trees.' But when he saw the old swing with the last of the summer roses climbing all over it, his artistic cup began to run over in a maelstrom of ecstasy. 'Jessica, Jessica, quick, here, sit on the swing for me.'

'He'll have you looking like something out of a Fragonard painting if you're not careful.' Mel laughed from behind her clipboard. There was more than a hint of cattiness to her voice. She was clearly put out that she hadn't got her way with the woods and fields.

'Something's not right,' Rodney said, disappointed, when Jessica took up her position on the swing.

'The clothes are all wrong,' Mel said smugly.

'Jessica, you look much too severe in that suit, could you be a real sweetheart and go home and change?'

'*Change!*' she squawked. Didn't this man have any idea how much this outfit had cost? And as for severe, well he'd get a dose of that in a minute if he didn't watch his step!

'Yes,' he carried on undaunted, 'slip into something soft and floaty for me, something summery. I know it's autumn, but we'll take a bit of licence with the seasons on this one. Mel, you go with Jessica and help her choose the right look. A long, wafty scarf would be a nice touch.'

Mel drove Jessica the short journey home in the hire car in which the crew had driven up from London. Kate opened the door to them. It was then that Jessica remembered Hattie. 'Hell's bells!' she said, 'what are we going to do? Hattie needs picking up in half an hour and Cecil B. DeMille is nowhere near finished.'

'I could fetch her for you,' Kate said.

'You're a life saver, Kate, truly you are. I'll dedicate the next book to you.'

Suitably attired in a simple cotton top and her longest and most revealing skirt – not her choice, but Mel's – Jessica was driven back to Willow Cottage. She found her mother artfully posing with a rake for the camera, there was even a small bonfire of smoking leaves in the background. Jessica noticed that Anna had removed her sling and was standing so as to disguise the fact that her arm was in a cast.

'Your mother's a natural,' Rodney announced as Jessica stomped her way across the lawn – *whose fifteen minutes of fame was this anyway?*

They filmed the swing scene next. It took nearly forty minutes to get it just the way Rodney had in mind and by the time he was satisfied with what his faithful monitor was showing him Jessica was shivering with cold. Floaty was all very well in the height of summer, but on a sharp autumnal day it was bloody freezing! Piers, she decided, would pay for this.

The filming went on.

And on.

Jessica's childhood was revisited in every shape, form and manner that Rodney could come up with. They filmed her sitting in her old bedroom. They filmed her studying her school reports, which Anna magically unearthed from some overstuffed drawer in the kitchen. She was made to read out her English teacher's comments about her appalling spelling and grammar – 'we want to show the viewer that anyone can be a writer,' Rodney not so tactfully enthused. They filmed her looking at her infant school photograph and had her point out, from the line-up of black and white faces, the smallest and ugliest and skinniest child as herself.

And only when all these avenues of humiliation had been thoroughly explored and Rodney was convinced that Willow Cottage had been fully exploited did he suggest that maybe they could call it a day and head back to London.

There wasn't even a single mention of it being a wrap. It was most disappointing.

After the film crew had packed up and gone, Jessica borrowed an old coat from Anna and walked home. It was nearly half past six when she let herself in. She found Kate in the sitting-room with Hattie; they looked very cosy on the sofa together with Hattie tucked under Kate's arm.

'I'm shattered,' Jessica said, flopping into the nearest chair. 'Remind me never *ever* to be so vain as to want to do anything like this again.'

Kate smiled. 'Cup of tea?'

'Please. That would be lovely. I'll go upstairs and change, I'm nithered to death in these summer rags.'

But she didn't make it as far as the stairs when the doorbell rang. 'Oh, Lord, what now?'

It was Tony. 'Was everything all right with Hattie?' he asked anxiously. 'I'm sorry I couldn't get here sooner. I've been in a meeting all afternoon.'

'Don't worry, she's fine and has been in more than capable hands.'

Hattie came running into the hall. 'Daddy, Daddy, guess who came for me at school.'

He picked her up and swung her round. 'I know who did, it was Jessica and wasn't she kind to do that? We're lucky to have such helpful neighbours.'

'Oh, no, it wasn't Jessica, it was Kate.'

'Kate?' repeated Tony. He turned at the sound of footsteps and as Kate appeared in the doorway he slowly lowered Hattie to the floor. He couldn't think what to say.

But Jessica did. She had written this kind of scene before and knew the score exactly. 'Hattie,' she said, 'why don't you and I go out for some fish and chips for everybody's supper tonight while Kate makes a drink for your father? He looks as though he could do with one.'

Chapter Forty-Eight

With Jessica and Hattie's sudden departure, the house fell eerily quiet.

'How are you ... how are you feeling?' Tony's words were hesitant and barely audible, and magnified the uneasy atmosphere between them.

'I'm fine,' Kate said.

He nodded, then looked down at his shoes. 'That's good. I'm glad. I'm glad you're all right.' He took off his jacket and carefully laid it on the back of a sofa. This was awful. Why couldn't he talk to her? Why was he so terrified? But the answer was simple. One wrong word from him now and he was sure he'd lose Kate for ever.

'How about you?' she asked.

'Me?'

'Yes, you.'

He shrugged. 'I'm okay.' He went over to the patio doors and pretended to look outside into the darkness, but all he could see was his own nervous reflection in the glass staring back at him. He turned away from himself. 'No,' he said abruptly, swinging round to face Kate, 'that's a lie, I'm far from okay.'

She looked concerned. 'Jessica told me about Amanda. I'm sorry, I never meant for anything like this to happen.'

Tony stared at her, then realised the mistake she'd made. 'No,' he said, 'no, you don't understand. Amanda taking things into her own hands is the best thing that could have happened.'

'So why –'

He took a few tentative steps towards her. 'So why am I not okay?'

'Yes.'

A few more steps. 'Yesterday at the hospital I thought you would blame me ... blame *us*, for what happened ... that you might not want to see me again.'

She lowered her eyes.

'I'm right, aren't I? That is what you thought.'

'Not entirely,' she said softly.

He was so close now he was almost touching her, could smell her light, fragrant perfume.

'I've left Alec,' she said, suddenly lifting her head and looking at him.

Nothing could have surprised Tony more. He stepped back from her and said the first thing that came into his head: 'Why?'

'Because, without meaning to, I changed. I wasn't right for Alec any more . . . and he was no longer right for me.'

He looked away, hardly daring to think of the consequences of what Kate had just told him. Did he have a chance? Was it possible that they could start all over again? And would she want that? Did she think they could be right for one another? An unlikely wave of sympathy for Alec swept over him. What must he be going through? He turned back to Kate and found that she was studying him in the same way she had that day in St Luke's.

'What is it,' he asked uncomfortably, 'why are you looking at me like that?'

'I was wondering if I would ever see you smile again, you look so earnest.'

He shook his head. 'Is it any wonder I feel earnest, Kate?' And with a sudden rush of nervous energy he moved away from her. He began pacing the room. 'Look,' he said, bringing his hands down with a bang on the back of one of Jessica's cream sofas. 'I'm just a simple guy. I'm not clever with words. I can't dress this up. But I'll say it anyway. I need to know where I stand with you. I'm not going to push you into anything and . . . and I know you need time to get over Alec, but . . . but can I see you from time to time? I'd like to do things properly with you.'

'Properly?'

'Yes. We didn't meet in the right circumstances. I want us to have a fresh start. I want to take you out for dinner and flirt outrageously with you, then drop you off at home and spend the next twenty-four hours ringing you up and agonising over when I'm going to see you again. How does that sound?'

'For a man who can't dress things up it sounds heavenly.'

He came to a standstill and stared at her. 'It does?'

She nodded and went to him. She raised one of her hands and let her fingers drift the length of his jaw, then she kissed him.

'Please don't stop,' he said, when at last he felt her pulling away.

She smiled. 'I'm afraid I need the oxygen,' she said.

He drew her further into his arms. 'By the way, where will home be?'

She lifted her head from his shoulder to answer his question. 'Knutsford. I'm going to stay with a friend until I've got myself sorted. The first thing I need to do is find a job. I don't suppose you'd consider employing me meanwhile, would you?'

'What, at Arc?'

'No, silly. You're going to need somebody to look after Hattie after school, it might just as well be me.'

To her surprise he shook his head. 'No,' he said firmly. 'It's out of the question.'

'But why? It would be perfect.'

'I can't do that. Everyone would say that I was using you.'

'And who's everyone?'

He shook his head again. 'Just people.'

'Well I don't have a problem with it.'

'But I do. I don't want you to be the hired help.'

'Then don't pay me.'

'Now you're being silly.'

She smiled. 'And you're not?'

He let go of her and walked away. He went and sat down. 'I just want it to be right between us, Kate,' he said. 'I did everything wrong with Amanda and I'm not inclined to repeat any past mistakes.'

'Good, so that's settled then. I'll pick Hattie up from school tomorrow.'

'Didn't you hear me?'

'I heard you, Tony. I heard you loud and clear, making life unnecessarily difficult for yourself.' She joined him on the sofa. 'I'm offering to look after Hattie because I'm very fond of her and it just so happens that she's the daughter of the man I'm even more fond of.' She kissed him and as Tony gave himself up to her embrace he realised that there really wasn't any point in disagreeing with Kate. Her mind was obviously made up.

Jessica crawled into bed like a woman suffering from sleep deprivation. She was shattered. Stardom wasn't all it was cracked up to be, especially when it was compounded by a star-struck mother and an evening of running to earth a fish-and-chip shop that was actually open. She and Hattie must have tried nearly half a dozen, only to find they didn't open until eight o'clock, which was no good when they were starving hungry at seven. In the end they'd tracked one down and had then headed for home and found Kate and Tony smiling contentedly like a couple of chipmunks on the sofa.

Love's young dream was written all over their faces and Jessica had felt pleased for them. They'd all sat in the kitchen with their plates of fish and chips, and cracked open a bottle of wine. When they'd finished eating, Tony had driven Kate to her friend's house in Knutsford.

The only downside to the evening for Jessica was that Josh wasn't there to join in. She had tried ringing him several times to see if he wanted to come over, but there was no answer, not even from his mobile. His house, like Alec's, was in darkness and with no sign of his car, she could only assume that he was working late, or was with Charlie.

She lay back on the pillow ready for a good night's sleep – boy, had she earned it. But sleep was to be denied her. The phone rang almost the second she closed her eyes. It was only ten forty-five, but rarely did anyone call her so late. She snatched up the receiver, a vision instantly in her mind of her mother in trouble.

But it wasn't Anna.

'Gavin!' she yelled into the phone, jerking herself into an upright position.

'Yeah, that's the fella. You knew him once. Alas, poor Gavin, I knew him well. And in this case very well.'

'Have you been drinking?'

'Just the merest, teensiest, weensiest bottle or two of Metaxa.'

'What do you want, Gavin?'

'Oh, Jess, don't you know?'

'No, Gavin, I don't.'

'It's you, Jess. I want *you.*'

'You had your chance and you threw it away,' she said nastily.

'But I've changed, Jess.'

'Prove it to me.'

'I've grown a beard.'

'A what?'

'You know, one of those hairy things men wear on their chins.'

'*Yugh!* Why?'

'I thought it would keep the women away.'

'And does it?'

'No.'

'Good-night, Gavin.'

'You're a hard woman, Jessie Lloyd.'

'Thank you. Any other compliments for me?'

'Oh, come on, Jess. I'm trying to tell you that I've changed, that I'm ready to settle down.'

'And I suppose you really expect me to believe that?'

'And why wouldn't you?'

'So let's get this straight. You're telling me you're ready for children and slippers and a Ford Mondeo?'

'Steady on, Jess, I only meant I was ready to settle down for a life of regular sex and a clean pair of trollies every day.'

'*Hah!*'

'Would it help if I sang to you? You used to like me singing to you when we were in bed together.'

'Well, we're not in bed together now, are we?' she snapped back at him.

'Oh, Jess, you've turned into a bitter woman.'

'I'm not bitter!'

'Well that new fella's obviously not treating you right, or you wouldn't be sounding so hard.'

'What do you know about Josh? Oh, don't tell me, Helen told you all about him.'

There was a long pause.

'Well?' demanded Jessica, 'answer me, Gavin.'

'I'm trying to look sheepish down the line, that's why I'm not saying anything.'

Jessica suddenly laughed. 'Gavin, go to bed. If you want to ring me, do so when you're sober.'

'But I'm more romantic when I'm a little the worse for drink, the words come easier.'

'That's a matter for debate.'

'Jess?'

'Yes.'

'I love you, Jess.'

'No you don't, Gavin. Good-night.'

Chapter Forty-Nine

'I can't see that you've any choice,' Charlie said bravely.

They were having breakfast and as a consequence of what Charlie had just said a deathly hush had settled on them, but Josh's anger as he continued obstinately to read the front page of the *Financial Times* was as palpable as the strong smell of the coffee Charlie had just made.

It was also as manifestly real as the black cloud of depression that had descended on Josh and it was at times like this that Charlie knew he was way out of his depth. As far as he was concerned, before MS had booted its way into his life Josh had never suffered from depression; the moodiest he'd ever been was when he'd been recovering from a hangover.

But this was different. A glass of Alka-Seltzer was no remedy for what Josh was experiencing. Charlie knew that once the grip of depression was on him there was no instant cure. Sometimes it would only last for a few hours, at others it could be days. He'd read an article once in a magazine about a guy who could never shake off his depression, it was always with him. The poor fellow had likened it to having a parasite in his stomach eating away at the guts of him.

Thank God Josh didn't have it as badly as that.

Charlie poured out the coffee from the cafetiere and pushed his brother's mug across the table. He deliberately placed it next to Josh's left hand – he could see that his right was too clenched to get a proper grip on anything.

Still Josh didn't raise his eyes from the newspaper.

'You've got to face up to it, Josh,' Charlie said, determined to pursue the point and to make Josh admit to what was so glaringly obvious. 'You've reached the stage where you need a stick. It would help you.'

But still Josh didn't say anything.

And he didn't need to. Charlie could see well enough what was going through his brother's mind. He knew that this whole MS thing was the most humiliating ordeal for Josh, that it was steadily eroding away his self-esteem, stripping him of his sense of worth. Resorting to a walking stick at his age was bound to be a hell of a blow to his pride. He probably viewed it as giving in to his MS rather than keeping up the fight against it.

But his attitude would have to change. He had no choice.

After work last night when everyone had gone home, Charlie had gone into Josh's office to go over a couple of ideas he'd had on one of their new lines and had found him inching his way round the room for a sample garment hanging on a rail some six yards away from him. Charlie had seen the strain in his face as he completed what to anybody else would have been a few easy steps, but what to Josh at that precise moment was the equivalent of running a half-marathon on one leg.

Much against Josh's wishes, Charlie had insisted he spend the night with him at his house in Hale. As he'd driven them home he had asked Josh when was the last time he'd seen a doctor. But all Josh had said was, 'I know how I feel, I don't need some bloody doctor telling me what I already know.'

And now, as he stared at Josh's sullen face, he decided the silence had gone on for long enough. Josh would have to listen to him. And act on it.

'I just think it would help you,' he said.

Josh lowered his mug of coffee. 'And how the hell would you know?' His words were slow and accusing.

'I'm making an assumption,' Charlie battled on, 'it makes sense, that's all, a stick would give you the support you need. It would stop you from –'

Josh threw down his paper. 'Well, why don't we just get straight to it? Let's not mess about with a stick, let's get me a wheelchair. Would that make you feel better?'

'It's not a question of how it would make *me* feel.'

'Oh, yes it bloody well is! You don't like the sight of me crawling round the office. It embarrasses the hell out of you.'

'That's not true.'

Charlie made a point of staying out of Josh's way that day at work. He knew that if he ventured into his brother's office another argument would ensue. There didn't seem any way of helping him. He appeared determined to ignore what was staring him right in the face. Something, or someone, had to explain to Josh that there were certain things he could do to make his life easier. The thought crossed his mind that perhaps Jessica could help. Could she be the one to get through to Josh?

He didn't have Jessica's phone number so he went in search of Mo. Josh had got her to ring Jessica once and with a bit of luck she might still have a note of the number.

Mo was an obsessive hoarder of bits of paper. Her desk was always a mess, as was the large drawer where she kept everything stashed away. 'I'm pretty sure I've still got it,' she told Charlie as she began taking out her pile of essay notes for that week's homework. At the back of the drawer she found a thick wodge of telephone messages and after sorting through them she finally came up with the one Charlie wanted. 'Why didn't you just ask Josh for it?' she asked.

'Because I'm going behind his back, so not a word, okay?'

'Hey, you're not trying to pinch Jessica, are you? Because if that's your game you can hand that over. I've done enough harm in that department without aiding and abetting you.' She tried to snatch the slip of paper out of his hand.

'Of course I'm not. I just need her help. Now remember, nothing about this to Josh.'

Jessica wasn't in when Charlie phoned her, so he left a message on her answerphone.

Jessica was at Willow Cottage. She'd just taken Anna shopping and now they were filling the cupboards and fridge with enough food to ensure that Anna wouldn't go hungry for the next six months. This was partially due to Jessica's desire to appease her conscience over her mother's welfare and also because first thing that morning George and Emily, just back from a holiday touring the west coast of Ireland, had phoned and when they'd heard about Anna's accident had immediately invited themselves to come and stay for a few days.

The arrangement suited Jessica perfectly. At least now there would be somebody keeping a keen eye on Anna. Not Emily, who was as irresponsible as Anna, but George, who was rock solid – forty years as a barrister specialising in Personal Injury had made him reliably cautious. Jessica was more than happy to entrust her mother's well-being to the capable hands of a man who would no more stand for her DIY antics than he would allow her to go bungi jumping.

'Right,' said Jessica. 'That's about everything stored away, do you want me to throw something together for your supper tonight with George and Emily?'

'Heavens no!' cried Anna, 'what have they ever done to you to deserve such a punishment?'

'You're all sweetness, Mum.'

'I know. I do my best. Now off you go and leave me alone. I've got things to do and you've certainly got a book to get on with. Kissy, kissy, bye, bye, and all that.'

Jessica drove home in a despondent mood. She would have liked to have lingered a little longer with her mother. It was silly, but she wanted to talk to her about Gavin's phone call last night. Silly because there really wasn't anything to discuss.

Or was there?

Hadn't she spent most of the night tossing and turning, thinking about Gavin and what he'd said? He'd never before said he loved her. Drunk or sober, the word love had never been a part of his vocabulary. So why, oh why, did he have to go and say it now? Why couldn't he have said it months ago when she wanted him to?

There were two messages waiting for her on the answerphone when she let herself in. She hoped that one of them was from Josh, but she was disappointed. The first was from Charlie asking her to ring him back and the second was . . . was from Gavin.

'I'm not drunk now, Jess, honestly,' he said, sounding hollow and tinny as the machine amplified and distorted his voice. 'And guess what, I meant what I said last night. Not the bit about you being a bitter woman, or being hard, but the other thing. You know, the bit when I said that, well you know, when I said that I –'

But the technology hadn't allowed Gavin time to finish what he was saying and Jessica felt slightly relieved. To have heard Gavin, without the aid of a gallon of Metaxa inside him, saying that he loved her was too much.

She replayed Charlie's message, then phoned him back. She listened to what he had to say. 'I'll try, Charlie,' she said when she'd taken in what he wanted her to do, 'but to be honest I don't think he'll listen to me.'

'But you'll have a go?'

'Of course, but just don't put all your hopes on me. I can't help but think that if you've failed to get through to him there's no chance of me succeeding.'

'It's got to be worth a try, Jessica. But whatever you say to him, don't let on that I put you up to it.'

'Okay.'

'And look, I don't wish to sound alarmist, but I'm convinced he's getting worse. Last night he could barely manage it to the car. If I hadn't been around I don't know how he'd have coped. And another word of warning –'

'Charlie, don't go on, you're making Josh sound like a minefield.'

'That's not a bad way of describing him in his current mood.'

355

'What do you mean?'

'Put it this way, his mood hasn't improved since the other night at Mum and Dad's.'

'Is he worse?'

'I'd say so.'

'Poor Josh.'

'I've seen it before. It's like he gets caught in a downward spiral and sucked into the darkness. All you can do is go with him and accept that you can't say or do the right thing. You just have to be there for him, a silent support act, you could call it. I only wish I could remember to do it myself. Unfortunately I managed to antagonise him thoroughly this morning.'

'Who's to say I won't?'

'But he feels differently towards you, Jessica. I'm just his boring old brother.'

After they'd finished their conversation Jessica tried to psych herself up for an afternoon of writing, but not surprisingly she found that she couldn't concentrate on *A Casual Affair*. Her thoughts alternated between Gavin, who had been so free and easy with her emotions, and Josh, who even though he was such a troubled person had made her feel like no other man had.

She had only known him for a short while, but within that time he had touched her in an exceptional way. When he wasn't battling with his MS he was all the things Gavin wasn't: gentle and sensitive, thoughtful and astute, and so very loving. She had found him to be the perfect foil to her own personality, which tended to be a little abrasive. She was aware, too, that what she felt for him didn't hinge on what he felt for her. It was almost as if loving him was fulfilment enough. Was this what selfless love meant?

If so, it was the antithesis of what she'd experienced with Gavin. The more she thought she'd loved Gavin, the more she'd wanted him to love her. But he never had.

Until now, apparently.

If he was to be believed.

But she didn't want to think any more about Gavin. He'd taken up far too much of her thoughts today as it was.

She reached for the phone and dialled Josh's mobile, a number which she knew by heart.

He sounded distant when he answered.

'Is it a bad time to talk?' she asked, thinking that maybe he had someone in his office with him.

'I'm a bit busy,' he said.

'Oh.' She wasn't prepared for such a lack of response from him. 'I tried ringing you yesterday evening.'

'I spent the night at Charlie's.'

'Oh.' She cringed. What was happening to her? She was a woman who made her living from words and here she was unable to utter anything more scintillating than *oh*. 'There was a lot of excitement going on last night,' she said, trying to inject some life into their joyless banter. *Why hadn't he asked her about her big day being filmed?*

'Oh?'

Oh great! Now he was at it as well.

She told him about Tony and Kate.

'Good for them,' Josh said uninterestedly.

His lack of enthusiasm annoyed her. He's tired, she told herself when she put down the phone. As Charlie said, this is a definite low period for him.

And just how on earth did Charlie think she was going to be able to broach the subject of Josh seeing a doctor, never mind the other thing she was supposed to bring up casually in conversation that evening – oh, and by the way, Josh, ever thought that a walking stick might come in handy?

So far there had been little conversation passing between them. There hadn't been so much as a kiss or a cuddle.

Nothing.

Zilch.

The atmosphere was distinctly chilly. Any cooler and they'd be chipping the ice off one another.

Jessica had resorted to switching on the television to provide a diversion. But yet another interminable medical drama was not what was required, especially when it was about a small child dying of some muscle-wasting disease. She quickly zapped the telly with the remote control.

Josh turned and gave her an odd look. 'What was wrong with that?' he asked.

Instantly she saw the trap he was setting her. 'Men in masks and gowns give me the willies,' she said. 'Another drink?' Hellfire, he was touchy tonight and obviously just waiting for her to put a foot wrong. Charlie was right. In his current frame of mind Josh really was a minefield.

She fetched the bottle of wine from the kitchen and poured the remains into their glasses. She put the empty bottle under the table and sat down next to Josh. Somehow she had to get him to talk. In the past she'd found it effortless to be light-hearted and flippant with him, but this evening she seemed incapable of the most basic small talk. What had happened to her?

Then she realised what it was. It was her reaction to what Charlie had described as Josh's downward spiral – it was destroying her confidence, making her fearful of him. She had to snap out of it. She might not be able to do anything about Josh's mood, but she had to work on her own.

Tentatively, she touched his hand. 'Josh,' she said, 'talk to me. You've hardly opened your mouth since you got here.'

'What do you want me to say?'

'I . . . I'm not sure.'

'Well, in that case, neither am I.' He removed his hand from hers and reached for his wineglass. He drained it in one go, but when he went to replace it on the table he misjudged the distance and the glass dropped with a soft thud on to the carpet by his feet.

Jessica made no move to pick it up – she'd learnt that much from being with him. Instead, she watched him retrieve the glass and place it with extreme care on the table in front of him.

'See,' he said, 'I managed it all on my own. How about that? Not bad for a disabled person, wouldn't you say?'

Jessica was either going to lose her temper or cry. And deciding that tears were for wimps, she resorted to her old standby. She leapt to her feet. 'Right, that's it!' she shouted at him. 'I've had enough. I've tried to be considerate. I've tried to humour you. I've even tried to do your brother's bidding, but enough is enough. I'm not a patient woman, I've a temper on me like a . . . like a, oh God, I give up, I'm hopeless at similes, but just hear this good and proper, I'm not going to stand here and let you use me like a punchbag. Have you got that?'

He stared at her, his eyes dark and narrowed, his lips drawn in a tight line. 'What do you mean, my brother's bidding?' His voice was frighteningly low.

Jessica's anger was suddenly checked. Damn, she'd given Charlie away.

'Did Charlie put you up to something?'

She swallowed nervously. 'No.'

'Liar.'

She swallowed again, her anger now straining to unleash itself. 'Okay then,' she said, 'you're right. And what of it?'

He continued to stare at her. 'I thought as much,' he said coolly. 'So the pair of you had a little confab behind my back, did you?'

Jessica's anger had fully returned now. And in triple strength. 'God, you're so self-obsessed,' she let rip at him, 'you're so full of self-pity you really can't see what you're doing to those who love you. Your poor parents live in constant fear of saying the wrong thing and as for Charlie, he's so desperate to help he'd chop off one of his own legs if he thought it would be of any use to you. And yes,' she continued, 'Charlie was worried enough to ask if I would talk to you. And what of it? Is that really such a crime? Doesn't it just prove how much he cares about you?'

A cruel smile came over Josh's face. 'Don't tell me, you were supposed to convince me that it was time to put up a neat little sticker in my car window and persuade me to buy the latest in disability accessories? Was that it?'

'If you had a broken leg you'd be more than happy to use a pair of crutches,' she blasted back at him, 'just tell me what the difference is.'

'The difference, Jessica, in case you hadn't cottoned on, is that I've got some fucking disease that is slowly killing me.'

'The only thing that's killing you is your bloody pride, you pig-headed, arrogant bastard!'

His jaw tightened and cold fury sprang into his eyes. 'Well, thanks for informing me of that, Jessica. I'll bear it in mind on the days when I can't put one foot in front of the other. Oh, that's all right, I'll tell myself, Jessica says it's only pride that's preventing me from being able to walk, it's got nothing to do with the gradual breakdown of my central nervous system.'

He began hauling himself to his feet. His movements were heartachingly clumsy. Jessica turned away. She couldn't watch him. It was too painful.

'I think we've said enough,' he said, when he was fully upright. 'In fact, we've probably said all that we ever need to say to one another. Good-night, Jessica. Or perhaps I mean goodbye, but there again that sounds too trite and clichéd even for a romantic novelist.' The bitterness in his voice was total. So was the contempt.

When he'd gone, Jessica threw herself on the sofa and buried her face in the cushion that he'd been leaning against. She could smell his aftershave on the fabric, the redolence of which brought forth the first of the tears; small, pitiful tears that quickly turned into painful sobs of remorse.

How could she have shouted at him like that?

How could she have hurt him when she loved him so much?

And how could she have let him walk away from her?

Why hadn't she tried to stop him? He was so weak, so worn down that she could have stopped him with her little finger.

The answer was ironically clear. The very same thing of which she had accused Josh had stopped her from saying she was sorry. Her pride and anger at the way she felt he had mistreated her, and those closest to him, had killed his love for her.

She had lost him.

Even if he would ever listen to her, which she very much doubted, there was no going back. Those damning words could never be withdrawn.

She stumbled upstairs to bed and cried herself into a restless sleep, tormented by images of Josh reaching out to her and her turning her back on his outstretched hands.

THE END

Chapter Fifty

While the stolid and reliable George was visiting a branch of his bank in Holmes Chapel and at the same time obtaining his daily fix of *The Times*, Anna and Emily had taken the opportunity to slip in a quick hour's worth of furtive gardening. They were working on the border opposite the back door where they couldn't be seen from the road or the drive, and where Anna had assured Emily that they'd hear George's car in plenty of time so that they could skip back inside the house and pretend they'd been doing nothing more perilous than washing up the lunch things. But their enjoyment of the while-the-cat's-away-the-mice-will-play situation was being marred by Anna's concern for her daughter.

'Do you think Jessica would talk to me?' Emily asked as she pushed the fork into the soft damp earth and waited for Anna to lift out the gladioli corm.

'You could try if you want,' Anna said, taking care not to bruise the corm in her hands as she removed the soil from its surface and cut away all but the last half-inch of its stem with her secateurs, 'but to be honest, I don't think it will work. I've never seen Jessica like this. She's never blocked me out before. We've always been able to talk to one another, but this silence from her is awful.'

Emily looked at her friend's worried face. 'Are you sure you're not over-reacting?'

Anna shook her head. 'I know what you're thinking, that I've got used to having her around and now I can't cope when she's got other things on her mind, apart from me. But it's not like that. Really it isn't. I've always been used to Jessica living away from home and being independent – it was what I wanted for her – and in all that time I've never been really worried about her. I've never needed to. Whenever there was a lack of communication between us I was always confident that she was okay. Don't ask me how I knew, I just did.'

'And you're not confident now?'

'No. It's like she's closed a door on me.' Tears came into Anna's eyes. She wiped them away with the sleeve of her old gardening jacket. 'I never knew that I could miss her so much,' she said quietly, 'or feel so worried for her. Perhaps it's a just punishment for the hard time I gave her when she was doing her best to look after me.'

It was nearly a week since Jessica had informed Anna of the argument she'd had with Josh, which had brought about the end of their relationship.

'I don't want to discuss it in any detail,' Jessica had said when she'd come out for a pub lunch with George and Emily last Saturday, 'I'm just telling you what's happened so that you don't go and say something stupid.'

Later that afternoon, when they were alone in the kitchen at Willow Cottage, using all the kid-glove diplomacy she knew Anna had drawn out of her daughter a few more details.

'It strikes me that all you need to do is apologise to one another,' Anna had suggested. She liked Josh and had entertained a very real hope that one day he might become her son-in-law. She felt strangely sad at her own loss.

But in response, Jessica had shaken her head with tears in her eyes. 'I tried ringing him this morning and he refused to speak to me. I tried to apologise, but he was so cold . . . so unforgiving. Now please, just don't talk to me about it any more. It's over and I've got work to do. I ought to go. Say goodbye to George and Emily for me.'

And she'd left, just like that, almost running out of the house. Since then, she hadn't phoned. The tables had turned and now it was Anna who was doing all the ringing to check on her daughter. Most of the time Jessica left her answerphone on and on the few occasions when Anna had spoken to her she had claimed she was either too busy to chat, or too tired.

'Shall I call on her when George gets back?' Emily pressed.

But Anna didn't get a chance to reply. 'Quick,' she said, pulling off her gardening gloves and handing her friend the box of lifted gladioli corms, 'it's George. Put those in the shed on the top shelf and I'll go and put my feet up and pretend to be having a snooze.'

'Jess, I can't sleep for thinking of you.'

'Why do you want to sleep? It's only four o'clock in the afternoon.'

'I don't mean now. I'm talking about when I'm in bed at night.'

'Then take something. Treat yourself to some chemically enhanced sleep.'

'So you've turned into a drugs dealer now, have you, Jess?'

'Look, Gavin, please, I'm just not in the mood.'

'I can't remember you ever saying that to me before. If I recall, you were always mad for it.'

'Leave me alone, Gavin.'

'You don't mean that. I know you don't.'

And he was right. These days Gavin was the only person Jessica could talk to without ending the conversation in tears. Over the past week his silly jokes and buffoonery had become a prop to her.

He'd phoned her on Saturday, the day after she'd argued with Josh, and she'd told him what had happened.

'I'm not sure I want to hear you blubbing about some other fella,' he'd said.

'Then don't ring me,' she'd told him through her tears.

'Shall I fly over and beat him up for you; would that make you feel better?'

'No.'

'What would?'

'I don't know.'

He'd phoned every day since.

On Wednesday he'd said, 'I can't hear you snivelling, does that mean you're over the awful fella or back with him?'

On Thursday he'd said, 'Why don't you give yourself a holiday? Dig out your bucket and spade and come and stay with me.'

'Don't be absurd, I've got work to do.'

'Oh, come on, Jess, you can write that penny-dreadful stuff in your sleep.'

On Friday he asked her again to go and stay with him. 'There's hardly any tourists here now, we'd have the place to ourselves. I could take you out in the boat.'

'I hate sailing, you know that.'

'We could have sex if you'd prefer. It could be good for you, you know, in a therapeutic, healing kind of way.'

'Is that your latest chat-up line?'

'Oh no, I've got a much better one than that.'

'Spare me, please.'

And now it was Tuesday and Gavin was complaining to her that he couldn't sleep. She hadn't slept much recently either.

She wondered if Josh was sleeping.

It was exactly eleven days since Josh had finished with her and for most of those days she'd seen him for the briefest of seconds. Every evening while working in her study she would wait for him to come home. Night after night she would watch him across the courtyard as

365

he dragged his tired body from his car to his front door. Not once did he turn and look in her direction. Not once did he even acknowledge that she existed.

But he still existed for her. And each evening the painful sight of him invoked a whole series of responses in her: anger, hurt, regret, but mostly an overwhelming sense of love. Oh yes, she still loved him. She wished that she could tell him that. But he would probably never believe her. His pride and anger would stop him from accepting that she loved him unconditionally; that his MS didn't affect the way she viewed him, that in reality it was just another facet of his personality that had become so precious to her. She wouldn't have cared that their future together would have been full of uncertainty – after all, there wasn't a person alive who could rest secure in the knowledge that his or her own future was clear-cut and perfectly defined.

But there was no point in going over all this. She had to face up to the truth that Josh had no desire to see her, which was why she had taken the step of booking herself on a flight to Corfu. With the first draft of *A Casual Affair* very nearly finished, and with George and Emily staying on for another week at Willow Cottage, she felt able to go away knowing that her mother was in safe hands. Other than Helen and Jack, she had told no one of her plans. But now she told Gavin.

'Great!' he said, 'I'll clean up a bit and change the sheets.'

'No, Gavin, I'm staying with Helen and Jack.'

'You're such a tease, Jess.'

'It's true. Ask them. It's all arranged.'

'All right, then, but let me pick you up at the airport.'

'Okay, that would be nice.'

'Jess?'

'Yes.'

'I'll change the sheets anyway, shall I?'

Anna couldn't believe it.

'What is it?' Emily asked when Anna put down the phone and went and joined her friends in the sitting-room.

'It's Jessica,' she said, 'she's going back to that fool Gavin.'

'What, that chap in Corfu?' asked George, lowering his *Times* crossword and peering at Anna over the top of his glasses.

'The very one.'

'For good?' asked Emily.

'She says she's just going for a few days.'

366

'Oh, well, I don't suppose too much harm can come of that,' said George, returning his concentration to seven down.

But Anna was far from convinced. 'That place and that man seduced her once before. Why wouldn't the same combination work a second time . . . and keep her there for ever?'

'When does she go?'

'Tomorrow.'

Anna had never interfered in her daughter's life before, but she had absolutely no qualms over what she was about to do. It's pay-back time, she told herself as she picked up the phone. All those years when I held my tongue and let her get on with making her own mistakes have to count for something. She dialled the number and waited.

And waited.

Dammit, where was he? Why didn't he answer?

Josh ignored the ringing from his mobile phone. Whoever it was, he didn't want to speak to them. He carried on reading through the latest wad of specifications from Hong Kong.

The ringing eventually stopped. Relieved, Josh took off his glasses and rubbed his eyes. He was unbelievably tired.

Tired of work.

Tired of his failing body.

Tired of trying to banish Jessica from his thoughts.

He was also tired of Charlie.

'For God's sake, ring Jessica and say you're sorry,' Charlie had shouted at him yesterday, 'your life's bad enough without doing this to yourself.'

It was advice he didn't want or need.

Even his parents had phoned him – no guesses who had put them in the picture – 'Are you sure you know what you're doing?' his mother had asked him, 'she seemed such a lovely girl.'

But what none of them could see was that there was no point in any of it.

So much of what Jessica had flung at him he knew to be true. He had hurt his family in the past and without knowing how to stop himself he would probably go on hurting those closest to him.

I'm not going to stand here and let you use me like a punchbag, Jessica had said. It was these very words that had sealed their fate. He could never continue a relationship with Jessica because he would only end up causing her pain and he loved her too much to do that.

His mobile started ringing again. He stared at it, still not wanting to answer it.

'Are you going to let that ring all day?'

It was Charlie. He came into the office and plonked himself in the chair opposite Josh. 'Well?' he said, 'answer it, then.'

'No.'

The ringing stopped and Charlie frowned. 'Who are you afraid of?'

'Nobody,' said Josh sharply.

'Liar.'

Josh leant back in his chair. 'Not another lecture, please.'

The mobile began trilling again. Charlie snatched up the small phone from the desk and answered it. 'No, this isn't Josh, it's his brother, Charlie. Oh, hello, Mrs Lloyd. Yes, we do sound alike, don't we? Hang on and I'll hand you over.'

Josh shook his head. He waved the phone away.

'I'm sorry, Mrs Lloyd, he's rather busy, can I pass on a message or get him to call you back?'

The conversation that followed was brief and to the point, and when Charlie had said goodbye he handed the phone to his brother and said, 'I suggest you speak to Jessica before it's too late.'

'What do you mean?'

'Apparently an old boy-friend is making his presence felt and has persuaded her to go back to Corfu.'

Josh's face dropped. He quickly regained his composure. 'To live there again?' he asked calmly.

But Charlie had seen the expression of alarm in his brother's face. 'I don't know,' he said. 'Her mother just said that Jessica was catching the early-morning flight tomorrow.'

Josh said nothing. He slowly got to his feet and struggled across his office. He came to a stop in front of a large notice-board. He ran his fingers over the samples of stretch denim that were pinned to the green felt. 'So what's any of that got to do with me?' he asked.

'What the hell do you think? Go home and talk to Jessica. Tell her what you feel about her. Be honest for once.'

'It's honesty that's got me where I am.'

'I don't believe that for a single moment.'

'Suit yourself.'

Charlie banged his fist down on the desk. 'It's not a matter of what suits me.'

'Good, so keep out of my life.'

Charlie leapt to his feet. 'I wish I bloody well could! I also wish I could get to the bottom of what's gone wrong between you and Jessica. She's the first woman who's made any real impression on you and you seem absurdly content to let her go. I don't know the full ins and outs of what you and Jessica argued about, you didn't tell me the whole story, but I bet your bloody pride is involved somewhere.'

Josh turned on him. 'The only reason you're so keen for there to be a neat package of Jessica and Josh is that you hope it'll let you off the hook!'

'*What!*' exploded Charlie.

'That's right. You want me to be conveniently hitched up with Jessica so that you won't have to worry about me any more, you'll have somebody else to do it for you.'

An anger that was raw and violent swept over Charlie. The blood drained from his face. He felt sick with rage. 'Don't ever, ever accuse me again of something as despicable as that.' He spat the words out and turned to walk away, but he changed his mind, and suddenly and without warning he slammed his fist into Josh's face.

Charlie stared in horror at his brother as he lay on the floor. It was a couple of seconds before he took in what he'd done and it took a further split second for him to come to terms with how easy it had been to knock Josh clean off his feet.

Josh's head was spinning. He could taste blood. He gingerly touched his mouth, then looked up to see Charlie offering him his hand.

'I'm not even going to say sorry for doing that,' Charlie said when he was up on his feet, 'you deserved it too much.'

Josh took out a handkerchief from his pocket and pressed it against his lower lip. 'I can't recall you ever hitting me,' he said in a shocked voice. Holding the hanky to his mouth, he went and sat down. 'Do I really get up your nose that much?' he asked.

Charlie pushed his hands into his trouser pockets. 'Yes,' he said simply. 'There've been more times than I'd care to admit when all I've wanted to do is thump the living daylights out of you.'

'So what's stopped you in the past?'

Charlie shrugged. 'Hitting somebody when they're down doesn't seem to be the decent thing to do, I suppose.'

'You mean until now it was pity that was keeping your fists off me.'

Charlie paced the room. 'Why do you have to make pity sound so derogatory? Look it up in the dictionary, it means sadness and compassion felt for another's suffering. I can't help feeling that way about you. You're my brother.'

Josh closed his eyes. His head was still spinning. The shock of Charlie actually hitting him was still with him too. Knowing that he'd pushed his brother to such an extreme appalled him. What had he become? What kind of monster had his illness turned him into? Whoever or whatever he was, he was no longer recognisable to himself.

'There's nothing wrong with people having a genuine concern for you, Josh,' he heard Charlie say. 'It's called love. And it's what Jessica feels for you.'

He flicked his eyes open. 'Yeah well, maybe you're right,' he said matter-of-factly. 'But it's over. We've said our goodbyes. And that's my final word on the subject.'

But Charlie was determined to prove his brother wrong.

Jessica's taxi came for her at the unearthly hour of twenty to six in the morning. It was pitch dark when she was driven away from Cholmford Hall Mews, and as the car negotiated the small bridge over the canal and she looked back at Willow Cottage she was reminded of the night she'd returned to England. It seemed an age since then, so much had happened.

But in reality, it wasn't the case.

It was just that what had gone on during the past few months had been so all-consuming. Love was like that, though. Once it got a hold of you it held you in its grip, giving you the impression it would never let you go.

But sometimes it did.

And this was one of those occasions.

At the airport she paid the taxi driver and made her way to the long row of check-in desks in the departure hall. After queuing for a short while she checked in her luggage and went in search of a café where she hoped to force down some breakfast. But the way she was feeling it was unlikely that she would manage it. Her churning stomach was leaving her in no doubt that it wasn't happy at being disturbed so early.

Josh opened his front door. 'What the hell are you doing here?' he asked, bleary-eyed and disorientated – it was six o'clock in the morning and his brother was on his doorstep. *Why?*

Charlie ignored Josh's question. He stepped in and closed the door behind him. 'Get washed, shaved and dressed, you're coming with me.'

Josh opened his mouth to speak, but Charlie raised his hand and pointed a forefinger at him. 'Not a word. Got it?'

Upstairs in Josh's bathroom, Charlie stood over him. 'You've missed a bit,' he said, watching his brother shave, then realising that Josh's hands were shaking and were too stiff to do a proper job he added, 'here, give it to me.'

'I know exactly what you're doing, Charlie,' Josh said above the sound of the razor.

'Good, so let's get on with it.'

'It won't work. I know it won't. It's gone beyond that.'

'Right now, I can't be arsed with your pessimism. Okay, that's the shaving done. Clean your teeth, then splash on something irresistible while I get your clothes. What do you think Jessica would like to see you in?'

'After the way I've treated her a coffin, probably.'

'Would that be teak or mahogany?'

When Charlie parked his car he switched off the engine and reached through to the back seat. He handed Josh a Jiffy bag. 'A present,' he said, 'open it and don't argue.'

'You bastard,' Josh said, when he saw what it was. But instead of there being anger in his face as Charlie had dreaded, there was a look of resigned acceptance as Josh inspected the specially designed fold-away walking stick.

'I got it through one of Dad's catalogues. At least it's black and matches your image.'

'Some bloody image.'

'There's also a slip of paper there for you . . . with some addresses you might like to follow up.'

Josh looked inside the Jiffy bag and pulled out the piece of paper. He read what was written on it and, without saying anything, pushed it into his jeans pocket.

They locked the car and slowly made their way to the lift as Josh tried out the new stick. Charlie pressed the button and the doors opened immediately. They stepped inside and as they dropped to the fifth floor Josh alternated between chewing the inside of his mouth and looking at his watch.

'Relax, we'll make it,' Charlie said, 'I checked earlier, the flight won't be called for at least another half-hour.'

'But what if she's gone through passport control already?'

'It never happens that way in all the films,' Charlie said lightly, needing to take the edge off his own apprehension.

The lift stopped, the doors opened and Josh froze. 'I can't go through with this,' he said, suddenly rooted to the spot. 'What if she won't talk to me?'

Charlie took him by the elbow and helped him out. He couldn't answer his brother's question because even he was frightened that Jessica would turn her back on them and simply get on her plane.

They looked everywhere for her, but couldn't find her. They checked out W. H. Smith, searching for her among the shelves of magazines and bestsellers. They moved on to Boots. Then across to the Body Shop. But there was no sign of her anywhere.

Miserable and depressed, Josh was all for giving up, but Charlie wasn't. 'I've got an idea,' he said, 'come on.'

Jessica's stomach was threatening to do its worst. For any normal person there was no decision to be made. It had already been made. The flight was booked. She was at the airport. She was all set for Corfu.

But was she? Was she really?

If she got on that plane there were certain things that would happen as a consequence. She just knew it.

She wiped the sweat from her palms and from her top lip. Lord, she was nervous! She hadn't felt this sick with indecision since that awful day in London with Piers. And as on that surreal day, she was now prepared to let her future be decided by a toilet.

A bloody toilet! I ask you!

To flush or not to flush, that was the question.

This is no time for joking, she told herself severely, just consider the facts, calmly and rationally.

If the toilet flushed first go, she would stay where she was – and that's Cholmford, not Manchester airport, she added for clarification – and she'd talk to Josh. She'd force him to listen to her; he had to realise she was sorry.

And if the toilet didn't flush then she would get on that flight for Corfu.

Well, that seemed clear enough, didn't it?

She reached out to the handle, knowing that she was seconds away from a decision. A crucial one.

Whoa! Just a cotton-picking moment. Was there to be no clarification on the second option? No definition of what Corfu actually stood for? Was the jury to be denied the full facts of the matter? Were the members of the jury not to be told that a few days spent languishing in Corfu licking her wounds was in actual fact an excuse for bailing out at the first sign of difficulty and running straight back into the arms of a previous lover?

She looked round guiltily. So what if it was? What was wrong in doing that? The situation was quite clear. Josh didn't want her. Gavin did.

And besides, a little comforting wouldn't do any harm. Because that's all it would be. She knew how to handle Gavin now. She wouldn't be taken in by those pouty, hurt, little-boy lips whenever he couldn't get his own way with her. Oh, no, those days were gone. She was a much stronger woman than the one who had left Corfu in the summer.

Yes, she thought sarcastically, you're a thoroughly empowered woman, so much so that you're letting a toilet decide your future.

No need to get nasty.

Then get on with it!

She took a deep breath and reached out to the handle.

'Would Miss Jessica Lloyd please go at once to the special assembly area opposite the Lufthansa ticket desk.' The tight nasal voice that came over the PA system threw Jessica into an immediate state of alarm. Something had happened to her mother. She'd had a heart attack and George and Emily were trying to get hold of her. Panic-stricken, she spun round in the small cubicle and head-butted the door.

'Miss Jessica Lloyd to the special assembly area. Thank you.'

'Be quiet you stupid woman!' Jessica muttered under her breath as she fumbled to unlock the door, and with an egg-sized lump already forming on her forehead, she belted out of the Ladies and raced across the arrival hall. Oh God, how could she have thought of leaving her mother? How selfish she'd been.

'Where's the Lufthansa ticket desk?' she shouted at one of the girls on the British Airways check-in desks.

'Straight on and to the right.'

Jessica ran, turned the corner, then stopped dead in her tracks.

She saw Charlie first, then Josh. All at once she realised that her mother was quite safe and that the only heart in trouble was her own. It was pounding so fast it was likely to burst out of her chest.

Charlie smiled at her. He said something to his brother, then walked away.

Josh came slowly towards her. Which was just as well as she was in such a state of shock she didn't think she'd ever move again – a shock that was compounded by the sight of him having its normal effect on her. Her mouth was instantly chalk dry; she thought he'd never looked more desirable. He was dressed in his usual black jeans and with a baggy V-neck sweater over a white T-shirt he reminded her of the teenage heartbreaker in the photograph at his parents' house.

She then noticed that he was using a stick.

A stick? Had Charlie finally got through to him?

She noticed, too, how terrified he looked.

He was standing in front of her now, so close she could see all the dazzling flecks of colour in his wonderful brown eyes and her stomach twisted itself into the kind of knot she'd learnt as a Girl Guide. *But why was he here? To wave her off? Or . . .*

'You've cut yourself,' she said, lowering her gaze from his eyes to his mouth.

'Charlie hit me.'

'He did what?'

'He said I deserved it.'

'And did you?'

'I think so, yes.'

'That's all right, then. I was brought up to believe that we always get what we deserve.'

'Sound advice. So what have *you* been up to?'

'Me?'

'You've hurt your head.'

She raised her hand and felt the bump on her forehead. 'Nothing gets past you, does it, Crawford?'

'I sincerely hope you're right.'

His voice was suddenly low, which in turn increased the pounding in Jessica's rib-cage. Hardly daring to ask, she said, 'Why are you here, Josh?'

'I would have thought that was obvious.'

She swallowed hard. 'A girl likes to have it properly explained, especially if she's a writer.'

He suddenly smiled. It was the first real smile she'd seen on him for what felt like for ever. Much more of this and she'd be the one needing that stick for support!

'Just my luck that I go and fall in love with a writer,' he said.

Love! He'd mentioned the word love. Was there hope? 'Hey, it could be worse. I could be a civil servant and want it in triplicate.'

He shook his head. 'Believe me, Jessica, nothing could be worse than falling in love with you.'

'I'm not sure how to take that.'

374

He took a deep breath. 'Look, I'm sorry for the way I've treated you, for all those things I said, please . . . I don't want you to go.'

'Not even for a holiday?'

'No. I hate the thought of you being with that Gavin character. Or any other man for that matter. I love you. And . . . and I need you more than anyone else ever could. Perhaps I . . .' But his voice trailed away and he lowered his gaze.

'Perhaps what?'

'Perhaps I need you too much.'

Hot, stinging tears pricked at her eyes. *He loved her . . . he needed her.* Nobody had ever said that to her before. Nobody. It was all she'd ever wanted to hear. 'You could never want me too much,' she said, and throwing her arms round his neck she kissed him.

When they finally parted he said, 'I'm completely knackered, do you mind if we sit down?'

Chapter Fifty-One

It was a cold, wintry evening in the middle of November and everyone had gathered in Josh's house to enjoy Jessica's fifteen minutes of fame.

Except for Jessica.

She was there with them all, but unlike the others, she held no expectation of deriving a single second of pleasure from watching herself on the television. And determined to put the dreaded moment off for as long as possible she was now opening the first of the bottles of champagne that Josh had specially bought to mark the occasion.

'I think a few toasts are in order,' she announced as she passed the glasses round.

'Oh?' said Anna, 'anything in particular?'

Jessica caught the hopeful glance her mother gave her left hand. 'Yes,' she said, 'for a start I think we should celebrate the removal of your plaster cast this morning and that, despite your worst endeavours, you've been given a clean bill of health.'

'Any chance of having that in writing from you, Jessica, dear?'

'Don't push it, Mum!'

Josh laughed and raised his glass. 'To Anna and her clean bill of health.'

'What's a clean bill of health?' whispered Hattie to her father after she'd taken a gulp from her own tiny glass and had felt the bubbles fizzing up her nose.

'I'll tell you later,' he whispered back. Then putting his arm round Kate, he said, 'I think we should also congratulate Kate on being offered a part-time job where she used to work.'

'That's brilliant news,' said Jessica. 'When did you hear?'

'Yesterday,' Kate answered.

'And after the way they treated you before, you weren't tempted to tell them to shove their job straight up their Dewey System?'

Kate laughed at Jessica. 'No,' she said, 'I'm much too practical for that.'

'You mean you're too nice,' said Jessica.

'Not really. I need the work and besides, for now, the hours are perfect. This way I'll still be able to carry on taking care of Hattie.'

Jessica smiled at Kate, then at Tony and Hattie. 'Well, here's to all three of you and your perfect arrangement.'

They raised their glasses one more time.

'I'm sorry,' Anna suddenly said when the room went quiet, 'but I really can't take the suspense any longer. I'm dying to see a bestselling author's mother on TV. How about it?'

Jessica cringed. 'Do we have to? Can't we have another toast?'

Anna groaned. 'What to this time? The weather?'

Jessica looked thoughtful. 'I know,' she said. 'To the new people moving into number three next week. May they be as –'

'As mad as you,' said Josh. 'At least then there'll be a chance of them fitting in around here.'

Jessica pulled a face at him. 'I was going to say, may they be as sweet-natured as you, lover boy.'

'Please!' cried a thoroughly exasperated Anna, 'before we all die of old age, can we just sit down and watch the video?'

'Okay,' Jessica demurred, 'but only on the condition that I'm in charge of the remote control and I'm allowed to have all the cushions to hide behind.'

'You could always go behind the sofa like you did as a child when you were scared,' Anna said. 'Now come on, I want to see how my garden turned out.'

They settled themselves down: Anna in the armchair nearest the television, Kate and Tony on the floor with Hattie on her father's lap, and Jessica and Josh on the sofa together.

Jessica pointed the remote control at the video, wishing that she hadn't made such a ridiculous pact with her mother and Josh last night – because Josh would be at work when the programme went out, he and Anna had insisted that none of them watched it until they could all be together that evening. 'Now if anybody laughs,' she said, 'I'm warning you, I'll switch it off.'

'Get on with it!'

Amanda was getting ready to go out to a party. As she switched off her hair-drier she could hear her mother arguing with her father downstairs. It was a familiar scene, but one which she had forgotten about until she'd left Tony. Living with her parents for a few months had seemed a good idea, but now it didn't. No wonder her father spent all his time with his head in the past. He had all her sympathy. And just as soon as she'd found herself a job she would be off.

Over the coming weeks she had several interviews arranged, one of which was a follow-up interview, and she was confident that she'd soon be back in full-time employment.

Meanwhile, there was the divorce to organise. Tony had so far acted very decently and had given in to all her requests – no more than he should after everything she'd done for him. Half the house was to be hers, just as soon as it could be sold, as well as a suitable sum of money, part of which was to compensate her for loss of earnings while being stuck at home looking after Hattie. And, of course, she had all that furniture in store just waiting for her to set herself up somewhere new.

When she'd asked her solicitor if it wasn't worth their while pushing for more, the woman's response had been a little disappointing. 'My advice to you, Mrs Fergusson, is to quit while you're ahead,' she'd said.

Well, maybe her solicitor was right. It wouldn't do to be seen as greedy. Not that she thought she was being greedy. In her opinion Tony had been prepared to hand over as much as he had because his conscience had made him do so. He had put no effort into making a go of their marriage and had been only too quick to stray into the arms of another woman. And if it hadn't been for her father catching Tony and Kate red-handed that day in Holmes Chapel, goodness knows how long it would have been before she'd have discovered what he was up to.

She finished applying her make-up and went downstairs. There was no sign of her father, but she found her mother in the sitting-room watching a wildlife programme. Amanda's stomach turned as she caught sight of a panther feasting on a gazelle. She shuddered. Predatory animals, weren't they just the worst?

It was Alec's fiftieth birthday. He wasn't celebrating it in the way he had imagined – in Venice with Kate – but he was enjoying himself. His dinner companion was proving to be good company, but then he wouldn't have expected anything less.

Getting over Kate hadn't been as bad as he'd thought it would be. Initially he had felt sorry for himself and had wanted her back. Unable to stop what he was doing, he had been rather pathetic and pestered poor Jessica and Josh about Kate. They had been very patient with him. And very tactful. When he'd discovered that Kate had been seeing Tony behind his back he had been mortified, distraught with jealousy. But in a way all that deception had helped

378

him to get over her. There was nothing like a little anger to harden one's resolve.

As time wore on, and from the little he could glean from Jessica, his reaction to what had happened between him and Kate changed. It shook him that he actually wished Kate and Tony well. He hoped that one day she would have the children she so badly craved. He was even thankful that it had been Tony who had taken Kate to the hospital that day when she'd lost the baby. He was glad that it hadn't been, as Kate had told him, a stranger who had helped her, but someone who really cared about her.

He saw now that he had fallen for Kate because he'd been unbelievably flattered by her being interested in him. What man wouldn't be? She had stroked and pampered his battered ego – Melissa's departure had left him more devastated than he'd realised at the time – and Kate had made him feel as though he wasn't such a disaster area after all. When it came down to it, it wasn't love that he'd felt for Kate, but gratitude. And feeling grateful to another person leaves you vulnerable – it makes you feel beholden to that person, that you could never be worthy of their love.

He now looked at the person sitting opposite him. Gratitude was something he'd never felt for Melissa – he'd felt a lot of other things for her, but a sense of obligation had never been one of them. Perhaps this was because they'd always viewed one another as equals. Since they'd formed Thistle Cards there had never been a time when they hadn't worked well together – even during their divorce the company had been rock steady under their equal partnership. When it came to business they were of one mind, with an uncanny knack for second-guessing what the other was thinking.

But they weren't conducting business tonight, which meant he had no idea what his ex-wife was thinking. Melissa was one of the most private people he knew and when it came to anything of a personal nature she played things close to the chest. Last week he had spoken to Ruth on the phone and when his daughter had taken a break from complaining about Kate – 'I feel very let down, Dad, decent child-minders are hard to come by' – she had told him that Tim was now history. 'Don't say I said anything,' she went on, 'but Mum sent him packing. She said she couldn't stand him any longer. Something about him having too high an opinion of himself and too low an opinion of others.'

It was certainly news to Alec. Melissa hadn't said a word about any of this at work. But then he wouldn't have expected her to confide in him.

379

And as they read their menus Alec decided to give Melissa an opportunity to put him in the picture. 'So how's things with you and Tim?' he said as directly as he dared, but at the same time hiding behind his menu.

'Tim who?'

Alec raised his eyes and smiled. 'Like that, is it?'

She didn't return his smile, but kept her gaze on her menu. 'I think I'll have the Dover sole.'

'No starter?'

'No. But you go ahead, I'll pick something from your plate.'

Alec was tempted to say 'like in the old days', but a comment like that deserved to be treated to the derision she would most certainly fling back at him – he and Melissa might spend their days constantly immersed in greetings card sentiment, but there were limits to what either of them would put up with after office hours.

They ordered their food and Alec poured their wine.

'Will you stay in Cholmford?' she asked him.

'I haven't decided yet.' Which was true. At first he'd thought he'd have to move, that he wouldn't be able to cope with seeing Kate's car parked outside Tony's, but when he'd seen the 'for sale' board go up at number two he'd decided to sit tight for a while. There was no point in running away when very soon there wouldn't be anything to run away from. And despite everything that had happened, he liked his house; it was home to him now.

Melissa raised her glass to him. 'Happy fiftieth, by the way,' she said. Then she reached down to her handbag on the floor and pulled out a small parcel for him.

'For me?'

'Who else?'

'You shouldn't have.'

'Save the self-effacing touch and get on and open it.'

He unwrapped the parcel. It was an uninspiring cheaply made notebook, the sort with which the Chinese continually flooded the market. 'Um . . . thank you,' he said.

She laughed. 'I know exactly what you're thinking, Alec.'

'You do?'

'You're wondering how to thank me for such a cheap and nasty present, aren't you?'

'Of course not.' Then he smiled. 'Okay, then, you're right. Have you bought me an expensive pen to go with it?'

She shook her head. 'That's the present, take it or leave it.'

'Oh, I shall definitely take it,' he said, 'gift horses and all that.'

'It's up to you what you use it for, but it's meant to be symbolic.'

'Of what?'

She reached for her glass of wine. 'Do you remember when I left you, I said I was tired of reading the same book?'

'Yes,' he said, 'I remember very well. I was extremely hurt by what you said.'

'I'm sorry I hurt you, Alec, but I said it because it was true . . . at the time.'

Alec had an uncomfortable feeling that he knew what Melissa was going to say next and he wasn't sure what to make of it. 'And now?'

'Well, let's just say that since then, and after what we've been through, both of us must be quite different.'

'You mean improved, like a good wine?'

'Let's not overdo the metaphors.' She smiled. 'What I'm saying is that you're a different book now and one I'd be interested in taking off the shelf. I'm prepared to take the risk . . . are you?'

He leant back in his chair and contemplated her. 'I think you've got a bloody nerve, Melissa,' he said slowly.

'But that's what you always liked about me,' she countered. 'You used to say that you admired my strength of character.'

'And what makes you think, after what you did to me, that I'd even consider taking a risk on you again?'

'It was *you* who invited me to dinner tonight.'

'For something called old times' sake.'

'Well, it could be a start.'

'Are you serious, Melissa?'

'We could see if it works.'

Alec shook his head. 'I don't know. We're not the people we used to be, it would be –'

'That's the whole point. It would be different.'

'I still don't know. What about sex?'

'What, right now?'

'*Melissa!*'

She smiled. 'That, too, would be different. I assume you've learnt a new trick or two from Kate. I know I have from Tim. Alec, I don't believe it, you're blushing.'

'Look,' he said, reaching for her hand across the table, 'I'm just an old-fashioned bloke who's beginning to feel his age. I'm not sure I'm up to all this.'

'Nonsense. You'll pick it up as we go along.'

He smiled at her, then laughed. 'You're quite amazing, you know that?'

'It's often been said. And while we're on the subject, you're not so bad yourself. Now, where's my sole? I'm hungry.'

He laughed again. 'There must be some wise-cracking response to that question, but I'm too stunned to come up with anything.'

'Good. Now pour me another glass of wine and let's drink to the future.'

'No, I've a better toast. Here's to better the devil you know.'

'You silly old fool, you.'

'You can come out now,' Josh said as Jessica's face disappeared from the television screen and the presenter of the programme moved on to discuss the relative merits of a home confinement.

Jessica lowered the cushions and emerged. 'I swear that wasn't me,' she said. 'I didn't say half of those things, they've dubbed stuff on afterwards. Nobody could sound that ridiculous.'

'You did say those things,' Anna said. 'I was there; I saw and heard all of it. I was rather good, wasn't I? That bit with the bonfire came across well, I thought.'

'You were both wonderful,' Kate said generously.

'Yes,' agreed Tony, 'quite the double act.'

Jessica groaned. 'My claim to fame, the unfunny half of a double act; the stooge.'

Josh squeezed her hand. 'You were fine, honestly.'

'But what about that bit on the swing?'

He grinned. 'It was the best bit. I'm going to watch it again later.'

She pulled a face. 'For that, you can go and get us all something to eat. And as a real punishment I'll come and help you.'

'Anything I can do?' offered Kate.

'No,' said Jessica, 'I want to bully Josh alone.'

He got to his feet and Jessica slowly followed behind him. When they reached the kitchen they could hear the others replaying the video and laughing out loud.

'Mum was pretty good, wasn't she?' Jessica said as she watched Josh open the oven and pull out a large dish of Cajun-style chicken wings. He placed the hot dish on the hob and gave the pieces of chicken a prod with a sharp knife.

'Perfect,' he said.

'Oh, come on, she wasn't that good.'

'I was talking about the chicken, but you're right, Anna played her part beautifully. So did you.'

'Really? Do you mean that?'

He glanced over at her and frowned. 'I've never seen you in unsure mode before. You okay?'

'Mm . . . I don't know, I think I need a hug.'

He put the chicken back in the oven, took off the oven gloves and held out his arms. She went to him like a small child needing to be comforted. He held her tightly. 'That better?' he asked.

'Nearly.'

He stroked her hair, suddenly worried. With shame he realised that lately life had been so good for him he'd hardly bothered to wonder if the same was true for Jessica. She always appeared so strong, so confident and positive, and had been such a support to him over the weeks that he had come to rely on her vitality to help him through any of his low periods. But had it been too much for her? Was he sapping her of her energy? And was she beginning to regret moving in with him?

A week after he'd stopped her getting on that plane for Corfu he had suggested that they live together and it had been her idea that she move in with him, rather than the other way around. 'Your house is bigger than mine and has the best views,' she'd said in her typically frank manner, 'let's see how it goes, shall we?' He'd thought that the arrangement was working perfectly. Jessica would work in her study in her own house during the day and when she had finished writing, not long after he arrived home, she would come across the courtyard to him. It had seemed an ideal set-up.

But maybe it wasn't. Perhaps she had seen too much of the real him. It was possible that she had found his problems too much to cope with, and he could hardly blame her for that, sometimes they seemed too much for him.

No, that wasn't strictly true these days. Having Jessica in his life and feeling secure in their love for one another had gone a long way to altering his perspective. Though not completely, there were still times when he panicked when he thought of the future, which was reasonable enough – Jessica's love could never be turned into a miracle cure, but it was certainly palliative. She had boosted his self-esteem, which in turn had put him on better terms with his brother and parents, and everyone at work including Mo. They were less cautious of him now. He suspected that this was because they had always taken their cue from him and now that he was more at ease, they were too.

He'd taken his mother out to lunch one day to try and apologise to her, to bridge the gap he had so ruthlessly forced between them. It had been difficult at first to find the right words to express himself because he had become so used to concealing the truth from her. In the end he had resorted to saying that he was sorry and to ask if she would forgive him. 'Nothing to forgive,' she'd said, but the tears in her eyes had told him that this wasn't the case. It also told him just how much he had hurt her.

Undeniably, his mental capacity to cope with his MS was stronger than it had been, which was just as well because it was showing no sign of easing up – but to be positive, it wasn't showing any sign of worsening. The stiffness in his leg was as bad as ever and sometimes it really got to him, but with the help of a physiotherapist whom he'd started seeing recently – and not forgetting the wretched stick Charlie had given him – he was now able to move about more freely. With regard to the wretched stick, his brother hadn't ever said the words 'I told you so', but Josh knew they were there for the prompting, which amused him.

It also amused him when Jessica tried to play the role of Florence Nightingale on speed. He'd found the perfect way to stop her. Instead of over-reacting and blowing up at her, he simply took her in his arms and kissed her till she couldn't breathe. 'A shame I can't do that to her myself,' Anna had said when he'd told her how he had got round Jessica's bossiness.

But it was Jessica's forthright manner that had helped him to take an important step, one that he now saw as being crucial for them both. That day at the airport when Charlie had presented him with the walking stick his brother had also given him the address of the MS Society, as well as the name and phone number of a man who belonged to a self-help group for MS sufferers in the area. His first reaction was that he would have none of it – what would he have in common with a bunch of people who wanted to sit around discussing how ill they were? But he hadn't bargained on Jessica taking things into her own hands. Without him knowing it she phoned the number Charlie had given him and asked the man if he would agree to meet them for a drink.

He came to the house late one evening. His name was Chris Perry and it was only when Jessica had made the necessary introductions that Josh realised what she'd done behind his back. But it was impossible for him to be cross, for two reasons. First, he found he loved Jessica too much to be furious with her and second, the man who had gone to such trouble to meet him was wearing an item of clothing that invariably caused most people to be on their best behaviour, including Josh.

'Sorry, I'm late,' he'd said, settling himself in a chair and taking the glass of wine Jessica was offering him. He knocked back the drink and began removing his dog-collar. 'Do you mind?' he asked, tossing it on the table, 'I hate wearing the damn thing, but I've just been dealing with a woman who thought her house was haunted. She needed the reassurance of a bit of Popery, 'course there wasn't a ghost in sight, just a case of noisy neighbours. Anyway, less of me, more of you, Josh. How's it hanging?'

The Reverend Chris Perry was in his early forties, an Anglican minister, married, with a young son, and before MS – in a relatively mild form – had entered his life, he'd been a compulsive potholer. 'Of course, these days the only hole I get near is the one I've dug myself into from the pulpit,' he told them. 'There's nothing like a controversial vicar to stir up the mob.'

On the face of it he and Chris had nothing in common, but the more the conversation progressed, the more similarities Josh could see between them. Despite the bravado Chris showed, Josh sensed that he was just as concerned for his own future as Josh was. 'I don't mind the possibility of one day being in a wheelchair,' he had said, while driving Josh to meet the rest of the group for the first time two weeks ago, 'it's the crap that goes with it I can't hack. If you can't walk, people assume that you're brain-dead.'

It was a view that was shared by everyone to whom Josh was introduced at the group that evening. If he'd thought the only common thread that would hold these people together would be their depressing list of aches and pains he was proved wrong – it was actually their spirited sense of humour that kept them afloat, offering each other support and understanding. Josh had come away impressed.

And a little humbled. He had a lot to learn.

Which was what Chris said to him in the car on the way home afterwards. 'It's not just about learning to confront the illness,' he'd said, 'it's learning to laugh at yourself. An illness like MS tends to bring out the worst in us, the challenge is to overcome that and dig out the best in ourselves. No matter how deep you have to go, Josh, just keep on digging.'

On reflection, it was quite a challenge and Josh wasn't entirely sure that he was up for it. But on the other hand, he was aware that in the past few days he'd actually caught himself thinking how happy he was. A milestone in itself.

But suddenly he wasn't so sure.

If Jessica wasn't happy, where did that leave him? Was it possible that she was still hankering for her old way of life in Corfu? Was that where she believed she really belonged? With Gavin . . . a man who didn't have half the problems he had? 'There's nothing wrong, is there?' he finally dared to ask Jessica.

She raised her head from his shoulder. 'No, not really. What made you say that?'

'I was just wondering if you thought that moving in with me wasn't such a good idea.'

'What an extraordinary thing to say. I love being here with you. I wouldn't have it any other way.'

'So why the long face?'

She sighed. 'It's called seeing yourself as others see you. I'm in shock. I looked and sounded dreadful on that programme.'

Relief flooded through him. Nothing had changed between them. Everything was all right. He kissed her. 'Now you know what I have to put up with every morning when I see you lying next to me.'

'You're all charm, now get back to your oven gloves.'

'No,' he said, still holding her in his arms and deciding that now was as good a time as any to let Jessica know what she meant to him, 'there's something I'd like you to ask me.'

'Mm . . .' she said, 'something you want *me* to ask *you*? Sounds a bit tricksy. Any clues?'

He nodded. 'You already know the answer to the question because I gave it to you that awful night at Tony and Amanda's. Do you remember?'

She stared at him, unsure. Then it slowly dawned on her – the flickering candle-light, the way he'd gazed at her and the heart-stopping moment when he'd said *I'd say yes*. She swallowed. 'You mean –?'

'I know I'm not much of a catch, a man who hobbles about with a stick and –'

'Don't go selling yourself short, Crawford,' she said with a smile. 'I know the score.'

He smiled too. 'So, is there any chance that you might ever want to ask me that particular question?'

'Do rabbits like hot-cross buns?'

He raised a puzzled eyebrow. 'Don't you mean carrots?'

'Hey, who's asking the questions? Now tell me, has this got to be a down-on-the-one-knee job?'

He laughed. 'I would think so. Properly or not at all.'

'Like this?'

'Yes, that looks about right.'

'Well, here goes then.' She looked up at him and cleared her throat. 'Joshua, will you –' But she got no further. The phone rang out, loud and shrill.

'I hope that's got nothing to do with fate,' Josh said, disappointed as Jessica got to her feet. 'I'll get it while you serve up the supper for the others,' he added.

He answered the phone, then covered the mouthpiece with his hand. 'It's Piers,' he said, 'do you want to take it in the study while I finish off here?'

Wishing she'd never been so stupid as to give Josh's number to her agent, Jessica picked up the extension in Josh's study. 'Hello, Piers,' she said grumpily, 'this had better be good because your timing is absolutely bloody awful.'

'And good-evening to you, too, Jessica.'

'Don't be sarcastic with me, you've just ruined the greatest moment of my life.'

'Well, if I can tear you away for a little longer, I was ringing to say that you weren't bad on the television this afternoon. Not bad at all. In fact, almost good. A shame you had to go and spoil it by showing your knickers on the swing.'

'How kind of you to share that with me, Piers.' *Argh!* Would he never change? Would he never pay her a clear-cut compliment?

'I'll be in touch.'

'No hurry. Good-night.'

She went back to the kitchen and found everybody helping themselves to something to eat. Another bottle of bubbly had been opened and they all seemed very merry. She wondered if they would miss her and Josh for a while. He came over to her. 'Everything okay?' he asked quietly.

'How's your leg?' she whispered.

'Pardon?'

'Could you manage a short walk?'

'Where to?'

'Just to the woods.'

'Any reason why?'

'I want to get you alone and finish what we started a few minutes ago.'

They sat on what they now referred to as 'their' fallen oak tree. It was a cold and blustery night, and thick black clouds scudded over a full moon; branches swayed, leaves rustled.

'It's like something out of a Hammer House of Horror film, isn't it?' said Jessica with a shiver as she stared up at the restless sky. 'All we need is a howling wolf to complete the scene.'

'And some swirling mist.'

'Vincent Price in a black cloak with blood-red silk lining would be a nice touch.'

'So would Peter Cushing.'

'We shouldn't leave out Christopher Lee.'

'You're right. We'd have to have all three.'

'But what about Boris Karloff?'

'Him, too, if you want.' Josh put his arm around Jessica's shoulder and drew her inside his thick overcoat. He wondered if she was beginning to change her mind. 'You're not getting cold feet, are you?'

She turned her head and smiled up at him. 'You wouldn't be trying to talk me out of proposing to you, would you?'

He suddenly looked serious. 'I wouldn't blame you. We can't pretend my problems won't affect –'

She silenced him by placing a finger on his lips.

'And what about Gavin?' he mumbled against her finger.

She removed her hand. 'I don't believe you. Now you really are getting desperate.'

'He was very upset when you didn't turn up in Corfu. How many times did he ring you?'

'Too many, that's how many. Now please, can we put all the prevaricating aside and get on with what we're here to do? And to put us in the right frame of mind, we'll kick off with a kiss.'

'You sound like you've done this before.'

She laughed and kissed him. And when they stopped, she stared up into his face. 'I'm sorry,' she said in a low voice, 'it's no good, I really can't go through with it. I've changed my mind.'

He looked at her with a horrified gaze. 'But –'

'Don't panic.' She smiled. 'It turns out I'm a traditionalist at heart. In my book the romantic hero has to do the proposing.'

He let out his breath in one long sigh of relief. 'In that case, there's nothing else for it. Miss Jessica Lloyd –'

'*Yes!*'

'I haven't finished. Would you –'

'*Yes!*'

'Do me –'

'*Yes!*'

'The honour –'

'*Yes!*'

'Of marrying me?'

'Yes, yes, yes, yes, yes!'

'Thank goodness for that.'

'Now what do we do?'

'We go home. I'm frozen to death sitting here.'

'You're such a romantic, Crawford.'

'But cute with it, wouldn't you say?'

She helped him to his feet and passed him his stick. 'And as we walk, we'll plan the wedding. St Paul's would be a good choice. We ought to think big.'

'Yes. But if it's booked, we'll make do with Westminster Abbey.'

'And Charlie can be best man.'

'Naturally. And Helen could be your matron of honour.'

'How about Chris to officiate?'

'Good idea. And to hell with convention, Anna can give you away.'

'Brilliant. She'll love doing that.'

'I can hardly wait.'

'Me neither.'

'Jessica?'

'Yes?'

'Where will we live?'

'Your house, of course. Why move again? I've a feeling it's exactly where we both belong.'

THE END
Or to put it another way

THE BEGINNING